PHANTOM IN THE DARK

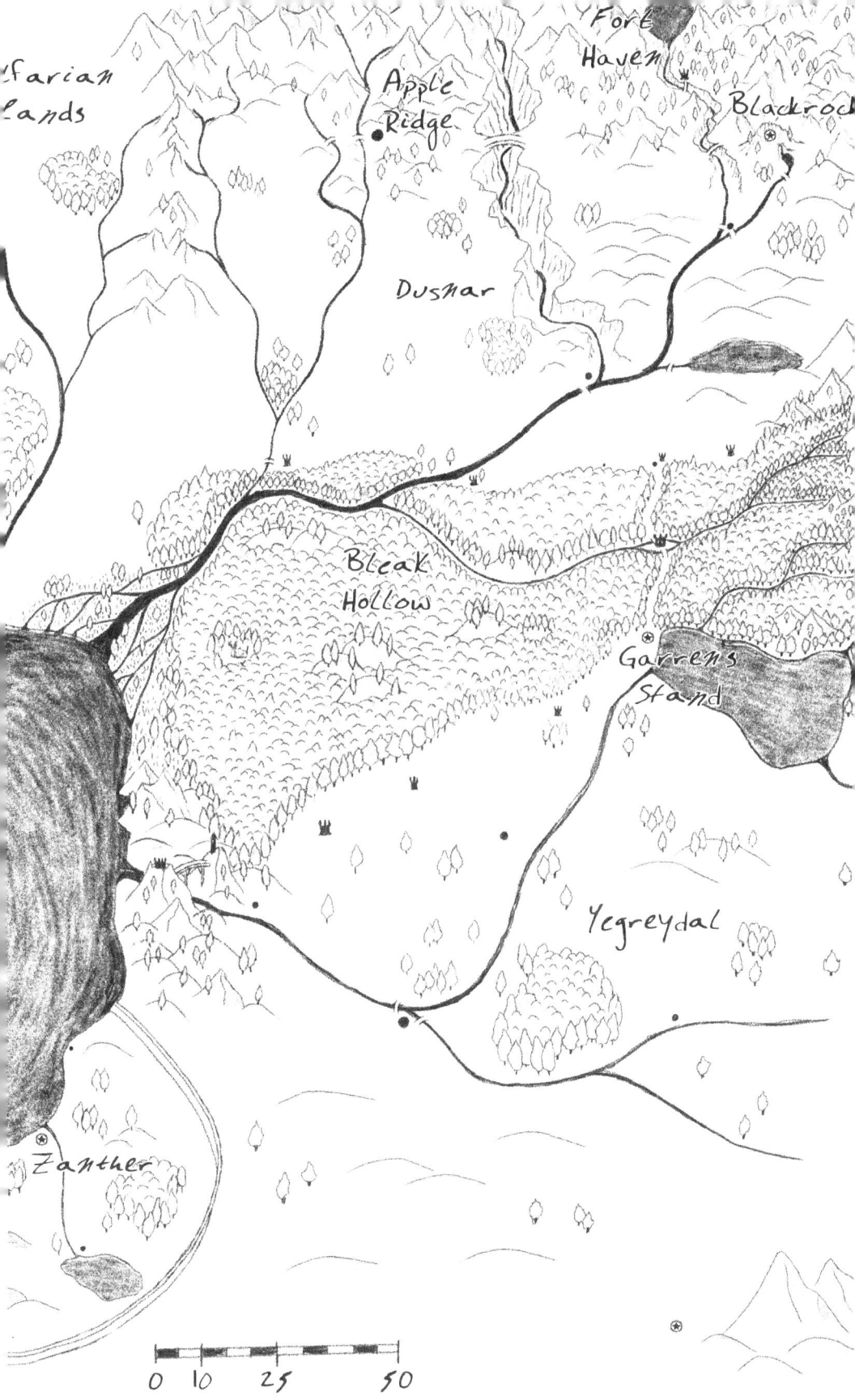

PHANTOM IN THE DARK

Ellie Lerum

RED RICHARD ARTS

Mom and Dad, thanks for never giving up on your strange girl.
I love you.

CONTENTS

AUTHOR'S NOTE

This book is a work of fiction, and all characters, scenarios, and events are imagined. However, it does explore themes of grief, abuse, pregnancy loss and trauma. There are also references to, but not described, instances of rape and sex. The author has approached these topics with care and respect, aiming to shed light on complex emotions and often unspoken struggles.

Reader discretion is advised, as individual reactions may vary. If you or someone you know is affected by similar issues, please seek support from a trusted professional or helpline:

- U.S. National Suicide Prevention Hotline: 988

- U.S. National Maternal Mental Health Hotline: 1-833-852-6262

- U.S. National Abuse Help Hotline: 1-800-799-7233

- U.S. National Mental Health Hotline: 800-273-8255

The author sincerely hopes that readers have not experienced the hardships depicted in this story. For those who have, please know that you are not alone.

THE JOURNEY BEGINS

J ean shifted, clutching the leather strap of her satchel tighter over her chest. She could hear her heart beating in her ears as the line in front of her inched forward at an agonizing pace, echoing the same worried, *'they'll stop you; they'll stop you'* repeatedly. The guards' distrusting gaze did nothing but make the rhythmic fear scream louder.

"Next!" a guard barked.

Again, Jean stepped forward as she pulled her hood tighter over her head. Her fingers brushed against the horns under her headscarf, spiking her worries before she inhaled deeply. "It'll be different this time," she muttered. "They've no cause to stop me this time..."

She lifted her gaze slightly as she saw the guard's boots before her. Slowly, as she allowed herself to look over the man, she realized that his hand was on the hilt of his sword and his eyes had narrowed. Their eyes met, and his became slits as he saw her crimson skin.

"Curseborn," he sneered, the word dripping from his lips like venom.

Stay calm. Don't show him it bothered you.

Jean straightened up, swallowed past the lump in her throat, and said, "I'm visiting family in Blackrock."

The guard didn't answer, instead leaning toward another soldier. They whispered, their faces unreadable, before the first one turned back. "Your kind don't travel freely. State your real purpose."

The crowd murmured behind her. She could feel their stares burning into her back, whispers of "bad luck" and snide comments about livestock cutting through the buzz.

Her grip on the satchel tightened. There was no turning back now.

After a moment, Jean sucked in another breath. "I'm traveling to visit my uncle and aunt in Blackrock. Their youngest has grown ill, and they've asked me to come and tutor him while he's home. I've got all the documents needed: the work visa, the letter asking for aid—"

"Hand it over, then." The guard thrust his hand out, a bored look thinly veiling the contempt on his face. "Hurry it up, you're holding up the line."

Jean glanced back at the crowd, ducked her head, and rummaged through her satchel. From a worn leather book, she pulled out a thin sheet of paper and a letter. Her uncle's signature stood out, scrawled hastily across the page. She placed them into the guard's hand and, silently, lifted her blue eyes to the sky.

Solaris, the sun god, never seemed to listen... but now was as good a time to pray to him as ever.

The droning whispers behind her only made her worries grow as the guard scanned each document painstakingly slowly before he finally tossed them back to her. "If it's a forgery, it's a good one. My suggestion: stay out of Zanther until you're forgotten... Jean Cassy. We'll be sending word to Blackrock that we'll require a letter permitting reentry."

What relief Jean had faded at his words, and she stammered, "I-I'm sorry? You can't bar reentry—"

"We will do what we want, husk." Once more, the guard's voice rose above the crowd. Jean knew he was doing this only to cause a scene as she clutched her papers to her chest. "You are only barely a citizen of Zanther due to whatever unfortunate couple it was who bore you." He then leaned in, his breath hot as he whispered, "Be glad we're allowing you to exit. Now... leave before I change my mind."

"Move it, cow!" a man said sharply from behind her. "You're in my way!"

Jean stumbled forward, caught the pages once again, and then hurried from the first gate.

A couple of people spat at her as she passed them, one mother clutching her son as though shielding him from a leper, and Jean pulled her hood even tighter over herself. Over and over, she murmured, "Almost out. One gate left, almost out."

She hated being the center of attention. It was a despicable thing, and as a curseborn, it only brought trouble. If detained, that'd delay her trip to Caxton, too. It'd be a tremendous mess, and others would assume she was a criminal for even a simple misunderstanding.

The courtyard between gates was just as busy as the first section, though this time guards were waving people through dismissively. It was the people wanting entry through the Great Wall of Zanther who had to wait, though Jean was detained a second time to verify that she hadn't slipped through unnoticed.

When she finally stepped out of the city, Jean inhaled deeply. It'd been years since her last visit to Blackrock, and it was a breath of fresh air to escape the stifling city. Now, though, she faced the journey through the nation of Yegreydal and into Dusnar.

With each step she took, spanning over several days, Jean focused on her goal. She needed to see her cousin. He was ill, his parents were both working, and there was no other person to tend to him. Initially, Jean's adoptive mother protested as there were other cousins to watch, but the pleading nature of her Uncle Flick's letter eventually won her over. In the back of her mind, Jean wondered why Adriata had been so reluctant to allow her to leave. They hadn't visited Blackrock since Jean was 8, and a decade was quite a long time. Aunt Anca had written before, Jean remembered seeing her letters, but they never came up in conversation. Even her Uncle Flick's notes, which were often addressed to Adriata under the guise of Aunt Anca, earned their place in the fire pit. Regardless, it was an overwhelming urge that made Jean beg to leave Zanther and trek across the country.

She'd expected her adoptive mother to say 'no' the moment Jean suggested the land route. Instead, she had offered a quiet prayer to the traveling twins, Drisis and Ireus, and wished her luck on her travels.

Jean reached Garren's Stand, the final checkpoint in the nation of Yegreydal, earlier than she had assumed. Its tall walls were intimidating, further punctuated by the large five-rayed star on the highest tower. The symbol for Solaris glistened in the rapidly setting light, as though Solaris knew Jean had arrived. Each amber inset around the star also shone weakly, and Jean muttered a half-hearted prayer to the pantheon as she stepped beneath orange and yellow banners.

A variety of people milled about the central courtyard. Many wore amber jewelry on their person. It mimicked the amber around the star of Solaris, and those individuals, though they didn't speak to Jean, glowered at her from where they sat. Absentmindedly, Jean reached for the amber pendant beneath her shirt, her fingers curling around it as she scanned the courtyard for a place to sit. The only available spot was near a squat stone building at the far end. A small group had already gathered there, huddled close to the glow of a lit brazier. Jean drew in a slow breath.

While sitting with other Solari worshipers was unpleasant at best, interacting with Kingsmen would guarantee that she'd either be reborn a curseborn once more or that she would meet an early grave. The two factions got along as well as oil and water, and she was in the middle of it.

Slowly, Jean moved to the brazier closer to the Solari temple. One man there shuffled his jacket to show his blade. The woman beside him, and the three young children, shifted to be out of sight. Each brazier that Jean approached met her with the same open hostility. Another group was so callous to call her a 'witch', but Jean didn't respond.

She'd been called far worse things before, by many other people. Being called a witch was the least of her concerns, anyway.

When she finally sat beside the Kingsmen temple, she pulled her journal out. A half-finished sketch of a small lizard stared at her, offering a welcome distraction from the heretics nearby. Still, Jean's curiosity grew, and she allowed herself a glance at the symbol on the temple.

A three-peaked mountain stood prominently above a small band of thorns.

She vaguely remembered her aunt wearing a pin with the same thorns, but that was a wreath instead of a band. All of Jean's tutors had said the Kingsmen claim that their god, HaMelech, was a being of three parts. That never came up during dinner conversations, and Jean didn't care to ask. It was a load of rubbish, and anyone who thought otherwise was a fool. No one knew Solaris to be present either.

Jean shook her head to clear it of the blatant disrespect for Solaris, muttered a half-hearted prayer, and returned to her illustration.

Eventually, Jean lifted her head. The avatar of Solaris was quickly setting, shooting rapidly from the zenith where she had last seen it. People were shifting uneasily and someone relatively close by murmured, "The caravan hasn't made it yet... do you think everything is okay?"

In the distance, to punctuate the worries, was a single, haunting laugh that cut like a knife through the air.

Silence fell over the crowd before several guards shouted. Jean's eyes snapped to the winch as a group of four struggled to lift the portcullis and a large caravan surged through. Dogs bigger than Jean led the group in a dead sprint. Following the dogs were the wagons and carts, running travelers, and a huge clockwork suit that walked backward behind them. It lit up the night and the forest outside of the fort and, as it fired its devastating weapon, more of the chittering laughter rang out before it fell away. Emblazoned on its chest was the Kingsman symbol, though this time it was a sword driven through the wreath of thorns. Armored knights shared the emblem as well, though their tabards bore various symbols such as apple trees, obsidian stones, or lions' heads. Several people wearing pins with the wreath of thorns and a dove followed behind on horses as well.

As the group entered, Jean shied back against the stone.

Few people looked at her as they passed, though she was sure it was because of the shadows that shrouded her. As she sat, however, she realized the hair on the back of her neck beginning to prickle.

The gates began closing as a cacophony of howls and otherworldly laughter rang through the air. Around her, mothers grabbed their children and any person with a weapon grabbed it with white knuckles. Jean's hand found its place on the repeating crossbow on her hip. She gripped the crossbow tighter, subconsciously checking the crystal's winding to ensure she had six shots before needing to reload.

Jean watched the gate fall shut just as the clockwork knight fired two more shots into the darkness. It briefly illuminated lithe forms that scattered from the light before it grew silent.

After a brief pause, the camp cautiously resumed its activities.

As Jean watched the gate, movement in the corner of her eye caught her attention. One dog had left the pack and was sniffing the gate with raised hackles. It growled, the sound loud enough to ring through the courtyard, before it paused and lifted its head. Jean sucked in a breath. It locked eyes with her before trotting in her direction.

Jean shifted a bit. These dogs were large enough to take down a bear, she was sure. While its ears perked in curiosity, she certainly didn't want to be eaten.

Before Jean could stand, a sharp whistle rang from where the Kingsmen guard had set up their bedrolls. One of them, a thin man with dreaded black hair, had turned towards them. He watched the dog for a moment before he whistled once more. "Nettles! Here!"

Nettles paused for a moment, his floppy ears focused on the man before he shook out his coat and made his way to Jean. She didn't move as he approached, his enormous nose sniffing at her foot, then her knee, arms, and finally her face. He was such a large dog that a single breath caught Jean's hood and knocked it from her head. Nettles' inspection left Jean's horns and head cold, but she remained still. She knew he could hear her heart pounding in her chest, though his brown eyes revealed nothing but a gentle curiosity. He touched his nose to one of her horns before he sat down, whined, and pawed at her leg.

Slowly, Jean shifted and then reached out. Nettles whined again before he bumped her hand with his nose. His tongue lolled as she pet his fur and scratched behind his ears, which made her chuckle. "Look at you... you are a big softie, aren't you?"

She didn't pay attention to the people around her as she pushed her journal from her lap to dote on Nettles, who was panting as his tail wagged vigorously. It wasn't until someone stopped behind the dog that Jean looked up.

The knight from before had come over, his arms crossed over his chest. A bit of a smile had crossed his face but, aside from that, he seemed serious. Jean shifted and stopped. "I'm sorry, I didn't mean to distract—"

"No, no, it's alright. You've done nothing wrong. I'm more annoyed that Nettles didn't obey." The man shook his head and then scratched Nettles' ear. The dog's tail wagged harder, and the man laughed. "I'm surprised he came to you."

Jean stiffened slightly and looked down. She pulled her hood up. "Ah... I see."

Her quiet answer earned a soft hum, and the knight looked at the sky. Then, he looked at Jean. "Nettles doesn't like many people, is what I'm saying. Nothing about who you may be or what you may look like. You're the first person I've seen him come up to like this." He scratched Nettles's head again and tilted his own. "He's an excellent judge of character, and his disobedience tells me that you are someone who has a way with him. Dogs are usually less affected by perception than people are." Another little smile flickered over his face before he patted his leg. "Come on, Nettles... it's time to rest. If you're joining the caravan tomorrow, miss, I suggest you do the same: we're leaving by first light and will not be stopping until we reach Last Hope. It's a long walk, and I'd hate for you to fall behind." He nodded at Jean, who offered a little smile back, and then lightly pulled on Nettles's collar. "Have a good night. I do not doubt that we'll likely see you again, given Nettles' perception of you."

The dog huffed, licked Jean's face, and trotted off behind his master.

That certainly was a strange man... but Jean couldn't help smiling slightly at his kind words and interaction. It'd been a while since anyone spoke to her like a person, outside of her adoptive mother Adriata, and even longer since someone had complimented her interaction with animals. Positive conversations were rare, too; curseborns rarely had luck in being seen as people, much less good at something. As much as Jean hated to admit it, a tinge of pride welled up in her chest as she returned to her sketch.

Maybe, just maybe, she could use whatever animal-handling skills she had in Blackrock.

That night, the laughing demons outside of the gate screamed in the darkness. This was the closest that Jean had been to chitters, and even their invisible shapes brought fear to the forefront of her mind. Quietly, Jean pulled her cloak around herself to cut the biting chill and haunting calls from her bones.

Jean awoke to a light nudging. She opened her eyes to find that she had fallen over while she slept, as her cloak was the only thing that kept her warm that evening. It wasn't light yet, which meant the avatar of Solaris had yet to rise, but Jean knew deep in her core that it was only a matter of moments before it would be fully bright. She sat up, slowly, and looked around to find that it was Nettles who had been bumping her arm.

He nudged her hand, and she briefly ran her fingers over his coarse fur, before she pulled herself upright. Her satchel was still securely around her shoulder while her journal lay on the ground. She brushed it off and placed it in her pack, grabbed a handful of nuts from her bag, and looked around.

Nettles had wandered to the knight from before, who had shouldered a bow with no string. He was chatting with a man who wore a crystal-powered backpack with a large ram's head, which was accentuated only by the ram's head gauntlet he wore... no.

Jean narrowed her eyes before she realized that the gauntlet *was* the knight's arm, which was a bronze prosthetic. The two were speaking to a woman on horseback who pet Nettles's head as they chatted. After a brief moment, the knight with the prosthetic shouted, "Gates are lifting as soon as light hits the ground! If you're leaving Garren's Stand for Last Hope or beyond, it's time to go!"

The courtyard, which had been lazily milling about, suddenly broke into a buzz of activity. Parents loaded sleeping children into carts, men armed their boltcasters, and guards (Solari and Kingsmen alike) prepared themselves to surround the gathering caravan. Jean kept to the outer edge of the caravan, her hood low and her satchel pulled close. She avoided the knots of travelers chatting near the carts, their laughter sharp as broken glass. Every step felt like walking a tightrope, one misstep away from falling into their scrutiny. As she did, she watched Nettles' ears perk slightly, as though he knew she was there, before he looked back at his master.

From beside her, one of the young men muttered, "Great, a husk."

She cautiously looked at him to see that he was glaring in her direction. His soft words stung, and Jean pulled her hood tighter over her head to shadow her face. Though her fingers were still visible, she could at least attempt to hide herself.

There was little time to move as the man continued to mumble, prompting the surrounding others to glare in Jean's direction. She did her best to straighten up. It was a weak attempt to show that it didn't bother her, as she had to focus on leaving.

The first light of the sun peaked over the trees while she thought. The knight with the clockwork arm barked out a couple of orders and the portcullis lifted, slowly, to allow the group to race into the sunlight and toward the only checkpoint in Bleak Hollow.

Last Hope.

Solari Pantheon

The Solari religion worships a pantheon of 6 sanctioned beings that have transcended into godhood. While there are some other 'deity' level beings recognized such as Telfaria, the Black Dragon, and Hamelech, worshiping outside the sanctioned 6 is strictly prohibited and considered heresy.

Common Solari Shrine

Solaris the Radiant
- King of the gods. Creator of life and source of divine magic.
- Each year he battles the Black Dragon for dominion of all Illeross
- Takes the form of a great golden dragon to interact with mortals.

The brothers Ireus and Drisis
- Gods of travel and commerce.
- Ireus guides the living while Drisis brings the faithful to their next life based on their Karma.

Zephin
- Goddess of harvest, festivals, good wine, and fertility.

Lunararia
- Goddess of those who travel where the light of Solaris does not reach.
- Exiled to the dark north for stealing magic from Solaris to give to mortals.
- Chased by Solaris who desires her and regrets the banishment he had made in a fit of rage.

Xolta
- Solaris' 2nd wife, goddess of war, justice, and the forge.
- Most high Inquisitor and general of Solaris' armies.

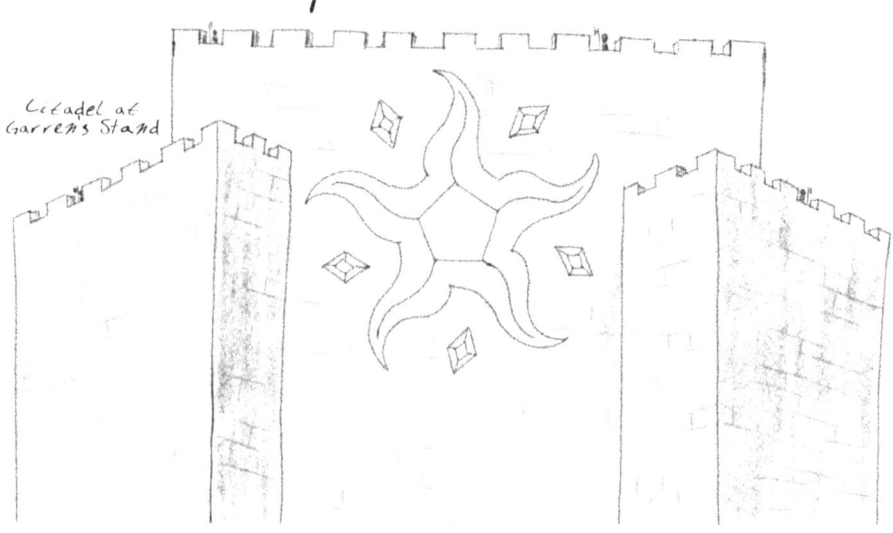

Citadel at Garren's Stand

BLEAK HOLLOW

As the caravan raced through Bleak Hollow, there was only enough time for Jean to recognize that the hard, packed ground beneath her feet was the only path cut within the trees.

Pine trees and twisted cypresses stood about sixty feet from the road, their shadows stretching toward the edges. Grasses grew wild and thick, threatening to smother anything that dared venture into the untamed forest. Jean couldn't see anything within the trees, but the prickling at the back of her neck told her something was there.

It was quiet, deathly quiet, aside from the sounds of feet and wheels on the dirt. Not even the babes with their mothers made a sound.

Jean swallowed, her eyes darting around as they walked. There were no birds, no animals, and only the feeling of being watched convinced her that there was life around them.

"We'll take a brief break for lunch once we reach the first checkpoint," a knight said lightly. Jean jumped at the sudden noise, as did those around her.

The knight offered a faint smile. "Sorry. It won't be a very long one, as we need to keep going, but our travels will allow us to rest for just a moment before we do so."

A brief murmur of agreement echoed through the gathered company, and then silence rang again.

As they slowed down, Jean found she had no way to move away from the caravan to eat in peace. They remained huddled together, silent, as they hurriedly ate. Nettles and his master, along with the four other big dogs, circled the group to keep an eye out for danger, while the clockwork knight and the man with the prosthetic arm focused on the woods to either side.

The only form of protection between the caravan and the forest was a short earth wall. Jean took what comfort she could from the wall as she slowly ate, all the while scanning the forest. Once everyone had settled, there was a soft bird note or the hum of a bug from time to time. It made Jean jump as she choked on a piece of dry bread, the sudden sound of her cough forcing the rest of the group into a disapproving murmur. It was further punctuated by a child making a soft sound of distress and his mother shushing him fiercely.

Those in the caravan looked around nervously before they went back to eating. Only Jean continued to look around. After a couple of moments, the birdsong hadn't continued to her right. She shifted slightly, slowly grabbing her boltcaster as she scanned the tree line.

Should she say something?

Noise should have continued from there; there wasn't a reason for it to remain silent unless...

Jean looked down at her boltcaster to ensure she had readied it, just catching the soft sounds of Nettles growling nearby.

Maybe she wasn't going crazy. She should tell them there was something there, right? Though... no one would believe a husk like her.

As Jean's throat tightened, a burst of movement from the forest caught her off-guard.

Lithe, gaunt rabbit-like creatures darted from shadow to shadow as a low mist rolled in. Simultaneously, ominous clouds blotted out the sun and plunged the group into eerie darkness.

Then the laughter began.

It was low, whooping, that grew into cackles and hollers that sent the caravan into a frenzied panic.

Mothers screamed as they grabbed their children and climbed into their wagons. Men struggled with their weapons, their cries of panic mixing with the baying of the large dogs that echoed through the darkness. Still, the chittering didn't stop.

Jean scrambled back as several of the demons launched over the earthen wall, their mouths oozing black bile that sizzled as it hit the ground. One launched towards Jean, and she lifted her boltcaster. With a quick movement, a bolt sprouted from its chest and it screamed.

Another took its place as Jean struggled to her feet. The surrounding people were panicking and knocked her down again, this time leaving her vulnerable as the mass ran and panicked.

Jean curled into a ball to protect her head as feet stampeded around before burning spread through her ankle. She screamed, reflectively kicking, and her foot struck something solid. When she looked, a small rabbit with black bile was standing before it got caught in the stampede.

Did it bite her?

Jean's mind raced a million miles a minute as she struggled to stand again, the burning growing worse. Chitter venom was practically a death sentence: if the venom didn't spread and kill her, an inquisitor would.

She had to hide it.

She stumbled as the pain crescendo before she found her fingers had clutched coarse fur. Beneath her hands, muscles contracted and rippled as she realized it was Nettles beside her. He snarled, snapped, and backed up, teeth bared and hackles raised, as the chitters lunged.

Jean caught her footing just as Nettles shot into the fray, followed by a golden arrow that sent the demons screaming. She didn't waste time looking to see where the arrow came from, instead slipping into the crowd as they tried to move away from the chitters.

As soon as Jean did, someone shouted. The hair on the back of her neck began to tingle and prickle just as another shimmer of gold, this one falling around the caravan, caught her attention. It felt like bugs running up and down her body, a stronger response than usual, before Jean realized that the arrow had caused this feeling, too: it was some sort of magic.

Her eyes flashed to the people around her and then the gold, which solidified into a large golden dome around them. Chitters launched towards it before Kingsman knights would catch them with swords that glowed golden, or magical arrows pierced them. The clockwork knight also unleashed its devastating golden light, striking large swarms of chitters before aiming somewhere else.

Now that she was safe, Jean quickly crouched to check her ankle.

There were two punctures in her boot. They both oozed the same thick, black spit that the chitters had running down their faces, and they stung horribly. Jean stared at it for a moment before she hurriedly pulled her headscarf off and tied it over the wound.

The air was cool on her head, and she did not doubt that, if people were paying attention to her, the two little horns poking out of her black hair would disgust them. With that brief thought, Jean's worries returned to the wound on her ankle. Her scarf did nothing more than add additional bulk to her boot, but it was at least a distraction from what it could be. She'd need to look at it closer, possibly when she reached Blackrock. She sucked in a breath and allowed herself to return to reality. It was deathly silent again.

Any sign of chitters had vanished completely. They'd scattered the moment the clockwork knight fired its light into their ranks, their whooping and cackling fading as quickly as they had. There was no way those creatures were natural- they had to be dark ethereals, demons, at the very least.

The knights and other Kingsmen wearing thorns with a dove circulated through the group to check for injuries, while other members of the caravan double-checked their families. Jean slowly reloaded her boltcaster, swallowed hard, and lightly waved off a Kingsman. "I'm alright."

"Are you certain?" the other woman asked. "Please, my job is to be sure that you and the others in this group are in good health to make it to Last Hope. Do you need to ride in a wagon, or do you need water?"

"I said I'm fine," Jean snapped. She pulled her hood over her head. "Don't worry about me. Others had injuries."

She ignored the Kingsman woman, doing her best to hide under her cloak. While a small part of her felt bad for making the woman jump, the rest of her refused to slow down this journey and cause more panic. It was just a little bite, after all... that wasn't bad, right? It could all be rumors that a chitter bite was so horrid. Besides, she couldn't risk showing the healer, even if it didn't guarantee her fate: the rest of the group would notice and report her instantly to those at Last Hope. It would seal any execution that awaited her.

Jean fell into the caravan once again. The healer and others circulated through the crowd and offered herbs, soft murmurs and, in rare cases, magical healing that made Jean's skin crawl. Finally, after several long minutes, they hurried through Bleak Hollow again.

It was hard to keep up after only a handful of minutes. The burning in Jean's ankle spread with each step, causing her to grip her satchel tighter. People didn't look at her, their own panic at the forefront of their minds, and it brought only a sliver of comfort to Jean. Then she'd take another step and have to bite her lip to keep from crying. Still, the fear that someone would report her to the Inquisitors once they reached Last Hope was enough to make Jean keep going, even with the pain.

Near nightfall, they reached the imposing fortress of Last Hope.

Its walls were massive to keep the chittering demons out, while a tower with Solaris's symbol and the other gods in the pantheon overlooked a ravine with an icy stream that surrounded it. As soon as the winter snow melted, the moat would be heavily flowing once more. The rough-hewn stones radiated a chill as the caravan entered, and the Kingsmen moved in to guide people through, directing them with quiet efficiency.

Solari guards then surrounded the caravan. Jean shrunk back as one of them, different from the rest, approached the man with the ram's head gauntlet. This Solari guard had pearlescent white armor, shadows hiding his face beneath his cowl, and a sword that sparked as though threatening to ignite. Each flicker of fire made Jean's stomach sink and nausea grow, especially as he said, "You have bitten among you."

"They're under our protection until the sun sets. I've had this conversation with you and any other inquisitors enough times to have memorized the treaty," the Kingsman said smoothly. He looked over the crowd. "My dove healers have already administered treatment to the injured: there is no need for your... judgement."

The inquisitor scoffed slightly and studied the crowd. "You make this claim, but we know your Kingsmen are lying snakes." He shifted and then addressed the crowd. "Good and faithful Solari worshipers!" His voice boomed, ringing through the fort. "The chittering demons bit some amongst you within these woods, spreading their darkness through you and forcing out Solaris's pure light from you! Fear not... for Solaris rewards those who walk willingly to his chosen. The chitters have defiled you, bringing you close to becoming like her!"

Jean found all eyes on her as the inquisitor pointed at her, making her shrink back.

"Do you wish to be reborn as a child of darkness? Or... shall those of you injured by the chitters, who cannot receive aid by the magic of Solaris's might, allow him to bring you to a new life of rebirth?" The inquisitor looked over the crowd again, his voice growing ever-so-slightly gentler. "Our surgeons are waiting if the wounds are too much for simple sunlight; Solaris will welcome you regardless of what may come."

He said nothing more as people moved forward. Children left their mothers and formed the line with adults who had been bitten. Each person approached the Inquisitor slowly, and he inspected their wound. Then, he'd direct them back to the group or gesture to the temple of Solaris. Those who entered the temple gave cries of pain after a few quick moments, but that did not deter the masses. It was a messy parade punctuated by the falling shadows and Jean, who wanted nothing more than to avoid any scrutiny, soon found herself on the outer edge of the gathered caravan.

While amputation was an offer, it wasn't extended to curseborns. It was a waste of materials and only kept her kind alive longer.

With that thought, Jean took a deep breath and slipped away from the group. She was near the shadows of the wall when a sharp "Halt!" caught her attention.

Two guards approached; their pikes lowered. "What do you think you're doing, curseborn? Back with the others."

"Please," Jean whispered. She swallowed, glanced at the caravan, and then looked at the guard. "I... was cleared already. They inspected me and said I was fit to enter the remainder of Last Hope."

"Did they now?" one retorted. He grabbed Jean's arm. "I don't suppose you would argue if we confirmed their inspection?"

Jean opened her mouth as a gurgle rose from the center of the town. Silence fell over the group and a sickening smell of burnt flesh and blood filled the air. Jean dared a gaze back to see the Inquisitor had ignited his sword and was systematically beheading those deemed infected beyond saving. Panic set in as Jean looked back at the guards. "No... No, I wouldn't... though... can it wait, please? It was a long journey, and I've yet to... use the facilities. I'm bursting, and... and I would hate to cause problems for the inquisitor. Solaris looks down on us as is, I'm sure it'd be worse if I were to piss myself and on the shoes of his chosen."

It was a horrible excuse, but Jean had nothing more to cling to.

The guards looked at each other, their noses wrinkled, and then the one holding Jean pushed her away. "Just like a husk to soil themselves... Fine, but you're to go into the stable with the rest of the livestock."

Jean stumbled back, barely stopping herself from crying as her weight pressed down on her injured foot. Pain shot through her ankle and up her spine, making her head swim. She blinked rapidly, then quickly turned away from the guard. "Thank you."

"Beat it," the guards spat.

She could feel their eyes following her as she approached the enclosed stable where the caravan horses would be placed. It was there that she sunk against a wall, panting through the pain, and then slowly took off her boot.

Two puncture wounds on her ankle stared back at her. They were black and oozed grey from pussy bile from the chitter, and thin black tendrils were running up her leg. She stared at it, fingers shaking, and then pressed against the wound.

It spurted blood and then the oozy mixture. Jean's vision faded and she inhaled sharply. There was no way she'd be able to keep up with the caravan with this injury, even if she tried, come morning. Slowly, Jean pressed on the injury again. The pain made her vision grow black once more, but she forced herself to do this repeatedly to clean the injury out. Each time, she smelled a bitter aroma wafting from the cut, as if it had been infected for days, not just a few hours.

As soon as Jean only received blood, she tightly bandaged the wound and slowly put her boot back on.

It didn't feel any better, but she could slowly stand and move further into the stable before the horses were brought in.

After the horses settled, and Jean had found an unsoiled section of straw, she caught sight of the dark-skinned knight and Nettles again.

The large dog had his nose to the ground again and was sniffing beside where Jean had originally looked at her wound. Then Nettles lifted his head and locked eyes with her. His tongue lolled, and he trotted to her while his master followed behind. Jean shifted slightly and scratched the dog as he approached. She didn't look at the knight, who had crossed his arms for a moment before he sat down beside Jean and pulled a canteen from his hip. "Are you thirsty?"

"No, thanks," Jean replied. She looked at the knight from the corner of her eye and then scooted over slightly. "Aren't you going to go rest with the other Kingsmen?"

"Eventually." The knight took a drink of water and tightened the cap again. He watched the caravan horses and then looked at Jean. "Aren't you going to go rest with the other Solari?"

Jean gave a dry laugh. "I think they like my kind even less than we like Kingsmen."

"We? You subscribe to the feud as well, then?" The knight raised an eyebrow as he shifted to get comfortable. "For someone who seems so observant, I'm surprised. The only argument the Kingsmen have with

Solari is about who the real God of this plane is... but that certainly is not an excuse for open combat in areas."

He offered a faint smile before he held a gloved hand out. "I'm Captain Rolandus of Apple Ridge. You've met Nettles, of course."

The curseborn woman looked at him, paused, and slowly took his hand. "Jean Cassy."

This was a change. Kingsmen rarely interacted with Solari worshippers, and the interactions of this knight in a friendly manner, though nice, were suspicious. Still, Jean slowly relaxed as Nettles laid down with a huff and put his giant head in her lap. She lightly brushed over his coarse fur, studying him, before she looked at Rolandus again.

He had taken a pipe from his breast pocket and was smoking quietly. As soon as he realized she was watching him, he cleared his throat. "I'm sorry, nervous habit... I can put it out if you'd prefer."

"No... that's alright."

Jean watched him smoke for a few moments and then rested her head against the stable wall. There was no sound except for the light breaths of the animals and the knight beside her, all of which was a lull that prompted Jean's mind to wander. Rolandus shifted slightly and her eyes snapped open. He paused as he stood, his face growing gentle. "I'm sorry, I was going to go set up my bed roll... You know you are welcome to stay beside the Kingsmen camp this evening, right? You don't need to stay here in the stable if you'd rather be beside others."

"And let the Solari see me?" Jean asked. "I have enough problems already; I don't need my people thinking that I'm a traitor."

The knight tilted his head. After a moment, he asked, "Jean... are they really your people if they treat their horses better than you?"

Jean jerked her head back.

The conversation wasn't one she had considered having with anyone, let alone a knight who seemed far too interested in her thoughts. It seemed rather suspicious that he was asking her questions and trying to get her to join the Kingsmen now. The Inquisitors, and high priests, in Zanther always warned the populus of Kingsmen trickery. They wanted nothing but to dethrone Solaris! Jean was lucky that her aunt and uncle never spoke of religion when she was there, but even their silence made her worried. Besides... even if they were right, worshipping the Usurper HaMelech resulted in death within the nation of Yegreydal; it was Solari run, and these Kingsmen were toeing a line. Now, as Rolandus spoke, she looked away. "You won't convert me so easily."

Rolandus' eyes widened. "No, that's not what I meant—"

"Enjoy your evening, Captain Rolandus. Good night."

Jean looked away from him and Nettles huffed before he settled once more. After a brief pause, Rolandus's steps retreated.

That night, Jean grew more and more worried. Each time she opened her eyes, it felt like something was watching her from the shadows. She pulled her cloak tighter around her to block the chill before she turned over and curled up beside Nettles, who sighed and shifted to get comfortable as well.

Finally, as dawn approached, a horrible scream rang through the air.

Chittering Madness

A sickness caused by prolonged exposure to chitters + chitter magic, often times leathal

Symptoms include hallucinations, manifestation, hysteria, paranoia an adversion to sunlight

Known Treatments: None

All Infected must be burned to prevent spread of the sickness.

By order of: **Fernando Alastar**

Solari Grand Inqusitor General

3

CHITTERS

Jean struggled to her feet as the sounds of a panicked crowd grew. Nettles lurched upright, growling, and padded to the stable entrance. The horses pranced nervously, looking at one another as Jean slowly put weight on her bad leg and followed the large dog.

Outside, people with lanterns ran through the Solari group. The scream had died down into soft sobs and a thin, broken, "My boy!" rose above the crowd. Jean held onto the stable door as the cacophony of worried people grew and finally the voice of the Inquisitor rose above the din.

"What is going on?!"

"He's dead! He's dead, and he was fine when I last nursed him!"

As the sounds traveled to Jean, her stomach turned. If a child died through the night, randomly, people would look for something to blame. They always did: if there wasn't an answer, they'd find one. Unfortunately, even though chitters were an option, Jean was the best scapegoat in the fort.

She held onto her satchel strap and took a shaking step into the darkness. Unlike before, where the shadows brought her comfort, nothing but worry and dread filled Jean. She swallowed back the pain and limped towards the gates, ever mindful of the crowd demanding answers.

From the Kingsmen side of the fort, she could hear them praying. It was a contrast that made the hair on the back of her neck stand up and her skin crawl, making her want nothing more than to escape this fort and get to Blackrock sooner. The guards were distracted, which allowed her to make it to the darkest section of the courtyard beside the gate with little issue.

The portcullis was shut, its thick bars the only obstacle between Jean and her escape.

It had taken far too long for her to get here, especially as she heard someone crying out into the darkness about a curseborn witch. The adrenaline spiked and Jean looked around.

All she needed was a gap to slip through... Her eyes traveled to the winching system, and she sucked in a breath. It was going to be too heavy, but maybe, just maybe, the fear she had would help her. With that thought, Jean slipped to the winch and used her full strength to turn it. It stuck, refusing to budge, before finally it gave a soft creak and Jean hit the ground as it moved. She did this twice more, praying that the growing mob covered the noise, and looked back at the bars.

It wasn't big enough.

Jean squeezed her eyes closed and forced the winch again, this time managing to lift the portcullis enough that she could slither under it on her belly. It hurt to stand on the other side, her ankle burning now and sending pain up her spine, but Jean pushed that away. She pulled her boltcaster from her hip, aimed it through the bars, and shot the rope holding the portcullis.

While it'd cause problems for the traveling caravan, it also prevented anyone from following her out or letting anything in.

She pressed her back to the stone wall, reloaded her clip and wound the crystal, before she took a deep breath.

Solaris's avatar would rise soon, and there would be no fear. Until then, she'd have to walk.

Jean took two cautious steps and her ankle gave out. She fell forward with an outstretched hand, but her fingers didn't touch anything. She began to somersault down the riverbank, her hubris her downfall as she had forgotten the dry moat, before she finally came to a standstill, inches from the stream.

That only caused the pain to grow worse.

After several moments, Jean sat up and double-checked her belongings. It seemed like everything was still there, her extra bolts included, which allowed her a single breath of relief before she slowly climbed out of the ravine and towards the woods.

The shadows seemed longer here, this time stretching towards her before they'd retreat as she looked in their direction. Jean shifted, looked around, and continued.

As she walked, the feeling of being watched filled her again. It wasn't until she could not deal with the pain any longer that she stopped, her eyes closed as she sucked in a breath and then looked around. The sun hadn't risen, and she thought it would have.

With nothing more to do, Jean pressed her back to a tree and held her boltcaster. She could at least wait for it here, sheltered from any prying eyes.

Her paranoia mounted with each moment as she watched the shapes of barren trees shake in the wind. Out of the corner of her eye, she saw a small light, and she stared at it before she rubbed her face.

It must be a hallucination.

The last time she thought she saw any orbs like this was when she was small, and it was an imaginary friend. At least, that was what her adoptive mother always told her. Adriata never put much stock into things like that, nor was she an incredibly doting mother. The only saving grace was the realization that Jean didn't enjoy actual school, and so she allowed her to study in the forest. Too much stress, she had said, going with other children. Perhaps it was a stress-induced vision; it certainly would make sense, given Jean's aptitude for worrying. Jean watched it bob closer before she offered a weak chuckle. "Osmond... I don't think I've thought about you since I was young... Look at me, I'm losing it." It had to have been caused by the pain.

Osmond moved closer, and Jean sighed. Even imaginary company was welcome at this point.

When Jean opened her eyes next, it was still dark. Osmond had gone, and she was alone in the woods. A thin mist rolled through the trees and Jean, as she looked at the sky, felt her heart sink. The sun should have risen. Why didn't the avatar of Solaris rise?

She looked around, slowly, before she caught sight of Osmond.

He was bobbing near a thicket where a lithe rabbit laid hunched. The rabbit stared at her, eyes locked on her face, as it placed one paw in front of the other. Jean's mounting worries grew as it snarled, exposing two long teeth that dripped with bile. It froze, nose twitching, before suddenly leaping towards Jean.

Reflexively, Jean swung her boltcaster.

The creature hit it with a solid thud, and Jean struggled to her feet. Her ankle hurt worse, and she sucked in a breath. She hit it hard. It was dead, right?

To her horror, the creature slowly stood up and shook itself off.

It locked eyes with Jean once more and then laughed.

A single bolt silenced it.

Jean breathed shakily, looking around as something else picked up the laughter, then another, and finally an entire pack of chittering calls rang through the forest. Jean lifted her boltcaster and swung it before a large chitter, this time bipedal with a sharpened bone, shot through the undergrowth towards her. Another small group with javelins appeared as well, but Jean wasted no time in running. Her ankle sent agony through her, forcing her to go slower than she'd like, and she turned back to see the chitters were gaining on her.

She fired the boltcaster once, removing one threat.

Desperately, she scanned the trees for a break. Osmond floated near the loudest section of the woods, but as Jean realized that he didn't steer her wrong with the chitterling that was stalking her, she allowed herself to swerve in that direction.

The slight course change didn't come with problems, though, as another chitter lunged out of nowhere with a knife.

The bile burned as it entered her arm, the knife blade sinking deep into her upper arm, and Jean, with a cry, struggled to keep going.

Osmond stayed beside her this time. Part of Jean wondered if he was helping her or if he was helping the chitters, but she didn't allow herself any additional time to think about it.

Jean's side cramped, and her left arm had gone numb from the pain. All she could do was keep running, the cries of the creatures just a step behind her pushing her forward. She broke through the tree line and tumbled down a steep bank, landing in a small grove.

The chitters had to be right on her trail as she could hear footsteps gaining on her faster than she thought was possible while she forced herself through the tree line.

A spear whizzed past her, grazed her already useless arm, and sent another jolt of agony through her. The throbbing in her arm, even with pressure applied, caused her to stumble over a log; she caught herself before looking back. They were gaining on her, and it wasn't simply small ones anymore: a large, wolf-shaped chitter with goat's horns had joined the rapidly approaching group.

Jean struggled to her feet before catching sight of a branch.

It was just low enough that she could climb, even with her arm and ankle. She had nothing left to lose, so she climbed up the tree. As she did, she brought her foot down as hard as she could on the first branch she used. It cracked, convincing her that there may be enough breakage to the load bearing portion to save her, and she scrambled higher.

She didn't stop until she was at least fifteen feet in the air, clinging to the trunk and shaking.

The chitters below her began to cackle and circle the tree while the one with goat's horns sped up and rammed it. Jean held tighter to the trunk before a headache washed over her. Between her arm, her ankle, and her head, Jean was lucky to cling to her perch.

Sucking in a breath, she looked around before she caught sight of a figure around her height in the undergrowth.

Jean narrowed her eyes to try focusing on the humanoid shape coming through the mist. To her horror, she saw a yellowed, gore-stained skull grinning back at her. It shared the elongated form of the deer skulls in Zanther's taverns, yet concluded with a predator's snarl. Two magnificent antlers were on its head, and sitting between the antlers was a large, unblinking black eye with a white pupil.

Nausea flooded Jean as she recognized it as the Eye of the Dragon, the deadly eye that rose once a year to bring about chaos and heighten carnal urges. Now, as it focused on her, panic and fear mounted in the curseborn as she dug her nails into the bark.

The skull lifted and two tiny white pupils followed the gaze of the eye. Now, as it was closer, Jean could see rotten hide and flesh hung off of what she once thought was a man, instead revealing a nearly skeletal form of a chitter... or, at least, what looked like one.

In its clawed, gnarled hand was an ebony staff. It glistened with a cruel contempt, outshining the rancid blood that dribbled over polished bone.

As Jean stared, the Eye of the Dragon narrowed in on her. The creature carrying the staff let out an unholy wail; the sound echoing both a thousand screams and the silence of nothing as its thin muscles twitched and pulsed with far more strength than its emaciated body should have. Black mist rolled up from around it, spreading through the air and towards her.

The sound pulsed through Jean's skull, sending one hand to cling to her temple while the other haphazardly attempted to hold on to the tree. All the while, she felt watched. It was like a hot breath brushing her neck, the feeling of a predator before its jaws clamped down on its prey.

The fog grew thicker and hid the chitters beneath her until only one hulking form remained. Jean could see its red eyes focused on her despite the darkness: chittering filling the air and sending dread through Jean. The tendrils had reached her now, wrapped around her body and neck as she choked.

This was strong, and it wasn't simply darkness. It had a thickness to it — almost viscous — as Jean struggled to breathe. It filled her lungs and made her hack as her head pounded, her vision growing hazy as the migraine grew worse.

She was busy focusing on trying to inhale anything but the mist when the tree shook violently, almost throwing Jean from her perch. She looked down to see the enormous creature that resembled a horned wolf with blood-red eyes had slammed its head into the trunk of the tree again.

Eyes and teeth filled the rolling black mist below. Once more, the tree shook, and Jean thought she could now see the creatures clawing their way up the trunk. Out of the corner of her eye, she could see a chitter leap off a branch above her.

Jean closed her eyes as she braced for impact.

The final blow never came, as she was still alone on her branch. Something was there, waiting in the darkness for her to turn and let her guard down, she knew it. She could feel the eyes watching her, glinting.

CRACK.

The tree listed to the side, and Jean tightened her grip on the rope behind her. She couldn't untie herself; she was going to fall headlong into a mass of waiting teeth regardless of what she did, and it'd be over. Her hand shook as she fumbled with her boltcaster.

She had to hit it. The sound of the boltcaster made her wince: why was her weapon so much louder? A scream made her double over as her headache compounded and her heartbeat echoed. The beast below still stood. Jean leveled her boltcaster and fired an uncertain shot into the darkness.

What vision she had was hazy from pain and tears; panic and despair had taken root, especially as she heard a growl to her left. She whipped around and fired in that direction. She thought she had seen a chitter up with her, but it faded away as quickly as it had come.

Was it only a hallucination?

Jean squeezed her eyes shut. "Please someone, anyone..."

In front of her, as she opened her eyes, was Osmond. The surrounding chaos dulled as though she were underwater as she stared at him. "Osmond, help me..."

Not a sound left the orb, but he drifted down and towards the mass of bodies below her. Jean watched as he found a place near the creature with the staff.

Jean lifted her boltcaster, aimed, and fired.

A scream filled the air, the sun broke through the fog, and the chitters shrieked as they ran for cover. The creature Jean shot crumpled to the ground with a cloud of thick black smoke rising off its form. Then it disintegrated to nothing more than a skeleton clutching its black staff.

"They turn to dust," she whispered, watching as a few chitters caught in direct sunlight melted away.

It didn't take long for her to scurry down the tree. The sun was uncomfortably hot from her perch, and she had a growing curiosity about the staff.

Jean studied it from a distance before deciding it was safe enough to approach. It was a smooth, black piece of wood that was very reminiscent of obsidian as she stared at it. Her curious face reflected her, and, despite the sense of dread, she stepped closer to trace over the piece.

As she did, soft voices filled her mind. She be respected rather than scorned.

Jean slowly closed her hand around the staff. In an instant, her troubles seemed to melt away, and she looked around.

It was the children she used to go to school with, mocking her and her appearance. One of them threw an apple past Jean, and she winced as she heard it hit behind her. "You're a demon! Your adoptive mom doesn't love you; she took you in because she pitied you!"

Jean turned to look towards where the apple had hit, prepared to see her younger self crying on the ground as she had done that day. Instead, she saw herself atop a massive wolf-like brute of a chitter, the staff in one hand and a ball of darkness in the other. A mass of chitters ran in front of them, their fangs bared as they descended on the children who had been mocking her.

The scene changed, and it was the men from the caravan who had whispered threats against her; again, chitters swarmed over them, and their faces full of contempt and hatred turned to horror and fear.

She looked around, and a small smile flickered over her face. This was all she ever wanted; people weren't looking at her with hatred, they had a mix of awe and fear. They recognized she was a person, and that she was better than they were! How tantalizing it was, the thought of reverence instead of revolt! A scream echoed behind her, and she slowly turned.

It was a mother holding a baby in her arms, absolute terror on her face as a chittering swarm converged and then consumed them.

Jean's heart shattered. This vision, the pure bliss she'd once imagined in being feared, wasn't limited to those who had hurt her. It was everyone, even strangers who had never laid eyes on her. She was a monster, worse than what they already believed her to be.

She shook her head to see Osmond hovering nearby, enough to make her snap out of it and let go of the staff.

Her fingers were stiff as though glued to the wood and Jean's horror mounted as she realized tendrils had wrapped around her hand and arm. They stuck to her flesh, burning through her body as the darkness that had choked her minutes ago seared her arm. Jean forced herself from the staff and then fell backward. The staff was only a few feet away from her before it began to dissolve into the same black mist that had risen when the chitters had died.

Jean stared at it, her head swimming, before a wave of exhaustion and pain washed over her. She staggered for a moment before her vision faded and she collapsed.

***

Nettles snuffled as he hurried through the woods, followed closely by Rolandus. The dog wasn't sure what was wrong, but the urgency in his master's voice as he spoke to the other humans made him nervous. Now, as he ran untethered before Rolandus, the sheepdog was looking for any scents that could reveal what his job was.

The caravan left without them.

It wasn't often that they did this, but Nettles enjoyed it. He was big enough to take on a chitter if needed, and his master had a blessed bow to help if it was too much.

From behind him, Rolandus whistled, and Nettles slowed down.

His master was crouched beside broken bushes. Nettles approached and sniffed before his ears pricked.

He smelled her.

Rolandus had no chance keeping up as Nettles took off. It was a quick run through the woods, jumping over logs and swerving through trees, before Nettles slowed to a stop.

In a clearing laid the girl.

She had several foul-smelling bites and black tendrils over her arms, her face was covered in dirt, and she convulsed slightly as she breathed. Nettles laid down with a whine before his eyes darted to the figure standing over her.

It was bright, with four sets of wings and an ever-shifting face. Its footprints changed, too, though the prominent directions had a hoof, a foot, a clawed paw, and a taloned leg sunk deep in the dirt.

From behind Nettles came Rolandus. He made it two steps into the clearing before he fell to his knees. Nettles watched as the Guardian turned, said something, and then faded away.

Then Rolandus stood and hurried to the girl.

Nettles approached as well, sniffing her, before his master gathered her and laid her over the dog's back.

"Come on, old friend," Rolandus murmured. "We need to get her to Godrick's Rest."

The Chittering Plague

Their high pitch laughter can carry for miles to call their brethren to the hunt

Adult chitters stand 3-4 feet tall with common fur color ranging from browns to blacks. Chitters always look emaciated but are far stronger and more energetic than they appear.

When killed the chitter's body disintegrates into a thick black smoke in less than a minute.

Chitters have no sexual dimorphism or even recognizable genders. The current theory is they reproduce asexually through the corpse of a human host. However they are also known to appear as if from thin air in dark areas during the Long Night as if the Black Dragon willed them into existence.

There are a small number of chitter anomalies that show up periodically, such as the brute, a massive wolf-like creature with ram's horns and boar's tusks, or a shaman, a humanoid figure with a deer skull head and a terrifying control of illegal dark magic.

This staff was left by the shaman when it vanished.

Chitterlings are assumed to be the juvenile form of their larger brethren. They are equally aggressive as their adult form. Chitterlings have been observed emerging from the corpse of one of their victims after 24 hours when the body is shrouded in darkness.

GRANDMA LETTY

When Jean awoke, she was lying on a plush bed with covers tucked up to her chin. A clock ticked faintly beside her and a bird, quietly, sung outside the window.

Where were the chitters? Where was she, and what had happened?

There was no way she could sit up: she tried, but the pain that flooded her body made her cry out and then sob. Out of the corner of her eye, she could see that there was a floating orb bobbing over what looked like a bedside table. Despite her pain, she couldn't help but give a weak little laugh at the sight of Osmond before a feeling of dread and fear settled over her again.

Haunting chitter laughter filled her head, making Jean squeeze her eyes closed. It wasn't real, it couldn't be real... right? She slowly opened one eye to find that the shadows were trying to choke her again, their clawing, grasping hands reaching out as they morphed into the chitters that had chased her through the woods. Jean struggled to sit up, gasped in pain, and then threw herself from the bed.

The hardwood floor beneath her sent a jolt of agony through her left arm and her ankle, and Jean shuddered as she tried to stand.

She had to leave... she had to get out...

"Grandma Letty, I can't just keep quiet. If the inquisitors or the doves find out you're harboring someone with chittering madness—"

"Young man," a thin voice interrupted, "I follow HaMelech's will, not theirs. I'm not asking you to lie, I'm asking you to avoid telling anyone if it doesn't come up. Now, my houseguest needs something to eat. I just heard her, I believe she's awake."

"Yes, Grandma Letty..."

The sound of a door shutting in another room made Jean suck in a breath. She looked around, and found Osmond was bouncing beside her, before the shadows closed in again.

This time, however, they retreated as footsteps sounded out.

From the door came an old woman, bent and gnarled with age. She had a cane in one hand, though the longer Jean looked at her, the more the cane looked like a spear and the woman looked like a large rabbit. Jean's eyes focused and unfocused on her as the curseborn tried to decide if this was a threat before the old woman held out a hand.

Her bony fingers morphed into claws as Jean watched. Jean scrambled back as best she could and bit back another cry of pain.

"Easy, child," the woman crooned gently. It sounded like she was trying to soothe a wild animal, which only added to Jean's rising fears. "Nothing will harm you here. The chitters cannot enter my home."

"No... no, you are a chitter. You are trying to trick me," Jean whispered.

The woman frowned and slowly found the rocking chair in the corner. She moved back and forth, and Jean watched her. It was almost mesmerizing, lulling Jean into a state of calm as the woman murmured back, "Your friend brought you here. He would not bring you to a place of harm... and the Guardian has stayed beside you. I will not hurt you."

Guardian?

Jean blinked at the woman, her mind beginning to swim. Finally, she whispered, "Who are you?"

"You can call me Grandma Letty, dear one." Letty stood and approached again.

The hallucination of the chitter over the woman made Jean flinch, but as Letty gently took her hand, a sense of peace washed over her. Letter helped her into the bed, patting the mattress to find the edge, before she laid Jean down. Then, after a moment of fumbling, she tucked the blanket over the curseborn again. Jean stared at her, taking in the features of Letty's face as the hallucination ebbed in and out.

Letty's face had wrinkles, and age spots coating most of her face. There were crow's feet and laugh lines, very little on her brow from frowning, and her hair was wispy around her face. Jean's gaze traveled to Letty's eyes, where sightless blue irises searched the ceiling as though looking for unknown secrets. Letty found Jean's hand and patted it lightly. "There, child... what's your name? Your friend didn't stay long; he said there was a caravan he needed to return to."

Friend? Jean racked her brain for a moment.

No one would have helped a curseborn from the forest, nor would they have spared her, if they were Solari. She didn't have any Kingsmen friends, though... Well, Captain Rolandus had done his best to interact with her. Was he the friend that Grandma Letty was talking about? He had Nettles, who could have tracked her... but why would he have brought her here?

"Child?"

"Oh... I'm Jean."

Jean blinked at Letty again, the hallucinations making her head foggy. Letty lightly patted Jean's hand again. "You rest. How badly do the bites hurt?"

"The... bites?"

"The wounds from the chitters. Did you tend to them, or do I need to clean them?" Letty asked.

"I haven't cleaned my ankle since Last Hope," Jean murmured.

Letty's eyebrows raised, and she hummed quietly. Finally, she said, "I'll be right back. Rest while you can, this part will not be pleasant... I'm glad Master Rolandus could get you here when he did."

So, it was Rolandus. Jean frowned as she watched Letty go. She had referred to him as Jean's friend, not his name, up till now. Was she trying to keep it secret? How did Rolandus know who Letty was? Had he brought others here?

As Jean's mind swam with questions, the sudden weight of the surrounding shadows seemed to grow heavier. She sucked in a breath and looked around. The shadows were growing, now forming eyes and fangs that threatened her from the darkness. Jean stared at them, her heart rate beginning to increase, before Osmond bounced into view again.

The shadows faded away from sight as though forced away by his light. Jean swallowed and looked around, finding that Osmond was gone as suddenly as he had appeared.

Letty slowly found her way into the room again, this time carrying a bowl of hot water with flowers floating in it. It smelled very nice, almost like cinnamon, with hints of lavender and chamomile. Jean inhaled, finding her eyes were closing as Letty sat beside her.

Jean's relaxation vanished as Letty worked on her ankle injury first. The warm water sent jolts of pain through Jean, who, despite her best efforts, began to cry again.

"Hush, dear," Letty murmured. "I know it hurts, but we must rid your body of the toxin."

She gave Jean another gentle squeeze of the hand before finding her ankle once more. She continued to wash it, silent, before she whispered, "This feels so incredibly raw and inflamed... How long ago were you bitten?"

"Just... just yesterday," Jean managed. She clung to the blankets underhand and sucked in another breath as Letty massaged the wound. When she dared look, dread filled her heart.

The wound looked awful. A single day's worth of festering had caused the immediate area around the bite to go black, swollen, and pussy. Letty seemed unbothered as she pressed on either side of the wound, producing a stream of bile and gore that coated her hands and the bedsheets. The old woman lightly blotted Jean's ankle with a cloth, then wiped the warm water over it, before she returned to massaging the wound clean again.

Jean swallowed. "I... I'm going to die, aren't I? If the inquisitors find out... I'm a curseborn, there's no way they'll simply amputate..."

Letty paused. "I'm sorry to say, dear, but even if you were not curseborn there would be no chance of amputation. The infection has spread and become rather severe. There's treatment to manage symptoms, but that's all even Kingsmen healing can do. Only HaMelech Himself could fully cure you if it was within His will." She didn't stop working on Jean's leg, though she did murmur, "The only grace you currently have is the fact that you hadn't touched any of their cursed weapons... I haven't dealt with many who have, but those who did..." she trailed off, her lips setting in a firm line. "The madness sets in worse for those who touch those weapons, and even symptom management may not be enough. Bites are easy enough to treat... Chittering sickness is troublesome, but able to be dealt with. Chittering madness is something entirely different."

She became quiet again. Jean watched her, the adrenaline from the pain now more than enough to keep her focused. The hallucination of a chitter instead of the ancient woman at the edge of the bed lingered longer now, as though threatening to consume Grandma Letty and all that she did. Every so often, Letty would press on Jean's ankle and the hallucination would solidify, leaving Jean breathless and shaking.

Jean remained quiet the entire time. She simply watched Letty, doing her best to wrap her mind around the entire situation.

She had touched the staff.

Her assumption was that it was a cursed weapon, especially as it had played with her mind. That meant that she really had chittering madness, right? Jean sucked in another breath, staring at the ceiling now. Grandma Letty said it was worse than just chittering sickness, whatever that was. It was all the same: there was chitter venom, and that was cause for execution. There was no second thought spared in removing the infected limb. One less curseborn was good enough for the Solari, and that could free her to be reborn differently.

The thought made Jean shift. That wouldn't be so bad... no, she had to stay safe, if only for Caxton's sake.

Her mind was so consumed by these worries that Jean didn't notice Letty had moved to her arm and was tending the cut from the knife now. It wasn't until Letty pressed on either side of the wound and sent infection splattering over Jean's face did the curseborn move, and she blinked and wiped the gore with her other hand.

Even in Letty's grip, Jean's arm felt incredibly heavy. It was the sudden realization that everything, absolutely everything, hinged on how well Jean handled treatment for chittering madness. Her eyes wandered over her arm, studying the black tendrils the covered her right hand and raced up to her shoulder. It was pretty, almost, and Jean couldn't help but stare before Letty patted her leg.

"Are you done?" Jean asked softly.

"I am for now. You need to rest, dear. The adrenaline will wear off soon, and I'm not sure how well you will handle it once that happens." Letty slowly stood, found her bowl of water, and began to walk out. She paused for a moment. "I'll be back in a moment with some food. Until I am, just rest."

Jean blinked and shifted.

The kindness was strange, especially after Letty treated her wounds. Perhaps she should leave?

Jean tried to stand, but her body was too weak to even sit up.

She hated this. Never had she been in such a position as this. She couldn't sit up, which meant she was unable to defend herself. Her arms were heavy, breathing hurt, and there was a keen sense of looming danger that refused to lift as she slowly scanned the room. The shadows swirled ever so slightly, and Jean sighed and closed her eyes.

There was still a buzz of worry in the back of her head, but it had grown dull amid the rising pain in her limbs.

When she opened her eyes, it seemed like her strength had vanished. Even the simple act of looking around made her tired, much less want to eat anything that Grandma Letty might have prepared.

The soft creaking of the rocking chair across the room alerted Jean to where the frail old woman was, and as her strained eyes found Letty in the corner, Jean simply sighed and closed them again.

Footsteps padded to her, and then a lightweight settled on the bed. A cool cloth found its place on Jean's forehead before Letty murmured, "Are you awake, sweetheart?"

"Yes."

Her throat burned as she spoke, making Jean cough and sputter slightly as she swallowed. It was worse than the day before, and a flash of fear raced through her. Then, as she looked at Letty, her vision clouded. A large chitter was superimposed over the woman, either a powerful delusion or a sudden attacker in the room. Jean tried to move away but her limbs had seized as though frozen over, causing more panic to mount in the curseborn. She sucked in a breath, her lungs constricted as the fear only grew, and Jean began to cry.

The vision of the chitter reached out and wrinkled fingers cupped Jean's cheek.

"Oh, Jean," Letty's voice murmured through the din, "you are doing worse than I thought... close your eyes, you are safe here. You'll need more treatment and sunshine."

Jean sucked in another breath, this time the feeling similar to sucking through a straw.

It took a few moments for Letty's hand to find the shutters, which she carefully threw open to reveal golden sunlight. The warm beams of light landed on Jean, filling her with a keen sense of uneasiness and dislike, before Letty then found her blankets and pulled them from Jean's body.

The sunlight dappled over her wounds, sending a rising pain and panic through Jean. She tried to scoot away from the light but found that it hurt too much. Then, as she bit back a whimper, she realized that the wounds on her ankle and her arm were bubbling under the sunlight. That was where the pain was coming from, as well as the wispy black smoke that seemed to fill the air and dissipate. Jean shifted before Letty asked, "What's going on?"

"There's black smoke." Jean didn't look at the older woman. Instead, she stared at the wound as it sizzled and slowly cleared up. The tendrils running up her arm from where she had grabbed the staff, however, didn't change. Jean closed her eyes as Letty brushed her hand over her head. As the blind woman's hand brushed over Jean's horns, and then tensed. Jean stiffened. It was only a matter of time before Grandma Letty would force her out and report her.

Before Jean could whisper a hasty promise to leave as soon as she was well, Letty smoothed her hair down again. "Get some rest, Jean. You aren't going to be well enough to travel for several days. I'm sure your family in Blackrock will understand, though we can write to them if you're worried. I'll get you some food and some tea to help soothe you."

She hobbled off and Jean, startled out of her hazy state, interrupted. "I didn't say I was going to Blackrock."

"No, you didn't," Letty answered. She continued to move through the room, using her foot to tap around any new objects in her home. "HaMelech spoke to me in a dream two days ago and instructed me to wait for a houseguest. I needed to restock my herbs, and as I was doing so, He then told me that you were going to Blackrock. I was to tell you that your little cousin will be just fine to wait as soon as you were well enough to hear the news."

Jean watched the elder leave the room, her mind swimming with unanswered questions.

How did HaMelech speak to Letty? Why did He care about a curseborn, and why was Letty so calm about Jean being one? Kingsmen didn't like anyone outside of other Kingsmen — save for potentially her aunt and uncle — and the moment Letty learned of Jean's amber necklace, she would force her out. Perhaps this was only buying Letty time to call for an inquisitor... though, any number of times, Jean was sure that Letty could have reported her. Instead, she took in an injured curseborn brought to her by Rolandus, which was another confusing point. None of it made sense, and Jean's head was beginning to hurt the longer she thought.

Instead, she closed her eyes and tried her best to ignore the gnawing anxiety that filled her. Inquisitors were going to find her. The Kingsmen would make her pay heavily for treatment, and she wouldn't be able to pay any tolls on the remainder of her trip. Worse, maybe she was going to be robbed by a seeing relative of Letty's at any moment.

A huge yawn made Jean stop momentarily, and she slowly settled. The smell of lavender and chamomile was wafting from another room, soothing her mind and coaxing her to sleep.

Whatever happened, she would have to wait.

She remained with Letty for three days. The first two involved brief movement and few answers to questions. Letty was a gentle caregiver: she aided Jean in sitting up, helped wash her face when the pain left salty trails of tears down her cheeks, and ensured that Jean was well-fed. There was little argument, though, of how Letty was to treat Jean's wounds and the mandatory sunshine time.

"It will assist in removing any venom that may linger," Letty had said. "Chitters cannot mix with the light, as they are darkness themselves. Just like the demons in the Holy Text, they stand no chance against light from HaMelech."

That wasn't the strangest thing Letty had said, either. Sometimes she spoke to herself, leaving Jean wondering if the old woman was truly hearing from HaMelech or if she was going insane. When Letty looked over Jean, for example, and lightly said, "Thank you for watching her for me... I can see them too, but I cannot do much more than pray to our Master," nothing but cold chills ran through Jean. Letty didn't explain herself, nor did she refer to anything above Jean, either. It made Jean uncomfortable: she didn't like this woman knowing more about Jean than what she had said, nor did she like thinking about where Letty learned this. HaMelech wasn't a god; he was a usurper. There was no power there, right?

Amid the treatment and the murmurings, Jean relaxed in Letty's care. The hallucinations of a chitter over Letty had faded, leaving only the gnarled woman and her weathered face. The tendrils over Jean's arm had faded, too, but despite Jean's protest, Letty insisted on giving her tea every couple of hours. Finally, after the sixth cup of tea, and the third trip to the bathroom, Jean asked, "Why do I need to drink this if I'm doing better?"

Letty paused in her rocking, her wrinkled hands marking a place in her book, and looked towards Jean. She was quiet for a moment and then said, "You have chittering madness, Jean, even if you don't feel its effects now. The tea is meant to help keep any flare-ups from occurring. The last thing you need is to enter a manic episode, or to hallucinate chitters into being. It's a nasty disease, and the Solari won't put up with you if they discover that you are ill."

"How do you know?"

Jean watched Letty look at the ceiling as though searching for an answer. Finally, her caregiver sighed. "When I was younger, I was fortunate to have been married when I contracted the sickness. My husband tended to me, but I could not fully recover. Overtime, it grew worse. I lost my sight, praise HaMelech, and I no longer suffered the effects. During that time, though, it was a constant danger to be out of our home. Dusnar had yet to create treaties protecting different religious freedoms, and the Solari inquisitors had every right to enter our home to end my life. HaMelech protected me and kept us safe... and now I listen and obey to ensure that those who come to my door receive the same chance that I got." After her soft explanation, Letty returned to rocking back and forth. She didn't look at Jean again, lost in thought, and Jean took the silence as her finality on the subject.

By the end of the third day, Letty confirmed that Jean could continue her travels. She cradled Jean's hands as the curseborn stood before her. It was an odd gesture, Jean wasn't sure why Letty was so fond of her, but she didn't argue as Letty said, "The Guardian will not be leaving your side anytime soon from what I can tell. HaMelech has placed him with you for a purpose, though I am not sure what." Jean racked her brain for an explanation as Letty pressed her hands. "May HaMelech keep you and guide you... may you soon hear His words and come to love Him, and know that He has not forsaken you."

Jean's skin crawled with the gentle prayer, her discomfort outweighing the slight semblance of appreciation. She shifted. "What is the Guardian, Grandma Letty?"

Letty's face softened. "A friend, Jean... someone sent by HaMelech. Outside of that, I can't explain much more."

Jean nodded faintly and then checked her satchel. A thin leather pouch looked back at her, containing the tea that Letty had painstakingly made for her during her stay. It'd be enough to get to Blackrock, at the very least.

The curseborn turned to go before she suddenly had Letty's arms around her in a tight hug. She blinked before she slowly hugged Letty back. "Thank you."

"You are so welcome. Travel easy, Jean, and may HaMelech allow me to see you once more."

BLACKROCK

Jean hurried toward the large gate of Blackrock. She did her best to stay away from the shadows while simultaneously avoiding the bright patches of sunlight. Both made her nervous, even when drinking her tea. There weren't any eyes manifesting, or hallucinations, but that only gave her minor relief.

As she passed the gatehouse, given barely a second glance by the guards, Jean fixed her hood again.

It'd been many years since visiting her aunt and uncle, and the hazy memories of her treatment by everyone else in Blackrock only brought concern of what may happen this time. The other fear, more to the forefront of her mind, was that her young cousin was getting sicker.

The letter in her satchel felt heavy at the reminder.

Aunt Anca and Uncle Flick hadn't sent any others, as far as she knew, but that didn't mean anything.

Jean sped up, following the twisting turns of cobblestone streets. She did her best to avoid getting distracted by the crystal-work toys being peddled on either side of the large courtyard, their shiny crystals glowing faintly as they unspun. Above her, a crystal-powered train raced along its track: its gears were perhaps the loudest yet most ignored sound, while the soft sound of a musician demonstrating his latest creation posed a beautiful juxtaposition. Everywhere, as far as Jean could see, people were using clockwork.

While it was there in Zanther, Jean avoided going into the city proper. She had forgotten about the six-legged carriages that jostled about the ground behind their charges, or the newest clockwork weapons that boasted superior firing power. Blackrock was almost dizzying as she suddenly witnessed the copper and bronze technology, but as Jean made her way towards the center of town and the sulfuric lake it boasted, she focused on her task.

The divide between Solari and Kingsmen residency was stark.

Buildings loomed over her, their black towers shimmering beneath the light. The walls of the caldera that hosted Blackrock did little to offer shade, and Jean finally sat beneath a shadow of a tree to see if there was a carriage she could hail.

In the distance, she could see the temple of Solaris towering over the Solari district. Amber stones dotted its visage, mimicked by the amber set into the houses and businesses that lined the streets in that direction. To her other side, the temple of HaMelech proudly proclaimed its deity. Houses around it almost seemed to be bowing humbly before it, as it was the tallest building that side of town. It wasn't fair to include the Telfarian district in the competition, as it was quite literally a black market and a dark mark in the area.

Jean shivered slightly and looked around.

A carriage was slowly making its way up the lane, and Jean lightly held her hand out to signal for it. The driver grimaced, but stopped. "What do you want?"

"I need to get to the other side of the lake, please. This is the address." Jean fumbled for the letter and held it out to the driver, who scanned it and then looked at her. Jean shifted. "I know it isn't far, but—"

"Payment is required first."

After a moment, Jean pulled out three copper pieces. The driver raised an eyebrow and took them, then held his hand out for more. Jean set her jaw before giving a single additional piece. It seemed to satisfy the driver, who jabbed his thumb back to the coach. "Climb in, but keep the curtains closed. I don't want anyone getting the wrong idea."

The carriage lurched forward as soon as Jean shut the door, and she watched the city quietly through a small slit in the curtain. She knew he overcharged her for this: she was all too used to paying double the fees for most services simply due to her appearance. As they went down the road, a small crowd began to gather towards a store front. Standing on a box, held by a chain, was a skinny man.

Like Jean, he had ruddy red skin and horns, though his were long and curving. Jean shrunk back slightly as an auctioneer began to call out bidding for a slave. It was a solemn reminder of the fate her adoptive mother saved her from, one that Jean did her best to ignore as the carriage continued to move. The local wildlife did wonders to help pull her mind from more stressful issues — which were beginning to morph in the shapes of rabbits in the shadows — as she continued to look through the window.

Rakow, funny griffins with bushy striped tails and beautiful black feathers, darted from fence to fence as they moved further from the city edges. Songbird noisily chided the creatures while the horses pulling the carriage didn't seem to be bothered by the mischievous bandits. The driver was another story as he began cursing at them, seemingly having been robbed by them in the recent past.

Finally, Jean looked up from her journal to see they had arrived at an imposing black manor. It rose above many of the houses on this street with its three stories, while a raven ornamented its large oak door.

"Out."

Jean wasted no time in doing as the driver commanded and was soon alone in front of the home. She took a breath and knocked on the door, looked around, and then sighed.

"We aren't taking any solicitors, young lady," a voice finally said.

Jean looked at the door to see a tall man with dark hair and eyes. His face was pale and gaunt, as though he hadn't had any chance to sleep for several days, though his eyes offered a mischievous light that countered his tired appearance. Over his shoulders was a black feathered mantle, each piece meticulously tended to while his dress seemed formal and neatly kept.

"Will you take a wayward traveler, then?" Jean replied, unable to keep from smiling.

The man chuckled and held his arms out for Jean, who embraced him and then withdrew. Her uncle hadn't changed much from what she remembered, though he was beginning to grow grey hairs that peppered his bushy, well-groomed beard. Jean stood still as Flick lightly turned her around. "You've gotten big since you were last here. I hardly recognized you. Come along. Anca is with Caxton now, I'll get you something to eat."

He allowed Jean in first and then shut the door behind them. Distant memories of Jean's last visit slowly drifted back as she studied family portraits along the entry hallway. Her uncle and aunt, much younger, sat with two teenagers while holding a small baby. Then, the group was older and in formal wear. Finally, there was a portrait of her aunt, uncle, cousins, adoptive mother, and Jean. It was an awkward painting, especially as the man painting had removed Jean from the family unit, but it was the family all the same.

"Is Caxton doing alright? I would have been here sooner, but I had some issues along the way..."

"He's doing alright, tired, most days, but we might be over the worst of it. It's still a long road to recovery, and very little we can do outside of keeping him comfortable." Flick put his hand on her shoulder. "Was it trouble boarding the ship?"

Jean glanced at him. His eyes were curious, especially as he seemed to look down at her gloved hands. Jean shifted slightly. "I didn't go by ship this time."

"No?" Her uncle directed her to the kitchen, where he began to boil a pot of water over the fireplace. He hummed softly, looked at her, and then began to chop vegetables. "Did you go by coach, then? I heard there was a new crystal-tech railroad put in that is rumored to go around Bleak Hollow."

The curseborn woman shook her head at him and he paused. In the silence, she shifted. "I went through Bleak Hollow. It wasn't too bad, though the chitters aren't very friendly." Flick didn't speak again and began to work on the soup.

Did he think she had chittering madness? Of course, he was correct, but Jean didn't want to think about that. The last thing she needed was for her family to know, as they had no true obligation to keep her around. Jean listened quietly to the water boiling before footsteps sounded by the entry. She turned to face the doorway to see a short woman entering.

Her long, curly blonde hair was haphazardly piled atop her head while her eyes had heavy circles under them. She was thin and well put together, wearing an orange dress and an apron that pinned neatly to it. In one hand, the woman held a couple of bottles of what looked like medicine. A worn book rested in her lap as she maneuvered her wheeled chair into the room, sighed, and put the bottles on the counter. Outside of her exhaustion, she looked accustomed to the life she and Flick had made together; clean, well-tended, and full of love.

Jean subconsciously smoothed her own wild hair down as the woman turned to face her with an tired smile. "Jean, you have gotten so big!"

The woman hugged her tightly and Jean smiled. "Hi, Aunt Anca. Uncle Flick said Caxton's doing a bit better; is he awake?"

"He's resting now, otherwise I'd invite you to come say 'hello'. How were your travels? Did it go smoothly?"

"As smoothly as Bleak Hollow goes, I suppose," Jean replied. She didn't want to bring up Grandma Letty, or what happened in Last Hope, so she carefully changed the topic. "How long as Caxton been sick? Haven't the healers been able to do anything?"

Flick stiffened slightly from beside the fire and Anca's eyes softened. Jean tilted her head as her aunt gave him a kiss. Instantly, his shoulders relaxed, and he sighed softly. "It's been a couple of months, now. The healers have done what they can, but it's entirely in HaMelech's hands. He's doing fine outside of the reoccurring illness. It's been a strain on all of us, Drop and Shatter included. They've done what they can to help us, but it's certainly not something that we can sustainably continue to tend to him with. They're tired, we're tired, he's tired... having extra hands is a huge blessing." He smiled a little at Jean, who shifted. "I was surprised that you wrote back. We hadn't heard much from you or your mother."

"My adoptive mother has been busy," Jean replied. The words, though she'd been using them since she was a child, stung in her throat. There was always the reminder that her birth parents didn't want her, and her adoptive mother only took her in for karma. The word 'mother' wasn't acceptable in any circle, not with what Jean was and the agreement that curseborn children are a sign of disobedience in the parent. "The

High Inquisitors have selected her to assist them with some information gathering…" She trailed off. Those were not details that needed to be elaborated on. It was enough that she knew that was happening; sharing it with Kingsmen wasn't wise.

Anca's smile turned sad. "I'm glad she's doing well, at very least, and I'm so glad that you're here, dear." She gave Jean another tight hug. "Why don't you get settled, and we'll eat together once you do. Caxton hasn't been sleeping more than a handful of hours at a time, and I know that he'll want to see you."

It took a moment before Anca slowly got up from her chair. Flick caught her arm, and she gave a faint smile, though Jean could see her body was struggling to walk.

"I'll be alright once I sit back down… Jean, be a dear and take my wheelchair up ahead of me, please. There's a crystalwork lift now that I use to go up and down the stairs, but I'll want to sit as soon as I get there."

With her husband's help—and Jean glancing back nervously—Anca followed her up the stairs to the third floor, where a cozy study had been set up. The bed was made with fresh linens, and the gas lamp had yet to be lit. Jean placed her handful of belongings into the wardrobe (where Anca insisted they'd shop for more clothes soon).

"You know that we are planning on paying you, correct?" Flick asked abruptly. Jean looked at him, one eyebrow raised, and he continued. "The last thing we want to do is take advantage of you being here, so we are going to pay you for helping with Caxton. It isn't much, but we can do a handful of coins each week. Room and board are included, of course, as well as weekends off. Really, it's simply tending to him while Anca and I are working. Is that alright?"

Jean blinked.

She hadn't expected payment, or any time off. Really, she had assumed that she'd be helping with Caxton as family rather than hired help. Still, the idea of payment brought a glimmer of hope to her as she thought it through. While she had the issue of being a curseborn, she would be able to purchase a simple home in Blackrock if she saved enough. It was safer than Zanther, and offered more chances at living a normal life than anywhere else. Besides, helping with Caxton would allow her to have a chance at good karma and rebirth. That's what they taught in the Solari services, at least. Any good deed would go towards a better standing in the next life; whether it truly worked that way for curseborn, who were born that way due to the errors of their former life, Jean didn't know.

"That sounds great!" she replied, pulling her attention back to her family.

The relief on her aunt and uncle's face made her give a very small smile, and she followed them back down to Caxton's room.

There, they ran her through the medicines and breathing therapies prescribed by the dove healers at the Temple of HaMelech, and eventually Jean sat beside her cousin's bedside to read.

The ten-year-old was sleeping with a cool cloth over his forehead. The illness had made his face paler than usual and had also sunk his cheeks in, but he seemed alright aside from that. Anca had obviously been combing his blond hair as he rested, as a brush sat on the bedside table beside them. Jean stayed with him for a little while before she joined her aunt and uncle in the kitchen, where they had a light soup and then retired to bed.

The next morning, Anca waved to Jean as soon as she had descended the stairs. "We were planning on you arriving later, so please feel free to explore Blackrock! I remember you were in ranger school when you last visited: there's a forest outside of the eastern gate that might bring back some good memories. They do man it, but it's easy enough to return to Blackrock if you leave."

Jean beamed, kissed her aunt's cheek, and then went upstairs to check on Caxton. He was still sleeping, prompting her to sigh and then kiss his forehead. She'd hoped to say 'goodbye' while he was awake, but this would have to do. She couldn't wake him, not when he needed desperately to get well.

She did her best to avoid people as she hurried to the gate, and then through the gate into the woods beyond. It was a welcome change from the city, especially as birdsong filled the air. Out of the corner of her eye, she saw Osmond had reappeared and was bobbing along. He hovered lazily over flowers, interesting rocks, and bugs that wandered around. Jean couldn't help but chuckle at the sight, though the back of her mind had a lingering concern about her mental state as she continued to see Osmond.

Finally, as she entered a clearing, she found herself surrounded by lush trees and bushes. She could hear the soft rustling of a nettle mouse under a bush, prompting her to inhale deeply and then sit with her back to a tree. There, she drew in her journal and take notes about her adventure so far.

It was an hour or two before Jean shifted, the keen sense of something wrong filling her. The hair on the back of her neck began to prickle with the fear of being watched, followed quickly by the realization that the birds had gone silent. Jean looked around, spotted Osmond resting on a flower, and then pulled her boltcaster from her side.

In a couple of moments, she found herself in the sudden presence of a magnificent, large, beast. It flapped two powerful wings as it touched down, releasing a dead deer from its front claws. It had the face of an owl with enormous amber eyes that morphed into the body of a striped cat with four legs. Its orange and black tail twitched as it stalked towards the deer and then chirped.

From Jean's right, something chirped back.

Another creature stalked from the bushes near Jean. As the plants split, she could see several large eggs hidden in the undergrowth. The two creatures, which reminded Jean more and more of the rakow in Blackrock, began to eat the deer together with loud growls and hisses. Jean quietly shifted back into the bushes and then hurried away.

She could still hear the sounds of the creatures eating behind her, but it wasn't their gnawing that made her stop.

Soft cursing came from deeper in the woods. Jean tilted her head slightly, checked that she had reloaded her boltcaster, and slowly made her way to the sounds. When she came upon the noise, she stopped and tilted her head again.

Laying on the ground, struggling to free himself, was a man caught in a bear trap. The metal jaws had clamped around his leg just below the knee. It was bigger than any trap Jean had seen before, and she opened her mouth to speak before the man stiffened and looked towards her.

Green eyes studied her briefly as he grimaced. His brown hair was long on top and tied in a knot on his head, his rough skin weathered from hard work, and age-old fights had left his nose crooked. His rough-spun tunic seemed relatively unharmed, though the trap had torn his pants to reveal bone and blood. He was perhaps the fittest man that Jean had seen, especially as he didn't seem to be in pain from the trap, but seemed more annoyed. When he finally spoke, Jean was surprised by the relatively gruff voice that held the slightest trace of an accent that she didn't recognize.

"Enjoying the show?"

Jean raised her eyebrows. "I'm not the one in a trap."

He stared at her, frowned, and then sighed. "I suppose I should be grateful that you are here. While you don't look too terribly strong, another pair of hands to get out of this thing would be nice." He shifted, winced, and grasped the trap again.

Jean approached and felt around the trap. The man beside her was quiet now, as though he didn't want to curse in front of her, before he mumbled, "Thanks for not walking off."

"Why would I?" Jean craned her neck to study the trap and then slipped her hands beneath the man's leg. "It's not every day that you run into someone caught in an oversized trap."

"Great horned griffin trap."

"What?"

"It's a great horned griffin trap," the man repeated. His hands found a place beside Jean's as the two worked on the springs and pressure plate. "That's the only reason it's so big."

"And somehow your leg didn't come flying off?"

A soft laugh answered her, and Jean looked at him. He was smiling slightly despite the situation, and as he shook his head, he murmured, "It takes a lot to mutilate a staros. You seem like a curious sort... daito."

"Daito?" Jean asked.

"It means mouse.... you're like a mouse." He swayed slightly and Jean carefully gripped his arm to stabilize him. He shook his head. "I'll be alright, just give me a moment... It's the adrenaline wearing off."

"I almost have it."

Jean found the latch on the trap and sprung it. The man pulled his leg free and laid on the ground, quietly, before he shifted. Then, as Jean was about to speak, he grabbed her arm. "Don't. Move."

The keen feeling of being watched settled over Jean, and she allowed herself to turn.

Sitting at the edge of the clearing was one of the striped creatures. Its head tilted to the side and its ear tufts were perked straight ahead. Its tail twitched ever so slightly, and Jean knew, in a moment, that this was a predator watching prey.

"I'll make some noise, and you run," the man whispered from beside her. "With my leg, I can't get anywhere. Deliver my bones to Fort Haven, would you? I know my colleagues would want to know what happened to me if I disappear."

"What? I'm not leaving you here for it to eat," Jean muttered back. She slowly stood and swallowed. Finally, after gathering her courage, she lifted her arms and let out the loudest yell she could muster. The creature blinked, stood, and twitched its tail.

"What the hell are you doing?"

"Go on, get!" Jean shouted, waving her arms at the beast. It worked with most other predators, it'd have to work now, too. It was a desperate attempt more than anything, but as Jean continued to stand over the injured man and attempted to frighten the beast off, she couldn't help but feel a semblance of pride at the fact that she had even thought of this. She continued to fuss at it before it huffed. With another tail twitch, it padded away.

On the ground, the man coughed. "I can't tell if you have balls or are stupid."

"Why not both?" Jean asked, offering a weak smile. She crouched beside him and tied his leg with a piece of bandage from her pack. If she had her headscarf, which she was sure had gone missing at Grandma Letty's, she would have used it instead. The blood was quickly soaking through the bandage, even as she tightened it with a nearby stick, and she murmured, "I don't know if you'll be awake by the time I get to Blackrock; you're losing more blood than any of my supplies can handle."

The man followed her gaze and then put his hands on his wound. "It'll be alright. Just give me a moment, daito."

"My name is Jean," the curseborn answered.

"Daito is cuter," he replied. He offered a brief smile. "I'm Popcorn, if it makes you feel better."

"Popcorn?"

He didn't answer her, and Jean shifted as the feeling of bugs crawling up her spine washed over her. It was immensely unpleasant, more than enough to make her want to run from him, but the sudden visual of the blood-soaked bandages clotting instantly made her eyes widen. She looked at Popcorn and found that his face had lost some of its pallor, though his eyes were slipping shut.

"Are you alright?"

"It just takes a lot out of me, that's all," the man said quietly after a moment. He nearly fell forward, and Jean caught him lightly. She took a deep breath, shifted, got her feet under her, and then helped him stand as well. Popcorn held onto her, his head lolled forward, and Jean wrapped one arm around him.

There was no way she could let him die out in the woods. Whatever magic he had done proved to be interesting, and he was already a rather strange man, given his appearance and calm demeanor about the entire situation. Besides, it was another point of karma that could change her entire fate after death.

Popcorn stumbled slightly, and Jean stopped. His breathing was growing harder as they walked, and Jean whispered, "Are you going to be alright?"

"I think so," he answered. "I've been through worse."

"How much worse?" Jean asked.

He smiled ever so slightly and shook his head. Jean, taking his soft refusal as a desire to conserve his energy, didn't press.

It took twice as long to get to Blackrock as it did to leave, and by the time Jean found a temple, Popcorn was nearly unconscious. Against her desires, Jean found that the HaMelech temple was closer to them than the

Solari one, and she helped Popcorn stagger in before she let him sink to the ground.

It was a whirlwind of commotion as dove healers hurried to them, some helping Popcorn stand and get to a room while others questioned Jean about what had happened. She did her best to help, though the looks she received when she didn't have an answer made her feel more useless than not.

Finally, after things settled down, Jean sat in a chair and waited.

Flick and Anca Alastar.
Caxton 5, Shatter 17, Drop 20,
Adriata Cassy, Jeam 13.

POPCORN'S RECOVERY

Jean shifted as she sat in the hallway.

The handful of dove healers who passed by glanced at her from time to time, but otherwise left her alone. At the far end of the quiet hall, Jean could see two whispering and pointing towards her as a stark reminder that she wasn't welcome. Out of the corner of her eye, Osmond bobbed lazily from stone to stone as though entertaining himself. He settled above Jean's right shoulder after a moment and then disappeared before reappearing across the hall. Jean tapped her foot, doing her best to keep from falling asleep in the silent hall.

It didn't take too long before a dove in a pale blue dress and apron approached. "Miss?"

"Yes?"

"You're the curseborn that brought Mr. Popcorn here, correct?"

"Yes, I am." Jean sat upright as the woman folded her hands in front of her. "Is everything alright?"

The Kingsman nodded slightly, paused, and sighed. "Surgery is taking longer than we had thought. He lost a lot of blood, but he should recover. Do you remember him saying anything else before you brought him here? Family we could notify, or friends?"

Racking her brain, Jean made a face. He was from Fort Haven, his friends were, anyway, and he was staros. She wasn't sure what it meant, but maybe it could provide some help to the dove?

"He said he was staros? Outside of mentioning Fort Haven, that's all I can say. Oh! And he did something to his leg before we came this direction," Jean said. The dove rose an eyebrow and Jean shifted. "He did some sort of magic, I think. It stopped the bleeding as far as I can tell, but I don't know what he did. It was weird, though." The dove's gaze grew darker, making Jean shift again. She felt like she was under a magnifying lens and she attempted, "I don't know if it was actually magic, of course. I don't dabble in it. It's illegal if Solaris didn't sanction it. I was under stress the entire time I was with him, anyway."

Osmond bounced into view again as Jean swallowed, her throat beginning to close. Around her, she was certain that the shadows looming closer, threatening to consume her. Red eyes peeked around corners, and Jean tightened her grip on her satchel. Then, as Osmond slowly moved around the room, seemingly unnoticed by the dove, the shadows retreated to their proper place.

The dove healer finally spoke. "Are you certain?"

"No... I mean, yes, about Fort Haven and his being a staros. Everything else is just speculation. I was so stressed as it was, it's a wonder I remember anything." Was she going to be arrested for his magic use? It was illegal, and she had opened her mouth about it; she'd be guilty by association. Maybe they'd arrest him, too. That'd remove good karma, for sure.

Jean bit her lip as the dove slowly nodded and then gestured to the seat. As Jean sunk into her chair, she watched the dove. "You said he is in surgery?"

"Because his knee is mostly beyond repair, we will perform a limb salvage surgery," the dove responded. She turned to go. "We're removing a portion of his leg and set it soon enough. It's a long process, and the healing will take even longer, but he'll be able to walk with a limp rather than require a chair after we're done." She paused again. "What relation did you say you were to the patient?"

Jean faltered for a moment. "I... am a friend. I mean, I found him in the forest, too, but I'm a friend."

The dove raised an eyebrow but nodded, seemingly satisfied with the answer.

Jean exhaled and put her head in her hands. Osmond bobbed to her side again, hovered over her, and vanished like a flame blown out.

Solaris was going to punish her for the lie, wasn't he? Technically, she hadn't fibbed, right? She was a friend, not an enemy, if she had helped him. Besides, she wasn't really sure of what he did when he healed himself. It could have been anything, especially during a stressful situation.

She took another deep breath and closed her eyes, this time to calm her racing thoughts down. She was getting tired now that the adrenaline was wearing off, and that left nothing but a desire to sleep and have something to eat. Still, as she waited quietly for the strange man to be placed in a room, Jean did her best to avoid nodding off from time to time.

It was a light shake of her arm that made her sit bolt upright, her eyes wide and hand on her weapon. A different dove was crouched before her, this one older with laugh lines around her eyes. She blinked at Jean. "I'm sorry I woke you so suddenly... I was to tell you that Mr. Popcorn is awake in his room and you are welcome to see him, if you wanted."

"Oh... thank you." Jean rubbed her eyes, her face hot. She really was tired, wasn't she? Her stomach gurgled as though to remind her it was still there, but she ignored it and started down the hall.

"Miss?" The dove stood. "You've been here six hours. Can I please get you something to eat and drink while you visit with him? I'll be bringing him a meal too and am happy to bring you one as well."

Jean paused and looked at her. She seemed earnest, but it could be a trick. Jean's prayer amber was visible, so everyone knew she was Solari on top of being a curseborn, which meant that this dove could be trying to take payment. Finally, as Jean's belly rumbled again, she hung her head and sighed. "I'll take a cup of hot water for tea, please."

"Are you certain? I can get a sandwich if you want something more?"

"No, just the water, thanks."

Jean avoided the dove's gaze as she started again. Then, as her face grew hot once more, she looked at the ceiling. "I... don't exactly know where I'm going."

The dove smiled, pointed at a door, and then hurried off.

When Jean entered the room in question, there were more empty beds than not. Each had a little curtain set up around it, most of them open, while the open windows pulled fresh air inside. The only bed with a curtain around it had soft voices coming from within, and Jean recognized one of them as a stubborn, "I told you, it's fine," rang through the air.

She paused outside of the curtain before she cleared her throat.

Another healer poked his head out, looked Jean up and down, and then returned to what he was doing.

"Who was that?" came Popcorn's voice, tired and raw from the surgery.

"A curseborn."

"Why did you just let her stand around, then? There's a chair; you're not using it."

"Sir, you need to lie down—"

"Take your hands off me, I'm fine. Daito, get in here... please."

Jean's eyebrow raised at the use of the nickname. He remembered it, and her, which she really hadn't expected. Still, at his request, she slipped into the little section.

Popcorn lay on the bed with his injured leg propped up. Bandages tightly wrapped around it, as well as a rawhide cord to keep it secure. Neatly folded on the on the bedside table were his shirt and pants, and blankets covered him up to his waist as he struggled to sit up. Now that he was in better lighting, Jean could see a multitude of scars crossing over his chest and ending in a rather prominent burn that had mutilated the skin from the back of his right shoulder to the front. It ended above several faded black patches, possibly tattoos, the flames had burned and destroyed.

When she stepped in, Popcorn looked at her. His brow furrowed, and his lips were set in a thin line, but they softened ever so slightly as he studied her. Finally, he waved the dove off. "Make yourself useful elsewhere. I'll send for someone if I need pain medicine."

"But—"

"I said—" Popcorn glared at him, the corners of his lips beginning to draw back in a feral, unnatural baring of teeth. "Go away."

Jean's eyes widened as she watched the threat display. She'd never seen someone able to do this. It was both alien and reminiscent of a predator, especially as Popcorn's lips pulled back to reveal the entirety of his teeth. The dove hadn't expected it, either, as he stumbled backwards, nearly tore the curtain from the ceiling, and then ran.

Popcorn glared after him before he moved his lips as though to remove tension and then smacked them. Then he looked at Jean. "You stayed."

"I didn't want to just ditch you in Blackrock if you didn't remember what happened," Jean replied. She sat in the seat as Popcorn gestured to it, shifted to make herself comfortable, and then frowned. Popcorn's eyes never left her, and she finally blurted, "What was that you did with your face?"

"Remember, I said you were like a mouse? Curious and questioning?" Popcorn asked. Jean's cheeks burned hot and he chuckled quietly. He settled back and closed his eyes. "I'm staros. Threat display puts people in their place. If they won't listen to that, then there's no point in using words anymore." He opened one eye to look at Jean, who tilted her head, and then closed it again. "Now, it's my turn. Was I delusional in remembering you yelled at a great horned griffin?"

Again, Jean shifted. Though he wasn't staring at her, she knew he was very aware of what she was doing. It was subtle, but she could see his muscles were tense and ready for a sudden movement. In the back of her mind, she wondered who this man really was, especially as he seemed to know more than he let on. Finally, she murmured, "No, that happened. I yelled at that creature."

"Great horned griffin," Popcorn corrected. He opened his eyes and slowly sat up again. "Those things aren't the nicest, and you managed to scare it off. Why did you do it that way, of all the ways, especially when I told you to run?" He didn't stop looking at her, and Jean swallowed past the lump in her throat.

"I figured that if we looked problematic enough, it wouldn't want to eat us. Predators don't often attack things that look threatening in their own right." Popcorn raised an eyebrow, and Jean continued. "You called it stupid earlier, but that's what I grew up needing to do. If you look too tough to bother with, then it'll leave you alone. It's kept me out of trouble before... though, I will admit that it was a gamble with that th... great horned griffin."

Popcorn nodded slowly to himself, and Jean frowned. He was deep in thought about something as he tapped his fingers against his thigh. Then, he paused, patted his legs as though looking for something, and then looked around the room. "Daito, did you grab my pack before you brought me to Blackrock?"

"Your pack?"

A string of foreign words erupted from Popcorn as he struggled to sit up. "Yes, my pack! It was on the ground beside me when you found me!" Jean recoiled slightly as another slew of words- curses, she assumed- filled the air. Popcorn flung the blanket off of his lap. "I need that pouch. There's research and efrage in there; I don't want any of that to get into the wrong hands."

Jean blinked before her eyes widened.

She remembered her adoptive mother storming home once from work at the brothel, raving about a client on efrage. What was it she had said...?

"Daito, focus," Popcorn said. The sound of his fingers snapping in front of Jean's face startled her from her thoughts, and she blinked rapidly. "I need you to go back and get my pack. I'll pay you, even, to do that for me. I need that pack."

"Where did you get efrage from?" Jean questioned quietly. "Isn't it... illegal?"

Popcorn looked at the ceiling, mumbled something under his breath, and looked at Jean. "It is not... not in the North, anyway. Look, I just need my bag. I'll answer more questions once you do that, alright?"

"You're trusting a stranger to go get your drugs and paperwork?"

The man sighed, rubbed his face, and then suddenly lunged. He caught Jean's hand, making her squeak, and stared her in the eyes. "I don't have anyone else here to send on this task, and I sure as hell won't ask the doves. You seem resourceful enough, and you know where you're looking. Please."

Jean searched his face before she slowly nodded. Relief flooded Popcorn's face, and he sighed again. "Thank you."

He released Jean's hand after a moment and settled back onto the bed. Jean, after getting her wits about her, slipped from the room. The dove from before was coming down the hallway towards her and stopped. "Are you leaving so soon?"

"Oh... I needed to go get something for Popcorn," Jean replied. She shrugged. "I'll be back in an hour and a half, give or take."

"It's getting late. Are you sure you'll be safe?"

Jean glanced towards the window, which had grown significantly darker as the sun rapidly set. She chewed on the inside of her lip, calculating what the trip might contain, before she finally nodded. "I'll be fine."

"Alright, but..."

"You're welcome to leave the hot water on the bedside table once I return. I do appreciate it," Jean said. She hurried away before the dove could say anything more, doing her best to duck away from any eyes who may be watching.

Her walk was brisk and accompanied only by Osmond. The orb bounced ahead of her as she traversed the dark forest, lighting shadows that seemed to be too dark or figures that threatened to pounce. It gave Jean a faint sense of courage, and she murmured, "Thanks, Osmond."

Her companion didn't answer, and she knew he wouldn't, but still in the back of her mind she questioned the light's appearance after disappearing years ago. As she approached the clearing and saw Popcorn's pack laying intact, she couldn't help but feel grateful to her imaginary friend reappearing and insisting on traveling with her. Jean gathered the pack amid the nighttime sounds and then opened it. She knew better, but the curiosity gnawing at her had her fingers fumbling for the latch before she could catch herself. Then, as she looked down at a closed journal, a handful of tightly rolled scrolls, and a small pouch, the curiosity faded into guilt, and she shut the bag. She held it tightly as she hurried through the woods again, her eyes darting around from shape to shadow as Osmond lit her way.

"You don't think he's some crackhead, do you, Osmond?" Jean finally asked.

The orb didn't respond, but he gave a bit of a bob as though he heard her. Jean frowned. "Maybe he is. I mean... wasn't efrage was banned a while ago, before I was born? Maybe he's a secret junkie and that's why he wandered into a bear trap? He was on a high and didn't register it? That could explain why he wasn't screaming."

Again, Osmond bobbed at her, and they walked in silence.

When Jean returned to the temple of HaMelech, she hunger and exhaustion washed over her once more. She should have taken that dove up on the offer of food, but her pride said otherwise as she slipped through the halls and towards Popcorn.

He lay on the bed with his eyes closed. His chest rose and fell rhythmically, as though he was sleeping, but he looked at her as soon as she placed the pack on the chair.

"You found it! You didn't open it, did you?" he questioned, sitting up before he grimaced.

Jean caught one of his arms habitually to steady him, her face growing hot at his question. She avoided his gaze. "I didn't see anything."

"So... you opened my pack?" Popcorn looked at her. Jean, under his gaze, nodded slowly. "Hm... but you didn't look at my belongings?"

"No, I didn't look at anything in the pack," Jean answered. Popcorn continued to stare, and she looked at the ceiling. "I saw you had a journal and scrolls, but I didn't open those. That felt too much like a breach of privacy... and I don't want to be like those people." As silence resounded through the room, Jean played with the hem of her tunic. Finally, she looked at Popcorn and murmured, "I'm sorry."

Popcorn blinked at her and Jean sighed before he softly said, "You didn't look through my things, so I do appreciate it... and I appreciate the honesty." A wide yawn interrupted him, exposing his tonsils and beyond. He sighed, settled on the pillows, and watched Jean for a moment. The curseborn, in return, watched him as well. Then, Popcorn said, "Thank you for what you've done. Can you hand me the small pouch in the pack?"

Jean did as he said and then watched. He opened the pouch, pulled out a small pinch of dusty lichen, and placed it beneath his tongue. In an instant, his pupils contracted, and he let out a long, breathy sigh. Once more he laid down, this time staring at the wall ahead of him.

"Do... you take efrage often?" Jean dared, quietly.

"Of course I do," Popcorn responded. Jean blinked as he continued, "No self-respecting staros would go through the withdrawal willingly. The headaches are one thing, but the entire 'slowly going to die' issue is another." He looked at her. "Why wouldn't I?"

"... it's illegal."

"For you southerners, dear daito. For staros, it's rinki.... life." Popcorn rose an eyebrow. "You have no idea about what staros are, do you?"

Jean shifted. She hadn't heard the term before, no, but being called a 'southerner' solidified that he was perhaps from beyond the Spineback mountains, which divided the No-Light zone from the rest of Illeross. That could explain his accent, and the words he continued to use in speech. How long he's been in the south, though, she wasn't sure. Jean shook her head faintly at his question.

Popcorn sighed, tapped his fingers on his thigh again, and looked at Jean. "We are from the north. Strong, wise... We are..." He trailed off, searched the ceiling for a moment, and then shrugged, "Staros. We are staros."

"Is that why you stopped your bleeding?"

Popcorn stiffened slightly. Jean watched as his tapping grew more frequent, betraying nervousness, before she slowly reached out and put her hand on his. He frowned but didn't pull away. "You don't have to tell me anything."

"Good... because I wasn't going to," Popcorn said lightly. He yawned again and Jean pulled away from him. "You head out... I appreciate it. It was Jean, right?"

"Jean Cassy," Jean replied. "And Popcorn?"

"Well... Baba Maze, but friends call me Popcorn. It's a dumb joke, given Baba means father in some languages, and maize is corn... anyway, just call me Popcorn, daito. Hope to see you around."

"You too."

Jean left the temple and made her way back to her lodging, where she retired to her bedroom and simply thought. Osmond drifted about the ceiling as she used him as a sounding board. "The magic is something other than being staros, I'm sure... I don't know what, but he seemed so hesitant to even have it mentioned. Maybe it's illegal, just like the efrage? I've never heard of someone needing to take drugs to function like that, but..." Jean trailed off and sighed, looked at the orb, and shook her head. "I'm going insane, aren't I? You're still here, and I'm talking to you. How is any of that supposed to make sense?"

Osmond simply drifted to the left, and Jean rolled over to go to sleep.

Blackrock, the City of Truces

Built out of the dark volcanic stones of its namesake, this city resides inside the caldera of a long dormant volcano and contains a semi-sulfuric lake. The city is divided into four districts. The trade district runs through the city and serves as a common ground while housing the central governing body. The other three districts are given a degree of self-governance and are divided by cultural and religious ideals. This is one of the only locations where people of the three primary religions are able to coexist semi-peacefully as their respective districts provide for religious freedoms.

Solari District

A safe haven for Solari worshipers in the predominantly 'Kingsman' nation. the largest temple outside of Solari controlled lands is here.

Kingsmen District

This is the largest district by population and is where my aunt and uncle live. This is also where the largest temple of Hamelech resides.

Telfarian District

Where anything can be bought in the Black Bazaar, and the laws on violent crime are near nonexistent.

THE OFFER

When Jean woke up, Osmond was settled beside the gas lamp near her bed. She carefully lit the lamp to see, yawned, and started to get ready for the day.

Her aunt was working, or should have gone to work extremely early that morning, and her uncle was staying home with Caxton again. This provided a second day of respite, then a third, before her shifts with Caxton began. Until then, however, she was going to enjoy the day and get her room set up as she wanted.

She was halfway through tidying her desk, deciding what books she wanted in order to better tutor Caxton, when there was a knock on the door. Her uncle Flick stood on the other side, studying the wallpaper until he noticed Jean had opened the door, then smiled at her. "Sleep well?"

"Pretty well," Jean answered. She offered him a smile back and then tilted her head. "Letter about service? I can watch Caxton-"

"No, not for me." Flick looked down at his hand before he handed the letter to Jean. "The courier said that a return letter wasn't required, as per the sender. A man named 'Popcorn'... the courier apparently asked around the temple to figure out who you might be, and Anca gave him our address. It certainly threw me for a loop, given that this is addressed to 'daito'...?" He watched Jean, one eyebrow raised. "Is everything alright?"

Jean nodded, stepped into her room, and Flick followed. She carefully opened the letter and scanned it. "It's from a gentleman I encountered yesterday. He's at the Temple of HaMelech, currently, because of a leg injury... it looks like he'd like some company this afternoon and wanted to speak to me again." Flick hummed softly at her and Jean looked at him. She raised an eyebrow back at him, paused, and grimaced. "Get that look off of your face. We're strangers, he just doesn't have anyone else to talk to."

"I never said that you were more than strangers," Flick replied. He shifted slightly against the wall. "Calling you by a nickname is an interesting choice, though."

"He was stuck in a bear trap, I'm sure it was the only thing he could do to keep from panicking." Jean rolled her eyes, read the letter again, and then placed it on her desk. "I'll go by this afternoon, as I wanted to get things cleaned up here first."

"Are you sure that's wise? You've barely met him—"

"I'll be fine. Besides, he had surgery yesterday, I'd be surprised if he could do anything," Jean interrupted. She shifted as Flick gave her a look. "I'll be careful; I'm a big girl."

"I just want to make sure you're safe," Flick said. "This isn't a matter of what he could do, it's a simple matter of my desire to keep you from harm."

"I'll be fine. In fact, I feel so confident as to say that Caxton could come with me. It'll be good to get outside, and I'd love to spend time with him." Besides, if Popcorn was interested in something more than just speaking to her, Caxton could very well result in deflection. While Jean wasn't entirely sure if it would come down to something like that (especially when she wasn't sure what the conversation was about), she had a deep feeling that it would be nothing more than pleasantries.

"If that's the case, and you'd like to, you're welcome to sit with Caxton until you decide to leave. He's awake and dressed, I'm sure he'd enjoy the company as well. After all, he has yet to see you; he woke up yesterday and wanted to know if you'd arrived yet." Flick paused and gave her a serious look. "Be careful, Jean. I mean it."

Jean smiled slightly, nodded, and watched her uncle go. Then she finished a couple of minor tasks she had been working on and made her way down the stairs to Caxton's room.

He was sitting up in bed, coughing into a handkerchief. When Jean knocked on his door, his greyish-blue eyes flashed to her and he gave a large, tired smile. "Jean! You're here!"

"Of course I am," Jean said. She sat beside his bed and put a hand to his forehead. While he was warm, he didn't feel feverish. "What do you think you're doing, getting so sick? You're supposed to be running about, causing trouble."

Caxton laughed before he coughed again. Jean winced as his chest heaved, waited to see if she needed to pat him on the back, and then gave him a sympathetic smile. He smiled back, sucked in a breath, and shook his head. "Dad said the same thing... and Mom... and Drop, and Shatter." He sighed, swallowed, and looked at Jean. "I didn't think you were coming."

"I decided that you could do with some time away from your family," Jean replied.

A pang of sadness hit her as she said this, though she didn't say a word. Family meant something different to them both: while he had two parents and two half-siblings, Jean knew full well that she didn't truly have anyone. Yes, she had her adoptive mother, but that didn't really mean anything. It was a good deed to take her in, that was all, and it resulted in a better place after death.

Caxton's eyebrows furrowed. "You are my family too, Jean. I want to spend time with you."

Jean met Caxton's eyes, surprise taking the place of sadness as she realized that he seemed more confused than anything. Without a sound, she ruffled his hair. "Yeah, you're right. Your dad asked me to take you to the Temple of HaMelech with me this afternoon. How does that sound?"

"Do I have to walk?"

She laughed at his words and shook her head. "Personally, I was going to get us a carriage, but we can if you'd like."

"Nope."

Caxton gave her another tired smile, and Jean smiled back.

They chatted for a little while before eventually making their way to the ground floor and outside. Flick had already called a coach for them and they entered it quietly. As they rode to the temple, Jean asked, "How far behind are you in school?"

"I've been sick since the beginning of the season," Caxton answered. He shrugged slightly. "Mom and Dad have been trying to tutor me, but I know they're tired—"A rasping cough interrupted him again, this time leaving him breathless and shaking. Jean gently caught his arms to keep him sitting upright, her face set in a firm line. He coughed for several minutes, drew in a shaking breath, and then continued to cough. All the while, Jean held tightly to him. Finally, when he finished and could breathe, he whispered, "I know Mom and Dad are exhausted... I hate it."

Jean's heart broke as she stared at him. His face was hollow and pale. His eyes, which had previously held a semblance of mischief, had gone back to tired and lifeless. Without a sound, Jean pulled him close to her side and stroked his hair as they continued to ride. Finally, she murmured, "They're tired because they want to be certain they can help you thrive, even in this illness. It's a sign of love."

"You think so?"

"I know so." The coach lurched to a halt, and Jean gave her cousin's head a gentle kiss. "Let's get inside and see what the healers say, hm?"

Caxton nodded and, with her help, exited the coach.

When a dove called Caxton back, Jean waited quietly outside of the room. She tapped her foot slightly, looked around the hall, and then paused as she heard, "Do your parents know that you're with a curseborn?"

Her blood began to boil, drowning out Caxton's response. As often as the Kingsmen claimed to welcome everyone to their temple, and that all were equal, it was comments like this that frustrated her. The Kingsman's infractions from the night before seemed insignificant, having happened out of earshot. This man speaking to Caxton clearly wanted her to hear it, and Jean did her best to hold her tongue.

Afterall, causing a scene might seal her rebirth as a curseborn yet again.

A coughing fit made Jean look towards the room with a heavy sigh. It was no wonder that her aunt and uncle were exhausted. Each instance sounded like Caxton was fighting to breathe, and round-the-clock care was going to be administered, if that was the case. Unable to take it any longer, Jean entered the room.

The dove was listening to Caxton's breathing while the boy shuddered on the examination table. Jean stood beside her cousin and took his hand, patting it lightly, before the dove glanced at her.

"You should be waiting outside."

Jean bit back her automatic reply. Instead, she murmured, "Caxton is under the age of 13. I'm here as his current guardian."

The dove healer scoffed and turned away, making Jean grit her teeth. Caxton leaned into her again, wheezing, and Jean asked, "Are there any medications you can prescribe for the cough?"

"We've given him what we can. HaMelech's hand is over this, it's a case of waiting now."

HaMelech hadn't done anything, Jean thought. Caxton couldn't breathe, he looked like he was going to blow over, and the dove didn't seem to care. "Have you tried mallow to soothe the throat?"

"Are you a healer?" The dove snapped. Jean's eyes widened as the dove stood. "I said we've given him what we can. Your constant pestering isn't going to change anything, husk."

Husk.

The word hung in the air, and Jean stared at the healer before her. His chest was heaving with anger, his eyes blazing, and for a moment, Jean kept her free hand beside her boltcaster should she need to defend herself.

Of course, he would call her a husk. That was what she was anyway, wasn't it? A husk of a body, with no soul? Jean's stomach clenched as she formed a response. He had no right to call her that. He was supposed to follow a loving god, and this wasn't at all what Kingsmen supposedly did; he should apologize or be rebuked or... Jean sighed and looked down.

"I'd like a report for his parents, please," she whispered.

The dove healer lifted his chin as though proud of what he had said. "I'll send it home with his mother this evening. Now, take the boy home."

The underlying tone told Jean precisely what he thought of her, and Jean turned away to help Caxton from the table.

As she led him from the room, he coughed and looked at her. "Why did you let him talk to you like that?"

"You might understand one day, Caxton," Jean murmured. "Until then, though, please don't worry yourself over it. It's my burden to bear."

"It was rude and wrong. That goes against the Holy Text," Caxton said. He looked up at her. "He should know better if he is a dove healer."

"All done, Caxton." Jean looked away from her cousin, took in a deep breath, and then plastered a smile on her face. "Would you like to meet an acquaintance of mine? He's here at the temple, and was hoping for some company."

Her cousin nodded, leaving Jean to lead him into the wide room that Popcorn's bed was. When they reached the curtained area, Jean could hear him muttering to himself in that odd language again. She cleared her throat, waited for him to acknowledge her, and then ushered Caxton to the chair. Popcorn raised his eyebrow when he saw the young boy and glanced at Jean. "I didn't realize you were a mother."

"No... no, this is my cousin, Caxton. Caxton, this is Baba Maze—"

"Call me Popcorn, kid," Popcorn said. Caxton smiled, tired, and Popcorn looked at Jean. "I didn't mean to interrupt in your day. If you need to get Caxton home, please do so."

Jean looked down at Caxton, who was watching Popcorn, and gave a small smile. "What do you think, Caxton?"

"I think I'd like to stay."

Popcorn nodded faintly and then pulled a string. In the distance, a small bell rang. Jean looked towards the sound before Popcorn gestured to the bed. "Take a seat while we wait for a dove healer. I'm wanting to get you another chair, and something for the boy to eat. He looks stick thin. Do you want anything, daito?"

Jean sunk onto the bed beside Popcorn's leg, which he carefully shifted away from her. The woman sat quietly for a moment before she looked at him. "A pot of hot water, please."

Now that she was sitting, she realized that the surrounding shadows were creeping in. Whether it was a hallucination or reality, Jean didn't want to test her fate. Osmond hadn't shown up, which was her only comfort.

Popcorn nodded slightly at her request, looked at Caxton, and then at Jean again. "Have you eaten?"

"I'm fine."

He gave her a look before a young woman came bustling in. She wore a sour look on her face, and she scowled at Popcorn. "What?"

Jean raised an eyebrow but said nothing. Popcorn, too, took it in stride. "I'd like another chair brought in for my friend, as well as a pot of hot water and a bowl of broth for myself and the boy."

"This isn't a maid service, you know."

"I'm aware. I am, however, asking for comfort for those who have kindly offered to spend time with me here. Look at the kid, anyway. He'll blow away should a heavy north wind strike." Popcorn watched the dove healer before he looked at Jean, and then the dove again. Then, after a moment, he said, "I see. She's an ae'shaur. You southerners have a penchant for making them incredibly unhappy. Here's the deal, miss. I would like my guest to receive the utmost respect while I have her here. You see, I don't ask for much while I am in the care of the doves here at the Temple of HaMelech. Never whine, never fuss, never demand. Today, however, I will be doing so should you decide to make her life miserable."

Jean shifted slightly as Popcorn leaned towards the dove, who had stiffened slightly. Heat flooded Jean's cheeks, and she looked down. This was incredibly out of the ordinary, and she didn't know how she felt. Caxton seemed incredibly interested in what might happen, especially as he looked at Popcorn and then gasped. "Woah, how does your face do that?"

He had bared his teeth again, staring down the dove, before he looked at Caxton. He offered a smile and looked at the dove again. "Why don't you go get that chair and the other items I requested?"

"Yes, sir."

The dove hurried off, and Jean looked at Popcorn.

"You didn't need to do that."

"Didn't I?" Popcorn settled back again and watched her. "I can only imagine what treatment you've received since coming in. I've always hated the blatant racism here in the south."

"So, why do you stay here?" Jean asked. Popcorn tilted his head and Jean continued, "I mean, if you hate the racism in the south, and you're staros, which you said are from the north, why do you stay in an area you hate? Aren't you from the north?"

Popcorn blinked at her and then laughed. As he did, Jean realized that she had opened her mouth too hastily and had done exactly what he had commented on. Caxton looked between them. "Why are you laughing?"

"I'm so sorry," Jean said, her eyes wide. "Please, I didn't mean to sound so ignorant—"

"No, it's fine, daito. I understand what you mean."

As Popcorn finished laughing, Jean suddenly realized that it was a rather pleasant sound. She blushed slightly as she had this thought, brushed some hair behind her ear, and looked at her lap. "I'm glad."

A light hand patted her own and Popcorn said, "I haven't been north in 14 years. Less opportunity, less chance to study creatures, less to do there. I would much rather deal with all the problems here than back in the cold." He shrugged and leaned back. "What about you? Are you from Blackrock?"

Jean shook her head, paused, and looked at Popcorn. He hadn't removed his gaze from her, and it made her shift slightly. Was it a wise idea to tell him where she was from, or anything else?

After a moment, Jean offered a small smile. "I'm from Zanther, visiting my family. Here for Caxton, specifically." She looked at her cousin and smiled. He was staring at Popcorn again, his eye huge and interested. "You haven't answered his question."

Popcorn raised an eyebrow. Then he shifted. "I'm a staros, kid. Have you ever seen a staros?"

Caxton shook his head.

"I come from the north, and that is how we communicate that there's a problem. It's sort of like a dog baring its teeth." The man waited for a response, which never came, and then looked at Jean.

Before he could say anything, Jean asked, "Why did you want my company?"

At this time, a different healer came in. She had a chair with her, and she looked back as though looking for something. Then she scurried off and returned with a tray. Just as Popcorn had asked, there was a teapot with hot water. Instead of two bowls, however, there were three. As she carefully divided the requested items, she looked at Popcorn and then Jean. "I'm sorry about how things have been going. One of my coworkers commented that you scolded her without warrant but I could tell there was more to her story than she shared." She shook her head. "I don't know what's going on with attitudes, but I do want to apologize."

Jean frowned as she sunk into the chair. She didn't trust this apology. It didn't feel natural. No one ever apologized to her kind, let alone on behalf of others. This might be a Kingsmen ploy to bring her guard down. She watched the dove, who dipped her head and ran off, and then sighed.

"Not used to that, are you?" Popcorn questioned.

"You called me something earlier."

"Daito?"

"No... the other thing. In front of that dove."

Popcorn thought for a moment. "Oh, an ae'shaur. Yes, I did."

"What does that mean?" Jean narrowed her eyes slightly. "Is it an insult?" She didn't want to deal with him if he was insulting her in his native tongue. That was the last thing she wanted.

Caxton slurped his broth and filled the silence before Popcorn cleared his throat. "It means horned one. You are a horned one."

"Does that bother you?"

Popcorn tilted his head, confusion filling his green eyes. Jean furrowed her brow as well. People usually had a clear opinion about curseborns, but Popcorn didn't seem to have one. It was strange, and uncomfortable. As Jean waited for an answer, she pulled her pouch of tea herbs to steep them. Lavender and chamomile wafted in the air, prompting her to sigh and close her eyes. When she opened them, Popcorn had pulled out his little pouch of efrage and started to chew on a clump of it. Finally, he shook his head.

"I don't know why you think it would. I mean, I suppose I get it, but it doesn't bother me. Horned ones have a place of honor in the north. It's the southerners who have it all backwards."

Jean blinked at him, and he shook his head again. "Regardless, I didn't ask you to join me in order to discuss the implications of your appearance. I wanted to talk to you about yesterday."

"Oh?"

"Yes. Are you currently working here in Blackrock, or are you looking?"

"Working. Popcorn, what is this all about?"

The man's gaze shifted ever so slightly to disappointment as Jean watched him. He shifted, winced as he moved his bad leg, and then sighed. "Well, I was hoping you hadn't found work. You've got balls, daito, and that's the type of person I was hoping to meet." Jean raised an eyebrow and poured herself a cup of tea as he continued. "You see, I've got a position open on the team that I'm running towards Apple Ridge.... west of Blackrock. Small research outpost in an old fort. I'm particularly interested in griffins, but any wildlife in the area will do. That's besides the point." He waved his hand slightly. Jean couldn't help but smile over her cup of tea, watching him quietly. Caxton was silent, too. "Regardless, I have a position open and was going to ask if you wanted to try it out. I can't pull you from any of your other responsibilities, of course, but... perhaps you could consider it? Room and board are included, along with weekly pay. Hell, if Caxton needs to come for whatever reason, we'll take him too."

This was a tempting offer, Jean had to admit. She'd be out of Blackrock, more or less adventuring as she had a chance, and would likely maintain good company. She loved her family, but this provided a new chance at living in Blackrock. As she mulled it over, Caxton coughed. She looked at her cousin, pulled him to her side, and shook her head. "I'm sorry, Popcorn, but I am in Blackrock to take care of Caxton for the foreseeable future."

"Do you have a schedule work around, or time that you would be open?" Popcorn questioned. He looked at her expectantly. "I don't want to lose the potential of having you join me; you've shown your resourcefulness, I would hate to see you go."

Jean twisted her lips. Finally, she murmured, "Let me speak to my aunt and uncle, and I'll let you know."

Nothing but heretics. They claim that HaMalech is the only god and that he alone can 'save' a person's soul. Of course, they also claim that he loves all despite being exclusive in 'saving', as he sends any who don't worship him to some sort of torturous existence. They are clearly delusional and unwilling to accept the consequences for their actions.

The holy symbol of HaMalech

Heretical Thoughts of Kingsmen

The Order of the Doves is a 'healing' group. Aunt Anca serves with them as an administrator. Caxton says that they will heal anyone who needs help with 'HaMalech's blessing', but I don't trust it. Only Solaris grants sanctioned magic; whatever unholy magic the Kingsmen are using must be dangerous.

Uncle Flick served as a Knight of the Long Road before Caxton was born. This is the 'guard' faction that protects those who travel, fight threats, and likely serve as executioners of those they call heretics or who have chittering madness.

The Solari city of Garren's Stand only tolerates them as they provide a free caravan guard to merchants regardless of faith when crossing Bleak Hollow.

The Grand Temple of HaMalech in Blackrock.

ACCEPTANCE

The remainder of the visit was pleasant. Caxton pestered Popcorn about griffins, Jean enjoyed some broth with them, and eventually, they parted ways.

Jean paused at the entrance of Popcorn's curtained corner and then looked back at him.

His green eyes hadn't left her, and he offered a small smile. "Thank you."

When Jean and Caxton returned home, the curseborn got Caxton to bed and sat beside him. He fell asleep quickly, his chest rising and falling rhythmically, and Jean smiled as she settled into her chair.

He was a good kid, though he didn't seem to understand the world. At least it was a protected innocence, and not naivety. Jean sighed and kissed his forehead before she began to read her book.

All the while, she thought about Popcorn's offer, the potential of a second job, and the future she could have if she saved and planned.

Eventually, there was a soft knock on the door. Jean looked up to see her aunt Anca, who slowly wheeled in and felt Caxton's forehead. "He seems to be doing better. Did you stay with him all day?"

"Most of it." Jean put her book on the nightstand. "We went to the temple this afternoon."

"I heard." Anca stayed beside the bed, stroking Caxton's hair as he slept. "There was a bit of an uproar there." Jean raised an eyebrow and her aunt continued. "One dove claimed you were attempting to undermine his authority. Another was flustered that a patient was so rude about bringing you a chair. I'm glad that he was there to stick up for you, whomever that patient is."

Jean shifted slightly and looked away. "It doesn't really matter, Aunt Anca. It happens." She cleared her throat. "Anyway, the dove didn't tell me anything about how Caxton is doing. He said he'd give you a report instead." Anca nodded and handed Jean a small roll of parchment. Jean, after reading it, looked at her aunt. "He could have simply said to continue administering medicine as you had been."

"He should have, but he decided to make things difficult." Anca replied. She looked at Jean. "I'm so sorry they treated you that way today. We should—"

"Aunt Anca," Jean murmured, "please stop." Anca frowned at her and Jean shifted again. "It's alright. I'm used to it."

"You shouldn't be, Jean," Anca replied. She sighed, shook her head, and then offered a tired smile. "Have you eaten yet, dear? Flick reheated yesterday's soup and it should be warmed through by now. Why don't you come downstairs and relax with us?"

Jean glanced at Caxton and then her aunt. Then, with a nod, she followed her aunt to the kitchen.

Halfway through the meal, Jean cleared her throat. "I've been offered another job."

Flick paused halfway through taking a bite. Anca, who was sipping on some wine, choked at the sudden announcement. "Another job? Working for who?"

"The man at the temple, Baba Maze." Jean looked between them and frowned. "I'm not planning on walking out on this one. I already declined the position as I'm here to help Caxton recover... but he did ask if I could consider any time working with him."

Anca looked at Flick with wide eyes. Jean looked between her aunt and uncle, steeled her nerves for an argument, but paused as Flick asked, "What would you be doing?"

"He didn't give me many specifics, but he said that there's a research post he'd like me to be involved in," Jean said. She blew on a spoonful of soup and shrugged. "It could be fun. Honestly, I would enjoy spending more time in the woods outside of Blackrock, but again, I have a duty to Caxton here. The last thing I want to do is to add additional stress to you."

Her aunt and uncle shared a look again before Flick said, "Perhaps we can find a way to let you explore this option, if you'd like. Weekends are yours, though I don't know if that'd be enough time to go wherever it is he'd need you."

"Are you sure?"

Flick nodded and Jean, caught off guard by the suddenness of this, could do nothing but give him a tight hug. Her uncle began to chuckle and patted her back. "Alright, alright. We'll have to see what we can do come the next couple of weeks, as it's all contingent on how Caxton feels. Whatever the case, we'll work through it." He patted her back again and Jean pulled away.

The rest of the evening flew by, leaving Jean to spend time in her room. There, she carefully journaled all that had happened, wrote about Popcorn, and then about how Caxton was doing. Doing so would keep her from growing forgetful, and, if for some reason she wanted to recount everything that happened, she could.

When Jean woke up the next morning, she found that Caxton was downstairs with Flick and Anca. He was coughing again, this time slightly less than the day before, and his eyes brightened as he saw Jean. "Jean! I was telling Mom and Dad about Popcorn!"

Anca smiled at Jean from across the table. "He sounds like an interesting man, dear."

"I think so. I was going to go talk to him later today about the job offer."

"Can I go with you?" Caxton asked.

Jean laughed and sat down beside her cousin. "Only if your parents say its alright."

"Probably not today, Caxton," Flick said. He sipped his coffee for a moment and shook his head. "Jean needs to discuss that offer with him privately, I think. You're welcome to go later, provided Jean doesn't mind." He looked at Jean and raised an eyebrow. "Anca and I spoke about this other offer, and we're happy to let you off early on Thursdays if need be. You already have the weekend to yourself, and if things change, we can always reassess."

"Thank you, Uncle Flick." Jean took a bite of bread and tapped her foot. "I suppose we should go over appointments as needed before anything else happens... the week's plan and such?"

She chatted with them for a while, sorted out the errands and tasks for the week, and then gathered her satchel before leaving.

The walk to the Temple of HaMelech was quiet, as was the temple itself when Jean entered.

Popcorn was snoring softly on the bed when she entered his little portion of the room. His pack was on the ground beside the chair while a notebook sat on the bedside table. He stirred slightly as Jean sat down, murmuring, "Wisteria..."

His peaceful appearance morphed into pain and confusion as his murmurs turned into whimpers and panting. Jean, unsure what to do otherwise, gently shook his shoulder. "Popcorn?"

In an instant, Popcorn's eyes flashed open. His hand shot out and caught her by the neck, his teeth bared, before his eyes focused on her face. Jean sucked in a breath. This was the face of a predator, and she was his prey. As she stared at him, trembling, Popcorn seemed to realize who she was and sighed. He released her and laid down again. Then, after a moment, he whispered, "I didn't think you would be by this soon."

"No... I was planning on later, but had nothing else to do this morning," Jean whispered back. She stared at him, swallowed, and murmured, "Are you alright?"

A mixture of emotions flashed over Popcorn's face as Jean watched him. First disgust, then sadness, before a wave of apathy washed over him. Jean wasn't sure what he had been dreaming of, or what 'wisteria' had to do with it, but a flood of grief filled her as Popcorn shook his head. "I'm fine, daito. Don't worry about me. It was just a bad dream, that's all."

He didn't meet her gaze. After a moment, Jean reached out and took his hand in her own. He tensed, looked at her, and then away. "I don't need your pity."

"It isn't pity," Jean answered. She shifted slightly. "It's... you aren't alone, whatever it is that you're dealing with. I mean, I don't know what it is you were dreaming of, but—"

"Daito?"

"Yes?"

"It's fine." Popcorn offered a very small smile before he squeezed Jean's hand. "Don't worry about it. What are you doing here so early, anyway?"

Jean shrugged slightly. "As I said, there wasn't much else to do. I figured you might enjoy having some company this morning, and then we could talk about that job offer if you're still open to it." She paused as she realized that she was still holding his hand, blushed, and gently released it. As awkward as it was, she had to admit that there was a certain charm to this man, one that left her relatively disappointed at having let go of his hand.

"The job offer? Of course, it's still open!" Popcorn sat upright, his eyes more awake now than before. "Did you speak to your aunt and uncle? I don't want you to leave your job watching Caxton, but I would happily take any time you have to help me out." Jean laughed as Popcorn rambled. It was endearing, especially as he struggled to grab his notebook from the bedside table and show it to her. "I'd have you at Fort Haven with me. It's two days' travel by foot, but you can reduce it to around a day's time, or less, if you go by horse or carriage. Like I said before, you'd receive a weekly stipend as well as room and board, and I'd train you myself for the position."

He fumbled through the pages of his journal, revealing illustrations of creatures and the corresponding scribbled notes. "It'd be you and me, Lyman, and possibly Park if he wants to get involved. You'll meet them in no time... There, here it is. We're doing griffin research, mainly, but other conservation work is just as important. Rakow, great horned griffins, fletchers... Cockatrices, too. Have you seen a cockatrice? They're ugly little buggers, but—"

"Popcorn?" Jean raised an eyebrow. "What will my job be?"

"Your job? Oh, yeah, that." Popcorn ran a hand through the long portion of his hair to untangle it. "While not quite yet, you'll likely take the position of wildlife expert. You're brilliant, resourceful, and have a keen eye about you. I think you'll do great. Once you're used to Fort Haven and our work, you'll fit in perfectly."

"Even with being curseborn?"

"Ae'shaur? You'll be just fine. If anyone gives you trouble, I'll deal with them." Popcorn smiled slightly at her and then held his journal towards her. "Take a look, tell me what you think."

Jean flipped through the various pages, scanning over them quietly before she nodded. "I want to do this. My aunt and uncle have given me the weekend to do as I please. I don't know if that'll be enough time to really do much if Fort Haven is so far away, but at very least we can start from there. I'm with Caxton at all hours outside of the weekend, and while I can bring him here from time to time, I know that he needs to rest regardless. Perhaps, once he's feeling better, we can see about him joining me if this works out."

She looked at Popcorn and found him staring at her with a gentle smile. She tilted her head slightly, and Popcorn shook his head in response. "Whatever we need to do, just let me know. It's the least I can do for the help you've given me."

Jean blushed again and looked down. She wasn't used to attention like this, especially from someone who seemed to have a position of standing. He had a large bid on this research at very least, which made her wonder what exactly he had going on. Still, the attention was nice.

Their conversation dwindled as Jean studied his notebook. A dove healer came in to give Popcorn breakfast, paused, and then hurried out. When she returned, she had a pot of hot water for Jean to use. The curseborn hadn't paid any mind to the shadows until now, which made her stiffen. They leered at her, threatening to consume her as she sat beside Popcorn. Stranger still, the shadows lingered over Popcorn as though he was a saving force. They didn't flee from him like they did some of the doves; instead they swirled around him as though an unseen force invited them to him.

After Jean had her tea, however, the shadows dissipated, and she studied the journal once more.

It was certainly strange, having witnessed that, but Jean didn't know if it was a hallucination or not. Regardless, she did her best to focus on the research that Popcorn had completed. Finally, she glanced at him. "How do you keep the cockatrices from pecking you? You state that they paralyze with their peck. What do you do to prevent this?"

"When we go in? Thick gloves. Otherwise, we leave them be."

"Why not wear lighter gloves? Thick gloves are rather unforgiving, aren't they?"

Popcorn tilted his head slightly, nodded to himself, and then said, "We could give it a try. I suppose that it'd be alright so long as the gloves themselves aren't too thin. Leather gloves should do enough... like the ones you wear. I haven't seen you take those off, by the way. Is there a reason?"

Yes, there was, but she wasn't about to tell him that. Instead, Jean gave a small shrug. "It's been cold as of late. Besides, I find I can grip a quill easier with these."

"Really?"

"Mhm." Jean returned to reading the journal. "How long do they think you'll need to stay here to heal up? It didn't sound like a minor surgery."

"I'm staros." Popcorn shifted, moved his leg, and grimaced. "Honestly, I'd give it a couple of weeks before they say I can start therapy. Normally, I'd think this takes a couple of months."

"Do staros heal faster, then?"

"Partially. Remember the ef—"

"I remember it, yes," Jean interrupted quietly. She looked around to see if there were any other people listening, especially a dove, and then looked at Popcorn. "It's illegal here, remember? Though... what exactly does it do for you?"

Popcorn raised an eyebrow, a bit of an amused smirk on his face. "Staros need it to survive, remember? It helps us heal outside of living. Look at my leg; if you pull any of that bandage off, I can guarantee that it's already scarred over and no longer needs stitches. Besides, if someone tries to arrest me for using, I can claim racism; I need it to live, and they can't deny me a right to live." He watched her. "That doesn't bother you, does it, daito?"

"You using drugs?" Jean clarified. He gave a bit of a nod and Jean shifted.

Did it bother her? She didn't want to be arrested if he was found out, nor did she want this secret to affect her chances at being reincarnated as something other than a curseborn. On the other hand, it really wasn't bothering her or anyone else. If Popcorn's heart stopped, that was his fault. She was mostly worried about her involvement, that was all. She certainly could care less about what happened to him, right? The thought of his potential death made a lump grow in her throat, but Jean swallowed that back. Instead, she slowly shook her head, and Popcorn gave a bit of a hum.

By the time Jean left the temple that evening, she and Popcorn had spent several hours talking about what he had hoped for her to assist with. Lyman, the wildlife expert as of current, was showing signs of potential retirement. Popcorn felt that Jean had enough gumption to fill his shoes after some training, and was willing to take that fall if it didn't work. They had tentatively planned on going to Fort Haven together in three weeks' time, where Jean would spend the weekend getting accustomed to Fort Haven before she'd return to Blackrock to help with Caxton. It seemed like an exhausting trip, but Jean looked forward to it all the same.

She spent time with Popcorn the next day, too, where they chatted and laughed about encounters they'd had in the woods. Popcorn recounted his first time seeing a great horned griffin while Jean, amid tears of laughter, described her first run-in with a black bear outside of Zanther. She found herself rather disappointed when she left that night, knowing that it would be a late evening if she tried to spend time with Popcorn after working with Caxton.

On Monday, she spent all day with Caxton. Her cousin did what he could to limit needing her, though his cough grew worse as the day progressed. Jean bundled him up in several blankets and sat him on the balcony to get some sunshine, where he leaned against her and watched the birds dart from roofline to roofline.

"Are you upset you have to stay in Blackrock with me?" he asked after several hours.

Jean looked at him. "Why would I be upset about spending time with you?" She met his tired blue eyes and sighed before she wrapped an arm around him. He closed his eyes as she brushed her fingers through his hair and murmured, "You are family, Caxton... whatever that means to you. I know that it means that I want to take whatever time I have available to be with you and to make sure you feel better. As for being in Blackrock, there's some disappointment, sure, but things will change. You're not going to be sick forever."

"That's what Dad says, too. He says that it's just a season, but I don't know how long that season will be." Caxton sighed. "I'm tired of being sick, Jean. Sometimes I just want to be done so everyone else can live normal lives."

"It wouldn't be normal with you changed, Caxton. This is a part of life, and it happens." Jean squeezed him lightly. "I wouldn't change anything about the time we get to spend together. Besides, when you're better, we can see about you coming with me. You have to focus on yourself first, though, before we can do that."

Her cousin gave a soft cough in response before he closed his eyes.

Over the week, Jean and Caxton worked through his schoolwork, with biology sparking a rare moment of enthusiasm. His fascination with griffins mirrored Jean's growing curiosity about her future at Fort Haven.

"Can you ask Popcorn about the griffins and why they look so funny?" Caxon asked abruptly.

Jean laughed. "I'll write it down. For now, focus on your schoolwork."

Eventually, the weekend came, and Jean returned to the temple of HaMelech to check on Popcorn.

He seemed to be in a good mood as he entered, especially as he saw her. "Daito! How was the week? Is Caxton doing any better?"

"He's doing just fine, Popcorn. How about you? Is your leg healing as quickly as you'd hoped?" Jean sat in the seat beside him and began to pull documents from her bag.

"Well enough, I suppose," Popcorn said, giving his leg a rueful look. "They don't want me to put pressure on it still, and are trying to convince me to use a cane. I'd rather not, personally. It only reminds me of the weakness I have."

Jean looked at him and raised an eyebrow. "I wouldn't think it's that big an issue."

"It is when you have an appearance to keep up." Popcorn shifted to look over her papers. "What's this?"

"Some thoughts I had while with Caxton. He wants to know why griffins look the way they do, by the way. We focused on chimeras during his biology this week and that was his latest question." Jean smoothed some papers down and then held them out to Popcorn. "It made me think about the cockatrice enclosure and some changes you could make."

Popcorn studied the documents as she spoke, nodded every so often, and folded the papers. "I'll get these sent to Fort Haven for immediate implementation. Hand me my pack, as I need to write to Park as well. You don't mind delivering these to a company heading to Fort Haven tomorrow, do you? Tamrin is reliable, as picky as she is, and I'd like to get these to Park sooner rather than later."

Jean passed Popcorn the bag and looked around. "When did you think you could leave?"

"Two weeks. I cannot stay here any later than two weeks. It's bad enough being cooped up here as it is." Popcorn scribbled on a piece of parchment and then handed it to Jean. "Take this to Tamin, by the west gate. It's hard to miss her establishment, though it isn't a pleasant neighborhood, but I think you'll be alright."

"What is her establishment?" Jean asked, fidgeting with the papers as she stood to go.

"Brothel. Take this, let her know I sent you directly. Get yourself acquainted with them, too. They'll probably be your transportation back and forth for a little while."

Rakow

Perhaps one of the more accustomed to urban life, rakow collect bits and bobs to impress their mates. Things such as knives have been found with these creatures as they can and will use tools to further their goals. A small group of rakow are able to distract people long enough to steal valuables.

Wings are for cooling purposes, as they are too heavy to fly

Sharp objects are not out of the question and may be used for mugging, self-defense, or wooing a mate

Attempts at impressing a female include stolen, flashy items. The noisier, the better.

9

FORT HAVEN

Jean quietly wandered through the streets of Blackrock, her hand on her boltcaster, as she made her way towards the brothel. She wasn't entirely sure if she wanted to think further about how Popcorn knew just how reliable Tamrin was, but the longer she allowed it to flit in her mind, the quicker she came to the conclusion that the brothel workers regularly attended those at Fort Haven. This idea disgusted part of her, more so as she imagined Popcorn inviting one of the workers into his quarters, while the other part understood. Morale needed to be kept up while in the middle of nowhere, and that was certainly a way to do it.

As she approached the west gate, her eyes flickered to a large wooden sign overlooking the street.

The faded blue background was a lovely host for the golden cursive writing, proudly boasting 'Miss Tamrin's Gilded Cage'. Outside, a woman wearing a slinky brown dress and a spotted fur was smoking a cigarette. The bags under her eyes betrayed her exhaustion, though she perked up slightly as she caught movement. Then, seeing Jean, her gaze softened. "What are you doing this direction? Certainly, you aren't visiting the Gilded Cage, are you?"

Jean shifted.

While she seemed nice, Jean didn't trust it. She shifted slightly. "I need to deliver some papers to Tamrin, please. Do you know where they are?"

"To Tamrin?" The other woman took a breath of her cigarette, exhaled, and then stood upright. "I'll show you where Miss Tamrin is. Come along, dear."

Jean swallowed, straightened up, and followed the woman in.

Exude confidence, act as though she was to be here. That kept her from getting in trouble at her mother's establishment, and it should work here. While she didn't have the benefit of a desk between her and others, just the air should be enough.

The Gilded Cage was a quiet establishment. There was a single desk at the front of the room and a set of stairs on either side that led to a balcony and several sets of rooms. Jean could hear laughter coming from a door to the right of the stairs, which the woman with fur led her towards.

She knocked on the door before she opened it and ushered Jean in.

There were fifteen men and women sitting in the room. Some lounged on a couch, others milled around a table with food, while still others applied makeup at vanity mirrors. No one looked towards Jean and the woman, prompting Jean to slowly relax. It was the breakroom, and they assumed that she was supposed to be here.

The woman led Jean further into the room and then cleared her throat. "Miss Tamrin? Someone is here to see you. She's got some papers."

"Papers? No one applied to work here."

Jean shifted as a short woman with red hair turned in her seat. She had half-applied her false eyelashes for the day, and the remaining lash hung limply in her hand like a dead bug. She looked at Jean for a moment before her face lit up. "Jeannie! Little Jeannie, look at you!"

Everyone turned to look at them as the woman stood and embraced Jean tightly. The curseborn, meanwhile, stood shocked before it clicked. "Miss Tamrin! Is it really you?"

"In the flesh, dear! You've gotten so big! Last I saw you, you were a scrawny thing doing homework behind your adoptive mother's desk. Everyone! This is Jean Cassy, adopted daughter of the famed Adriata Cassy of Zanther, Mistress of the Redlight District!" Tamrin grinned at Jean and then gestured for a chair to be brought to her. "What are you doing in Blackrock?"

Jean sunk into the chair. "I am here to help with my cousin. Oh! I have documents for you. Popcorn — Baba Maze — said you could get them to Fort Haven for him? Deliver them to Park?"

"In a moment, in a moment. First, tell me everything!"

Jean found a cup of tea pressed into her hands as Tamrin returned to doing her makeup. Without anything to lose, she recounted her travels to Blackrock (leaving out the issue of chitters) and meeting Popcorn. Then she shrugged. "He wants to get back to Fort Haven within two weeks but wanted to get this sent ahead of him."

"Well, that's wonderful news! I'm excited to finally have a woman to talk to at Fort Haven. Ingrid!" Tamrin looked at the woman with the spotted fur. "Tell Jefferson we'll need another seat in the caravan to account for Jean when she joins us. We'll be bringing her from Fort Haven when we finish our circuit it seems."

"Right away, ma'am." Ingrid dipped her head, winked at Jean good-humoredly, and hurried out.

"Is it alright that I catch a ride with you? I know I'm curseborn—"

"Just think of it as a favor to your adoptive mother, hm? It's good karma all the same, and I'm helping you with yours." Tamrin grinned through the mirror and adjusted her amber earrings. "Are you going back to Popcorn, dear?"

"Later today, yes," Jean answered. "Why?"

"Would you kindly remind him that Park has yet to complete his portion of the ledger? Funds are low, and they're our final clients that need to pay."

"Yes, Miss Tamrin."

After her cup of tea, and their chat, Jean returned to the Blackrock streets.

She milled the vendors as she made her way to the temple. There were many beautiful wares to look at, each handcrafted painstakingly: leather-bound notebooks, hats, bodices... She did stop at a small cart full of canes to peruse them. While Popcorn said he didn't like the idea of using one, he'd likely be more open to it if the cane itself was elegant and didn't look like it belonged to a man three times his senior.

Jean looked through them before one caught her eye. It was towards the bottom of the pile, as though forgotten, and made of a light antler. She carefully pulled it out and studied it closer only to find that it had what looked like runes carved into it. Something about the entire thing drew her to wanting to at least know what the runes said, if nothing more.

"How much is this?"

"Four copper pieces."

"I'll take it."

With her purchase under arm, Jean hurried back to the temple.

Popcorn was sleeping when she entered, this time silent. She lightly shook him, and he cracked an eye open to look at her. "You're back."

"Yes. Tamrin said that Park had yet to pay for services, and she wanted to remind you of that."

"Of course she does." Popcorn sat up, stretched, and looked at Jean again. "What's that?"

"It's for you. The only stipulation is that you let me figure out what those runes say." Jean held the cane towards him and Popcorn, after a moment, took it. With a single glance over it, he went incredibly quiet and simply stared. "Do you like it?" Jean ventured after a moment. "I know you said that you didn't want a cane, and this might be overstepping, but—"

"No, I like it. Where did you find this?"

"There was a vendor that I stopped by on the way here. Are you sure there's nothing wrong?"

"No. No, nothing's wrong. I just... haven't seen anything from the north outside of my personal possessions, is all," Popcorn said softly. He turned it over in his hands, traced the runes, and murmured, "It's a traditional staros blessing, written in Ivumi. I recognize the hand that wrote it, too. Thank you, Jean."

Jean tilted her head slightly, watching him. He seemed caught up in thought as he continued to study the runes, finally speaking. "Lor mi tuni fasta, un mi lash ingtu."

It was beautiful, lyrical even, as Popcorn said those soft words. Jean didn't dare open her mouth and ruin the sacred feeling that hovered over them. Finally, as Popcorn put the cane down, she whispered, "What was that?"

"May the hunt be swift, and the bow be light," Popcorn said quietly in return. "I have that same saying on my bow in Fort Haven."

"And it's from the north?"

"From my people." Popcorn was quiet for a moment. "I haven't met another staros in many years. The language fades for me, even when I use it. It is a breath of fresh air, a hishan, to hear it again." He chuckled, shook his head, and looked at Jean. "When we get to Fort Haven, remind me to show you my shield and bow. They're vital for surviving in the north, between protection from predators to shelter from the hailstorms. I think you'd find them beautiful."

Jean nodded slightly, giving him a small smile of her own. "I think I'd like that. Do you show them to many people?"

"Only those I think are worth sharing them with, daito." Popcorn answered. He eyed her, making her fiddle with the hem of her shirt. "I appreciate everything you've done for me while I've been trapped here. Thank you."

"Of course. That's what friends do, isn't it?"

Several weeks passed this way. Jean split her time between Popcorn and Caxton, doing her best to care for each of them as she could. Caxton's breathing grew stronger over time while Popcorn, begrudgingly, began to do therapy for his leg. His gait was awkward, confirming the need for a cane, but he was adjusting quickly. As for Jean and her chittering madness, it had begun to grow more troublesome as the days wore on.

Shadows lingered longer than they should have. Eyes manifested around corners, soft laughter came from darkened hallways, and Jean swore that, in the corner of her eye, there was always a tall, thin creature holding a staff.

It was never there when she looked, but the feeling of being watched never stopped.

Popcorn seemed to notice this once, when Jean was drinking her tea and watching his therapy session. He didn't mind her there as far as she could tell, nor did he see the shadows looming towards her. When Jean finally snapped and slammed her teacup down to cover her head (clutching it seemed to help), he stopped and stared. While her weak explanation that she burned her tongue seemed to satisfy him, she didn't believe that he fully trusted her answer.

Finally, after a month, Jean stood at the west gate with Popcorn. She shifted, scratched the back of her leg with her foot, and looked at him. "You're sure the supply caravan is going today?"

"Positive. Park wouldn't reschedule it. He's too anal about things like that." Popcorn leaned heavily on his cane as he lazily watched the street. "You'll find that out soon enough."

"What does he do again?"

"Foreman."

Jean raised her eyebrows and looked away from Popcorn. He certainly was outspoken, wasn't he? She couldn't dare say anything about people in higher standing than her... or anyone, for that matter. Jean sighed softly at the thought and looked around as a large wagon, driven by a team of oxen toad, slowed down near them. There were three other carts behind it, all of which pulled by antsy looking mules, while the drivers sat on the seats with rather annoyed faces.

"What's with this, aye? Why's there a curseborn at the pickup spot?" the lead driver questioned. "What do you think you're doing here, sullying the streets? The stockyard is down two roads. Go on, your master will be missing you."

Jean looked down. Beside her, she watched as Popcorn tensed and stepped forward. "Master Ellinger."

"Oh! Didn't see you, sir. Dealing with the riffraff. Are you headin' to the fort?"

"Yes, with my colleague. We've business to attend to now that I am well." Popcorn gestured to Jean, who looked up at the inclusion. "Miss Jean Cassy, this is Master Ellinger. Ellinger, Miss Cassy."

Ellinger gave a groan as Jean dipped her head. Then, as Ellinger began to complain to Popcorn, she stared at the shadows beneath the coach.

It glinted even in the shadows as she stared, looking back at her. The ebony staff. Jean felt her stomach twist in a knot as it began to whisper to her again, begging her to join it in a power-hungry run.

It was Popcorn's gentle nudge that snapped her out of it, and then the appearance of Osmond, that brought her attention to the conversation once more.

"Are you alright?" Popcorn asked.

"Yes... I'm fine, just... nervous." Jean smiled at him, though she wasn't sure if it reached her eyes. Popcorn frowned back but didn't argue. Instead, he helped Jean into the wagon and then climbed up beside her. Osmond followed, prompting Jean to scowl at the orb. As soon as Osmond was close enough, and Popcorn seemed preoccupied, she hissed, "You've been gone for nearly a month."

"What was that?" Popcorn asked.

"Nothing! Just commenting that you've been away from Fort Haven for several weeks. You don't think Park will be angry, do you?" Jean asked. She waved her hand past her head as though batting a fly, though it was more to knock Osmond off his seemingly random path.

The slight breeze made Osmond tumble through the air and then land on a sack of flour where he sat, pouting.

Popcorn, not noticing the little ball of light, laughed. "I can do what I want, daito. Park can complain, but he won't argue." He pulled his notebook out. "Now, where to begin?"

By the time Jean and Popcorn had exhausted their conversation, they were rolling over a creaking wooden bridge. It spanned fifty feet over a gorge, which was home to an old water wheel. Jean hummed slightly. They must use it to charge any kinetic crystals they had in their possession. Paths crisscrossed up and down the steep walls and betrayed the well-used courses. Jean craned her neck to look at where they were going and paused as large, worn stones towered over them. Popcorn followed her gaze. "Beautiful, isn't it?"

"It's amazing... it must be from at least the Golden Age."

"Or older," Popcorn said, nodding. "There aren't many relics to date it, but I've theorized that the Golden Age bears the characteristics that echo this building. I'd argue that it could be from the First Age, even, but it isn't quite old enough."

Jean looked around as they entered the fort. It was overgrown, aged, and poorly maintained. A dead garden lay beneath an oak tree with fading orange leaves, and the cottages built into the walls appeared to have been repaired just enough to remain livable. The best-kept cottage sat across the courtyard, partially hidden behind a cluster of dead bushes. "That's the lord's quarters. Park's office is in there. It leads to some other resting areas and the kitchen." Popcorn explained. "Most cottages are taken, though we'll clean one out for you to use when you're here."

The curseborn nodded, shouldered her bag, and hopped out of the wagon as soon as it stopped moving. Popcorn climbed out after her, leaned heavily on his cane, and sighed. "Good to be home."

Now that Jean was still, she could better catch sight of various workers. Laborers were working on the high walls overlooking the land. Others were tending to what looked like a meager attempt to till soil to plant winter crops, though the garden was abandoned. Still, more were surrounding what looked like a large chicken coop.

Popcorn patted Jean's shoulder. "We'll find Park first, to get you on payroll."

As she followed him, Jean was keenly aware of people beginning to stare. Ellinger snapped orders to some of his men, prompting a flurry of activity as the wagons were unloaded and inhabitants of Fort Haven hurried about. Just as Tamrin had said, Jean was the only woman.

"Get moving! Lyman, kindly get yourself into a useful state and get those men around you to move it!"

The voice came from the lord's quarters, where a lanky man with glasses perched atop his nose stood. His trench coat fit him poorly, his hair gave him the appearance of a wet bird, and his scruffy cheeks reminded Jean of a man who had little time for anything but worry. Popcorn beelined towards him, leaving Jean to hurry behind him.

"Park!"

"Gods above, what is it now... Popcorn! You've made it." The man turned to look at Popcorn, a dead expression in his eyes. "Several days after you assumed you would, but you made it. Welcome back."

He turned away, paused, and looked at them again. This time, his amber ring flashed in the sunlight. Jean shifted, aware of his scrutiny, before Park looked away. "Any reason you brought a curseborn with you? Tamrin usually brings new girls with her caravan; did you special order?"

A little growl left Popcorn. Jean stepped forward. "I'm Jean Cassy. Popcorn hired me to work here."

"Popcorn hired...?" Park looked at them again. This time, his eyebrows were furrowed and lips set in a thin line. He began to rub his forehead. "Popcorn, we talked about this. I understand that you want to expedite the hiring process, but there are standards that you have to follow."

Popcorn shifted, an easy smirk covering his lips. Jean glanced at him as he shrugged. "I decided we need another expert on the command team."

"Command team?" Jean questioned. Popcorn glanced at her, briefly, and she shook her head. "You never said I'd be a part of a command team."

"I said I was going to train you, didn't I? That entails a rather hefty position, I think," Popcorn replied. He paused, faced her fully, and frowned. "That doesn't frighten you out of the job, does it? The last thing I want to do is to make you uncomfortable here."

Park scoffed softly and Popcorn elbowed him. Jean shifted before she said, "No, but... with traveling back and forth to Blackrock, is there enough reason to put me on a command team? I'm not here full-time, and the trainings—"

"It'll be fine, daito," Popcorn soothed. "It'll be just fine. I'm willing to make accommodations in exchange for your skills."

He smiled at her and Jean, slowly, relaxed. It was different, but welcome, as Popcorn let her move closer. As he and Park began to chat, she watched the people around them busily move crates and bags. No one seemed to pay them much attention amid the rush, but the longer that Jean watched, the sooner she realized that there were people glancing towards them. One of them was a rather rough looking man with a smattering of scars over his torso. He stood up, brushed his hands on his legs, and stared at her. After a moment, he turned to the nearest person and muttered something. Then, both of them looked at her and the pattern continued.

Jean shifted, glanced at Popcorn, and then back at the man.

"I don't have any cottages open for her, either," Park said. "She'd have to stay with someone, and I honestly don't trust any of the men to keep their hands off."

"She can use my cottage while we tend to hers," Popcorn countered.

"I'll be fine wherever you put me," Jean said. She looked at the two. "I've dealt with worse. Besides, I won't be here for much longer, as I'll be returning to Blackrock at the end of the weekend. Just put me where you can."

Popcorn gestured to Jean and grinned. "With that, my friend, we'll be heading out to take a look at the cockatrices and get Jean accustomed to the area."

"I'll go with you, otherwise I'll have to answer a million questions that I certainly don't want to deal with." Park cleared his throat. "Well, Miss Cassy, I hope you enjoy little developed, partially tended to areas."

"Better than most places I've been," Jean returned lightly.

With a chuckle from Popcorn, and a sigh from Park, Jean followed the two men deeper into the fort.

Tower w/ roosts

Lord's Area and Main office living area

Park and Popcorns

West gate

Kitchen and store room

Coop

Dead garden

Stables

Communal fire

Main gate

Cottages

Solari Shrine

Draw bridge

Mill for grinding wheat and charging kinetic stones

Fort Haven

Road from Blackrock

10

SECRETS

The three moved slowly through the fort. Popcorn limped heavily beside Jean, who looked around quietly. Park didn't say much either, especially as they passed workers hurrying back and forth with supplies.

Jean was surprised with the activity compared to the state of the fort. Doors seemed to be attached just enough to allow entry and exit, but nothing more, and the stones were strewn with ivy and moss. Popcorn didn't seem bothered, nor did Park, so Jean didn't question it either.

All the while, she listened to the brief interactions that the two men exchanged, her interest piquing as Park asked, "Any word on ashura in Blackrock?"

"No, none. Seems you're still safe, friend," Popcorn replied.

Try as she might, Jean couldn't recall anything about ashura. It might have been some sort of creature, especially if Popcorn was interested in them, but that didn't explain why only Park had been affected. She frowned and tapped her fingers on her leg, brushed her hand against her bolt caster, and then looked around again.

Park sighed. "Good. Last time Ellinger came by, he said he saw some masks in the Telfarian district."

"Not that I heard of."

"What do masks have to do with ashura?" Jean finally asked.

Park glanced at her, his already expressionless face taking on a deeper, darker look. "You aren't familiar with much outside of where you're from, are you, Miss Cassy?" Jean opened her mouth, closed it, and frowned. The foreman shook his head. "Of course not. My hope is that you at least know the Solari tenants, else you're really in trouble."

Indignant heat flooded Jean's cheeks, and she straightened up. "I know about things that pertain to my life, and until now, none of this—" She gestured to the fort. "Did." Popcorn was watching her now, one eyebrow raised and the corner of his lip quirked up. Park continued to stare at her as she continued. "As for my faith, I know enough to know my place, which people enjoy reminding me about regardless of what I know, and I'd very much prefer that you refrain from involving yourself in it."

The foreman stared at her and Jean, as the warmth from her cheeks faded, realized that her hands were shaking, clenched fists. With a soft breath, she shifted. Before she could say another word, though, Park's expression shifted ever so slightly into amusement. "Keep up the attitude, Miss Cassy, and you might be okay here at Fort Haven."

Again, heat raced through Jean but she smiled despite her embarrassment. Popcorn lightly nudged her, and murmured, "Well done, diato." Then, they continued on their way. Jean didn't bring up the masks, or ashura, again; Park had done a good job in deflecting the question, and she didn't want to be seen as a fool once more.

Park brought them to the lord's quarters first, where a desk cluttered with papers and a poorly kept bed lay. There, he handed Jean several documents to sign. "Customary, liability wavers, payroll authorization... all the important things."

"How do you have enough to pay for everything?" Jean asked. She looked between Popcorn and Park. "This has to be an expensive operation, especially with all of the people and what upkeep there has been."

"We have a benefactor who donates regularly." Park shrugged as Popcorn shifted on his bad leg. The staros man sunk into a chair, sighed, and nodded as Park continued. "He's the one who keeps this place going. Though, I do want to talk to him about getting things winterized soon. It'll take a hefty sum, and with Popcorn being laid up the last month and a half, we're behind schedule."

Popcorn rolled his eyes. "It'll be fine, I'm sure."

"Coffers are low," Park countered.

Jean shifted and sat beside Popcorn. He looked at her, smiled, and shook his head as he looked back at Park. "It'll be fine, Park."

"Popcorn—"

Beside Jean, Popcorn tensed. She looked at him to see that he had begun to bare his teeth at Park, his eyes narrowed into dangerous slits. Park, however, seemed unphased. He rose one eyebrow at his friend, sighed, and shook his head. "Fine. It'll be fine. I won't continue this conversation."

"Good." Popcorn righted himself and looked at Jean. "I want you to meet Lyman, and then we go look at the cockatrices."

Jean nodded slightly, ignored the shadows that were beginning to grow on the wall, and followed Popcorn out.

Now that the supply caravan was unloaded, the business of the fort had died down. Men milled about, chatting idly, though they stopped as Jean left the lord's quarters. Popcorn kept himself straightened, prompting Jean to copy him, and then looked at her. "Lyman is over there, leaning against the wall. Found him in the Telfarian district peddling wares... leather, specifically. Anyway, I offered him the job after a couple of minutes of chatting. Established hunter, good with a knife, understands wildlife."

Jean glanced at Popcorn. The shadows seemed to grow longer at the mention of Telfarians, especially as flashes of the blood thirsty bandits who had managed to get into the gates of Zanther flooded her memory. Coupled with the Long Night, a night of deranged madness caused by the Black Dragon, and it was a recipe for nothing but brutality and death. She absentmindedly put her hand on her boltcaster, drew in a shaking breath, and closed her eyes.

It did nothing for her.

The memories of men advancing as she tried to hide in the alleyway were all to vivid, as was the irony smell of blood that flooded her senses as she witnessed another man brutally impale her assailants before he, too, turned with a sick grin on his face.

Something grabbed her arm, and she whipped around, boltcaster leveled. As she sucked in another breath, her eyes focused on a face that faded in and out. One moment, it was the deer-skulled monster who had held the staff in Bleak Hollow. The next, there were concerned green eyes searching her face. "Jean?"

Familiarity rang through the voice and Jean blinked before she whispered, "Popcorn... I'm sorry..."

"Are you alright?"

Slowly, Jean nodded and looked around. Osmond was hovering behind him, bouncing lightly through the air as he seemingly inspected the area. People were staring at them, especially now that Jean had her boltcaster aimed at Popcorn's gut. Her friend had one arm up, the other firmly planted on his cane.

He didn't move for a moment as Jean regained her bearings. Finally, when she took another breath and felt her shoulders sag, he carefully tilted her boltcaster down. "Are you certain?"

"I... don't know if this position will work out," Jean whispered. She shifted, stared at the ground, and shook her head. "Is he a Telfarian?"

"Lyman? No, no, he wouldn't have been able to keep up with them if he was. Terrible work ethics most days," Popcorn said. He put a hand on her back. "Why don't I introduce the two of you, and then you sit down. You look like you saw a ghost."

Jean slowly nodded. Popcorn didn't move until she looked up again. The concern that flooded over his face washed away as they approached the gruff man with scars. "Lyman!"

"Boss... and a curseborn." Lyman pushed himself off of the wall, one eyebrow raised. "Whatcha doing in the woods, sweetheart?"

The liquor on his breath and the glint in his eye made Jean's hand find her boltcaster again. She swallowed and straightened up. It was like the brothel. She was supposed to be here, and she wouldn't just lay down for him to take what he wanted. "Orientation."

"Orientation?" Lyman began to laugh as he shook his head. "Popcorn, you serious? What did we need, a gardener? Solaris above, you'd think we're hiring women here to take care of business!" He wiped his eyes as Jean frowned, her hand still firm on her weapon.

The longer she stood next to this man, the less she liked him.

Popcorn cleared his throat, his eyes narrowed. "Enough, Lyman."

"No, seriously! What did you bring her here for? You don't often special order from Miss Tamrin's Gilded Cage, did she catch your eye while you were in Blackrock? We don't need a woman here!"

Jean squared her shoulders. "I'm not a whore." Lyman's attention snapped to her. Popcorn's did as well, though he had a faint smile tracing over his lips where Lyman was beginning to scowl. The curseborn swallowed. "I'm not a whore, though I expect your respect regardless of my profession."

"Respect? You're a curseborn, girlie."

"My name is Jean Cassy, and Popcorn hired me to join the command team once training is finished." Jean kept her hand on her boltcaster. "I was assured that my heritage would have no effect on my standing here."

Lyman snickered softly. "Really? Who promised you that?"

"I did," Popcorn said. Lyman's gaze snapped to the staros and a mixture of emotions flashed over his face. Popcorn rose one eyebrow. "So, Lyman, you were saying?"

"... Welcome aboard, toots." Lyman stood upright and gestured towards a ramshackle coop with a nod of his head. "Cockatrices are over there, ugly things. Mind your fingers: it'd be a shamed if they paralyzed you." He gave a dark laugh as he plodded away, leaving Jean beside Popcorn.

A queasy feeling had filled her stomach, enough to make Jean try to swallow bile back, before she looked at Popcorn. He was watching Lyman walk away, his knuckles white on his cane, before Jean cleared her throat. Then, he looked at her.

"He's a lovely character, isn't he?" Jean questioned quietly. "Seems pretty polite... unwilling to question orders."

"Your sarcasm speaks volume, daito," Popcorn said, shaking his head. "I'm impressed that you stood up to him. No one likes to do that."

Jean shrugged slightly, bit back another snide remark, and followed Popcorn to the cockatrices. All the while, she did her best to ignore the shadows that had decided to make themselves noticeable again. Popcorn glanced back at her once, his eyebrows raised, before he looked away again.

When they approached the coop, Jean was met with three rather scraggly, disgusting creatures. They were bathing their warty bodies in a patch of sunlight, their toad-like hind legs kicking up dust to cover their sparse feathers. One lifted its chicken-like head, without feathers on its neck, and gave a croaking call. In an instant, all three of them were upright and nervously pacing the fence line to get away from Jean and Popcorn. They tripped over each other's tails, each one no longer than six inches and covered with dull feathers that protruded from its warty skin. Jean had never seen one of these creatures before, cockatrices as she assumed, but the strange cross of a toad and a chicken was enough to make her forget about her current issues.

Popcorn leaned against his cane. "They're certainly a sight to behold, but they're fascinating. These three were caught in a snare a couple of miles away from the fort. Lyman has said they're healing up fine, but I haven't been able to support the claim." He shrugged slightly. Jean could see he was watching her out of the corner of his eye, especially as he shifted and said, "Think you could catch one of them using those new ideas you wrote down?"

"I'm not sure if that's a good idea, Popcorn." Jean said. She looked at the warty cockatrices, a small stone mouse no more than three feet in front of them, and then at Popcorn again. "What if they peck me?"

"We have antivenom... somewhere." Popcorn chuckled softly to himself, murmured something in Ivumi, and looked at Jean again. A strange mix of emotions flickered in his eyes, catching Jean off guard, as he murmured, "I'll be right behind you."

Jean nodded slowly. She was more focused on trying to identify whatever it was that he was thinking of, especially as she saw a tinge of what had looked like admiration or adoration cross his face, than the cockatrices as she stepped into the coop.

All three griffins froze, staring at her with their large eyes, before they scattered with a flurry of wings and frightened croaks. Jean threw her arms over her face to protect herself from any stray beaks or talons as the cockatrices raced around her. One arm wrapped around her as Popcorn found his place by her side, shielding her with his body as the griffins spooked and then, ever so slowly, calmed down. Jean slowly lifted her head to look at Popcorn. "Are you alright?"

"I'm fine. They can't get through my pants to peck me." Popcorn released her gently. "Time to redeem yourself, daito."

Jean nodded again. This time, as she pulled on her leather gloves, she took a deep breath and slowly approached. The cockatrices had huddled into one corner of the cage to watch her, frozen. Jean took two steps, paused, and then a third. The beasts didn't stop staring. As she closed the distance, the cockatrices shifted nervously before she reached one hand out and murmured, "You're alright. I'm sorry I scared you; I don't want to hurt you."

They blinked at her, Popcorn shifted behind her, but Jean simply stood there. Finally, slowly, she reached out and gently lifted a cockatrice.

She could feel its heart pounding in its breast as it squirmed in her hands. The warty toad legs dangled as she held it like a chicken, allowing it to look around nervously. Jean put one hand on its back to help ground it before she turned to face Popcorn. He was grinning ear to ear, which was quite unnerving given his ability to bare all of his teeth, and he looked expectantly at Jean as she returned to his side. "Look at you! I think I made an excellent call in offering you a job. Let's see here... yes, we'll start on the basic griffin anatomy..."

Jean and Popcorn remained at the cockatrice coop until the sun had nearly set. Popcorn was a gentle teacher as he used the cockatrice to demonstrate various details across all griffins, his voice soft and his hands slow. The cockatrice fell asleep in Jean's arms as they worked, checking over each former injury and getting measurements off of the creature to keep an eye on potential recapturing. Popcorn had Jean bend a thin metal band around one of its legs. "It's to monitor it if we find it after release."

When they put the cockatrice to roost with the other two, Jean followed Popcorn to the center of the fort.

A blazing fire had been made in the middle of the courtyard, shedding light over the gathered assembly. Now that everyone was gathered and mostly stationary, Jean was surprised to see that there were no more than twelve people, including herself, this far from Blackrock. They all looked towards her as she and Popcorn approached, and most of them seemed to tense as the firelight washed over their faces. Popcorn sat heavily on a log and Jean, with nowhere else to sit, sat beside him. Park was on the other side of the log, sipping from his flask, before he cleared his throat. "As many of you have heard, our fearless leader has returned." Popcorn waved his hand slightly as Park continued. "Comprehensive reports are due from each of the contingent groups, including repairs, as winter will be approaching soon. Might as well catch him up, hm?"

There was a very soft wave of murmurs around the fire. The hair on the back of Jean's neck prickled. A keen sense of danger wafted through the air, as though each of her new colleagues were frightened of a predator in the area. Then, she realized that everyone was looking directly at Popcorn. Nervous shifts, subtle twitches of muscles, and the ever-so-slight flaring of nostrils made Jean put her hand on her boltcaster. Something about him scared them, though no one moved to betray that secret.

"Well, out with it." Popcorn rested his hands on his cane. "I've been out a month, my hope is that pay wasn't wasted. Park informed me that coffers were low, and they'd better be low due to earned wages and not loaf-abouts."

"Yes, sir!" one of the men said quickly. Everyone's attention snapped to him, and, after a moment, he began to stammer about the winter repairs and fortifications. Jean tuned out after a moment, not caring to listen about how much lumber they'd gone through in a month and instead studied each of the others around the fire.

Only one person was staring at her through the firelight, his face set in a thin line and a lack of fear in his eyes. Lyman was playing with a hunting knife across from her, his gaze never once leaving her face. Jean felt like a cornered rabbit as he leaned forward, watching her, before his eyes slowly moved to Popcorn and back to Jean.

He was gauging Popcorn's attention.

Jean swallowed slightly, unhooked her boltcaster, and laid it across her lap. Lyman smirked, sat back, and then watched the man return to blubbering about the broken saw they were dealing with. All the while, Jean knew she was still being watched.

The firelight was seeming less and less inviting as she sat there, an almost grasping darkness rolling in. No one else noticed, leaving Jean to shift in the choking blackness. Osmond was nowhere to be seen: she had decided that he was a rather unreliable imaginary friend, or guardian, or whatever he really was. With those thoughts, Jean slowly looked to her left.

There were eyes in the darkness now. Just pinpricks of white pupils, the remainder black, as they stared at her. They were taller than any of the other chitters, and the form moved slightly to betray the bleached bone of the monster that held the staff once again. Rotten flesh hung off of its antlers, its thin fingers curled around the ebony weapon that it had expertly wielded before. This time, though, the flesh was pale red, not the ghastly mummified pale flesh it was before. Jean's throat ran dry at the realization that this... thing... was the new wielder of the staff before her.

Besides the shaman was another small handful of chitters. They were pushing through the blackness, their fangs dripping with bile, as though testing the strength of the firelight that kept them at bay.

It's just a hallucination, Jean thought. They cannot hurt me, it's not real.

The piercing laughter that filled the night shattered every illusion of safety as Jean stood with her boltcaster drawn. Others at the fire startled, including Popcorn who stood up with a grimace. "Where the hell did that come from?"

"The west gate!"

"Then close it!" Popcorn spat. The unease in the camp skyrocket as he began to bark out orders, limping swiftly towards the gate. "The rest of you, prepare for a swarm! Torches and weapons up, do not let them bite you! We don't have any Kingsmen here who can tend to your wounds, nor are there any of those Solari bastards who'll cull you! Your only salvation comes from whatever the hell I can do!"

A controlled panic flooded the group as men raced to do as Popcorn ordered. Jean stared at the spot where she saw the shaman and summoned chitters, watching as the monster took one slow step. The firelight dimmed as it did so, making Jean stumble backwards, before she fired her boltcaster.

The shaman stopped, jerkily tilted its head, and began to laugh.

Smoke rolled out of its skull, its eyes never leaving her, before it held the staff out.

You could stop this.

Jean shook her head. "No... no. Just leave me alone!"

You could have power, girl.

Jean's boltcaster clicked softly and she fired it again. Once more, the shaman laughed.

Then, in one smooth move, it snuffed out the flames with black tendrils and the chitters around it surged forth.

Shouts and cries erupted throughout the camp as darkness suddenly overtook them. Jean broke into a dead sprint away from the courtyard, doing her best to recall the layout. The dying oak tree wasn't too far; she could reach it and provide fire.

She could hear the footsteps of the chitterlings behind her as they raced after her, prompting her to grab the closest branch to her and swing up as quickly as she could. Laughter and chittering came from below her, but she did all she could to calm her heart rate and focus on where the shaman was.

It had slowly followed her, creaking softly on some steps and others giving a horrid squishing sound as rotting tendons contracted. All the while, Jean could see its eyes.

As she leveled her boltcaster, a flash of red across the camp caught her attention.

She wasn't sure what it was, but as she watched another splash of red rise and then morph into a crystalline weapon that glowed ever so slightly, her stomach dropped and the feeling of spiders racing over her began. There was magic there, just as strong if not stronger than the magic causing her rapidly mounting headache.

The woman shook her head and leveled her boltcaster again. With two deep breaths, she fired.

Just as quickly as it began, it was over.

The bolt sprouted itself in the middle of the shaman's skull and it crumpled into a smoldering pile of rotten flesh and bone. The staff lay on the ground, abandoned, before it slowly disappeared into a wisp of black smoke.

With the oppressive darkness gone, the camp's torch light grew stronger and the sounds of the chitters eventually faded.

"Sound out, now!" Popcorn shouted.

Slowly, voices answered the man. Jean sucked in a deep breath, not responding until Popcorn called out, "Daito? Are you still here?"

"I'm in the oak."

Torchlight filled the area. Jean climbed down from the tree and met the group beside the bonfire, which Park was desperately trying to relight. Everyone was quiet before Popcorn said, "Did anyone get bitten?"

"I did, boss." One of the men shifted, holding his bleeding forearm. Jean winced at the bile that bubbled on his skin, though her grimace became one of pain as Popcorn sighed and held his hand out.

"Alright, let me see what I can do. Lay on the ground. Lyman, Brutin, hold him still. Jean, take my cane."

Jean took the horn cane and stared, wide eyed, as Popcorn knelt beside the man. He put his hands on either side of the wound and closed his eyes. In that instant, three things happened.

The first was a blood-curdling scream from the man. Second, Jean felt as though she was going to vomit while the third, and perhaps most gruesome sight, took place. Blood and bile began to rush from the wound. It covered Popcorn's hands with gore, flowing backwards, and began to swirl in a ball above the man. Lyman and the other worker struggled to hold the man down as he screamed again. Several others turned away and Park, from beside Jean, lightly turned her to face into the darkness.

"Best not see the rest, Miss Cassy," he said quietly. "Blood magic is rather nasty business, and if Popcorn can't remove all of the venom then... well..."

Jean looked at Park with wide eyes and then over her shoulder as the man convulsed. Then, she turned away and whispered, "How does he know blood magic? Isn't that banned?"

"No one knows, and no one asks," Park murmured back. He was silent for a moment before he said, "Let me get you to your cottage. We'll clean up and introduce you to everyone tomorrow."

"Are you sure?"

She glanced back at where Popcorn was, the sick feeling growing even stronger. Park nodded silently and the two slipped into the darkness. Park let her into Popcorn's cottage, a small hut crammed with papers and books, and excused himself. Jean, with nothing more to do, made herself a cup of tea, barred the door, and then fell into an uneasy sleep.

Baron Baba Maze
'Popcorn'
Lord of Fort Haven

A curious man, as he prefers the company of animals to people. Popcorn hails from the Northernmost region of the torus. His native tongue is Ivumi, and he often reverts back as he forgets words. 'Daito' is a nickname he has given me in Ivumi, and it means 'little mouse'

Baba   —□—□
Daito =□Π◊

⎢ΙΙ□ ᚷᚨ ᚲ/ΙΙᛟᚲ —ᚨ >ᛁᛁᛋ □Πᛖ ᚷᚨ —ᚦ —ᚨ ΤΓΙᛋ⸲
May the hunt be swift and the bow be light. -Traditional Staros blessing

Blood Magic

One of the more taboo forms of magic as it uses blood from either the caster or a victim as its fuel source. As a primary offensive or defensive magic, the caster can form crystalline structures from the blood. This can serve as armor or as deadly weapons. Though they are not as durable as steel, the crystals can be easily reformed and replaced. With additional focus, a blood mage can control their own blood as a method of healing; bleeding can be slowed and poison can be expunged in this manner. This can be applied to others though the difficulty increases to nearly impossible should the target be unwilling.

11

BETRAYAL

The next morning began with a cup of tea, and then Jean was at the cockatrice coop studying the creatures.

The fort was eerily calm as she did so, especially as a soft fog had rolled in from the canyon. Jean put one of the cockatrices down and turned to find that Popcorn had joined her. He was sitting on a stump nearby, writing quietly, though he looked up when Jean cleared her throat. For a moment, they simply stared at each other. Then, Popcorn said, "You weren't injured last night, were you?"

"No. The man who was... is he...?"

"He's alright, just on bedrest for the next several days," Popcorn said softly. "That takes a lot out of a person."

Jean nodded slowly, looked at the cockatrices, and then at Popcorn again. "That was blood magic." She watched his brows furrow, then relax, as he shut the journal. For a brief moment, she was worried that she was going to discover why everyone seemed to be afraid of him. Then, he nodded slightly. "Was it blood magic when you stopped the bleeding, when we first met?"

Again, Popcorn gave her a nod.

The curseborn woman shifted slightly before she murmured, "That's banned in this area."

"Do you think I care, daito? If I need to stop bleeding, or clean up some blood, I'm going to do so," Popcorn said. He put his journal into his pack, stood, and leaned on his cane. "It's a dangerous world, Jean, and you've got to figure out what you're willing to do in order to keep yourself, and others, alive." He searched her face, and Jean straightened slightly under his gaze. "I'm sure you're all too familiar with that, aren't you?"

"I would rather not talk about what I've had to do, Popcorn," Jean said quietly.

Popcorn nodded faintly, turned, and started to walk away. "I want you and Lyman to check for traps in the woods surrounding Fort Haven. You'll see them before he does, and if something should happen, both of you are capable enough to get help."

"Why won't you be coming?" Jean hurried after her friend. "I'm not familiar with the forest, I may run into trouble as it is."

"Park needs to go over paperwork with me today, I'm afraid. As much as I'd love to get back into the woods, he takes precedence, I'm afraid." Popcorn shook his head. "However, before the two of you go out, I'd be more than happy to have some breakfast with you. We can go over what you determined in studying the cockatrices and figure out a schedule for all of the additional training I want you to have."

Jean stopped in her tracks. "You... want to eat food with me? Where other people can see us?"

Popcorn stopped and looked back at her. "Why wouldn't I?"

Her cheeks began to grow hot, and she looked away. Whatever her answer was, he'd likely think she was foolish. Still, she murmured, "People don't often like to be seen with curseborn, is all. I thought, at the temple, you were eating with me as no one could see us with the curtains." She shifted ever so slightly. "You have to remember, curseborn are seen as black marks here in the south; we're little more than livestock to many people, and slaves for others. It's very out of the ordinary for anyone to want to spend time with us in public. Honestly, my aunt, uncle, and cousins are the only ones..."

For a moment, Popcorn stood quietly. Then, he said, "That is the stupidest thing I've ever heard. I would rather eat my breakfast in peace with someone I've come to cherish over the last several weeks than alone. Come on, it's cold out and my leg is starting to feel it."

Jean watched him limp off, her mouth slightly agape. What did he mean by that? Did he like her, romantically, or was she simply a friend? She'd never assumed someone could want to spend time with her, let alone due to 'cherishing' her. She shook her head and caught up with Popcorn. Neither of them spoke, but the slightest smirk over his lips told her that he knew she had reached his side again. They went into his cottage and Jean sat in the overstuffed chair by the fire as he began to busy himself with making a porridge. As he did, Jean looked around the full cottage once more, this time her eyes lingering on various documents and relics that littered the room. "What's the bow say?" She asked, finally noticing a large recurve bow beside a segmented shield. "It has Ivumi on it, doesn't it?"

"Same blessing as the cane... same hand," Popcorn replied. He didn't take his eyes off of the boiling pot. "Only things I kept form the north. I told you that it's beautiful."

Jean nodded, leaned forward, and studied the bow. It was quite polished and worn from many years of use. Looking at Popcorn, she was surprised that he could draw a bow of that size back. Still, he said he was staros, and she assumed being staros meant he could handle a weapon like that.

Popcorn sat back on his heels, looked at Jean, and tilted his head. "Daito?"

"Hm?"

"I hope you know that you are safe here."

The soft words made Jean shift, a little smile playing on her lips. She wasn't sure if she completely believed him, but as they sat together, listening to breakfast boil on the little fire in the hearth, part of her whispered that it was true. Jean, in turn, allowed herself to rest in the highbacked chair as Popcorn got comfortable on the floor in front of her. He leaned against her legs ever so slightly, prompting her to absentmindedly play with the long section of his hair, before the spell was broken by a knock on the door. Popcorn muttered under his breath— Jean didn't catch what he said— and pulled himself upright. Then, he limped to the door and opened it to reveal Lyman standing impatiently there.

"Where's the curseborn?"

"We're eating breakfast, and she will join you shortly. It isn't like you to want to do work, what changed your mind?" Popcorn questioned. Jean peered around him to see that Lyman's arms were crossed over his chest now.

"Breakfast together?" Lyman gave a dry laugh. "Careful, boss, the others will think you two are involved." As he said those words, Jean felt the hair on the back of her neck prickle. Popcorn shifted his weight to his good leg, his knuckles now white on the cane he held. Then, Lyman seemed to realize just what he said as he took a step back. "Anyway, tell her I'll meet her at the west gates. I want to head out before the fog lifts— if there's anything out there, we'll be better concealed in the mist."

With that, he hurried off.

Jean frowned and began to ladle the porridge into two bowls. "I don't like him."

"I don't think anyone does," Popcorn answered. He shrugged and sat beside Jean, took a bowl, and blew on its contents. "However, until you're ready to take his place, he's here."

Jean glanced at him. He had said she'd be a part of the command team, nothing more than that. "So, I'm his replacement?"

"Isn't it obvious? Who do you think put the existing policies in place before you showed up?"

"I thought you did, boss?"

Popcorn looked at her, his face set in a stern frown, and Jean began to laugh. He looked comedically serious as he held his bowl in one hand and a steaming spoonful in the other, both eyebrows lowered. As she began to laugh, his eyebrows shot up in surprise, which only made Jean laugh harder. Soon, she was laying on the floor gasping for breath. Popcorn didn't stop watching her, and as she wiped the tears from her face, she managed, "Do you really think that I'd assume that you put those into place? You care about the cockatrices. As far as I'm aware, Lyman was only interested in keeping from being pecked!"

He continued to stare at her before he shook his head. "Jean, I was very worried you were serious. I thought I'd need to find a replacement for you, too." A little smile flickered over his face and Jean beamed at him. Then, in a quick movement, she cleared her throat, sat up, and began to eat again. All the while, Popcorn watched her. Finally, he said, "You have a nice laugh."

"I do?"

"You do." His words made Jean blush and tuck a strand of hair behind her ear. "It's very nice."

"Well, thanks. Not many people are willing to compliment a curseborn." Jean said quietly. "I mean, they'll happily comment on horns, and skin tone, but..."

"Not the person themselves?"

"No."

Jean shifted and shrugged. There was a lot to think about now, especially as she finished her breakfast and stood. "I'll be back by lunch, I assume. Lyman doesn't want to be out once the mist rises, and I'm sure that Solaris' Avatar will clear it quickly once it reaches the zenith." She stepped to the door, paused, and looked at Popcorn again. He had started to gather dishes to wash but did look at her. Once she had his attention, she said, "I enjoyed this. I... don't think I can say that I've had a friend to do this with before, or anyone else, for that matter. Thank you."

Popcorn smiled slightly. "Thank you for joining me. It's a breath of fresh air to have a woman's laugh and smile in this cottage. Hopefully we can do this again."

"I'd like that."

The curseborn tucked her hair behind her ear self-consciously again, her face hotter than before, straightened up, and then hurried from the cottage.

Lyman was waiting for her at the gate. He had a hunting bow over his shoulder and a full quiver, a small satchel, and a scowl as Jean approached. She quietly flipped the safety off of her boltcaster as she approached. "Shall we, then?"

"After you." Lyman gave a mockingly grand gesture towards the open gate, and Jean swallowed as she stepped through it.

Act larger than she was, pretend to be more of a danger than she really was. Prey would be consumed; predators would be ignored. The brothel taught her that much, and now was the time to hope that she remembered how it worked. Part of Jean cursed her for not telling Popcorn about her worries. The other part, however, screamed that she'd be no better than the others if she did. She wasn't weak, and she could take care of herself. Lyman wasn't much bigger than she was, and if he tried anything, she had her weapon.

That thought brought only a sliver of comfort to Jean as they ventured further into the mists.

"Where exactly are we going?" Jean questioned.

"Looking for snares, kitten." Lyman looked at her. "They catch things—"

"I know what a snare is, and don't call me kitten." Jean interrupted. She put her hand on her boltcaster. "I'm your equal, and you need to treat me as such. Popcorn said—"

"Popcorn said what? That he's willing to give you whatever you want if you sleep with him?" Lyman whipped around and caught her arm with one hand. Jean stared at him, her mouth gaping slightly as he yanked her closer. "Tell me... were you a good girl for him? Or are you still waiting for one of us at the fort to show you a good time?"

"Let go of me, Lyman," Jean whispered. She tightened her grip on her boltcaster, her hand shaking. "Let go of me, now, or I... I..."

"You what? Are you going to tell on me? What's that cripple going to do, hm? He's laid up with his bum leg, he can't do anything to me. Just because he could tell us what to do during the attack doesn't mean he's back to himself. You can't do anything, either." Lyman pushed her back against a tree and Jean winced.

Flashes of the Long Night struck her again, and she stared at Lyman as the memories raced through her mind. Her breath hitched as he began to fiddle with her corset, the sheer realization of what was happening hitting her like a stagecoach.

All the while, the shadows began to grow longer and deeper.

"Lyman, please!"

"I like when girls play hard to get, you know? Act like your tough, as though you can control yourself..." Lyman whispered.

Jean managed to pull her boltcaster from its hook and pressed it to Lyman's stomach. He pulled back slightly, looked down at the weapon, and back at Jean. "You wouldn't dare ruin your karma streak, would you?"

Would she?

The question echoed in Jean's mind for just a moment, more than enough time for Lyman to grab her wrist and force her to release her boltcaster. She struggled, eyes wide, before she froze.

If she was the prey, she was going to have to force the predator to give up.

With this new vigor, Jean brought her foot down onto Lyman's. He grunted and tightened his grip on her wrist, his other hand working faster to remove her belt as he threw her corset to the side. Jean gritted her teeth, trying to wrench her wrist from his grasp, and stared at his face. He had nothing but carnal lust in his eyes, the same sickening look that she saw in Zanther. Jean's heart sunk as she realized that struggling wasn't doing anything, before a slight glimmer of hope struck her.

With nothing more to lose, Jean tilted her head down and lunged towards Lyman's face.

She felt her horn hit bone as she did so, and Lyman yelped at the impact. He reached towards his cheek and Jean, taking that moment, ducked under his arm and began to run. She could hear Lyman shouting obscenities after her, but that did nothing to deter her.

The pounding of blood in her ears and the shadows threatening to cling to her only fueled her panic, making the woman tear through the woods in an absolute panic. As she continued to race through the trees, she caught sight of things running in the darkness around her. They made the mist swirl haphazardly, enough to make Jean run faster, before she burst from the tree line and onto a rutted road. As she looked around, weaponless and out of breath, she caught sight of Osmond just out of reach.

"Osmond... Osmond... you're here..."

Osmond didn't answer. Instead, he started down the road and deeper into the mist.

Jean swallowed and followed him. It was cold as she did so, especially as her tunic had been ripped from her run and her corset was gone. Eventually, she caught sight of something large lurching through the mist toward her. Osmond remained steady at her side, before the shape whinnied.

The draft horse pulling the cart spooked as it saw Jean, and the driver began to curse. Jean covered her face to avoid any hooves. "Please, stop!"

Once the horse settled, Jean looked up at the driver.

Sitting atop the seat was a familiar woman. She blinked at Jean before her eyes widened. "Jean! What in Solaris' name are you doing out here? What happened to your clothes? Why aren't you at Fort Haven?"

The immense relief in seeing Miss Tamrin made Jean break down into tears. She recounted her struggle with Lyman and run through the woods as Tamrin climbed down and pulled her close. Jean held tightly to the mistress as she was led to the back of the caravan.

"Jefferson, help Jean up. We'll be skipping over Fort Haven; some things have come up, and I am not planning on going there until it is completely smoothed over. Ingrid, get Jean something to wear as we make our way to Blackrock." Tamrin crossed her arms. "All of you get some rest."

Jean looked up at the musclebound man in the cart. His hand was outstretched to her, and she shied back. Tamrin patted her arm. "He won't hurt you, dear."

Ingrid, the woman from The Gilded Cage, poked her head out. "It's alright, Jean. Come up, we'll get you warm. Poor dear, we could hear what you were telling Tamrin." Jefferson nodded silently as Ingrid continued, "We have warm water for tea, and blankets. Let's get you settled."

With the soft reassurance, Jean slowly took Jefferson's hand.

The caravan was full of resting places, costumes, and provisions for the road. There were ten individuals, not including Jean, who had settled along the cart to rest. Ingrid carefully wrapped a blanket over Jean's shoulders. "Come sit on the bunk. He didn't have his way with you, did he?"

"No... no, I headbutted him. He wasn't able to do anything before that happened." Jean swallowed.

The performers murmured quietly at the statement as Jean sat down. Ingrid put her arm around Jean. "Miss Tamrin will figure this out. We may be in the sex trade, but she will not stand for rape, even if you aren't one of our number."

Jean nodded slightly. Her exhaustion was beginning to catch up to her as she yawned, her eyes slowly closing.

She should have said something. She should have told Popcorn that something felt off around Lyman, or that she didn't trust him. She was foolish for assuming she'd be safe on her own.

Ingrid rubbed her shoulder gently. "I hope you aren't beating yourself up for this."

"No... Yes. I could have stopped it."

"You gave that bastard the benefit of the doubt. You won't make that mistake again," Ingrid murmured.

Jean nodded again, closed her eyes, and sighed.

When she awoke, the caravan had stopped moving. The various members of The Gilded Cage were leaving the warmth of the cart to enter the establishment again. Ingrid was leaning over her, her spotted stole tickling Jean's nose. "Wake up, dear. We're in Blackrock."

"Thank you," Jean whispered. "I'm sorry I ruined whatever other stops—"

"No, it wasn't you. You're lucky we found you. The fog didn't lift, so there is a high likelihood that Solaris knew what had happened." Ingrid shrugged. "Come along. Where are you staying?"

"Um... other side of town. If you send a message to the Kingsmen guard, one of them can find my uncle." Jean held the blanket tightly around herself. "Is that possible?"

"More than. Tamrin will also be sending a letter to Fort Haven explaining the situation—"

"Situation?"

Ingrid paused. Then, she shook her head. "As I said, Miss Tamrin is against everything that happened. She'll be informing Lord Maze that we will not be offering services to any of the men in that fort until things have been corrected."

Lord Maze? Corrected on her behalf? This was far too much for Jean to follow, though she wanted desperately to ask questions and receive answers. Instead, she nodded at Ingrid and leaned into the woman.

They entered the staff room together, where Ingrid laid Jean on a sofa. Then, she called for a courier and sent a message requesting Jean's uncle to escort her home.

It took several hours before Flick arrived, and he was more than apologetic about his delay as he did so. Neither her nor Jean spoke on the walk to his home, nor did Jean explain what happened.

Instead, she stared at the wall, trying to wrap her mind over everything that happened, before she fell asleep.

Karma, Rebirth, and Curseborn

Curseborn are only technically human, having done something in their past life to anger Solaris. This could be anything from heresy, to criminal, to simply forgetting to tithe.

Cases of adoption are quite rare. In the unlikely event, a Curseborn must always use 'adoptive' when referring to their caregivers. This is to ensure the act of generosity isn't confused with baring a Curseborn.

Horns come in a variety of shapes and sizes.

In some areas, the practice of buying and selling of Curseborn as livestock is common. When I was young, I saw an auction where they sold Curseborn like cattle. While I know we are little better, the sight has haunted me. Recently, this has been in my nightmares, amongst other memories.

12

AVENGED

"I don't think I'm going to go back," Jean finished quietly, holding her mug tightly in her hands.

Anca and Flick glanced at each other, and her aunt gently put a hand on her leg. "I don't think you should, sweetie. It doesn't sound safe... and that's the most important thing right now."

Flick nodded slowly. "We need to speak to your employer, though. This sort of thing can't happen to anyone else... it's awful that it happened to you; now is the time to try to keep others from dealing with it. I'll write to him, personally, and inform him of the incident, if you're alright with that."

Jean swallowed and nodded, staring into her mug.

She spent the next three days quietly tending to Caxton, who was already feeling much better. He was absolutely intrigued by the cockatrices that Jean had seen, and Jean was more than happy to tell him about the chitter attack, but that was all she spoke about.

On the fourth day, there was a solid knocking on the front door.

Anca was the one to open it, as Jean and Caxton were in the sitting room playing a game of chess. Jean paused in lifting the knight as she overhead the soft talking, and then footsteps hurrying towards the room.

"Popcorn!" Caxton exclaimed, nearly knocking the chess table down.

"Hey, kid."

Jean turned to face the man, silent as he stared at her. His face was set in that stern line again, his knuckles white on his cane, and his chest was heaving. Quietly, she gestured for him to sit. Anca gently gathered Caxton. "Let them talk, dear. Jean, do you want me to stay or get Flick?"

Jean shook her head slightly. "I'll be alright."

"If you're sure, honey. We'll be in the room next door if you change your mind. Come along, Caxton."

"I wanted to hear about Fort Haven—"

"Later, I promise," Popcorn said. He offered a smile at Caxton, waited until the boy and his mother was gone, and then approached Jean.

Despite being in no danger, and feeling nothing but familiarity towards Popcorn, Jean flinched back. Accusations were flooding her head, that this was her fault and she should have said something. The voices continued to scream louder and louder as Popcorn knelt before her, reached up to cup her cheek, paused, and then did so. "Are you okay, daito?"

Jean stared at him. When she tried to open her mouth, she broke down and began to cry instead. Popcorn's eyes widened and he haphazardly shifted to hold her close. Jean clung to him, one hand balled into his tunic while the other pressed against her own chest, as she cried and struggled for words. "I should have said something, I'm sorry!"

"Sh, no, Jean, don't start blaming yourself. I should never had sent you out alone with him; I didn't think he would..." Popcorn trailed off, his grip growing tighter on her. "This isn't your fault, not at all. He knew what he was doing." He ran one hand through her hair. "As far as I can tell, he isn't aware of my knowledge of this matter. Tamrin sent me a letter, and I came as soon as I received it."

"I should have told you that I was worried—"

"No, you kept quiet because you were afraid." Popcorn held her at arm's length, searching her eyes. "You are ae'shaur in the south. You have no power, and there is no voice given to those with no power. This is all you know. Fort Haven is different. You do have power, and a voice. You must learn to use it, even if it's just with me."

It was an easy thing for him to say. He never experienced life as she did. Though Jean didn't know much about him, she knew that he wasn't curseborn, and she was almost certain that he didn't follow Solaris, given the lack of amber on his person. Despite her reservations, she gave a little nod and found herself in his embrace once more.

As she took several deep breaths, she found herself being lulled into a state of relaxation by his rapidly beating heart. Then, after a moment, the calm was replaced by concern as his heartbeat fluttered, stopped, and then returned to normal. Jean frowned to herself and remained silent. He was a smart man; she was sure he knew about that... right?

They stayed like that for several long minutes before a gentle tap on the archway made them pull away. Anca said, "If you need to go back to Fort Haven to settle things, Jean, we can tend to Caxton tomorrow. He needs to go to the temple for a breathing treatment as it is, so he can remain with me while I work." She looked between them and then focused her gaze on Popcorn. "Regardless, I trust that the issue will be resolved, and Jean will not be placed into harm's way again."

Popcorn nodded slightly. "The issue will be completely resolved."

"Good."

After a brief deliberation, Jean did agree to return to Fort Haven. There was a gnawing lump in her stomach as she sat behind Popcorn atop his horse, though she didn't speak about it. Popcorn was silent, too, as they rode. She could only imagine what he was thinking about, but part of her didn't want to risk finding out. Instead, she pressed her head against his back and closed her eyes to think. Osmond had settled on the haunch of the horse, just above its tail, as though taking a ride. She watched the orb, ever grateful for her imaginary friend leading her to find Tamrin. There was still the growing curiosity as to what Osmond really was, especially after each time he showed up. Either way, Jean didn't put too much thought in it and instead did her best to rest as they rode.

It was nearly nightfall when they arrived at Fort Haven, and Popcorn helped Jean down before he shouted, "Everyone, bonfire! Now!"

There was a sudden surge of activity as Popcorn led Jean to the firepit, where people were scrambling to find seats. The curseborn flinched slightly as she realized Lyman was there. He had a scowl over his face, one eye bandaged tightly while a scabbing-over wound under it rang of what Jean had managed to accomplish.

The feeling of danger washed over her as she looked away from him. His gaze didn't leave her, and she was afraid that he'd attempt to finish what he started should anyone turn their back on them.

Before anything could happen, however, Popcorn strode to Lyman, grabbed him by the collar, and punched him in the face. His entire weight was thrown into it, causing blood to spray over the gathered company as a loud crack filled the air.

In that instant, everyone took two steps away from Lyman, who Popcorn released. The man staggered back, holding his broken nose. "What the actual hell, Maze?"

"Why don't you tell the company about what really happened to your eye, Lyman," Popcorn retorted, his teeth bared. He circled Lyman menacingly, never once taking his eyes off of the man. "Go on, tell them again about how brave you were, trying to keep Jean from harm when she spooked." Lyman looked up at Popcorn, his face significantly paler now as the staros continued. "Tell them about how you tried desperately to keep her from running into the forest, but as you ran after her, you lost your balance. Go on, tell them everything."

Jean's stomach turned as she watched, her knuckles white on her satchel.

Lyman coughed slightly. "I don't know—"

"You don't know what, Lyman?" Popcorn snarled. "You don't know how to admit that you attempt to rape her?"

A silence washed over the crowd. Jean looked away, the discomfort growing further. Then, there came a headache.

She looked around, trying to find the reason behind it, before she locked eyes with the swirling red blood coming from Lyman's nose and the drying spatter from before. It congealed together, shining in the firelight, before it rested over Popcorn's arm in the form of three vicious, crystalline claws. He stalked towards Lyman, who began to scramble back.

"She's just a husk, that doesn't matter! It's a kindness, really! No one else is willing to do it, I was going to give her a good time!" Lyman stammered. "You shouldn't care! You never blinked an eye when Tamrin's girls—"

His words were cut off by a gurgling scream as Popcorn rammed the blades into his stomach. His teeth were bared, his eyes narrowed, and his chest heaved. "Tamrin's girls give consent... unless you decided to have your way with them, too." He twisted the blades, eliciting more screams as the blood surged up Popcorn's arms and formed jagged, crystalline armor. "Jean is not a plaything. Rape isn't a kindness, but this? This is."

Popcorn pulled the blade from Lyman and then ran him through again. More blood splattered over the group. Jean turned away, doing her best to keep from joining the men who vomited at the violence in front of them. Park, who was nearby, didn't look away from what was happening.

The sounds of gore and screams didn't dissipate for a while, and when the screaming did stop, Popcorn didn't. The silence of the camp only broken by the rhythmic sound of the beating. When Jean finally dared to look at him, he was standing, shaking, amid a brutally mauled and utterly destroyed corpse. The blood on his arm had reformed into liquid and was dripping from his fingertips, a testament to the murder, as he looked around the camp. "If anyone dares think about touching her, or any other woman without consent, your fate will be worse than that pig's," he hissed. "Is. That. Clear."

Silence answered him and he shouted, "Is that clear!"

"Yes, sir," came a smattering of answers.

Jean stared at Lyman's broken, bloodied body. His once-mocking eyes were glazed over, his face twisted in fear and pain. Despite the short time he had been lying there, a trail of ants was already winding its way around him. It was a horrifying testament to why those at Fort Haven feared Popcorn, and Jean didn't blame them.

"Park!" Popcorn snapped.

"Sir?"

"Send his final pay to his family, and if there isn't a family, then give it to an orphanage. Best not let it go to waste." Popcorn stooped to get his cane and then sat heavily on a log.

He hung his head, breathing heavily, and Jean watched him. His chest was still heaving, prompting him to wince ever couple of moments.

Not wanting to ruin his image, Jean stayed quiet for a moment. Then, after brief consideration, she said, "You two, take the body and dispose of it... properly. We don't want anything coming to scavenge the corpse while we sleep. The rest of you, dismissed."

The men looked around, unsure what to do. Popcorn snarled from his log, "She said the rest of you were dismissed!"

There was another scramble as two men took Lyman's corpse and hurried into the darkness, and the other men scattered to their respective cottages. Jean slowly moved to Popcorn, who had his head hung still.

"Are you alright?"

"I'm fine!" He snapped. Jean flinched, and he grit his teeth. "No, I'm sorry... I'm fine."

"You don't look fine. Is it your heart?"

Popcorn stiffened slightly as he took a deep breath. Then, he whispered, "Why do you say that?"

"It wasn't rhythmic earlier. Are you dying?"

Jean sunk down in front of him, staring at his shadowed face as he sat there. Finally, he shook his head. "No... not dying. Just... sore."

They were quiet for a long moment. Popcorn continued to raggedly breath while Jean wrapped her head around it all. It was a lot to come to terms with, especially as they sat surrounded by blood and viscera from Popcorn's display. "Why did you kill him?" Jean finally asked.

"To prove a point."

"That they should be scared of you?"

Jean held Popcorn's gaze. His eyes met hers with a tired, irritated look, but after a moment, he sighed and looked away. "Fear is a wonderful deterrent, Jean." He slowly stood, wobbled slightly, and straightened up. Jean stood as well to catch his arm, which resulted in a head shake. "You learn what works, and you take full advantage of it."

"I've lived my entire life in fear... even now, I'm afraid—"

"Are you afraid of me?"

The question was so sudden and so soft that it startled Jean.

Was she afraid of him? He was violent, incredibly so, but... perhaps the means were justified? He hadn't done anything to harm her or make her worried about being harmed. Still, she couldn't say that she was at ease at this time, either. Finally, Jean sighed. "That's a very loaded question."

"Are you, though?"

They started walking to the cottages, Jean's arm entwined with Popcorn's, as she thought again. "I am not... not currently. Worried, yes, but I think that's fair given the last week." She looked at him. "I don't often return to places where I've been attacked or nearly taken advantage of."

"Has it happened before?"

Again, Jean was silent. She nodded slowly after several minutes before she murmured, "When you're a curseborn, it tends to happen. Following Solaris... curseborn don't have much of a say if things happen. My karma is bad, I was reborn to reap the consequences of my past actions. If I do things differently, I may be able to be reborn looking... different."

"Different?"

"Normal."

The word hung heavy in the air as they stopped at the cottage, and Popcorn stared at her. He seemed to be doing better now, especially as he took a deep breath. His free hand gently took Jean's, and he said, "I think you look like Jean, and that isn't a problem. I like your horns— especially that you could draw blood with them, that's quite impressive— and I like the way your skin looks. You're beautiful, perfect even. I don't think you need to be reborn to look normal."

Jean looked down. "You aren't curseborn... a husk. You are staros—"

"And I don't subscribe to the Solari nonsense that you do... I don't believe in HaMelech or whatever the Kingsmen say, either, but what I do know is that you are meant to be this way." Popcorn interrupted. He released her hand and brushed some hair from her face. "I hope you know that, even if it takes a while."

Heat flooded Jean and she shifted. Was this too soon? Was this too sudden, especially after Lyman's attempted attack and then his death? Did he even truly like her? Perhaps it was his drink speaking, or adrenaline. There was no possible way that he could care for a curseborn. Yet, at those thoughts, Jean felt tears beginning to streak down her face.

Maybe it was a potential.

She stared up at Popcorn, who was still looking at her, before she whispered, "Is this okay to do?"

"This being...?"

"Any of this?"

Popcorn tilted his head slightly. His lips set in a thin line and his eyes, though still on her, darted about as he thought about something. Finally, he answered. "If you think so, then yes. Otherwise, no. Regardless, you're still my daito, you know that, right?"

Jean couldn't help but smile slightly as he said this, and she shifted. "I think I'm alright with it."

"Good."

Popcorn tilted her chin up and lightly kissed her, sending butterflies through Jean's stomach and making her knees weak. She caught herself on his tunic, kissing him back, before she pulled away. Popcorn looked rather pleased with himself, lightly trailing his thumb over her lips before he pulled away. "Sleep well, Jean."

"You too, Popcorn." Jean watched him go before she paused. Ingrid had called him Lord Maze before, and Jean hadn't questioned it. This was entirely a mistake if he had some sort of title, wasn't it? She cursed herself for not asking him and went into the cottage.

She found Popcorn by the cockatrices the next morning. He didn't say much amid writing in his journal, nor did Jean as she sat beside him with her cup of tea. She blew the steam into the air and then glanced at Popcorn. "So... Lord Maze?"

"Hm?" Popcorn paused, looked at her, and raised his eyebrow. "Who told you that I was Lord Maze?"

"Ingrid mentioned it, one of Tamrin's girls. She said Tamrin would write to you. What land do you own?" Jean asked, sipping at her drink.

Popcorn closed his notebook. "Fort Haven, and the surrounding land. It's my barony, my property, and my livelihood." He looked around, a bit of a smile on his face. "It's come a long way since I first acquired it."

"Any reason you didn't tell me?"

"I didn't want you throwing yourself all over me for the potential of land." Popcorn shrugged. "Besides, I thought it wasn't that important."

Jean's blood boiled slightly, but she pushed it down. "I kissed a baron."

"No, a baron kissed you."

Jean gave him a look, which earned a chuckle, before she shook her head and watched the cockatrices. "Did you want to go out to the woods today to finish looking for snares? Lyman and I never got to that point when I went out with him..."

"We can do that. Have some lunch, too?"

"Please." Jean smiled slightly at him before she drank her tea again. "How far are you wanting to go?"

"With you? Depends completely on your comfort," Popcorn replied. Jean's attention snapped to him, and he raised an eyebrow before he cleared his throat. "Ah. Within a mile of Fort Haven, no further. It'll give us time to look around, and we can return to where you saw those griffin nests."

Jean's face grew hot again. She shifted, looking away from him, and murmured, "Sounds good."

Did he really think... Well, that was another shock. Jean wasn't sure what to think of that, nor did she know how she'd respond if he had asked her the same question. Of course, it was a misunderstanding, but it also brought butterflies to Jean's belly again. Either way, she gathered her things. "We can probably forage on what's left of berries and nuts— spend less time here and more time in the woods, no?"

Popcorn grinned. "A woman after my own heart, daito. Let's go."

The two set off towards the west gate. Then, they began to explore the forest in search of snares and other creatures. Jean captured a byri, a small orange lizard with a sail-fin on its head, and studied it quietly as Popcorn dismantled a snare. Later, Popcorn revealed a small, winged mouse that perched delicately on the end of his cane in order to study them.

When they finally approached the site of the great horned griffins, Popcorn sat down and patted the ground beside him. "These are my favorites. They're so incredibly clever, and beautiful... I've a theory on their venom, you know. There's some sort of anticoagulate in their saliva. That's the only way they can take down a draft horse, their preferred prey, without sustaining injuries. A single attack, a quick bite, and their prey bleeds out while they wait. It's a brilliant means to their survival."

He continued to go on about the griffins as Jean watched one of them stalk through the undergrowth. It was when she put her hand on Popcorn's leg that he stopped speaking and stared, enthralled, at the creature.

The griffin in question flicked its ear tufts at them before walking past with a twitch of its orange tail. Popcorn released a breath and Jean looked at him with a little smile.

He was at peace here. As she sat there, listening to his breath, Jean found that she didn't want this moment to end. So, bolstered by the crisp air around them and her newfound sense of self, Jean lightly pulled Popcorn to her and laid back in the moss.

He blinked at her before his eyes softened, and he murmured, "Are you sure?"

"... more than I have been before," Jean answered.

Popcorn chuckled quietly and shook his head, but didn't argue.

Fletchers

Fletchers are a migratory species that travel between Blackrock and the Emptiness due to the weather. Hard to find, they are a blip of color and are then gone.

Thin beak for sipping nectar

Earth toned body, jewel toned feathers

Tail for balance

Each of the 3 primary tail feathers are valued between a month and a year's worth of pay depending on the length and quality. Primarily worn by the social elite.

Cockatrice

These creatures are made of pure anxiety and deadly venom. As such, captive raised cockatrice are few as they do not put energy into growing their valuable feathers while stressed. Their bite delivers a toxin that paralyzes skeletal muscles and thickens the blood; this allows for their prey to remain alive and fresh while being eaten.

Warts are unpleasant to the touch.

Feathers are red, blue, and yellow

FALL OUT

It took several minutes to fix their clothes after their encounter in the woods. Jean smoothed her hair down while Popcorn watched her, admiration in his eyes. She cast a glance at him, blushed, and looked away. "I don't suppose we'll be doing this again, as we are supposed to be professionals."

"Maybe, maybe not." Popcorn sat up, fixed his tunic, and then stretched. "I won't mind making this a regular occurrence."

Jean grew hotter and she murmured, "If that's the case, we'll need to take precautions. I.can't get pregnant."

Popcorn stiffened at the words. He shook his head. "No. No, you can't. I'll see what I can do on my end for you, alright?"

"Is something wrong?"

"No," Popcorn said sternly. He shifted as Jean frowned; her eyebrows furrowed. Then, he said, "You weren't on birth control?"

Jean gave him a look. "Do you think I'm often sleeping with people? Of course, I didn't think about birth control!"

Popcorn began to rub his forehead. "Alright... Damn it, I'm sorry Jean. I should have thought ahead. You're my employee, and I—"

"Wait, are you... regretting this?" Jean questioned. She stared at him, her mouth beginning to hang open. "You said it was okay if I was fine with it!"

"I got caught up in the moment!"

The two stared at each other before Jean shook her head. "I should have realized that you'd change your mind once you realized that you slept with a husk. Go ahead and keep your excuses; you can claim it's the employee, employer relationship that's causing issues all you want."

"Jean, don't—"

"No, you don't! You should have said no before I slept with you! If you didn't want to do this, you should have said something!"

A fire lit in Popcorn's eyes as he struggled to stand. "How am I supposed to say no to you? I care about you, Jean! I do care, but this—" He gestured wildly between them. "This can't happen!"

Jean ignored him, beginning to walk towards Fort Haven. Popcorn continued to curse behind her in Ivumi, and she did her best to stop listening.

She should have known this was a ploy. She should have assumed that he wasn't truly interested in her, and that maybe, just maybe, Lyman had been right. Still, in the back of her mind, Jean knew this was her fault as well. She should have thought things through, realized that the desire she felt for Popcorn was nothing more than a desire for connection, and that there really was no true relationship possible. Jean gritted her teeth at the thought. She wanted nothing more than to go home, cover herself with the blankets, and sleep the remainder of the week. That wasn't possible, though, as she knew there were responsibilities that had to take precedence over her emotions, such as the research she was hired to do and the position she now held in Lyman's stead.

She entered Fort Haven alone. A handful of workers glanced in her direction, but she waved them off quietly. They returned to what they had been up to and Jean, with nothing else to do, returned to the cockatrices.

The remainder of the weekend was filled with nothing but awkward encounters. Popcorn didn't meet her gaze, and she refused to look at him. Once, she overheard Popcorn and Park speaking in the office as Park scolded the staros for letting his emotions get the best of him. The resounding echo of flesh on flesh made Jean flinch and her heart, once tender towards Popcorn, hardened.

He was a selfish man, caring only for himself. It was a shame that she hadn't realized it sooner.

Just before Jean was to return to Blackrock, Popcorn approached her. He shifted, his weight uneven on his cane, and refused to look at her. Jean wrinkled her nose slightly, tossed her satchel into Miss Tamrin's cart, and said, "Are you wanting to speak to me, or are you attempting to make me feel bad?"

"No... Damn it, Jean."

Jean narrowed her eyes. "You slept with me and then decided no more than five minutes after that that it was a bad idea. Don't say that I've assumed anything, especially when you're the one who decided to make me feel like nothing."

"You feel like nothing? The last three days, you've been walking around like a kicked puppy. Even Park commented on it—"

"Park told you not to get involved, and you hit him. You know you're in the wrong, Baba Maze, but you're far too thick-headed to admit it!"

Jean stared at him, her chest heaving, before she realized that his face had set in a firm line.

The air began to grow colder in that instant. At the same time, his green eyes had narrowed dangerously and an inky black film had begun to take over his irises. His free hand clenched, the other on his cane was white knuckled, and, for a moment, Jean could have sworn she saw the other workers backing away. "Watch your tongue, girl."

The voice wasn't Popcorn's.

It was guttural, full of malice and hatred that rang through Jean's bones.

"You have no idea what you've cause; all of the trouble, unraveling what I've made."

The air around them seemed to grow colder. Jean shrunk back slightly, pressing against the caravan as she stared at Popcorn. This was a side she wasn't sure she'd witnessed. Even the brutality of Lyman's death seemed pale in comparison, and Jean wished, in that moment, that someone had found her boltcaster.

Popcorn slammed his hand into the caravan beside Jean's head. He leaned in, all of his teeth bared. "I suggest you run, girl, and never come back. You and that dammed staff that keeps following you." His pitch-black eyes darted to the left and he began to growl. Jean followed his gaze to see that the shadows were moving again.

Instead of focusing on this, she looked back at Popcorn. The same blackness was there, but it was beginning to fade. Park was hurrying towards them, as was Tamrin. Jean straightened up slightly. "I don't know who you are... but Popcorn hired me, not you. And... and I will come back, if only to make you and him miserable."

Popcorn's hand wrapped around her throat in an instant and she began to choke. Rage had flooded his face, a silent killer as he stared into her eyes. Jean grasped his wrist and struggled for breath. Park grabbed Popcorn's shoulder and yanked him off. Tamrin, meanwhile, pulled Jean back and began to look over her.

Jean ignored the questions, instead staring at Popcorn who, as his eyes returned to green, staggered backwards with a hung head.

"You should be ashamed of yourself!" Tamrin scolded the man. "You could have killed her, and for what?!"

"I don't... I don't know..." Popcorn said, leaning heavily onto his cane. He sucked in a breath, looked at Jean, and then grit his teeth. "I... need to lay down." He began to limp off, paused, and looked around the camp. "What are you standing around for? Back to work!"

Everyone flinched at his shout and quickly obeyed. Jean watched him go in silence before climbing into the caravan.

As much as Ingrid fussed over her in the caravan, Jean was unable to take her focus off of what happened.

She wasn't sure what it was, but she knew that wasn't Popcorn. It was a dark change, a sudden change, that left her wondering who, and what, he was. Couple the shift of character and the blood magic together, and Jean was sure that it was supernatural. She shivered ever so slightly, ran her fingers over the tender marks in her neck, and looked at Ingrid. "Have you ever seen Popcorn do that before?"

"The whole 'I'm going to rip your head off' thing?" Ingrid questioned. She shifted nervously, petting her spotted stole, before she pulled it over herself. Her sudden shift from human to a dalmatian cote surprised Jean, but she didn't comment on it as Ingrid continued to pet her fur as though attempting to calm herself down. "Not like that. I mean, typically the boss man looks like he's going to kill you, but that... that was terrifying. I can't believe you spoke to him like that."

"... I can't, either," Jean admitted quietly. She held onto herself, quietly, before she murmured, "Ingrid? If I were to have... involved... myself with someone, how would I know if..."

Ingrid's eyebrows furrowed. Then, as if realization hit her, she squeaked and covered her mouth. Jean felt her face go hot as her friend looked around and then murmured, "Was it Popcorn? Is that why you were arguing?"

"That doesn't matter, does it?" Jean asked. She looked at Ingrid, shifted, and then sighed. "Yes, fine, it was Popcorn."

"Oh, my Solaris... wait, didn't your mother ever tell you about things like this?" Ingrid asked.

"My adoptive mother, who was busy running her brothel? The one who said that I wasn't allowed to go home with any strange men, ever?" Jean questioned. "Yes, she was open about protection but..." she sighed. "I messed up, Ingrid."

"I'll say." Ingrid shook her head slightly. "You'll want to watch your monthly courses. If you're late, that's fine, but skipping them could mean there's a child."

"That won't help; I'm not regular enough to watch."

"Well... there's other signs, too..."

The remainder of the ride to Blackrock was a bolstering of spirits, especially as Jean wrestled with the potential of being pregnant. On one hand, it could be seen as a blessing from Solaris; if the baby wasn't curseborn, then she was on the right track for being reborn herself. On the other hand, it was a bastard child with no hope of a future with her as a mother. Jean thought long and hard about this fact, finally settling on not wanting to dwell on it unless absolutely necessary.

It was three months of a terse working relationship with Popcorn whenever Jean was in Fort Haven, and three months of gentle tending to Caxton, who was steadily regaining his strength. Towards the end of the fall season, he was nearly without cough and was able to remain standing for a majority of the day.

Jean was packing to return to Fort Haven when he knocked on her door. "Jean?"

"Yes?"

"Can I go with you, this time?"

Jean paused halfway through putting a pair of pants in her satchel. She looked at Caxton, who had leaned against her doorframe, and then sighed. "Caxton, you know it isn't up to me. I'd have to talk to your parents, and Popcorn—"

"You don't talk about Popcorn anymore. He's still alive?"

His sudden remark made Jean laugh, and she tried to choke it down as quickly as she could. As she cleared her throat, she shook her head. "He's fine. We... just had a disagreement a while ago, and we're still working through it."

Working through it? Jean managed not to scoff at her own words. 'Working through it' was merely avoidance, or sharp glances from across the camp. Popcorn hadn't tried to speak to her, and she refused to speak to him. He had used her, after all, to have a good time and nothing more. Park had approached her, once, to attempt soothing her anger, but she had politely declined. "He knows what he did, Park. Until he shows me that he's sorry, and that he means it, there's nothing to me working here outside of making sure that things run smoothly."

Caxton lightly shook her arm. "Jean?"

"What?"

"If Mom and Dad say it's alright, can I come with you?"

Jean stared at him. It wasn't the safest place for a child, especially with the men she worked with. Popcorn, however, seemed to like Caxton, and he certainly demonstrated a penchant for sorting problems should they arrive. So long as Caxton stayed in the fort's walls, and with Jean, he should be safe.

With those thoughts, she sighed again. "You know what, we can use it for your science course. I'll talk to them, and we can figure it out, alright?" Caxton's smile was contagious as he hugged her, and she couldn't help but hold onto him for a handful of moments longer before she released him. "I'll speak to them after dinner, alright?"

Caxton nodded and bolted out of the room. No more than a few seconds later, he slid in front of her door. "Thank you!"

"Go on," Jean laughed, waving her hand at him.

Once he was gone, she sat down on the bed and sighed. Bringing Caxton would bring a plethora of problems. Park wouldn't enjoy having a kid in the area, simply due to liability, and Popcorn... Jean flopped back on the bed. This was going to open up more arguments, she knew it. Regardless, she told Caxton that she'd speak to Flick and Anca, and she'd keep that promise.

She waited until Caxton excused himself from the dinner table, his older siblings Drop and Shatter following after him to help set up a small diorama. Jean had enjoyed seeing her older cousins, though it was certainly strange now that they were both serving as Kingsmen guards. She always thought Drop would have served well as a hostess for one of the prestigious clubs given her appearance, but her cousin had instead decided to work as a Knight of the Long Road. Shatter followed in his older sister's steps, though he was training specifically to serve with those in Bleak Hollow.

Jean nodded politely to them as they left and then looked at her aunt and uncle. The two were chatting quietly, though they paused as they realized that Jean hadn't left the table. "Is everything alright?" Flick asked.

"Yes... well, partially. I'm packing to return to Fort Haven this weekend, and Caxton interrupted to ask if he could join me," Jean explained. "I told him that it was entirely up to the two of you, but we could possibly use it for his science course to maintain his schoolwork. He's excelling in biology; this could be a wonderful way to solidify his skills and get him potential work habits." As Jean spoke, part of her cringed. For not wanting him to join her, she had to have some of the best reasons for him to go.

Anca glanced at Flick. "He's been coughing less frequently, and the doves have told me that his breathing has evened out nearly completely."

"Then that isn't a limiting factor, though I'd want to be sure his medicine goes with him just in case," Flick murmured. He watched Jean quietly. "How long would you have him there? Winter is encroaching."

"No more than a month, at the absolute longest," Jean said. She looked towards the darkened window. "I haven't seen any signs of frost yet, so my hope is that it's moving slowly as it is. At the first sign of snow, he'll be home."

"Popcorn won't mind?"

Jean stared at them. Finally, after heavily weighing the potential consequences of lying, she murmured, "Popcorn seems to enjoy Caxton from when he interacted with him. If it does bother him, he'll probably comment on it and move on." She fiddled with her tunic hem under the table, looking down at her empty plate.

Anca rose an eyebrow and looked at Flick, who kept his eyes on Jean. Finally, Anca said, "I think I'll leave the two of you to finish discussing this. I'm alright with it, Flick, if you are." She kissed Flick's cheek, and then Jean's head between the horns, before she slipped out.

Flick nodded after his wife. He waited until Anca was out before he looked at Jean again. "What happened?"

"What do you mean?"

"I mean, something's wrong. Normally, you talk about Popcorn and whatever it is that you've discovered. Now, you've been tight-lipped and rather off-putting whenever work is mentioned."

Jean sighed. "I don't want to talk about it, please."

Flick raised an eyebrow before he shook his head. "Alright, Jean... I won't press. We are here for you, though, no matter what you think. We're family." He offered her a smile and took her hand. Jean looked up at him and returned the smile, though she was sure that it wasn't very convincing. Her uncle's eyes softened, and he kissed her head. "Go ahead and take Caxton with you. It'll be good for him to get out of Blackrock for a little bit, and I think it'd probably be wise for you to have family in Fort Haven, too."

"Thank you, Uncle Flick." Jean offered him another smile before she slipped out of the dining room and to her bedroom.

The trip to Fort Haven was longer than usual as Caxton asked the driver as many questions as he could muster. Jean couldn't help but gain some satisfaction from the driver's frustration, especially as conversations with him usually resulted in insult and muttered commentary about livestock. Instead, he bit back comments as Caxton asked him, for the fifth time, about the odd construction of his cart.

When they rolled into Fort Haven, Jean was pleasantly surprised by Park, who held a manifest that then went to the driver. "Your cottage was finished over the week, Jean..." He trailed off as Caxton hopped down beside her, one eyebrow raised as he looked up at Jean. "Miss Cassy, why is there a child?"

"Think of Caxton as my intern," Jean replied. "He'll be staying with me, and I'll take a pay cut in order to ensure his rations are paid for." She wrapped an arm around Caxton and raised an eyebrow at Park. "I'm happy to discuss his joining, if need be, but that'll be after he has had dinner. You and Lord Maze are welcome to join us so you can properly get acquainted with my cousin. Otherwise, I'll talk to you later."

"Miss Cassy—"

"Kindly show us to the cottage, if you please?" Jean interrupted. She straightened up. "It's cold, we've had a long journey, and I have a hungry preteen that I want to get fed before the night gets any later."

Park rubbed his temples. "Fine, alright... Let's go."

He led Jean across the courtyard and towards the cockatrice coop. Caxton dallied for a few moments as he studied the wonderfully ugly creatures before he hurried after the two adults. Park gestured to a little building. "This is yours, and there's been a lock installed with a single key. I've left it on the table for you. Tomorrow morning, plan on a debrief with Popcorn and I—the boy can come— before we set about our tasks again."

"Gladly." Jean watched Park go before she sighed and opened the door to the cottage.

Caxton stepped in first as Jean found the gas lamp and lit it. She appreciated the light that shone through the room, especially as her stress had begun to mount at the idea of meeting with Popcorn and Park both. Jean shook her head slightly to clear it, placed her satchel on the ground, and then paused.

The cottage was already furnished. A small table with two seats sat beside the small counter top and a nicely stuffed chair was in front of the fireplace. Some kindling had been placed in the hearth for Jean's use. In the other room, there was a made bed and a small wardrobe as well. Jean frowned, looked around, and then paused as she noticed a folded parchment on the table.

She lifted it and read it; her lips set in a firm line. It was an apology from Popcorn, and a request to speak to her privately. Jean folded it and put it into her pocket.

Caxton had flopped into the chair and was reading a book when she lit the fire and sent a warmth through the cottage. Then, she made a quick stew and served them quietly. Caxton glanced at her. "Who was that, Jean?"

"Park?" Jean questioned, blowing on a spoonful of broth. "He's the foreman. Nice guy, a bit upright, but nice all the same. Scared of masks for some reason, though. He keeps bringing it up every couple of weeks... masks and ashura."

"Ashura?" Caxton asked, perking up. "He knows about ashura?"

Jean raised an eyebrow. "I guess? I never asked. Why?"

"I've always wanted to see Ashuran! They have some of the coolest technology, ever! Did you know that they supposedly can use kinetic crystals to make lights?" Caxton jostled his stew, very nearly spilling it. Jean caught it as he continued. "The ashura wear masks because they're too beautiful to be seen! Maybe Park is from Ashuran, but escaped!"

"Escaped?"

"Yeah! Maybe he was working in the mines finding kinetic crystals and then ran off!" Caxton bounced again, this time spilling the stew across the floor. He frowned. "Sorry, Jean."

"It's alright, kid. You go get a towel and try not to move so much next time." Jean watched her cousin hop off of the chair before she sighed and watched the fire.

Was that what it would be like if she had a child? She began to rack her brain, the stark reminder of potentially being pregnant enough to send her into a worried spiral. Would she live in Blackrock, or Fort Haven? Would Popcorn be involved? No, likely not... it seemed like she'd be alone in all of this. Jean thought back over the last several weeks, her stomach falling deeper. She wasn't regular by any means, but there still was no monthly course. She could be expecting. Would she even tell Popcorn?

Jean was startled out of her thoughts as Caxton took his bowl from her hands. He smiled at her; she offered a smile back and then went back to eating.

Caxton took the bed that evening and Jean remained in the chair by the fire. It was better lit there, and warmer, enough to help soothe Jean to sleep despite her worries.

A strange bond
between humans
and animals,
cotes are
individuals who
have the ability
to use animal
hides, or mantels,
to transform
their own
appearances into
a creature similar
to that which wore
the hide first.

While fish and reptile
variants exist, it's far more
common to find cotes of avian
or mammal appearance.

Cotes are created in two ways; they are born into a
lineage of cotes (born) or an animal hide grants
them the ability through a variety of circumstances
(chosen)

Born cotes typically
receive their mantels
as part of coming of
age. While Chosen cotes
may receive a mantel
at any time.

Cotes

14

SILENCE

Jean woke before Caxton did. She started the stew back up for him to eat, made herself a cup of tea, and started to the lord's quarters first thing.

Park and Popcorn were already there. Popcorn had a cup of tea in his hand while Park, as usual, had a flask of brandy that sounded half-full. They turned to look at her when the door opened and Popcorn, fumbling with his tea, stood up. "Jean! I didn't realize you were back already—"

"And I'll be here, continuously, for the next month... provided the weather cooperates," Jean replied evenly. Popcorn sat down and she strode to the seat beside him. She didn't look at him, nor did she want to; there was a heavy ache in her heart, fully from the desire to make the amends that she refused to go near. He wasn't allowed to hurt her again, even though he could and likely would. She wouldn't let him hurt her again. "What was this meeting to discuss?"

Park looked between the two. "First, it was to inform Popcorn that you brought a child back to the fort with you."

Popcorn's eyes grew huge and looked at Jean. She looked at him, her lips a thin line before she sipped her tea. "He means Caxton, Lord Maze. Caxton came with me this time; I've already decided to take a pay cut to help with the purchase of his rations."

Her reassurance seemed to be enough for Popcorn, who lightly waved his hand. "Don't take the pay cut. He's too young to be paid himself, so we'll consider his payment room and board. Is he staying in your cottage?"

"Yes."

"Then there's no concern there.... outside of the griffins. It's mating season, and the last thing I want is for your cousin to be seen as prey."

"He won't be, not when I'm around." Jean replied. She sipped her tea and exhaled as the shadows around them faded. Her eyes followed Osmond as he bounced from shelf to shelf behind Park. He'd begun appearing more frequently again, often serving as a reading light or a welcome distraction during dull tutoring sessions. This time, he seemed to know that Jean was getting tired of being in the same room as the two men, and he was offering a reprieve. Jean looked at Park. "Now that that's out of the way, what's the other point?"

"This," Park said instantly, gesturing between them. "I don't know what happened, but this needs to stop. The snide looks, the interruptions, the avoidance. You two are supposed to be on the command team, with me, and I've had to shoulder all of the work! I don't care how angry either of you are, but this is ridiculous!"

Jean's head reared back. Beside her, Popcorn stiffened. In an instant, both of them began to speak.

"He's the one who can't take responsibility!"

"She won't accept an apology!"

"At least I am willing to accept whatever happens because of you!"

"You aren't willing to accept anything else!"

Park rubbed his temples for a moment as Jean and Popcorn argued over each other. Finally, he slammed his hand into the table. "Shut up!"

Jean fell silent, but Popcorn continued. "I said I was sorry, and that it crossed a line! You don't think I feel bad, then fine, but I hate the distance that's been created! I hate not having my daito to speak to and going alone into the forest!" He blinked at her and Jean straightened up, her teeth gritting.

"I hate not knowing if I'm pregnant, and being well aware that, if I am, I'll be alone to raise a child!" She snapped back.

"Wait, wait, there was more than just a make-out session?" Park questioned, holding his hands up. "The two of you...? Solaris above, you messed up, Popcorn."

"Shut up, Park," Popcorn growled. He looked at Jean. "You can't get pregnant! You just can't!"

"Well, it's too late if it's happened! Guess who isn't regular enough to be able to tell right now? That's right, I'm living in suspense, too!" Jean looked at Park. "Are you done with this conversation? You know why it's been so terse; you have a thick-headed employer who slept with one of his employees... a thick-headed employer who attacked one of his employees, no less!"

"I never hurt you!" Popcorn said, his eyes wide. "I would never—"

"You began to strangle me!"

"Enough!" Park shouted.

Jean and Popcorn looked at him. A large vein was beginning to bulge in his forehead as he rubbed his temples. "The two of you are causing more problems than I thought. You need to be done. This is tearing the command team apart, and I need you both working accurately and together if we're going to actually research anything before the snowfall. Please, for my sake, figure it out. Jean, I don't care if you're expecting. That's for the two of you to discuss. Popcorn, keep it in your damn pants! There are things to do that don't involve laying with people—"

Popcorn began to growl at Park, who ignored him.

"—that are far more important than this! Apologize, move on, something! Now, get out of here before I run out of my brandy!"

"Fine." Jean stood up and stormed from the room.

Popcorn struggled after her, cursing at Park in Ivumi, before his uneven footsteps followed Jean. "Daito—"

"Don't call me that."

"Fine, Jean. Wait, please."

The curseborn set her jaw and turned to look at him. "What do you want, Lord Maze?"

"I want to fix this." Popcorn said, leaning against his cane. He sucked in a breath and looked up at her. "I get why you're being so icy—"

"So, you're going to insult me in the same breath you apologize in?" Jean asked. She raised an eyebrow. "You certainly have a way with women, you know that?"

Popcorn bared his teeth before he took another breath and them muttered, "I'm trying to fix this."

"How? Popcorn, I don't know if I'm pregnant or not. I assume that, if I am, you're not going to want anything to do with me or it given your immediate reaction after we had sex," Jean said. She looked around and then at Popcorn. "I have been dealing with the burden of keeping that to myself for three months. Three! Do you have any idea how lonely that wait is, knowing that the man you partnered with regretted it moments after you connected? Do you have any idea how worthless that makes me feel, or how undesirable I have become as I now have nothing to my name, especially as a curseborn?! Even if I were to be sold into the sex trade, I'm worth less as you took my virginity! I have nothing, Popcorn! Nothing!" A couple of the workers who had come from their cottage looked towards them, and Jean glared in their direction. They hurried off, and she looked back at Popcorn. "I had assumed that maybe, just maybe, my friend would have stuck by my side even after we made that mistake. But I was wrong. Instead, I have a man scared of commitment, who is unwilling to take responsibility for anything that happened."

Popcorn stared at her and Jean swallowed. She couldn't read his face, but she assumed that it was his way of trying to keep her from seeing how angry he made her. There was no change of his eyes this time, but she could tell that he was mad. Whether it was from what she said, or what he was realizing, he was still upset. Jean looked away from Popcorn before he whispered, "I'm sorry, Jean."

"You should have apologized three months ago. I've been dealing with this apprehension for three months."

"I know... I know. Look, it'll be okay, alright? Maybe you aren't pregnant, and things can go back to normal—"

"How?" Jean questioned. "You don't want to talk to me and, frankly, I don't want to talk to you after you used me."

"I didn't use you."

"Then what was that, Popcorn, when you slept with me, hm? What was that?"

Popcorn opened his mouth and then closed it. It took him a moment before he finally said, "Fine, I'll say it. I was selfish and slept with you for my own gain, alright? It's been years since I've laid with a woman, and I got caught up in the moment."

"That's a pretty awful apology, you know." Jean started walking again. Popcorn hurried after her, cursing again in Ivumi.

"Daito! Damn it, woman, stop being such an ashkin!"

The woman stopped, turned, and drove her fist into Popcorn's nose. It gave a satisfying crunch under her hand, the warmth of blood splatting over her bare arms while her hands, covered by her gloves, were untouched. Popcorn fell backwards, hit the ground, and then clutched his now-broken nose. A string of Ivumi words that Jean hadn't heard before erupted from his lips. Jean, meanwhile, stood over him. "Until you figure out how to treat me, Baba Maze, I'm not speaking to you. Not as a colleague, not as a woman." She watched as his eyes flashed between shocked, to pain, to awe, before they settled on furious.

With that, Jean backed up as Popcorn struggled to his feet. "I swear, Jean—"

"To what? You don't believe in anything but yourself!"

Popcorn blinked at her, the slightest quirk of his lips masked beneath pure anger. Before he could continue, however, Caxton's voice rang out from the cottage. "Popcorn!"

He sighed, shook his head, and looked towards the boy. "Caxton! You are here! How are you, kiddo? Better than last I saw, that's for sure!"

Jean crossed her arms, one eyebrow raised. Caxton shook Popcorn's hand before he paused. "What happened to your face?"

"A..." Popcorn trailed off. "A rather irate female—"

"A griffin did that? Cool!" Caxton chirped.

The reaction made Jean turn away to keep from chuckling, especially as Popcorn rubbed the back of his neck. "Yeah... a griffin did this. Say, kid, why don't you follow your cousin around while I get my face cleaned up, alright? Later, we can go out to the woods, and you can see the real griffins."

"Really?"

"Really."

He gave Jean a pointed look before he left, and Jean rolled her eyes.

The remainder of the day was spent accustoming Caxton to the fort and the inhabitants. Park decided he was to remain in the office whenever Caxton was out, especially after the first conversation centered on the potential of the foreman having escaped Ashuran. To Caxton's credit, Park never argued and instead deflected the questions. Jean assumed that Popcorn knew whatever it was that had happened, and so she didn't pry.

Unfortunately, Caxton's visit didn't simply affect Park. Jean and Popcorn found themselves constantly working together again, despite their best attempts. Caxton was insistent on their expertise together, especially when it came to the great horned griffins. It was bittersweet to watch Popcorn direct Caxton gently as he pointed out different features of the beasts, the same passion on his face as the day that he and Jean had been alone in the forest. Jean listened quietly, taking notes and sketches in her notebook, before she paused.

"So, these two should be the only griffins in the three-mile radius, then?" she clarified.

Popcorn nodded, looking over Caxton's blond head. "Yes. Unless there's a loner wandering, which could happen, it'd be just these two. Given the fact that they're doing rather well, being plump and all, I'd say that there aren't any interlopers."

Jean hummed softly, returned to her notebook, and paused again. "If there was a loner in the area, how would we know? I wouldn't suppose they'd be sharing any kills, which means there'd be a real risk for emaciation?"

"If there was a loner, then yes. We'd probably be seeing an increase of territory marking as these two," Popcorn gestured to the mated pair, "would notice it first. We'd probably also find an increase of half-eaten kills, which is problematic because...?" He looked at Caxton, and Jean followed his gaze, before she smiled slightly.

The younger boy had fallen asleep while leaning against Popcorn. He was snoring softly, just loudly enough for Jean to detect. Popcorn sighed and shook his head. "I was hoping he'd be awake to answer the question."

"Give him some slack," Jean murmured back, "he's still recovering." She paused before she looked away from Popcorn, mentally cursing herself for breaking her self-made oath of silence unless Caxton was involved. With that in mind, she turned back to her journal as she finished scrawling some notes down. "On that topic, we should get him back to the fort. He's been tired as of late, and I want him to rest peacefully to keep that cough from coming back."

"Jean—"

"No," Jean murmured. She looked at Popcorn and shook her head. "No, I'm not speaking to you until you figure out how to treat me, alright? For Caxton, it's one thing; I don't want him to be caught up in the entire... issue. It isn't fair to him, especially when he wants so desperately to be involved." She carefully gathered Caxton, staggered under the ten-year-old's weight, and took a breath. "He respects you a lot. You know that, right? I've only seen him look up to his father and older brother the way he idolizes you and Park. Don't you dare shatter that for him like you did me."

Popcorn watched her walk away. She could feel his eyes in the back of her head as she slipped through the trees, all the while being mindful to look for any changes to this section of the forest. Like Popcorn said, it wasn't a high probability of a loner, but she wasn't willing to take any chances. Eventually, Popcorn caught up and they walked quietly together to Fort Haven.

The remainder of the month was just as terse.

Jean remained cordial enough when Caxton was around, but she avoided Popcorn whenever able. Popcorn did the same, though Jean couldn't tell if it was because he was still angry about his nose or if he hadn't yet figured out how to apologize. Caxton, meanwhile, was oblivious to the issue and happily spent time with them in the forest, studying the cockatrices, or standing atop the fort's wall to watch the waterdog he named 'Gerald'.

When it was time for Caxton to return to Blackrock, the day after the first frost, he presented Jean with a unique issue. "I want you and Popcorn to both bring me back, please."

"Both of us? I was planning on us taking Miss Tamrin's..." Jean trailed off and sighed. She couldn't put Caxton in the caravan of a mistress. There were questions that she needed to remain with his parents, not with her, and those were certainly in the unwanted category. "I can talk to Popcorn about getting a cart to go with us, but he might be unavailable. He's a busy man, kiddo."

"I know, but maybe we could wait until he's available?"

Jean sighed, rubbed her forehead, and finally nodded. "Alright, Caxton... we can at least see when he's available and go from there."

She watched as Caxton ran off, presumably to find Popcorn, before she shook her head and returned to packing. Whether she was going to stay in Blackrock or return to Fort Haven after getting Caxton home, she hadn't decided. Either way, the knot in her stomach made her think twice about eating food before talking to Popcorn, so she opted for her cool tea as she watched Osmond light on various books in the cottage.

"What do you think, Osmond? Has this feud gone on long enough?" She asked quietly.

Osmond paused, gave a little shake, and returned to bouncing. Jean raised an eyebrow. She still wasn't sure if that was a yes or a no.

Either way, she watched the dying embers in the hearth as she thought, absentmindedly running a hand over her belly.

She wasn't sure if she was pregnant or not, and she was sure that she wouldn't until she reached Blackrock. Someone in the temple, be it the Temple of Solaris or the Kingsmen temple, should be able to tell her. There was still the worry in the back of her head, but she shoved it to the back as there was a soft knock on the door frame. She turned to see it was Popcorn, as Caxton was by the cockatrices.

The lord of Fort Haven leaned against the door frame. His usually charming face was tired today, and he was breathing harder than usual. Jean frowned and stood, but he waved her off slightly. "Caxton said he wanted me to escort you both to Blackrock."

"Yes. Sit down, you look like you're going to hit the ground."

"It's... just a bit of exhaustion," Popcorn murmured. He looked at Jean, offered a weak smile, and sighed. "I can have a cart ready for us to go by dawn, tomorrow. Does that work?"

Jean nodded silently before she crossed to him. He stepped back but she caught his arm. "I need you to sit down before you pass out. You're going pale, and I can feel you shaking. Is it your heart again?"

"I'm fine, daito," Popcorn said again.

He didn't argue as Jean led him to her armchair and made him sit, instead leaning forward with his head in his hands. Jean turned to get him some water before the hairs on the back of her neck prickled at the telltale feel of magic. She didn't turn to see him until the feeling dissipated, and then she handed him a mug.

"You need to see a healer while you're in Blackrock."

"No, they won't be able to do anything."

"Then at least get that verified." Jean shook her head. "You look awful, like you've been up all night. Please, do it so Caxton can see you again."

Popcorn followed her gaze to the coop, where Caxton was offering fresh blades of grass to the griffins through the fence. A little smile crossed over Popcorn's face as he nodded. "Fine... for Caxton."

The next morning, Caxton sat bundled in a blanket beside Jean in the back of a cart. Popcorn was driving, the old draft horse pulling the wagon steadily moving forward. No one spoke until near noon, close to the halfway point.

"Jean, are those griffin talon marks in that tree?" Caxton asked.

Jean followed his pointing finger, her face twisted slightly. "I think so... though, they look rather small for the pair we've been watching. What do you think, Popcorn?"

"On that tree?" Popcorn slowed the draft horse down to look at the marks, his brow growing dark. "They aren't from our griffins, no. Keep

your guard up. There might be a roaming loner through here, and I don't
want to risk the horse."

Jean nodded and pulled Caxton slightly closer, scanning the trees
around them for any signs of danger. The birds around them continued
to sing, but the horse's ears twitched from time to time. Jean finally
murmured, "Popcorn, we should release the horse."

"I can't lose—"

"It's stalking us, Baba," Jean whispered.

Popcorn looked around and Jean did the same. "The bird have stopped
singing, and the horse is nervous. If we release the horse, it'll have prey that
it prefers. There aren't any confirmed griffin attacks, correct?"

"Correct... but I don't know if that'll work. If it's starving, it might go
for the smallest prey."

Jean looked down at Caxton, whose eyes widened. She held him tighter,
shook her head, and scanned the trees once more. "Caxton isn't the best
target right now. Kiddo, go sit with Baba at the front. He's bigger than me,
he can scare it off."

"What about you?"

"I've got a boltcaster. It's not mine, but it'll do." Jean smiled slightly at
him before she helped him onto the bench with Popcorn. As she did, she
caught sight of something moving in the large, gnarled oak branches above
them. The horse realized there was something there as well, as it spooked
and lurched forward. Popcorn caught Caxton with one arm while Jean,
barely catching herself on the cart, looked up to see a thin, bony griffin had
leaped from the tree and towards them.

It was all Jean could do to protect her face as it landed heavily on the
cart beside her. Caxton began to scream while Popcorn, with one hand on
the reins, pulled the boy to his side to shield him from any rough attacks.
Jean ventured a peek at the griffin, met with a drooling beak and narrowed
golden eyes. It was beautiful, terrifying, and heartbreaking all in a single
breath, especially as she saw the hunger in its gaze before it lunged and
caught her arm in its beak.

Jean cried out, pulled her boltcaster from her hip, before the griffin
yanked her from the cart and to the ground. She could hear Popcorn

shouting after her as he struggled with the cart, but that was lost as the blood pulsed in her ears.

Griffin venom was going to work fast, and she only had enough time to keep this beast from rending her further before it ate her.

She began to kick and scream, trying to be bigger than she really was, but she knew the blood loss was taking a toll. Her legs were already heavy, especially as she sucked in a breath and tried to roll onto her side.

The griffin circled her, chirping softly as though speaking to itself, before Jean felt the back of her neck prickle again. This time, nausea shot through her and she watched as her blood lifted from her wounds and formed on Popcorn's arm. He charged toward the griffin, slicing at it with his newly acquired crystalline blade. It didn't take long before the griffin fell, and he rushed to her side, letting the blood drip into her bite. "Damn, it broke the bone too. Jean, can you hear me?"

His words were fuzzy, but Jean nodded slightly.

He brushed some hair from her face and held her. "Alright, this is going to hurt. Caxton, get my pack! Bring it, now!"

With that, he pressed his hands to Jean's broken arm. She gave a guttural scream as it felt as though her very soul was being ripped in two, only able to hear his apology before her vision faded.

Great-Horned Griffin

The apex predator of the Thetbrook Forest, standing 6 feet tall at the shoulder, it is one of the largest creatures in the area. Its diet consists of deer, foxes, large birds, spider-wolves, and anything else it can catch. Given its surprising stealth and ability to swoop from above mixed with a deadly anti-coagulating venom, there is little that is spared from their hunt. Unless they are particularly hungry a great-horned griffin doesn't often prey on humans, though they will not hesitate to kill if their territory or mate is threatened!

MHORYGA

A soft ticking sound was the first thing that Jean heard as she slowly regained consciousness.

Her throat was dry, and raw. Her head felt heavy, her arm hurt and... Jean was unable to finish her mental notes as the sudden and overwhelming urge to vomit filled her. She managed to roll over fast enough to puke into a bucket that had somehow appeared, and a gentle hand rubbed her back as she did so. Jean vomited for several minutes before she laid back again and closed her eyes. The lights were too bright here. There were too many sounds, and not enough moments of peace. Even the blanket was too loud, as she shifted ever so slightly.

She sighed as the hand gently stroked her hair down and wiped her face with a cool cloth.

It felt nice.

Jean allowed herself to open her eyes and look towards her caregiver only to find Popcorn's worried green eyes were fixed on her face. Then, as she winced and scanned the room, she began to take in what looked like the Temple of HaMelech around her. She was hooked up to a couple of machines, her arm was wrapped tightly and placed in a sling, she had several bandages where she had been mauled by the griffin. Popcorn had Caxton beside him, the little boy sleeping in the chair. Around them were the steadily ticking machines and equipment used by the doves at the temple.

"Is Caxton alright?" Jean whispered.

"Yeah, yeah, Caxton's okay. You're who I'm more worried about. You've been asleep for two days, the doves weren't sure when you were going to come out of it," Popcorn said quietly. He smoothed her hair down again. "You puked quite a bit. That's a good sign. Your stomach is still working. And you can hear me alright?"

"Yes." Jean looked around again before she focused on Popcorn. He smiled a little bit at her before he sat back.

"Good. I'll let them know you're awake. Your aunt and uncle stepped out for food; they should be back soon." Popcorn stood, holding onto his cane, before Jean caught his hand slightly.

"What about the griffin?"

The man's shoulders sagged slightly. "It had to be put down. I really didn't want to but... there was no way to keep you safe if it was still moving. Either way, Jean, I should go and find a dove. They wanted to do some comprehensive tests once you were awake, making sure that you are alright."

Popcorn gently squeezed her hand and then hurried out of the room. Jean watched him go before she looked around again.

Nothing really happened until after Popcorn returned.

He had a dove healer with him, who looked Jean over a couple of times before she started to fiddle with some of the machines. Popcorn sat down by Caxton again. Jean ignored the dove as she watched Popcorn.

He was focused heavily on Caxton, checking on his breathing and ensuring that he wasn't getting a crick in the neck. Jean couldn't help but give a little smile as she watched. He cared, he seemed to genuinely want to check in on Caxton, and... for a moment, Jean couldn't help but wonder what it would be like if he was, in fact, a father.

Jean shifted as the dove poked her in the stomach, before she murmured, "Full bill of health?"

"Outside of the broken arm, and the blood loss, you're just fine," the dove said gently. She glanced at Popcorn and Caxton, and then looked at Jean. "There's a diagnosis that I think would be best for you just you, as you are not related to either of these gentlemen. Lord Maze—"

"Yes?" Popcorn perked up instantly.

"I'd like to speak to Miss Cassy alone, please."

"Is everything alright?"

Jean shifted to take his hand. "I'm fine, Lord Maze."

"Popcorn, please," he said quietly. "Jean, it's okay. Please, you can call me Popcorn again. I want you to call me Popcorn, please. Not Lord Maze."

Jean squeezed his hand. "I'll be okay... Popcorn. You go get something to eat. Caxton will be fine while he sleeps."

The man slowly nodded, though he took a moment to leave. Jean looked up at him, nodded, and then watched him leave. She looked at the dove, tilted her head, and asked, "What is it?"

The dove waited until Popcorn was gone, and she was sure that Caxton was asleep, before she said, "What were you thinking, being so reckless while pregnant?"

The words made Jean freeze, and she blinked at the dove as the other woman went on a tirade about responsibility. All that Jean could think of, though, was 'pregnant'. She really was carrying Popcorn's baby, and as it had happened so long ago... she was nearly four months, wasn't she? It was near the end of this year and... yes, it was four months. Jean's face ran cold, and she felt tears begin to sting her eyes. She couldn't cry, though, as the dove continued to question her. She didn't answer, either. Instead, she sat numbly, let everything wash over her, and then looked up at the ceiling.

Osmond was there, circling lazily as though he was a dandelion seed caught in the wind. He drifted close enough to Jean that she exhaled and sent him spiraling into the air. This apparent dismissal annoyed the dove healer, who said, "There seems to be no responsibility in you!"

"Sister Lin," another voice said lightly, "that is absolutely no way to be speaking to a patient, regardless of what happened. Kindly step out of the room to calm down, I will continue administering treatment."

Jean glanced to the side to see another dove was standing there. Her hands were folded in front of herself, and she raised on eyebrow at Sister Lin, who hurriedly ducked her head and ran out. Then, she looked at Jean and smiled gently at her. "I'm sorry, dear. We've been rather frazzled recently. That's no excuse, I know." She came further into the area and began to check Jean over again before she pressed a handful of pills into her palm and then held a water cup. "Painkillers. That was a rather nasty break in your arm, and it'll likely hurt the next few days as it heals. Your friend was wise in bringing you as quickly as he did; any later, and the blood loss might have done you and the baby in."

"So... I really am pregnant?" Jean asked after she took the medicine. "You're absolutely sure?"

"We are, but not to worry; whatever you're doing now has brought about a healthy pregnancy," the dove answered with a smile. "I'm sure you'll be glad to share that news with the father!"

A little nod answered the healer, who went about her way. Popcorn returned after a little while, this time joined by Flick and Anca. He looked at Jean, his eyebrows raised as though silently asking if everything was alright, and Jean shook her head dismissively. It didn't concern him, not as much as she'd like to admit it did.

As her aunt fussed over her, Jean watched as Flick and Popcorn spoke softly. Caxton was groggily watching them too. She couldn't tell what they were saying, but Flick lightly shook Popcorn's hand, and she gathered the sense that it was thanks for what he had done.

"We should get you back home, Jean," Anca said softly. "You need to be resting, and the last thing I want is for you to have another accident. Between the incident when you first started and this—"

"Those were accidents, as you said," Jean answered. "Fort Haven is as safe as Blackrock, if not safer. The treaty is in effect there, and there wasn't any Telfarians. It'll be alright if I go back."

Popcorn and Flick looked at her, and Popcorn raised his eyebrow. "Are you sure? Jean, after the last three months—"

"I would rather be back in Fort Haven, doing my best to continue to support myself, than have Caxton and my family needing to care for me,"

Jean said. She shifted slightly. "I love you, I really do, Aunt Anca and Uncle Flick, but I don't want to be a burden."

Anca reared back slightly. "A burden? Jean, no, you're never a burden." She stroked some hair out of Jean's face, minding her horns, and kissed her forehead. "You're family, this is what family does. But... I suppose if you want to return to Fort Haven, we have no right to stop you."

"Are you certain that you'll be alright with your broken arm?" Flick asked. "It's your dominant hand; I don't want you getting into trouble if you need to shoot."

Jean nodded and looked at Popcorn. Living at Fort Haven would give her a better chance at hiding her pregnancy, even around Popcorn and Park. Her aunt and uncle had a child together: they'd know what signs to look for, and they'd question suddenly layering to hide any pregnancy bump. At the fort, it was transitioning into the snowy season. By the time she delivered, it would be sudden. There'd be enough time to remain secretive without anyone questioning her, and when she was ready she could go to Blackrock to deliver. It'd be best to make it to Blackrock from time to time, but she could always claim that she was checking on Caxton. Yes, that should work.

"I'll be fine," Jean reaffirmed after her thoughts.

Popcorn stared at her before his eyes softened, ever so slightly. "Good. Then I'll expect you at work sooner rather than later."

"Are you leaving her now?" Anca questioned. She looked at Jean. "He didn't leave your side the two days you were sleeping. Sent for a courier to get Flick and I, and even the trips to the latrine or to find something to eat were brief."

The man in question shifted, almost in embarrassment, when Jean looked at him again. He rubbed the back of his neck with one hand. "Insurance would be a pain, that's all. Park would have my head if he didn't know the prognosis, and that'd look bad for a multitude of reasons, you know. Besides, Caxton wouldn't let me live it down. Kid loves you, don't cha?" He ruffled Caxton's hair, receiving a soft chuckle, before Caxton wrapped his arms around Jean.

She kissed his forehead, winced as he bumped her broken arm, and then smiled as he said, "You're the bravest person I've ever met, Jean."

"I thought I was?" Popcorn asked.

Caxton grinned at him and Jean chuckled. "Alright... I know I've just woken up, but I need to rest. I'll be fine."

Her aunt, uncle, and cousin filed out after hugs and kisses. Popcorn lingered for a moment more, though Jean stopped him as he started to leave. "Popcorn?"

The softness in his eyes made Jean pause, and she shifted ever so slightly. "Thank you for keeping Caxton safe."

"I know he means a lot to you, daito... and I wanted to make sure he was alright while you recovered." Popcorn offered her a small smile.

He turned to leave again, and Jean murmured, "Thank you for getting me here."

"... anytime, Jean. You get some rest. Once they give you a clean bill of health, I expect you to return to Fort Haven." He shifted slightly. "And... I'm sorry. I really am sorry, Jean, for... everything."

Jean blinked at him, looked down, and shook her head. "I appreciate it, but I've decided that I'm over it. It was a mistake. A mistake that..." she trailed off, sighed, and closed her eyes. "It's a mistake, that's it."

"Jean—"

"Please, I need to rest."

Popcorn nodded slowly and limped out.

When Jean was released the next week, she found Popcorn was waiting for her. He was sitting atop a cart that was full of crates, tapping his foot nervously. "I hope you don't mind; we need to take a detour while in town. I have a delivery to make."

"Delivery? Where?"

"The Telfarian district."

Jean was silent as they drove, unable to pull herself into asking any questions. Before she had managed to gather her nerves, they had stopped in front of a dingy brick-and-mortar warehouse.

Before they had time to even approach the door, a man wearing a black mask had opened it and gestured for them to enter. People in masks were running around the main floor in a frenzied sort of dance as they moved crates and boxes from one place to another. Standing on the balcony above was a woman in a stunning purple gown and a white, full-face mask. Her red hair had been piled elegantly atop her head and pinned in place under a hat with four cockatrice feathers— a display screaming status.

She stood there for a moment, watching everyone before her gaze landed on Jean and Popcorn. The strange woman's eyes seemed hungry as she descended the stairs, never once moving from Jean.

In an instant, Jean realized that the work ethic wasn't out of a frantic need to get tasks done but the same fear-driven movements that overtook people at Fort Haven when Popcorn was in a bad mood.

Popcorn's voice snapped Jean from her thoughts. "I'm Baba Maze, the contracted artifact retriever. Are you—"

"Mhoryga, yes." The woman in purple held her hand out and Popcorn gave it a light kiss. "And who, pray tell, is your companion?"

"This is my research assistant, Jean Cassy."

"Pleasure," Jean said.

She forced herself to meet Mhoryga's gaze, a bit of a sick feeling in her stomach as a pungent aroma filled her nose. A second form, this one a man in black robes with a gaunt, skull-shaped mask, had taken his place beside Mhoryga.

"Ah, Ankou, back just in time. Why don't you help Mr. Maze bring in his shipment of artifacts and go over them with the foreman? Miss Cassy, I've yet to have my afternoon tea and would very much enjoy company if you'd rather not help the men with their tasks," Mhoryga said.

"I... suppose I can join you. If you don't mind, of course."

"Wonderful." The woman in purple led Jean up the stairs and to a room. "I'll be changing into my tea attire, do you happen to have something more... fitting, for a tea?"

"No, ma'am. I didn't realize I would be having tea this afternoon."

"Pity. I'll send my handmaid to you, and she'll get you settled then," Mhoryga replied, waving Jean off. "Wait here."

The handmaid led her into a room to change into a fine blue gown with silver threads. Jean protested but was ignored and then brought back to the first room to wait again. Movement caught her attention and Jean approached one of the windows facing a garden of tropical plants. She realized it was, in fact, a window into a large room rather than the outside when a feathered creature limped out from behind a bush. It blended with the dark greens and lush purples of the flora it moved through, and it lifted its head to regard Jean. Two huge eyes met her and it clicked its mandibles through the window. All Jean could do was stare in awe as it approached the glass, intelligence radiating from it as it studied her.

"Beautiful, isn't she?"

Jean turned to face Mhoryga. "I'm sorry?"

"Jezabella, that's her name. Isn't she beautiful?"

"Oh! Yes, she is. Have you had her for long?" Jean inquired, looking back at the beast in question.

"She and her boyfriend, who's currently hidden under that tree fern, came to me many years ago from the other side of the torus. Jezabella sustained an injury that rendered one of her legs useless. Had she stayed with her pack, there is no doubt that she would have been ripped into two as the weakest link."

Jean watched as Jezabella made her way to the male. "Are they a breeding pair then?"

"No, they are not; she's unable to lay eggs, the poor thing."

The two women watched the creatures for a moment more before Mhoryga led Jean into a second part of the room. This one was as lavish as the first, this time lined with artifacts rather than wallpaper. An eerie whisper filled Jean's head as soon as she stepped foot into the room, and she spared a glance to find its source. It was far too familiar for her to let her guard down, especially when her gaze landed on an ebony staff resting in a case across the room. Jean shook her head to clear it before she blinked and it was gone, a green marble staff in its place.

She must have imagined it, right?

"So, Miss Cassy." Mhoryga sunk onto a lounging couch and gestured to one across from her before she placed a satin tea bag into her cup. "Have you a preferred tea?"

"I carry some with me, thank you." Jean placed her herbs into her teacup as a servant wearing another polished mask stepped forward to pour the hot water. "Thank you for the invitation to tea. I hope this isn't a problem for you."

"Not at all. I enjoy the company of other noble ashura when I happen upon them." Mhoryga lifted her teacup in time with a silk napkin held by the servant beside her. It completely blocked any piece of her natural face and piqued Jean's curiosity before the woman lowered her cup and then stared at her. "Though it does make me wonder why an individual with your blood isn't in Ashuran, Miss Cassy."

Jean paused as she reached to take a cucumber sandwich, taking a moment to collect her thoughts before she admitted, "I don't know what you mean. I've never been to Ashuran, nor have I considered it."

"And yet, you have the blood of a noble." Mhoryga leaned in. "Surely you know your bloodline? Ashura do not leave Ashuran, which means you must have been removed when you were young... adopted, perhaps?"

Jean returned to her chaise and stared at her host, no longer hungry. "I'm not sure how you can make that claim—"

"I can smell it, Miss Cassy; your appearance masks your ashura breeding, but I can smell the noble blood that lingers in your veins. It's tainted, but it is still noble." Mhoryga leaned into her couch as she took a bite of a tea cake. "Your parents likely gave you up due to that fact."

Jean murmured, "Please, explain to me the difference between a noble and an ashn?"

"Oh, dear child..." Mhoryga shook her head with a sigh. "You have lost your heritage. Purebloods, noble ashura more aptly as purebloods are few and far between save for me and a select handful of others, are the desired race: beautiful, intelligent, powerful. They are the ones who must hide their faces behind a mask to protect the lesser from gazing upon their glory and thus dying. The ashn..." Mhoryga trailed off and snapped her fingers. From the corner of her eye, Jean watched as a man with cloth wrapped around his face, leaving only a slit for his eyes, hurried from where he had been resting. "They are the lowest of the races. Look at him, my dear. Under that wrap is a face that not even a mother can love. They are weak, they have no use aside from mining crystals for our use and other work that we as nobles mustn't be forced to do."

Jean stared at the ashn man and pity filled her as she saw his gaunt state. Mhoryga waved him off, "It is all in the natural order of things, Miss Cassy, and the unnatural on the other side of the spectrum are the ascended, those who have decided to attempt godhood, lose any semblance of sanity, and are plagued to a life of feasting on others. They're as disgusting as the ashn, though their stench is only slightly more tolerable." Mhoryga focused on Jean again. "Returning to the discussion of nobles, you must have left Ashuran before you received a proper adult mask. It's a pity; it would have allowed you to show your status in the city rather than the ill-treatment you receive for looking like this."

Mhoryga took a bite of the cookie that she had held until that point, her voice soft. "Now, tell me, Miss Cassy... why is it you're working with Mr. Maze instead of pursuing the magics? I know you heard something when you came into this room."

Jean stiffened. "I haven't an idea what you mean," she said, sipping her tea. "I was admiring the artifacts you've on the wall." If not for the cover on Mhoryga's face, Jean would have sworn the noble was smirking at her.

"Fair," she murmured, "but should you decide to be interested in the magics in this world, do reach out. You have a potential, Miss Cassy, that I've only seen a handful of times before."

Once they finished their tea, Mhoryga ushered Jean from the room to where Popcorn and Ankou were waiting. Popcorn gave Jean a soft smile. "Did you enjoy your tea?"

"I did, yes. And thank you again, Mhoryga."

"Of course. Please come again," Mhoryga replied, staring at her.

Jean offered a faltering smile before her gaze landed on Ankou once more. She had seen him before; she knew she had. There was a strange sense of familiarity, one that made Jean's eyebrows furrow. Popcorn took her hand as she finally ventured, "Do I know you?"

"It doesn't matter," Ankou replied. "You can see yourself to the door."

Popcorn ushered Jean out of the warehouse. The further they got from the man in black robes, the easier it was for Jean to breathe. "Did he smell to you?"

"Who?"

"Ankou?"

"He's ascended," Popcorn answered. "Though, you don't exactly mention that to anyone."

"How do you know what ascended are?" Jean questioned.

Popcorn glanced at her; his eyebrow raised. "You can't work with a former ashn slave for five years and not know the entire hierarchy of Ashuran," he replied. "Besides, when he spends enough time complaining about the noble walking around Fort Haven stinking—"

"Slow down. I've only been informed about nobles, and ashn and... I'm very confused. How do you know all of this?"

The man glanced at her once more. "Park's ashn, and so am I. Well, I'm part ashn. He's told me about what it's like in Ashuran as he spent most of his adult life slaving away in the mines. It's part of the reason he doesn't enjoy having you around. Nobles tend to smell. He hasn't said anything to you, though, since you aren't fully a noble, and don't have a mask. The noble that you had tea with, however, and the ascended with her, will keep him from entering Blackrock any time soon."

Jean hummed softly. So, Caxton was right. She didn't ask any additional questions as they drove back towards Fort Haven, instead staring towards the sky. Mhoryga's words hung heavy in her mind; there was something more there, and she didn't trust it. She also didn't trust the staff she thought she saw. Unless it really was there.

16

ADMITTANCE

J ean's welcome at Fort Haven was quiet, but there all the same. Popcorn helped her from the wagon and hesitated, briefly, before he finally gave her a gentle embrace. It surprised Jean, and she tensed up slightly at his touch before she closed her eyes and pressed into him.

In an instant, all of the hurt, all of the sadness, and all of the fear melted away. She took a deep breath at the sudden realization. It wasn't something she wanted to admit, or enjoy, but she cherished it all the same. Popcorn pressed his face into her hair, ever mindful of her horns, and took a breath as well. After a moment, he whispered, "I'm glad you're back, daito. You need to get some rest, alright? I'll see you in the morning."

The curseborn was suddenly left with a cold feeling of loneliness and hopelessness as Popcorn pulled away. She stared up the staros man before she nodded. "Yeah... I'll see you in the morning."

When she was alone in her cottage, Jean laid down on her bed and inspected her belly. There really was the slightest change there. It was so incredibly small that she thought she was imagining it. Jean sighed, rolled over, and fell asleep.

It was business as usual in the fort when Jean woke up. She tended to the cockatrices and then slipped into the forest, where she watched the great horned griffins amid the frosty landscape. The cloak she brought was a saving grace, and she wrapped it around herself as a shudder slipped down her spine. The griffin carefully shifted on her nest, revealing three large, oval eggs. Jean took painstaking measures to sketch what they looked like, especially as the female shifted again over the clutch and looked at Jean.

Jean offered a weak smile, her broken arm throbbing as though remembering the beak that had snapped it, and she murmured, "Good griffin."

The griffin, in return, clacked her beak and ruffled her feathers before she settled further on her nest of dying leaves.

"How do you do it?" Jean finally asked, making the griffin open one eye. "You have a devoted mate, you're content with raising your chicks. There's more to life than that, isn't there? You're huge, you can wander and find new territory; you don't have to stay in one spot and give everything to raise offspring."

Again, the griffin snapped her beak a handful of times and rested her head on her front paws. Jean sighed, leaned against a tree, and watched Osmond move slowly from bush to bush. He lingered by the griffin, who twitched her tail and knocked him off course. The movement made the griffin look towards the ball of light and, for a moment, Jean wondered if she could see Osmond as well.

Jean returned to sketching the griffin before she yawned. It wasn't like her to be tired at this time, or growing hungry, and she had no doubts it was the pregnancy. She grumbled to herself as she stood and gathered her things.

The griffin gave a little growl as Jean did so, and she looked at the creature. Her hackles were raised, and she was staring into the bushes. Jean pulled her replacement boltcaster from her hip and fumbled with it. It took a moment to ensure that it was loaded with one hand, and by the time she had, she discovered there was a fanged rabbit stalking through the underbrush.

It didn't seem to notice her, yet, and Jean swallowed as she realized that it was a chitterling.

This was the closest she'd seen one to the fort, and that worried her.

As the thought crossed her mind, the chitterling froze and looked at her. Jean blinked at it and then bolted as it began to laugh.

Any worries about the griffin and its clutch were gone as Jean ran for her life, the howls and laughter echoing behind her menacingly. She avoided looking towards the sides of her forced path, not wanting to see the eyes that raced after her. Osmond shot past her, leading her through the obstacles. As she rushed to the fort, she stopped breathing for only enough time to shout, "Chitters!"

Whether they could hear her or not, she didn't know.

She was still several hundred yards away from the fort when she heard something large crashing through the underbrush behind her. The chitterlings were close on her heels, nipping and biting as best they could. Behind her, though, Jean knew it was the largest of the chitters that was brutishly destroying flora to reach her. She managed to grip her boltcaster ever tighter, ready to fight, when sounds from ahead forced her out of her panicked stupor.

Was she surrounded? Jean looked around wildly, finally catching sight of an oak with one branch that she could possibly swing onto. It was a gamble, especially with her bad arm, but there was no other option. She wouldn't be able to reach the fort before the brute reached her, and she wanted desperately to see another day. With that in mind, Jean veered to her right.

Her bolt caster hit the ground as she abandoned it to use her good hand, and she struggled to pull her weight up with one arm. Her feet slid against the frozen bark, leaving her dangling before she found a single foothold and managed to pull herself up.

One leg wrapped around the branch, leaving Jean upside down. She had to get up. She had to go further.

Panic surged through her as the brute crashed through the undergrowth, a swarm of chitterlings and chitters close behind, brandishing bone knives. They charged toward her, and she scrambled in vain to pull herself higher onto the branch. She was eye to eye with the brute now. It stared back, its maw twisted into an eerie foaming grin.

This was it, wasn't it?

Jean shied back as the chitter closed in before more shapes broke through the brush. Through her panic, Jean really couldn't tell if it was another group of chitters or something else. Their appearances shifted between man and monster, especially as the hair on the back of Jean's neck rose with its uncanny revoke of magic.

The larger of the newcomers raced towards the brute, who swerved to meet it. They slammed into one another, inhuman screaming and guttural cries echoing through the forest as they ripped into each other. Other forms began to pick off the chitterlings and chitters, their shapes solidifying on various mercenaries from Fort Haven. Jean managed to get herself onto the branch, breathing heavily, as the two groups brutally attacked one another and then, as quickly as it started, it was over.

Standing in the middle of the group, breathing heavily, was what looked like another brute. Then, as Jean's fear began to dissipate, she realized that it was Popcorn. He had a bite on one shoulder but otherwise looked fine. His teeth were grit as he pulled what looked like a ball of blood from his injury, his hand shaking as the ball separated into a red viscus liquid that seeped back into the wound and black bile that hissed and popped as though burning in a fire. He flicked his hand and the bile sizzled in a beam of sunlight. Then, after he looked around at his men, he looked at Jean.

The worry on his face flickered to confusion and then anger. "What the hell were you doing out here alone? You could have been killed!"

"I'm alright... you got here in time."

"That's the only reason you're alright! Your arm is broken, you were struggling to escape when we arrived, and if we hadn't, you'd be dead!" Popcorn exploded. "You should have taken someone with you!"

Jean stared at Popcorn, her face and her heart falling. He was right, she should have had someone with her. No one understood though, he was busy, and the griffins didn't wait. She looked down as he continued to admonish her, finally saying, "I thought I could handle myself."

"You can't! Not right now, not with a broken arm!" Popcorn stormed to her and pulled her from the tree. He wasn't overtly rough, but it certainly wasn't as kind as Jean would have preferred in her state. He set her down, his chest heaving and face pale. "You could have died, Jean! Don't you understand that? First the griffin, now chitters! If I didn't know any better, I'd assume you really were cursed with the luck you have!" He sucked in a breath, leaned heavily against the tree, and swallowed. "You have to stop putting yourself into harm's way!"

"Baba—"

"I can't lose you, too!"

Jean stared at Popcorn; her mouth dry. She wanted desperately to ask why it was a 'too', but that didn't come. Instead, she whispered, "I'm sorry. I really thought I'd be okay. I didn't think there'd be chitters this close."

"That's no excuse!"

"I know," Jean whispered. She glanced at the mercenaries, who were shifting nervously as they watched Popcorn. Jean swallowed back her own worry and put a hand on Popcorn's arm. "I know, and you're right. I should have had someone with me. I didn't want to bother you, and I didn't want to bother others. I'm sorry."

Popcorn's gaze flashed to her, and he frowned. Then, as she touched his arm, he sighed. "I want you back in Fort Haven while Park and I discuss what to do. You can't be out here on your own, and I can't risk anything happening to you. Not now, not ever."

"I think I have a say in it, too, don't I?" Jean asked.

The look he gave her solidified that she was treading on thin ice. As much as Jean wanted to argue with him, and plead her case, she mumbled, "At least let me sit there and listen."

"Fine, you can do that," Popcorn said. He seemed dazed as he stood there, leaning against the tree. Jean rubbed his arm for a moment before she turned to the group of mercenaries.

One of them stepped up despite her silence and slung one of Popcorn's arms around his shoulder to help him stand upright and the group slowly started to Fort Haven.

Jean ensured Popcorn was comfortable when he was laid down, and she remained with him until after he had fallen asleep. She wouldn't admit it, but seeing him in that state, where he seemed to be in a stupor, scared her.

Eventually, it was settled that she would remain in Fort Haven unless accompanied by someone. The restriction would be lifted once her arm was fully healed, which took about a month, and she would be able to do her full research without any quarrels. The month came and went, Jean returned to Blackrock to have the cast removed and the pregnancy checked on, and she returned to life as she knew.

It wasn't until after she returned from Blackrock and was admiring her small bump in her mirror, now showing ever so slightly, that she was found out. As she inspected herself, there was a knock on the door as Park spoke from beyond. "Miss Cassy, Popcorn said that you use a tea blend that has begun to run low in our supplies. Do you mind sitting down with me to—" He opened the door and Jean whipped around, but it was too late. He stared at her, his eyes wide, and Jean rubbed her temple.

"Most people wait until they're invited in, Park," she said dryly. She adjusted her tunic to hide her pregnancy again and crossed her arms over her chest. "The tea?"

"Are you... carrying?" Park questioned quietly. He looked around and then at Jean again. "This isn't a great place—"

"I'm well aware," Jean interrupted. She scowled at the ashn foreman. "Are you going to actually discuss the tea, or has this turned into 'question Jean about her life choices' time?"

Park shut the door and looked at her. "I think it is valuable to discuss the future. Does Popcorn know? Are you returning to Blackrock after you deliver?"

"No, and no." The curseborn woman shifted under his gaze, then she lifted her chin in defiance. "Does it really matter?"

His questioning was beginning to irritate her, even after just a handful of moments. First, he barged into her home and then began to pester her about something rather private. It was inconsiderate, and nosy, and she didn't enjoy it. Park shook his head slowly. "You'll need to inform him. I'm sure there's various tasks you'll be asked to leave for him to complete, and you'll be going to Blackrock for appointments—"

"Park!" Jean snapped. He looked at her, and she glared back. "Shut. Your. Mouth." The foreman frowned but remained silent as Jean said, "I don't want this to be made into a big deal, got it? I can still function. They removed my cast—" she waved her arm about, "—and gave me a clean bill of health. My pregnancy isn't a condition, it's a stupidly natural thing to happen when men don't keep it in their pants, and make you feel like you're the top of the world before they say it was a mistake!"

The foreman stared at her, and Jean blinked angrily back. Then, she said, "It's chamomile lavender, I don't know where you can get any of the other additives as it isn't a common blend. I'll write the list for you. Now, get out and keep your mouth shut."

"You don't need to be so rude," Park replied.

Jean picked up one of her pots and threw it at him. He narrowly dodged it, raced out the door, and then looked back before he hurried away. The curseborn glared after him before she flopped into her chair and stared at the fire.

What if Popcorn found out?

Her fears were realized during the nightly bonfire, where they ate dinner as a camp and discussed the weekly happenings. One of the men beside Jean laughed as she finished another helping of roasted boar. "Starving, are we Cassy? The way you keep up, your weight gain will be normal!"

A healthy amount of laughter answered the man's commentary. All Jean could do was stare at him. Park shifted a bit and Popcorn, who was next to Park, raised an eyebrow. Finally, Jean finished her bite and then slapped the man. He held his cheek with wide eyes, Popcorn began to laugh, and Jean's attention drew to him. The others around the fire seemed significantly more worried now, especially as Jean questioned, "Do you think that's funny, Lord Maze? Do you think it's funny when discipline is enacted for a man commenting on my body weight?"

Popcorn shook his head slightly. "No, no, Jean... what's funny is the sudden change in your attitude! I saw you just miss Park today with a cooking utensil, and now this! Whatever it is that's got you mad, I would hate to be it!"

In one fluid motion, Jean grabbed Popcorn by the collar. He grinned up at her, clearly dazed from the mead he'd been drinking. The stench turned her stomach, and she swallowed back a wave of nausea. "Get these men in line, Baba Maze; you're going to want to make sure that no one else suffers the ire of your spawn's mother. I'm not going to be playing nice."

She released him, realized what exactly she had said, and met Popcorn's gaze. She'd never seen a man sober up as quickly as he did, and he struggled to his feet before Jean hurried from the fire.

"Daito, wait! Damn it, Jean... wait!"

Around her, the shadows were beginning to swirl. Worries about what might happen now that Popcorn knew flooded her mind, and she grit her teeth to try ignoring the eyes that watched her. She made it to her cottage, where she ignored the door as she set to work brewing herself a cup of tea. She sunk into her chair as the water began to boil, just as Popcorn hurried in. "Jean, what the actual—"

"I'm pregnant, and it's yours. And now, as you know that, I'd like to enjoy my last moments of peace with a cup of tea before you demand that I remain in Blackrock until the baby is born," Jean snapped.

She didn't look at Popcorn, instead focusing on the fire that brought about a soft comfort to her home. As she did, she could feel the frustration melt into grief: everything was changing, and it was all due to her pregnancy. All of the previously determined acceptance was fading, too, and instead left room for disappointment, worry, and that sense of hopelessness she remembered having in Bleak Hollow. Out of the corner of her eye, she watched Popcorn limp heavily to her and then crouch beside her chair. She sighed, shook her head, and shifted away slightly. "Go ahead, regret it. I'm regretting it, too. I absolutely ruined everything, especially any chance of making myself a home anywhere." The woman gave a bitter laugh. "I've got a baby to think about now. I can't do much while dealing with that."

It was silent for several moments. Finally, Popcorn whispered, "Daito, why didn't you tell me?"

The soft words surprised her, and she slowly looked at Popcorn. His eyes were fixated on her face, his hands holding tightly to the arm of her chair. His cane laid abandoned beside him, and he teetered slightly on his toes as he focused on her. As she looked at him, his gaze moved over her form before they snapped back to her eyes. "Why didn't you tell me that you were pregnant?"

"Why would I? You had made it clear that you regretted sleeping with me, and I supposed you'd want nothing to do with me once you learned about this."

Hurt flashed across Popcorn's face, and he shook his head slightly. "No, Jean... no, no, that's not right. No..." He found her hand and took it. It took every ounce of Jean's being to keep from pulling away, but her pain slowly faded as Popcorn whispered, "I'm so sorry that you felt the need to hide this from me."

Jean swallowed past a lump in her throat. This was a new side to him. She'd never seen him like this, even after the griffin attack. There was worry, hurt, and... hope. She wasn't sure hope was something he'd ever experienced before, but as she stared at him, she realized that it was very much there and very much alight. Absentmindedly, she rubbed over his hand with her gloved thumb before she mumbled, "You really don't need to be involved, Popcorn. I know that this is a commitment that... I'm not ready for it either."

"No, Jean. This is happening, and I've got responsibility to take." Popcorn continued to stare at her and Jean, after a moment, sighed and moved his hand onto her stomach.

She didn't know what she was doing. It's not like he'd feel their child moving within her, but the feeling of his hand over the small bump brought about emotions that she really rather not think about. Still, it felt right to allow him to feel the small lump that was there, and she couldn't help but smile as Popcorn's eyes grew wide. He stared at her stomach for a moment, silent, and then looked up at her. "Everything is going well? You're healthy, the pregnancy is alright?"

"As far as the healers said at the Temple of Solaris," Jean mumbled. "They suspect I'll be due towards the beginning of summer."

"That's a good time for delivery," Popcorn said with a little nod. "More food, predators aren't strapped for finding meals, and the snow will be gone."

Jean glanced at him; her eyebrow raised. "That's an oddly specific thought process."

"It's what kept my people alive all these years," Popcorn replied. He lightly ran his thumb over Jean's stomach, his voice thoughtful. "Are you going to stay in Fort Haven after you deliver?"

"I don't know."

They fell into an uncomfortable silence, where Jean quietly stared at the fire and Popcorn rested a hand on her thigh. Eventually, Jean whispered, "I don't want the remainder of the pregnancy to be any different than before you knew."

"It'll be alright." Popcorn shifted. "Look... I've got some digs I need to take care of before the Long Night comes. I'll be away until likely the last minute, as I really can't reschedule things like this. We don't have to say anything to the rest of the fort, and we can give you a monthly stipend of time in Blackrock, just like we did when you were tutoring Caxton. I just... you have to be careful, promise me that you'll be careful."

"Why do you care so much?"

"Because..." He hesitated for a moment. "I just do." Popcorn pulled away from her. "I've got to take care of the bonfire. You made a nice scene; we can deal with that later. Right now, go ahead and get comfortable, it's business as usual tomorrow."

Jean nodded and Popcorn slowly left. She sighed as she watched him go, finally relaxing as she sipped her cup of tea again. Did that mean that she and Popcorn were going to parent together? There certainly wasn't any prospect of marriage in her future, and whether or not Popcorn was actually going to stay was the true question. Jean couldn't help but give a little smile, the potential just there, before it slipped away, and she closed her eyes. She almost believed it, but she couldn't.

Happy endings didn't come for curseborns.

Broad-Breasted Robin

I am particularly fond of their odd 'bibbit' call, especially when I can see their little chests expand before it happens. They seem to know that their cries can be rather startling when people don't know they're there, which makes me all the more pleased to hear them.

Broad-breasted robins seem to remain near orchards or quiet towns. I've heard them once or twice while at Fort Haven, but that could very well be my imagination.

Broad-breasted robin have the cutest antlers, though I'm sure they do nothing but convince females of potential mates. Do they perhaps shed and then grow back each year? Likely not, but the idea of a velvety pair of antlers on their tiny heads makes me giggle despite the situation.

THE LONG NIGHT

The months came and went quickly. Her secret wasn't kept for long as her pregnancy began to show. The commentary, however, remained minimal. Popcorn had left to go adventuring, having explained it as securing funds for the fort's benefits. With that, preparations for the Long Night were well underway, especially in the weeks leading to the 36 hours of darkness.

Jean had taken to spending her time in the forest to watch the griffins. Their eggs were to hatch likely in the next several months, the longest that Jean had seen any incubation period as. Outside of the forest, she also spent many hours tending to two rakow kits — Icey and Grabby, as she eventually decided to call them— she had found abandoned in Blackrock. It was a huge change, especially in waking randomly through the night to feed them or to wash them, but she supposed it was practice for when she had her own child.

They were wonderful bundles of fluff and beak, and Jean realized just how much she enjoyed the little bodies cuddling into her as they grew larger.

She also found great amusement in the little bodies racing after her as she tended to various denizens of the fort, more so as the rakow batted at her ankles and tried to chew on her hair. It was a welcome change as the pregnancy progressed. Jean was exhausted most of the time, ready to deliver. Her body ached, her lungs burned, and it took everything she had just to stay on her feet.

She took a deep breath as she handed some nails to one of the carpenters. "Did Park say when Lord Maze was going to be back?"

"Um... I think he's supposed to be back within the next couple of days," he answered.

Jean crouched and lifted her satchel. "It'll be nice to see him. How often does he go on these excursions?"

"Every couple of months. Hasn't really done a long one since before you showed up." The man shrugged slightly and looked at Jean. "Why don't you go sit? You're flushed... more than usual."

"Hah, funny," Jean replied. She slipped away at that, though, and flopped beside the oak tree outside of the lord's quarter. It was rather quiet as she rested, a sunbeam on her face and a solid feeling of gratefulness. The child within her squirmed slightly and she chuckled. "Alright, alright..."

The sound of hooves and wheels creaking made Jean lift her head. She was groggy, making her realize that she had fallen asleep, and then pulled herself upright to see that Popcorn was driving his horse and wagon into the fort. He looked around, paused at he saw her, and waved. Jean couldn't help but wave back. After he had gotten the horse tended to, he beelined Jean.

Jean shifted slightly before she closed the distance. Popcorn wrapped his arms around her, and Jean, after a moment, returned the embrace. She pressed her face to his chest, listening to the arrhythmic beating of his heart, before she sighed. "Welcome home."

"It's good to be back," Popcorn answered. he smoothed her hair down gently and then pulled away. "How are you doing?"

His question made Jean shift again. "I'm doing alright, I guess."

"Are you sure? You're, what... 7 months, nearly?"

"Yeah, almost 7 months," Jean said. She offered a weak smile. "I can't believe it's been that long."

Popcorn's eyes softened. "It's getting hard, isn't it? The baby's heavy, and you're sore, aren't you?"

"You know an awful lot about pregnancy, don't you?"

He shrugged slightly. "Living in a village gave me a good amount of perspective, daito." He smiled a little at her. "Why don't I make you dinner, and I can tell you about everything."

Did she want to do that? Did she want to have dinner with him? Jean stared at him before she sighed and nodded. "That sounds nice, but I won't be able to do much to help."

"No, that's fine; I don't want your help to make dinner. I'll make dinner, you can rest," Popcorn replied. He lightly took Jean's hand and started leading her to the cottage, then he stopped. "Oh! I have something for you!"

He took off and Jean tilted her head. Then, he returned with a small bundle in his arms. "These were in the ruins I was exploring."

Jean took the package and pulled back the cloth. Nestled in her arms were two silver weapons, shaped like her boltcaster but with glowing blue orbs above the triggers. Etched into the handles were tiny, three-peaked mountains. She stared at them, chewing her lip in silence. "These are beautiful, but I won't have any use for them soon enough." The words caught in her throat as she continued to study them. She finally exhaled and offered a little smile. No, she'd use them. She wasn't sure how, but she would. This baby was a change, but, just maybe, there was a chance that she could continue to live and work in Fort Haven. With that thought, she glanced at Popcorn and gave a little smile. "Thank you."

"You're welcome. Let's get you inside and some dinner had."

Their conversation was quiet as they ate, and after dinner, Popcorn and Jean sat before the hearth. Popcorn absentmindedly rubbed one of Jean's legs, prompting her to sigh and close her eyes. Then, she murmured, "May I stay in Fort Haven after having the baby?"

Popcorn paused. "Why wouldn't I let you? You're your own woman, and I'd prefer my child close by than in Blackrock." Jean looked at him.

His eyebrow was quirked, and confusion was clear on his face. "It's a baby, that's all."

It certainly wasn't the answer Jean expected, but she was appeased all the same. With that, she closed her eyes again.

The week finished quickly, and soon the Long Night loomed before them. Preparations had been completed, and all was on course for the 36 hours of darkness. Food was stored, the shrine to Solaris was polished, and the fort had done what it could to fortify walls and palisades. Jean looked up as a horse whinnied in the distance, followed by a plethora of footsteps that sounded an alarm. Popcorn and Park followed her gaze before they started to the gate. Jean followed.

As they arrived, they were met by a man atop a mount, his armor and tabard well taken care of. An apple tree with red apples was emblazoned on his chest, his sword was hung on his hip, and he looked rather worried.

"Halt," Popcorn called. He limped forward, glanced back at Park and Jean before he jutted his head forward, and they joined his side.

The knight's charger pranced nervously as they approached, and Jean put a hand on Popcorn's shoulder as the charger moved towards him. Popcorn held himself upright, one eyebrow up. "Who are you, and what brings you here?"

"Captain Arthur Hornswoggle, sir. Member of the Riders of Apple Ridge, escorting a caravan of cider and additional knights. We're passing through to reach Blackrock for training. This said, I've come to request aid. One of our wagons broke a wheel several miles away. We won't have time to make it to the city, let alone here, if we don't have any assistance. If you have a carpenter, we're happy to pay for your services as well as serve here during the Long Night, given the pressing time."

Popcorn glanced at Jean and Park, both of which nodded. Jean folded her hands in front of herself, resting them on her belly gently, looked about the fort, and murmured, "We'll need to figure out who's going to go. They'll need to receive fair pay for doing this, and depending on the payment given, it could very well be a disagreement between carpenters."

She looked at Captain Hornswoggle, one eyebrow raised. "Will you be paying in coin or wares?"

"Wares— coin is tight for our travels, but we've got cider brewed in Apple Ridge that we're happy to part with."

Jean hummed quietly. Park leaned to Popcorn. "We could very well offer respite for caravans through here, if it's a hard cider. Our men would very much enjoy the wares."

"My thoughts exactly," Popcorn said lightly. "Fetch our carpenters, and we'll have them draw straws. That should make it less likely an argument of who stays and go."

Jean chuckled quietly. Anyone who learned that alcohol on the line, regardless of what type it was, would have happily accepted the task. Less of a problem provided was less of an issue for everyone involved. She shifted as the baby kicked, lightly caught herself on Popcorn's arm, and exhaled. He glanced at her, one eyebrow raised, and she shook her head at him.

Their wait wasn't long before the three fort carpenters arrived, and after a brief explanation, one ecstatically held out a short straw. He left with Captain Hornswoggle and they returned together, along with three large carts and 15 other people, shortly before sundown.

In the bustle of people arriving, Jean and Popcorn had managed to set aside some firewood for the caravan to use while they determined the best place for them to stay. There was a soft murmur of gratitude from each of the caravan members, and Jean was startled out of her thoughts as a redheaded woman approached. "We can't thank you enough for allowing us to rest during the Long Night here. We wouldn't have anywhere else to go and, quite frankly, I'd rather go anywhere but the forest." She laughed lightly and shook her head. "I'm Marin, by the way. Marin Lott of the Doves of Apple Ridge. It's a pleasure to meet you."

"It's very nice to meet you too, Marin. I'm Jean Cassy, leading wildlife expert here at Fort Haven." Jean shifted. She hadn't expected anyone in the caravan to interact with her but, as she looked around, the realization that Marin was the only woman in the caravan struck her. With that, Jean was sure that it was a sense of loneliness that made Marin approach her, and Marin likely assumed that Jean desired the interaction of another woman at this time.

"How far along are you?" Marin asked.

Jean's eyes flashed to her belly, and she offered a small smile. "Seven months. The baby is growing healthy and strong. I'll be happy for the Long Night to end and the stresses to fade before I deliver."

Marin smiled at her, nodded, and looked around. "That'd be ideal. Well, I should see to finding a place to stay tonight and the rest of the Long Night—"

"I could let you stay with me, if you'd like," Jean offered abruptly. She blinked slightly, surprised by her quick suggestion. "It wouldn't be bad to share a space with someone else during the Long Night."

"Are you sure? I don't want to intrude on you and your husband," Marin said, her eyes wide.

Jean shifted slightly. "I'm unmarried. Curseborns don't have luck in that department." She shrugged. "Regardless, you're welcome to stay in my cottage with me."

For a moment, Marin looked like she was going to decline. Then, she got a strange look on her face and then nodded. "I would like that, please."

The curseborn smiled at Marin before she started to her cottage in question. Each of the windows had been boarded up to prepare for the harrowing Long Night, and Jean gestured inside. "It's not much, but we can at least enjoy the Long Night from the safety of a home."

"It's just fine," Marin answered. She put her small rucksack down on the floor and looked around. "I'll happily take anything."

They chatted idly for a while before the sound of a horn blew. Jean's head shot up and she began to curse. "I'm so sorry, Marin, I need to run. The blessing of the ambers is taking place, and I'd really rather not become listed as an unfaithful." She scrambled to her feet, winced as a sharp pain shot through her belly, and then hurried out without another word.

She met Park and the other Solari workers beside the shrine of Solaris; Popcorn and the Kingsmen were notably absent. The entirety of the ceremony was an hour, just before the sun set. Jean held her amber necklace to the shrine, praying quietly that she and her unborn child would be able to see the light of the sun. Deep down, even though she knew it would happen again, Jean was afraid that the sunshine would not return. Perhaps they were too unfaithful, or the Kingsmen were too many, and Solaris would turn his back. Maybe, just maybe, there wasn't anything to expect after the Long Night set in.

Either way, with another pang in her belly, Jean started to her cottage. She met Popcorn halfway there, who lightly grasped her arms. "Stay inside, alright?"

"I'll be fine... we're not in Zanther, I can hold my own here."

"You say that, but now there's more than just you to keep safe," Popcorn said. He smiled slightly at her before his brows bunched. "Is everything alright?"

"I'm fine," Jean said. "It's just... stress, you know, from the Long Night setting in... worry about our home..." She offered a bit of a smile to him and shook her head. "Please, keep an eye out for any chitters that might be hiding. I'll see you when the sun rises, alright?"

"Of course." Popcorn hesitated for a moment before he embraced Jean. "Get some rest."

Jean held tightly to Popcorn for a moment, allowing her eyes to close before another pang struck her. This one was sharper than before, enough to knock her breath from her lungs. She inhaled deeply and then pulled away from Popcorn. His eyes were wide with worry. Before he could say anything, Jean murmured, "I'll be alright. I just need to rest."

She started back to her cottage, feeling his eyes around her all the while.

She and Marin chatted idly for a while before Jean shifted in discomfort again. She was having a hard time remaining comfortable, especially as the pains in her stomach grew more and more intense. Marin watched her, her lips twisted slightly. "Are you doing alright?"

"No... yes? I don't know. It's just some cramping is all; I haven't dealt with any yet with my pregnancy, but this is a lot." Jean exhaled slowly and leaned against the table. "I'm sure it's fine."

Her newfound friend came to her and put a hand on her back. "Can you talk through it?"

"Kinda... I need to stop and breath but... but they're getting stronger, and..." Jean trailed off, grit her teeth, and gave a shivering breath. "Marin, do you know what's happening?"

Marin frowned and nodded ever so slightly. "I think so, but I pray to HaMelech that I'm not correct. Now isn't the best time, and you certainly aren't ready."

"Aren't ready?"

"You're in labor, Jean," Marin murmured. "At very least, you're going into labor. I can see what I can do to stop it at least for now."

Jean stared at her, her blood running cold. Finally, she whispered, "Marin, I'm scared. Will the baby be alright?"

The other woman was quiet for a moment before she sighed and rubbed Jean's back. "I don't know. Right now, regardless of what happens, I need you to focus on breathing. I don't have any pain medication with me, and I wasn't prepared to deliver any babies while on leave." She laughed softly, but the sound was dry. "This certainly wasn't my expectation for the Long Night."

She guided Jean to the bedroom, where Jean clung to the bed frame, trying to steady herself against the waves of pain. Marin boiled water over the fire, speaking softly as she explained what to expect. Her words offered only a sliver of comfort as the pain intensified, each contraction crashing through Jean like a tide. Eventually, Jean stripped down and Marin draped a blanket over her. "You're doing great, Jean. You're shaking now, that's a sign of transition into active labor."

"H-how long has this been going?"

Marin brushed some hair from her face. "It's halfway through the Long Night. That doesn't matter right now, though, alright? You've been doing beautifully; this is the part that takes the longest. You're going to transition into active labor and then, once your body is ready, you'll start pushing. Don't rush this; it's alright. Do I need to get you anything?"

Jean swallowed, shook her head, and then hung it. After a moment, however, she whispered, "I-I want Popcorn here. I want Popcorn in here, please."

"Popcorn?"

"The man with the cane. I need him here, please."

Marin rubbed her back. "I'll see if I can find him, but with the Long Night, it might be harder than not."

The healer grabbed her cloak to go, checked on Jean one more time, and started to the door. Before she could, however, it burst open. A cacophony of sound rang from the outside world, chitters and battle cries, and the door was shut again. Popcorn had Park slung over his shoulder, his face pale. "He needs healing. The Eye of the Dragon caught up to him."

"Did he hurt someone?" Marin asked, hurriedly helping Park to a chair.

"No," Popcorn answered, his lip curled in disgust. "He drank himself into a stupor. He's just barely conscious, but the damn fool went through our liquor store. It was locked, and he had the key."

"Make him vomit— it'll clear his stomach. He'll need to sleep it off, I'm afraid... You're Popcorn, correct?"

"Yes.... I need to get back; there's some chitters—"

"No, there's a matter in here that requires your immediate attention," Marin interrupted.

Jean lifted her head again to watch before she groaned, which made Popcorn's attention snap to her. His face paled, his hands began to shake, and he limped to her side. Marin followed, though she was silent as she checked over Jean again.

"Daito, are you in labor?"

Jean nodded weakly and Popcorn, with a soft curse, pulled her close. She clung to him, and he began to sway her, his hands tight on her hips. It helped relieve some of the pain, and Jean pressed her forehead to his chest. "I've got you, daito. I'm here, I've got you."

By the time Marin gently said it was time to push, Jean was spent. She leaned into Popcorn, her eyes half closed, and he held her up. Park was sleeping in the other room, the smell of vomit strong while still others came in to have wounds bandaged. Jean spent several long hours pushing, enough that Marin quietly asked Popcorn to ready additional hot water and find her a sharpened knife if it continued any longer. Finally, Jean gave a cry.

Popcorn held her tightly and then helped her lay down, stroking her hair. "You did it, Jean, you've done it. You're done, you're alright."

The room was oddly silent. Jean caught her breath, clinging to Popcorn as he continued to whisper to her.

Even though she wasn't familiar with childbirth, she knew there was something wrong. It was a feeling deep in her gut, one that struck only once before in her life as she was caught out in the Long Night. She stared up at Popcorn, and then whispered, "The baby?"

"Marin has him, Jean, she has him." Popcorn brushed her hair from her face again before he stiffened slightly. Jean watched as his face went from worried, to angry, to grief-stricken to numb.

"Baba?"

Popcorn didn't answer, and Jean lightly shook him. "Baba?"

Marin approached then, a tiny, wrapped bundle in her hands. The silence was deafening now, especially as Marin whispered, "I'm so sorry, Jean. I'm so, so sorry."

Jean took the bundle from Marin and looked down. The baby's eyes were closed, his little body curled as though he was still within Jean's womb. There was no breath, there was no life, and as Jean stared, willing for him to move in even the slightest, tears began to streak down her face. "He's just asleep. He's... he's just asleep." She held the baby tighter, her body beginning to shake. "Please... please, wake up. Please!"

"Jean—"

"Do something Marin, please," Jean begged amid her tears. "Please, do something!"

"Jean, I can't," Marin whispered. Jean stared at Marin, just barely able to see the dove through her tears. "His time was called before he entered the world. Sometimes it happens and... I'm so sorry, Jean."

The curseborn stared at the baby again, and then she looked at Popcorn. He was staring at them, his hands clenched in his lap. Jean willed him to say something, anything, instead of sitting in silence. His shoulders shivered, and, finally, he murmured, "I'm sorry, daito. I'm so, so sorry."

His hurt words made Jean break down again, and she turned into his side to hide her face as she sobbed once more.

As soon as the Long Night was over, Jean and Popcorn stood together over a small grave. Jean held tightly to the man, who had his arm wrapped around the curseborn. He was shaking again, but she wasn't sure if he had ever stopped. It almost hurt how tightly he had a hold of her, but in that moment, all Jean felt was numbness and a cold sense of knowing. Behind them, Park and other members of the fort waited for them. Jean sniffed and whispered, "I'm going to go lay down."

"You should at least bathe, help yourself feel better," Popcorn murmured. "There was a lot of blood—"

"I don't want to bathe. I don't want food, either. Just... please, leave me." Jean pulled away from him and slowly plodded to her cottage. She laid down, stared at the wall, and closed her eyes to ignore the shadows creeping around her and beckoning her into them.

AUGUR

J ean stared at the wall.

It'd been three days since she delivered, and regardless of how many times people asked her to eat, she declined. Marin decided to stay in Fort Haven to watch her, especially as she was doing so poorly. Popcorn, too, stayed in Jean's cottage in an attempt to offer solidarity. Still, Jean didn't speak and didn't move.

Her body hurt, though it didn't hurt nearly as much as her heart. Even the rakow kits, as they curled against her with soft whines, brought nothing about.

Popcorn gently rubbed Jean's back, his voice quiet. "It's not your fault, Jean. I hope you know that none of this is your fault."

"I did something to cause him to die," Jean whispered back. "Solaris gave me a dead child for something I did."

"Solaris is nothing but a name that someone gave to the sun, daito. It had nothing to do with this, and you did nothing to cause it." Popcorn brushed some of her hair out of her face. Finally, after a moment, he whispered, "What did you want to name him?"

"He's buried; a name will do nothing."

"No, that's not true. He's still our son, whether or not he has breath in his lungs. My people,

we name all children. Even if they do not join our tribe in life, we still honor them in death. I want to name our son." Popcorn whispered. He rubbed Jean's back again, murmuring to her in Ivumi.

Jean, at his quiet words, began to sob.

Truly, she didn't believe him. He didn't understand this pain; he didn't carry the baby for seven months only to hold a lifeless body. He didn't know what it was like to feel the baby kick, or twist or anything like that. Anger bubbled in Jean's veins, and she finally gave a gut-wrenching, voice-breaking scream. Popcorn jumped at the noise before he pulled Jean tightly into his arms.

She continued to cry, Popcorn held her, and she let out another sob. He pressed her face to his chest, humming and whispering in Ivumi as he rocked her. "It's alright, daito... Irinmo no sunab..."

Though Jean didn't know what he was saying, the faintest trace of comfort filled her. Osmond bounced around the room before he, too, settled beside Jean. The rakow clambered onto the bed, as though knowing that Jean was going through this yet again, and she sucked in a breath. "I don't know if I can do it... I don't know if I can name him..."

"Sh, you can think about it. It's alright," Popcorn mumbled.

As Jean kept her head against Popcorn's chest, she could hear his heart skipping beats and slowing down again. It scared her, even more so after losing the baby. Jean squeezed her eyes shut and shivered. "It isn't alright."

"... I know." Popcorn stroked her hair and sighed softly.

After several minutes, Popcorn reached across Jean and pulled out her hairbrush. He began to brush her tangled locks, mindful of her horns, and Jean shut her eyes.

The shadows were growing wild again, and she whispered, "I want it to stop."

"I can stop, that's fine—"

"No... not you. The shadows."

Popcorn paused, briefly, and looked at her. "What do you mean?"

Jean exhaled.

There wasn't anything left to live for, was there? Jean shifted slightly and pulled her gloves off. The black scars and tendrils from touching the shaman's staff were seared into her skin as a silent testimony of her condition, one that she had been ever-so-careful to avoid people seeing. Now, as she laid there, she hoped Popcorn saw it.

She hoped that he killed her, whether out of mercy or fear, to free her from this misery. Once more, Jean shut her eyes and sighed.

Popcorn's brushing stopped again, and he slowly lifted her hand. Then, he muttered, "You summoned the shaman that night, didn't you?"

"They just show up. I don't summon anything, they just show up." Jean kept her eyes closed. Even without watching him, she could hear his breath hitch as he seemingly realized what that meant. The woman sighed. "It's getting worse... and I just want it to stop. I hate this, and I hate feeling so incredibly... like nothing."

Popcorn shifted beside her and then he stood up. Jean squeezed her eyes slightly to prepare herself for a blow, but it never came. Instead, a blanket laid over her shoulders and then Popcorn limped out.

So, he was going to get the rest of the fort on board.

Jean sighed, allowed her body to relax against the bed, and merely waited.

Eventually, Popcorn's uneven steps and cane entered. It was just him, barely enough to rouse Jean from her numb state.

"Get up, daito."

Another sigh left the curseborn and she did as Popcorn said. She kept the blanket over her mostly bare body, looked at him, and stepped forward. "Public execution, then?"

"No. A bath. I need you to snap out of this, at least enough to have a will to live. I've got a fort to run and I need you to help me do so. Come on, the tub has been set up by the fire." Popcorn gently supported Jean's arm and walked her to the other room.

All the while, Jean tried to wrap her head around why he was doing this and not culling her for her chittering madness. It was dangerous to keep her around, he might as well remove the problem while he could. The thought made the shadows swirl around her before Popcorn lifted her into the hot bath.

In an instant, everything in Jean's mind vanished. She sighed and let her eyes shut. The rakow kits jumped against the wooden bathtub. Jean peeked one eye open to see what was going on in time to receive two very sad sets of eyes staring at her. She sighed, lifted them, and perched each one on a knee. Popcorn sat beside her and began to wash her hair, shockingly silent.

Jean didn't dare look at him. Instead, she focused on the kits who were watching her. They didn't seem to be much for kits anymore, though, as their fuzzy fur had fallen out and they were as sleek as sleek was. Jean scratched under their beaks and sighed. Finally, she asked, "Why are you washing me instead of executing me? I have chittering madness."

"I have a bad leg and a heart that's failing," Popcorn replied. "You're not special in the case of diagnoses." He scrubbed her scalp vigorously, splatting soap about the water in front of Jean and into the hissing fire. One of the rakow on Jean's legs batted curiously at the foam before it chattered at Jean and hopped into the water between her legs.

The curseborn cursed and lurched forward, surprising herself with her quick movement, before she caught the sopping wet kit. It mewled pitifully, its feathers soaked, and she sighed. "Silly thing..."

"I missed this side of you," Popcorn commented softly.

Jean looked at him, surprised to see the small smile on his face. She sighed and looked away. "I don't know why."

Popcorn poured some water over her curls, paused, and murmured, "Because you are my diato. Even if we aren't anything more than friends— friends who make mistakes together— you're still my diato." He began to wash her hair a second time, this time more gently, and rinsed it once more.

"You shouldn't care; not with me having chittering madness and being curseborn."

"I do care, regardless of those things," Popcorn said patiently. He shifted slightly and lifted the rakows from Jean's knees. They made plaintive sounds at him and then curled up beside the fire to groom, working tirelessly to preen their feathers. Jean watched them quietly, her head against the side of the wash basin.

Neither she nor Popcorn spoke, nor did they talk after Popcorn helped her from the cooling water, wrapped her in a towel, and then helped her back to bed.

Finally, after he made her drink some bone broth, she whispered, "I liked the name Ashur."

"Ashur... I like it," Popcorn mumbled back.

Marin had returned to tend to her at that time, and she looked up at the curseborn with a soft, sad smile. "I think that's a perfect name for him, Jean," she said softly. "I can ask one of the carpenters to make a second headstone, one with his name, if you'd like." Jean nodded and the dove healer returned to checking her over. Eventually, the redhead said, "I'll be heading to Blackrock tomorrow, if you think you'll be alright without me here. Physically, you're doing great. The herbs I gave you helped dry your milk supply, and the poultices will continue to aid in the swelling and tenderness. As for everything else..." Marin trailed off and shook her head. "I'm sorry to say but only time can heal those wounds for either of you. I pray to HaMelech that comfort comes, and that you can lean on each other during this time." She shifted, sighed, and then took Jean's hands. "Can I pray for you now, before I retire for the night?"

Jean shifted.

No one had ever offered to pray for her before, and part of her was afraid to accept. Popcorn seemed strangely detached, but when Jean gave a small nod, he lowered his head and stared at his boots.

Marin rested her head against Jean's, her voice cracking as she whispered, "HaMelech, You are the ultimate source of comfort. You know all of our pains, You've experienced them Yourself.... from the first stone that was thrown, to the final battle against the Black Dragon, You've encountered grief, heartbreak, and agony in ways we could never understand... and now, my King, I ask that You spread Your incomparable peace over Jean and Lord Maze during this time of pain. Keep them near, and show them who You are. You love them dearly and want nothing more than to show them that love... and so I ask that their hearts soften as You hold them gingerly in Your hands. Thank you for Jean's smooth delivery, for people here who can help her during this process. Thank you for the moments she and

Lord Maze had with their son, Ashur, before You fully claimed him to join Your embrace. Thank you that he was warm, and safe, and loved the entire time... and thank you for allowing me to have attended Jean during this painful transition."

The words faded from Jean's hearing as she cried quietly, the overwhelming heartbreak welling up again. When Marin said, "amen", she pulled Jean into a tight hug. The younger woman sobbed into her chest, and Marin stroked her hair. "If you would like, my friend has experienced this far more than I could ever imagine. I can ask her for advice and bring you back a letter when I head back to Apple Ridge, if you'd like."

"I guess..."

"She suffered much before she delivered Caxton, her son," Marin murmured.

Jean sniffled and looked at Marin. As much as she wanted to ask, her voice was stuck in her throat. Instead, she simply nodded and then laid down as Marin left. Popcorn climbed into the bed behind her and held her, absentmindedly stroking her stomach, as she fell asleep.

After a week of recovery, Jean ventured out of her cottage. The rakow kits stayed close to her heels, only ever wandering away to get to Popcorn, and the cockatrices seemed to know that something was different, too. The fort was somber. It felt like a cloud had fallen over them as Jean wandered through the courtyard, even more so as the shadows dipped and danced around her. In the back of her mind, she could hear the soft whispers of the staff, pleading with her to let it enter her grasp. Each time she turned to find it; however, she discovered that she was alone.

Osmond trailed after her for most of the day. She didn't know if he was trying to offer some small measure of hope or courage, but she didn't question it. Once again, she ate her lunch seated beside Ashur's grave.

It had been beautifully decorated with some rocks and the small headstone, displaying 'Ashur Cassy'. Jean and Popcorn had decided it best that he didn't take the Maze name; it would result in too many rumors, and neither Jean nor Popcorn cared to deal with that. Jean brushed her fingers over the daffodils that had begun to spring up, her voice soft. "You would have enjoyed the spring, my dear... the animals wake from their slumbers, and they begin to have... have..." she trailed off, wiped her cheeks, and sighed.

Perhaps speaking to her aunt would be a good idea? If she truly did know loss like Marin said, maybe there was a semblance of comfort that could come? Still, Jean didn't want to bring this up. They were Kingsmen; she was lucky Marin had stayed after learning that Jean was unmarried.

The woman slowly plodded through the fort and into her cottage again. This time, she sat in front of the fire and quietly sketched one of the rakow kits.

It was then that the door burst open and Popcorn, limping quickly, beelined for the fire. "Get a blanket."

"Get a blanket?" Jean stumbled to her feet and did what he said, despite her confusion. Popcorn gingerly opened his satchel as Jean held the blanket for him and, in a moment, she had a football sized egg in her arms. She blinked at it, sunk in front of the fire, and then looked at Popcorn. "Where...?"

"The nest is empty, griffin pair A," Popcorn explained. He put his hand on the egg and then shooed Jean closer to the fire. "All of the eggs were hatched out except this one. It was still warm when I got to it, so they moved on within the last couple of hours— the female probably wanted to get her chicks going and didn't care to wait for this one."

Jean blinked again and pressed her ear to the egg. Inside, she could hear the faintest sounds of chirps and movement. She tightened her grip on the egg a little more. "It's still alive. What are we going to do with a great horned griffin, Popcorn?" The woman shifted, ever so slightly, and whispered, "What if I kill it? Did you think any of this through?"

"I did, which is why I need you to be a good mama griffin and keep the egg warm." Popcorn began to wrap her in a second blanket, tucking her securely and then feeling the griffin egg. "This is an experiment, and it most certainly won't be your fault if it doesn't make it; nature is cruel, and attempting to turn fate is something that not many are successful in. I think, though, that after the success with the rakow—" He glanced at the pudgy, fat griffins curled in their basket by the fire. "— I think you'll do just fine with a griffin chick."

Jean looked at the egg and then at Popcorn.

A million questions, fears, and whispers flooded her. The shadows grew darker, even as Osmond lazily lifted himself from the book he had been sleeping on, and Jean sucked in a breath. Popcorn looked around and slowly crouched beside Jean.

Then, he murmured, "You are a resilient woman, daito. Even in the midst of all of this pain, you've stayed resilient. I know you can do it."

Jean finally gave a sniffle and Popcorn sat down completely, rubbing her back as he pulled her close.

Relegated on griffin duty, Jean spent the next two days beside the fire, stoking it as she turned the egg from time to time and listened for any noise. Finally, at the turn of the evening, Jean lifted her head from her journal to see that the egg was shaking, and a small crack had become noticeable. Popcorn, who had taken to staying with Jean during this time, was chopping vegetables for their stew when Jean, suddenly, said, "It's hatching!"

She laid on her belly in front of the egg as she watched the crack slowly expand and a small piece of shell popped off. Jean lifted the piece, her eyes wide. It was a thick piece of shell; far thicker than any other egg she'd seen. Watching the little beak poke out of the hole, gasping for air, the reality of how cruel nature could be set in.

If this chick didn't survive hatching, it wouldn't have survived a life as brutal as the great horned griffin population did.

Popcorn's hand rested on her back, and they sat, silently. Minutes turned to hours. Popcorn eventually returned to chopping vegetables, and Jean, unable to pull herself from watching the egg, whispered, "Come on, you can do it." She carefully stabilized the egg, doing her best to remain positive.

She couldn't help it hatch. This was the way for the population to be strong. None of the cockatrices ever opened their hatching eggs, and she was sure that the rakows didn't have aid, either.

After a little while, Popcorn returned. He sat beside her, stroking her hair as his gaze lingered on the egg. "If it doesn't hatch by noon tomorrow, I need you to be prepared for the reality of what's happened."

"It will make it out by noon," Jean said firmly, her voice shaking. "It will hatch in time... I know it."

"You can't help it, daito. This will make it stronger," Popcorn murmured.

Jean looked up at him, trying to keep from crying. Instead of speaking, however, she turned away from him and stared at the egg again.

She remained awake the entire evening, trying to coax the hatching griffin from its shell. Every so often, it'd give her a soft cheep before struggling in the shell again. Jean allowed herself to touch its beak as it poked through again, a surge of warmth spreading through her at the gentle smoothness and the little noises that the chick made. Every fiber of her being wanted to help it hatch, but she refrained from doing it. Popcorn's arm, slung across her hips, a stark but gentle reminder of why she couldn't do anything, and so she obeyed.

Morning came and the chick still hadn't made a hole large enough to hatch. Popcorn's face had set into a firm frown and Jean, looking between him and the egg, finally murmured, "It's exhausted, Popcorn. It can't keep doing this. The shell is too thick, and there is something wrong. Shouldn't it have pushed through by now?"

"... the piece of loose shell simply hasn't been pushed off enough," Popcorn said. He looked at Jean. "You can carefully remove it but be aware it might have dried to the chick by now."

Jean's fingers shook as she received the permission. With her breath held, she carefully held the egg in one hand and peeled the piece of shell away from the egg just as the beak pushed through. This time, a damp, downy head appeared. Two eyes were squeezed shut and, as the chick realized it was free, it began to wiggle to get one paw out.

The sight made Jean's breath catch in her throat. An overwhelming urge to protect this fragile life surged through her, especially when she saw that its second paw was not fully formed. The chick whimpered, half-tumbling from its shell, and Jean instinctively reached out and lifted it.

Popcorn didn't argue, nor did he reprimand her as he got a towel and began to dry the chick off. Jean, meanwhile, struggled with her blouse. Griffins had feathers and fur to warm their chicks— she had neither.

Instead, she placed the chick on her chest as Popcorn rubbed it vigorously. The chick nuzzled into her, cheeping weakly, before it fell silent.

Grim determination settled over Popcorn's face and Jean looked at him. "It's alive, right?"

No response.

"Baba, the chick is still breathing, isn't it?"

"I don't know, Jean," Popcorn finally snapped. "I'm trying to get it to breathe again, alright?"

Jean stared at him, her eyes wide. He hung his head, sighed, and shook it. "I'm sorry, I'm just... I'm stressed. Give me a moment, please."

Neither of them spoke as they waited. Eventually, Popcorn sighed. "Jean, I think we need to ease its suffering; I don't know if it'll make it through the night."

The woman stared at him, looked at the chick, and back at him. As she did, the griffin on her chest shivered ever so slightly; it was still alive, albeit cold and weak. With that in mind, Jean pulled a blanket over them and shook her head. "No. No, it will make it through the night."

"Jean—"

"Don't you even think about taking it, Baba Maze," Jean interrupted. She swallowed. "I lost our son. I lost our son, and I still feel guilty for it all. This chick may not be a child, it most certainly won't take the place of Ashur but... but if there's even a chance to nurture something, to try and heal those wounds and the pain I feel from losing our boy, then please, don't take it from me. Please, please don't."

She watched as his eyes grew glassy with tears. The staros man mumbled under his breath, far too quiet to be heard, before he sighed. "Alright... fine. We'll see if it makes it through the night."

"Thank you." Jean whispered.

They were silent a majority of the day, as Jean whispered to the chick in an attempt to coax it into growing stronger, before night fell. Jean woke once to see that Osmond had taken his place beside the chick, shedding a soothing light over the little body. With that gentle, calming reminder, Jean stroked the small chick's feathers and fell asleep once more.

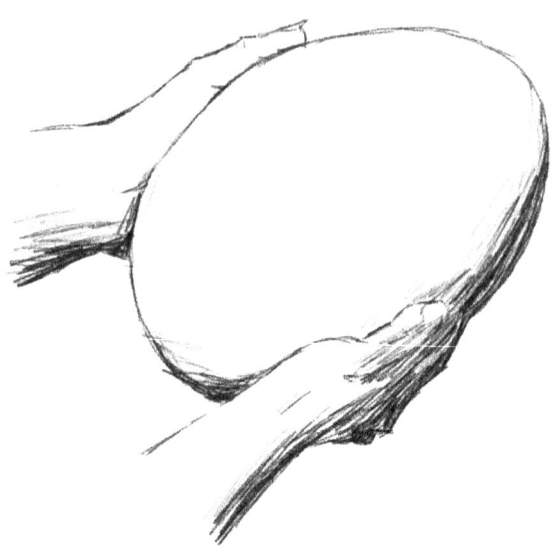

The egg is rather large and requires constant heat. Both parents would provide, which means we are going to have to be present for imprinting in order to ensure that the chick recognizes us as family.

Chicks are sopping wet for three hours, even after toweling dry. Claws are sheathed and the chick, while eyes are open, tends to gravitate towards warmth.

Great-Horned Griffin Hatchling

After three days, Augur seems to want to walk. Is this sooner for chicks who have all limbs?

Finely chopped meat seems to suffice for a newly hatched chick.

Downy feathers start disappearing at 5 days, making way for the awkward phase.

THE LIGHTCASTERS

J ean awoke to a weak chirping on her chest where the tiny griffin, who had been quiet the majority of the night, was struggling to stand. Its eyes had opened ever so slightly to peer around it, revealing beautiful blue eyes that Jean assumed would eventually become amber like the adult griffins she had spent so long watching.

Beside her, Popcorn shifted, and Jean shushed the griffin.

"I know... hang on, let me find some meat for you."

She struggled to her feet, holding the cat-sized chick, and slowly plodded to the door. Outside, around the corner, was the root cellar that they stored a majority of the fresh vegetables and curing meats. Opening the door, Jean crawled down the roughhewn stairs and, with a yawn, rummaged through the dried meat storage. She found a small piece of jerky that had been dried and returned to the cottage. There, Popcorn had groggily sat up and was looking for her. "Where were you?"

"Getting him some breakfast. We'll need to see if there's any way to increase our mouse and rat population— as cute as I think they are, we're going to have to feed this little guy and show him how to hunt," Jean said softly. She gently lifted the griffin and placed him on Popcorn's bare chest.

It startled the staros man but, as he held the griffin, his tense shoulders relaxed, and he offered a bit of a smile. "That's fair; I can speak to the carpenters about making a dedicated 'grain spill' area to try and encourage the vermin population. So long as we keep our stores locked tightly, we should be fine."

The griffin on his chest began to mewl and squirm, lifting his head to search for Jean through bleary eyes. The sight tugged at her heart, and she quickly hurried to the counter to grab the jerky, slicing it into smaller pieces.

When she did, she carefully offered pieces to the chick's open mouth, watching with awe as the creature swallowed it down and continued to mewl for more.

"He has an appetite," Popcorn mused. "Stark difference from yesterday."

"He slept and regained his energy... thank Solaris, as I was worried he wouldn't make it."

Jean watched the griffin, her face turning sour as she said the name of Solaris. Why she thanked him, she didn't know. He took her son from her and cursed her with nothing more than heartbreak and a horrid appearance. Solaris didn't care enough for her to let her have a little beast to nurture as a means for healing her heart... and she didn't expect HaMelech to do that for her, either. He, after all, was a usurper and didn't care for anyone who didn't follow Him.

She was pulled from her thoughts as Popcorn handed her the chick. "I'll go get the 'grain spill' going, and we'll hopefully have some mice for our new friend," he said. He started to the door and then paused; his eyes soft. "Are you going to be okay? I haven't really left you since Ashur..."

Jean looked down, stared at the chick, and shrugged. "I won't do anything while I have this griffin to watch. Someone needs to raise it and keep the rakow out of trouble."

Popcorn chuckled, ran a hand through her hair, and pressed his forehead to hers. It was an odd feeling, but Jean allowed herself to close her eyes and lean into his touch with a sigh. Finally, Popcorn pulled away. "Why don't you get some fresh air? You've been stuck inside for a while."

"I went outside before you found the egg," Jean countered.

"Yes... but I know that you've been visiting Ashur each day, just as I have... and I know that you haven't been able to since the egg showed up." Popcorn gave her a sad smile. "I'll go with you, if you want."

Jean shifted. "Are you sure? It may be too cold for the chick."

"I think he'll be alright." Popcorn took Jean's hand. "Are you not wanting to go?"

Is that what she was trying to do? Stall?

She wasn't entirely sure, but it made her uncomfortable to think of an answer all the way. Maybe she was wrong in trying to give excuses, or maybe it was simply worry that Popcorn would judge her for crying still. He had remained as stoic as ever with his pain, a sudden loneliness that echoed amid her grief. Finally, Jean sighed. "I don't know if I can grieve with you there."

"You don't think..." Popcorn trailed off. "Daito, I want to grieve with you. He's my son, too."

"You don't grieve like I do, and you just... you don't get it. You didn't carry that baby for as long as I did only to see him dead." Jean's lips tightened and she swallowed. "You can walk away from this without caring if you really want to."

"But I don't, daito."

"You should," Jean snapped. The griffin shifted in her grasp, and she looked at the ceiling. The two rakow lifted their heads and watched her, chirping quizzically as she searched for words. "You can walk away from this and forget it happened."

"Daito—"

"You rejected me once, why don't you just do it again? I killed our son—"

"It wasn't you!" Popcorn shouted.

Jean flinched as she stared at him. His eyes were wide, his hands clenched on his cane, and his breathing was beginning to labor, just as it did any time he grew upset. "Jean, it wasn't your fault! I can't believe you managed to carry him as long as you did!"

"What... do you mean?" Jean asked softly.

The man gritted his teeth, muttering in Ivumi. Jean could catch some of the curses he used when he was truly angry and, as he did so, she stepped away to avoid any rage directed towards her. Finally, he mumbled, "I rejected you as soon as I realized you could be pregnant. My children, regardless of anything I try, don't live long... if they even make it to birth." Jean's mouth went dry at his admittance, and she blinked as he shook his head. "I was hoping that you wouldn't be pregnant, that you wouldn't have to deal with the heartbreak if something happened and... I was hoping that you'd lose the pregnancy early if you were with child. It's not your fault."

"You... let me carry Ashur without telling me any of this, Popcorn," Jean whispered. The fear boiled into heartbreak, and the anger, as she shouted, "You could have spared me from this pain, you selfish man!"

Her comment made Popcorn's head jerk back, putting only the slightest bit of satisfaction in her, before it faded and an odd sense of remorse filled her.

He was trying to grieve, too.

"Fine, you're right. I was selfish, and I was hoping that you'd be alright... that I'd be alright," Popcorn mumbled. He didn't look at her as he rubbed his temple. "Look, I'm going to go and sit with Ashur for a little bit. You're welcome to join me if you really want to." He turned from her and Jean frowned.

"You should have said something."

"I should have, and I didn't. Go ahead, hate me for it," Popcorn replied. He began to limp towards the door. "I messed up, and I hurt you... again."

"You're walking away from a problem you caused."

"I am." Popcorn opened the door. "I'm walking away because I know how this ends, Jean."

Indignant heat flooded Jean, and she stuttered for a moment before she growled. "You don't know anything. I'm coming with you."

She could have sworn Popcorn smirked as she hurried after him, wrapped tightly in her cloak as she carried the griffin chick. The beast in question looked around, chirped softly, and then snuggled into Jean again.

The walk to Ashur's grave was short, and Jean sunk down in front of it as she always did. Those raw emotions flooded her once more and she bit back tears as she stared at the headstone yet again. Popcorn placed a hand on her shoulder and sat beside her, where she eventually rested her head on his chest, and they sat silently. Finally, Jean murmured, "Do you think he would have liked griffins?"

"I think he would have loved them," Popcorn replied quietly. "I think he would have taken after you and loved all manner of wildlife."

Jean offered a weak smile and looked down at the griffin. He had fallen asleep, prompting her to mumble, "Do you think that this griffin is some sort of second chance?"

"No, but I think he's a means for you to heal." Popcorn stroked Jean's hair and sighed.

"I don't know if I'm willing to try carrying again, for anyone," Jean mumbled after a long while. "I'm too scared to think of what might happen."

"As far as I know, daito, I'm the only person you've had a relationship with," Popcorn answered. "I'm not planning on this happening again."

The silence grew between them as they sat. It was only when the griffin chick began to whine for food did they leave Ashur's plot to feed the little creature. Jean watched it struggle with the mouse, her voice thoughtful, "I think Augur is a good name."

"Augur?"

"He's a sign of change... though I'm not sure what sort," Jean answered. "It is a he, right?"

Popcorn chuckled and lifted the griffin. The content chirps changed to rather ferocious growls as Popcorn turned it this way and that, gave a soft grunt as the beast bit his finger, and then sat it down. "Healthy male."

"You're bleeding! Do I need to get a tourniquet?" Jean asked, her eyes wide.

She barely remembered the events of her griffin attack, but knowing the dangers of the venom made her sick to her stomach as Popcorn staunched his wound with a cloth. He shook his head slightly. "No, I think we're good. It's clotting already, which only proves that these guys develop that venom later in life." With that, he crouched and waved a finger in front of Augur. "Feisty fellow, isn't he?"

Jean nodded, smiling slightly. The griffin certainly was doing better than when he had hatched, especially being only 24 hours later. In fact, as Popcorn looked at Augur again, the chick began to growl and snap toward him once more. The staros laughed, scratched under Augur's chin, and went back to cooking.

A couple of weeks later, after Augur had begun to follow Jean unsteadily through the fort, Popcorn approached her. He gently rested a hand on her shoulder, one eyebrow raised. "Do you want to get out of the fort for a couple of hours with me?"

"And do what?" Jean asked, brushing her hands off on her apron and began to hang it up. "I don't want leave Augur without someone keeping an eye on him. He's been prone to getting into trouble as of late, and has been very interested in the cockatrices." She looked at the griffin chick as his tail twitched, his eyes half-closed in the sunbeam he laid in.

Popcorn smiled a little and crouched to stroke Augur's back. He clacked his beak at the man, but settled as Popcorn said, "I already spoke to Park. While he wasn't happy with the idea, he did agree to watch Augur while we step out. As for what we'd be doing, I know you haven't had time to use those new weapons I got you. I saw them on the mantel earlier; it's been a while since you've practiced your aim."

Jean smiled ever so slightly.

It had been a while, and she missed going to the forest to shoot. With all of the stress of losing Ashur, hatching a chick, and general life, she had all but forgotten the joy of spending time in the woods. As she thought about it, Jean realized that Popcorn had already produced the box of weapons. They shone, tantalizingly so, and finally Jean shook her head with a little smile. "Alright, you've convinced me."

"Excellent!" Popcorn beamed at her and then paused. "Are you going to wear your gloves while we're out there?"

Again, Jean had forgotten about her gloves. He didn't say much about them unless he realized she had taken them off, and then it was a quiet reassurance that he didn't mind seeing the scars and dark tendrils that ran up the length of her arms. She shifted. "Probably not, once we're alone. I don't want to skew the accuracy of my shot while first figuring them out, but I'll probably start putting them on as we go."

Popcorn nodded and gathered Augur, who chirped indignantly. "Alright, I'll meet you by the gate then, alright?"

Jean watched him go before she gathered the weapons and her cloak. Then, as she waited for Popcorn to return, she looked around at the blossomed spring foliage and the budding trees. In the trees above her, especially the oaks that waited for their leaves to unfurl, she could see acorn gremlins scurrying about the branches. Their long tails curled around the branches to keep them from falling, just large enough for her to see the movement, and she couldn't help but wonder if they liked the dead oak in the courtyard as well.

If they were active, the nettle mice and humming badgers should be, too.

She was startled from her thoughts as something touched her leg, and she looked down at the two rakow cubs. They were nearly fully-grown, pudgy things that stretched up to grasp at her tunic's hem. Jean crouched and began to rough them up, eliciting croaks and caws as they batted at her hand and gnawed on her hand with their black beaks. Jean laughed, flipping one, and then paused.

Would her son have enjoyed playing with the rakow?

One of the cubs batted her hand to pull her from her thoughts again and Jean, more subdued, pet their coarse fur. Then, as Popcorn approached, she stood and wiped the tears from her face.

"You ready?"

"Mhm, lead on."

They walked from the fort and to a clearing, not too terribly far from where Lyman had attempted to take advantage of Jean. She could feel her body stiffen slightly as she approached, and she paused and looked at Popcorn. "How much farther?"

"Just here, I found a spot where there's a log available to shoot," Popcorn said. He frowned. "Is everything okay?"

"I don't want to go much further."

Popcorn's eyebrow raised but he didn't press. Instead, he held Jean's gloves as she carefully took them off and then pulled the weapons from their box. Her skin instantly prickled, the keen feeling of something bigger than her interacting with her frame, and she swallowed. "You didn't steal these from a Kingsman, right?"

"No, I found these while on the job," Popcorn answered. "Don't know how to use them, don't know who last used them. What I do know is that they were in a ruin filled with relics from the First Age. Their owner is long dead."

Jean hummed, lifted one towards the wood in question, and pulled the trigger. There was only a soft click, and Jean frowned. "They might be broken."

"Give me a go?"

The curseborn handed it to him, watched as he mimicked her actions, and shook his head as there was, again, just a click.

"Sorry, Jean, I thought they'd work. They're in great condition."

Jean took them back and shrugged. "They look like a great accessory, at least." Teasingly, she lifted the weapon towards the sky and held the trigger down. "It's an intimidation factor, at least."

A humming caught her attention and Jean's eyes flashed to the weapon. The blue orb at the back had begun to glow, as did two twin helixes that sat above the barrel. Realizing that it was armed, Jean pointed it at the stump and released the trigger.

In an instant, Popcorn lunged and pulled her to the ground as the blue energy raced towards the log. Jean hit the ground, and Popcorn sheltered her as the log shattered in an explosion of splinters, making the woman press her face to his chest as he grunted in annoyance. As she laid there, she could hear the arrhythmic beating of his heart once more before it stopped.

Popcorn went limp over her and Jean, struggling, rolled him over. "Baba? Baba?"

He didn't answer, his eyes wide and his lips slightly parted. Jean stared at him before she hurriedly gave a scream for help and then began to do chest compressions.

It didn't take long for her to get some movement from the man, and he grasped her wrist. Sickness flooded her being and she did her best to keep from puking. Popcorn sucked in a breath. "Stop... it hurts..."

"Your heart—"

"It's fine... I just... It was too much, that's all..." Popcorn clung to her wrist and Jean, after a moment, pulled him to her chest in an embrace. His breathing remained shaking, and she stroked his hair, the reality of what happened suddenly sinking in.

She could have just witnessed him die.

"I'm fine, daito... how did the weapons work?" Popcorn whispered.

Jean looked at the stump, nodded, and whispered, "It's decimated... holding the trigger down must make it stronger."

"Nice," Popcorn said. He coughed and Jean held him a little tighter. "We should probably head back. I'm sorry... I know you wanted to be out longer—"

"No, Baba, your heart stopped. I don't know what you did to keep from... to keep.... but I need you to rest, please."

She helped him stand, he clung shakily to his cane, and the two slowly started to the fort once more. As they walked, Jean looked through the trees. A sharp sense of being watched crept over her again, more malicious this time than when she had first lifted the lightcasters. Her hand slowly found one, her gaze scanning the surroundings until it landed on a rabbit.

The shadows were beginning to consume it, revealing the long teeth and black eyes. Jean lifted her lightcaster and held the trigger down, briefly, to fire a bolt of light at it. There was a gut-wrenching scream from the creature, and Popcorn frowned. "Jean, that was a rabbit."

"I..." She trailed off, the shadows concealing the still form just in front of them.

"You thought it was a chitter, didn't you?"

Jean nodded mutely and Popcorn squeezed her, ever so slightly, as they walked. "It happens, I suppose."

They continued to walk, and as the shadows swirled around them, Jean caught sight of several more rabbits. She swallowed and lifted her chin.

She wasn't willing to shoot another rabbit again, as they really were just minding their business.

It wasn't until one let out a chittering laugh that Jean realized it wasn't true, and she hurriedly lifted her lightcaster in an attempt to defend herself. The first beam shot the chitter, prompting Jean to hold tighter to Popcorn, and the two broke into a run. Jean shot behind her where she could, though her attention was more on her friend. He clung to his cane, limping beside her, before he swung it in an arch and struck a laughing chitterling that had jumped at them. The demons came out of the woods in a torrent, forcing them to a stop where they pressed back-to-back in an attempt to defend their blind spots before more footsteps joined the fray.

Jean aimed one of her lightcasters at a large brute of a chitter that had approached, but the weapon didn't fire. "Damn it!" she cursed. The second did the same, and she threw them to the ground to retrieve her boltcaster before realizing that the brute was fading into a mercenary from the fort. Then, the other large chitters did the same.

As the mercenaries flooded the area, firing their boltcasters at chitters and slicing through them with swords, Jean found herself in Popcorn's arms again. He pressed her face to his chest, and she closed her eyes. Then, in an instant, it was over.

The group slowly moved into the fort, where Jean helped to her cottage to rest. She sighed, sat on the edge of the bed, and whispered, "I thought you died."

"It'd take a lot more to kill me, daito," Popcorn laughed weakly.

Jean nodded ever so slightly, sighed, and then slowly laid down beside the man. Popcorn's eyes widened but he wrapped his arms around her all the same. Jean sighed and closed her eyes. "I... I keep thinking about Ashur."

Popcorn sighed and pressed his face into her hair. "I know... I do too."

"I could have done something... and now, I'm moving on and I feel so guilty..." Jean trailed off as Popcorn pressed a gently kiss to her forehead. "I'm so sorry I lost our boy. I nearly lost you, too... it frightened me. It'd be all my fault."

"There's no fault, Jean," Popcorn whispered. "It wasn't your fault."

Jean nodded before she stiffened. "I... I dropped my lightcasters. I didn't pick them back up."

"In the forest?"

Jean nodded, the guilt overwhelming her as she began to cry. Popcorn sighed and rubbed her back. "I'll find them later, daito, calm down."

When she woke up, Popcorn was gone. He returned with Augur, placed the chick on the bed beside her, and shook his head. "I couldn't find them, daito. Someone might have picked them up. Why don't you go wash your face and take the rest of the day, hm?"

Per his suggestion, Jean quietly stood and went to the wash basin. As she splashed cool water onto her face, the slightest shine of scars on her wrist caught her attention. They were situated directly between the black tendrils on her left forearm, two little diamonds that hadn't been there before. She ran her fingers over them, frowning, before she hummed.

She wasn't sure where they had come from, but they certainly were interesting. The longer she focused on them, though, the sooner she realized that something was shimmering, almost manifesting in her hand. Jean tilted her head, focused on whatever it was, and soon held a lightcaster in her hand.

She dropped it in her shock, watched it disappear, and then, with a shaking hand, focused on the weapon once more.

Again, it appeared in her hand.

Whatever these Kingsmen weapons really were, they were certainly more than she had assumed.

Fully automatic hand boltcaster

It takes roughly 2 seconds for the bolt caster to reload.

The Kinetic stone is good for about 10 reloads on a full charge.

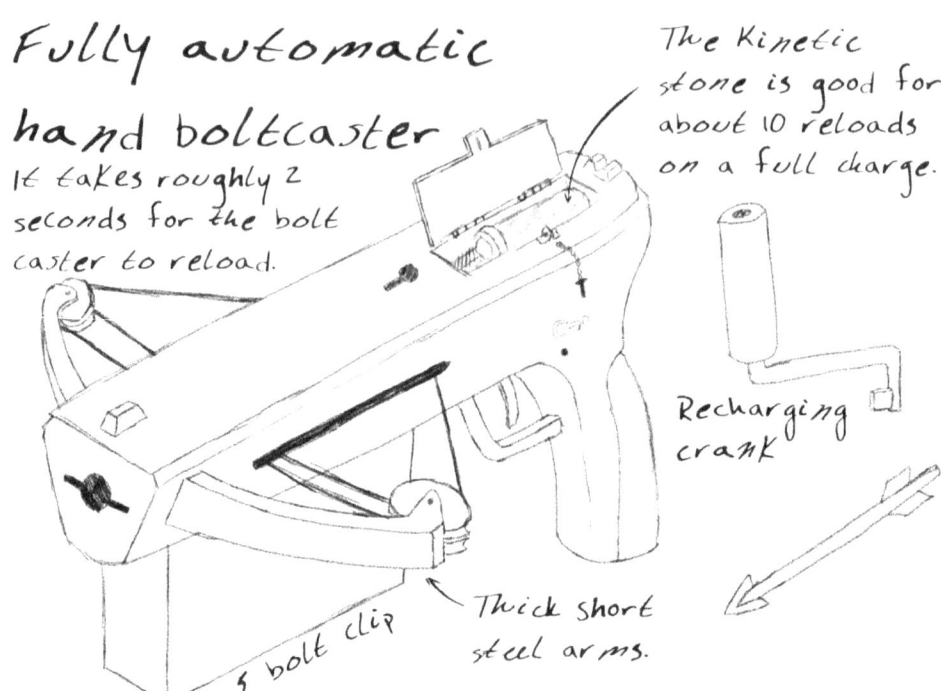

Recharging crank

Thick short steel arms.

5 bolt clip

Crystals, or Kinetic stones, are at the center of modern technology. Each crystal can store many times the potential energy of their predecessor the steel spring. This energy is released relatively slowly but at a constant force.

About 2/3 of all Kinetic stones are exported by the city nation of Ashuran.

The charging process involves rapidly applying concussive force to one end while applying a constant compressive force to the other end.

Hitting the crystal temporarily disrupts its structure, preventing it from expanding and allowing it to gain potential energy.

A fully charged crystal is as little as half the length of an uncharged crystal. As it charges, the crystal grows darker and more opaque.

Hard Light Weapons

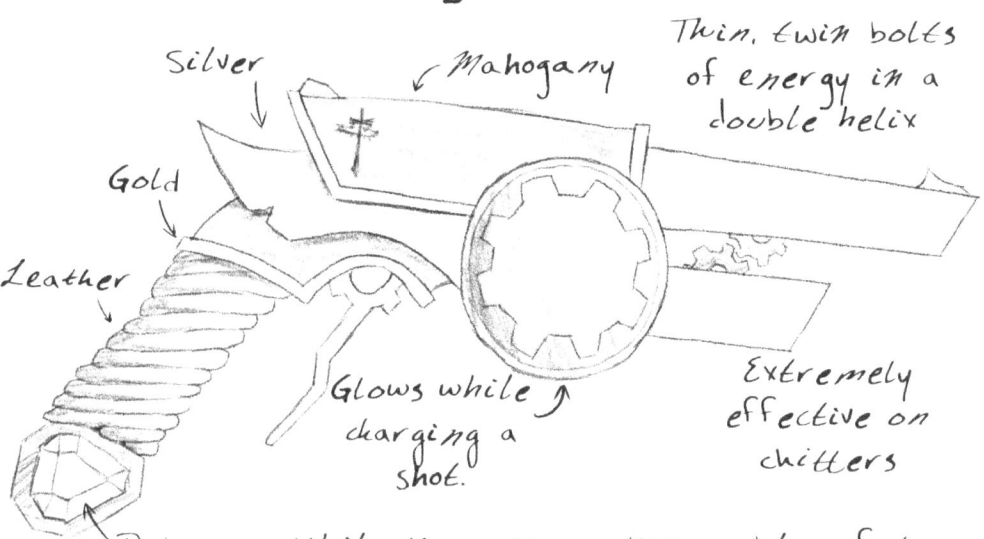

Silver

Mahogany

Thin, twin bolts
of energy in a
double helix

Gold

Leather

Glows while ↗
charging a
shot.

Extremely
effective on
chitters

Ruby

While there is no discernable safety,
the trigger does not activate the
weapon if the wielder isn't
intentional in firing, is Popcorn, or if
it is 'accidentally dropped' onto the
arm of a chair.

Hardlight Weapons and Kingsmen

Hardlight weapons are standard issue
for Kingsmen military orders.
Weapons are duller than a butter knife until
wielded by a Knight, in which the edge glows gold
and becomes razor sharp.
Apparently, these weapons seem to have a mind
of their own, as they may refuse to work
depending on the wielder's intent.

SIX YEARS STANDING

The longer Jean interacted with Popcorn after his heart attack, the more she couldn't shake the feeling that she had forgiven him for rejecting her before. She didn't like it, nor did she like the desire to be with him whenever he was available and open to it. Augur seemed to notice this change as he followed her on his unsteady legs, chirping at the curseborn and then bounding towards Popcorn. Even the rakow cubs, who didn't care too much for the staros man, seemed to prefer his company over any other worker in the fort.

Preparations for summer were well underway once Jean paid attention to them.

The cockatrices were to be moved into a large aviary before the fall, if possible, and the fort was working on expanding a garden patch inside the courtyard. Jean had protested that she was no good with plants, but Park insisted that she'd do better than any of them.

Everyone was pulling more weight than usual, if only to get things moving forward before the weather inevitably turned. Jean still returned to Ashur's grave to eat her lunch there, silent as she stared at the marker and wondered what could have happened. As the days went on, however, she found that the visits became more like a reunion with an old friend, bittersweet and full of hope, rather than the bitterness that she had felt for so long.

Miss Tamrin's crew returned to the fort after the Long Night as well. The workers at Fort Haven certainly were depraved, as Jean had only a moment to embrace Ingrid, who had been sending her letters, before the cote was whisked away. It wasn't until the next morning that Jean saw her friend again.

After she had carefully pulled away from Popcorn, who had taken to sleeping beside her after an onslaught of nightmares— which he refused to discuss, though Jean was beginning to understand the Ivumi he whispered beside her— and made herself a cup of tea, she sat beside Ashur's grave to watch the fog slowly lift. There was some lingering darkness around her, too, but as Osmond bounced from plant to plant and then rested above her knee, Jean sighed and simply focused on her thoughts.

"Early morning, even for you," Ingrid said gently. Jean glanced at the dalmatian cote, not too surprised to see that Ingrid had donned her mantle and was covered in the spotted fur to keep warm. The brothel worker had a faint smile on her face, though it faded when she saw the marker Jean was sitting beside. "Is this where...?"

"Yeah," Jean murmured. She scooted over for Ingrid, who sat, and sighed. "Usually Popcorn joins me, but he's sleeping in today; his nightmares are getting worse."

"So, are you two together, then?" Ingrid asked.

"No, we aren't." Jean sipped her tea and shook her head. "I just know that he's sleeping better with someone beside him. Those nightmares... I can't shake how awful they must be. He woke up crying last week, but he didn't want to talk about it. I don't know what it was but..." She trailed off before she offered a weak smile. "Enough about our issues. How are you? The men seem to enjoy you and the others being back."

Her friend laughed and nodded. "It's good to be back, really. I'll be honest, though you mustn't say a word to Park or Boss Man; we take full advantage over their lack of companions here. It pays the bills and keeps mouths fed, but I do feel ever so slightly guilty."

"You, guilty?" Jean asked, one eyebrow raised. "I would never have imagined it."

They shared a chuckle together before Jean's gaze returned to the grave marker. Ingrid lightly nudged her. "You're doing good, Jean. Grief is an awful thing, but you're doing a good job working through it."

"I don't believe you."

"You've grieved alone, you've allowed Boss Man to grieve with you, and you're slowly recovering," Ingrid murmured. "That's a feat in itself."

Jean didn't answer her and instead focused on her tea. Maybe she was recovering too well. It wasn't something that you just get over, and she didn't want to just get over it, but she really wasn't sure. Eventually, she finished her drink and stood. Ingrid joined her, and they walked arm and arm through the fort.

"Things seem to be busier than usual," Jean mused softly. "Is there something going on that I haven't heard about?"

"The only thing I can think of is the six-year anniversary of Fort Haven starting," Ingrid replied. She shrugged. "I guess Boss Man didn't celebrate five years, which would have made more sense to me, so maybe it's going to be a big one this year?"

"Maybe?"

They wandered aimlessly before Jefferson, from the caravan, whistled for Ingrid. "Time to go!"

"We'll be back next week," Ingrid said, giving Jean a tight hug. "Stay out of trouble, won't you?"

"Absolutely no promises," Jean answered.

She watched her friend run off and then climb into the caravan, holding herself as she turned and began her daily tasks.

By the time noon came around, the entire fort had gathered for a meeting. Jean settled herself between Popcorn and Park, the later pulling out his flask and offering it to Jean.

She'd noticed he'd been drinking more lately, especially after Popcorn had informed him of the ashura in Blackrock. Unfortunately, the alcohol poisoning during the Long Night did nothing to lessen his bad habit, and Jean lightly shook her head to decline the offer to indulge. She saw what it did to him; bloodshot eyes, a trembling hand, and a general air of not liking people. Park shrugged at her, downed the contents of his flask, and then stood up. He gave a slight sway, held one hand up, and cleared his throat. "Alright, alright, settle down!"

There was a soft hush over the assembly, punctuated by the pops of the fire as it roasted that evening's boar.

"As many of you have noticed, if you're perceptive enough to care, we're getting ready for our six-year anniversary. Lord Maze has decided it's been long enough, and you've worked diligently enough, to warrant a celebration." Park went to take another drink of his brandy and paused, a sour look on his face as he realized it was empty.

One of the men across the fire chuckled. "You mean we've dealt with you long enough!"

Park grumbled at him and the company laughed. It was only when Popcorn tapped the base of his cane on the ground twice did, they become quiet, and Park nodded at Popcorn before he continued.

Jean tuned out at that point. Really, there wasn't much expected of her beyond making sure the cockatrices didn't escape while the guard was down. As she watched the fire, Popcorn gently nudged her.

"Hey, after the celebration, next month, I'm planning on heading towards Apple Ridge for some field work."

Jean raised an eyebrow. "Field work by Apple Ridge? What are you going to be studying?"

Popcorn smiled slightly. "Palgraves, have you heard of them?"

As Jean shook her head, he murmured, "They're sort of like rakow. Squirrel chimera, if you will." He watched Park speak for a moment, a mischievous smile on his lips before he looked at Jean again. "I wouldn't normally offer for anyone to come with me, but I think you'd enjoy getting out of the fort and into the woods for a bit. There's a lot of memories here, and I know I like to be relieved of them from time to time. Besides, this is a good chance for you to return to field studies and observation."

"Will you be alright traveling with your leg and heart?" Jean asked.

The staros chuckled, rolled his eyes, and then nodded. "Of course I will be, daito. Remember, it takes more than that to kill a staros." He stared at her for a moment, his green eyes searching her face, and Jean couldn't help but stare back. Then, abruptly, she turned away from him to look at Park as the foreman continued to speak.

She didn't like how that made her feel. It was far too close to making her grow closer to Popcorn, allowing herself to forget everything that had ever happened between them. She refused to release that betrayal he had caused; it was keeping her safe, something that wouldn't come if she moved anywhere near the man. In that instant, she began to question the validity of a trip to study palgraves, regardless of where it was. It would be just the two of them, after all, and she couldn't risk loosing whatever boundary she still had up. As she sat beside him, though, his presence began to overwhelm her with warmth, and she sighed.

It wouldn't hurt, would it? Really?

As though he had read her mind, Popcorn's hand lightly brushed over hers as they sat. It started with his fingers lightly touching hers, and then his hand covered hers, and he gave it a light squeeze before he removed it. Jean's gaze snapped to him again and, as she met his eyes, he gave the smallest smile.

The meeting concluded quickly, and the workers separated to go towards their respective duties.

Popcorn stood, leaning heavily on his cane, and Park turned to look at them. "Don't think I couldn't tell that you two weren't paying attention."

"Whatever do you mean?" Popcorn asked, the smirk slipping over his face again.

Park's face fell flat, the sheer epitome of annoyance and no cares left. He looked at Jean, and then Popcorn, and back at Jean. "If you're going to make my life harder, at least be upfront about it."

"Nothing to bother the fort, Park," Jean reassured. Popcorn stepped behind her and she swallowed, consciously keeping from turning to look at him. There was something palpable there, more than she realized after he had spent so many evenings with her in her cottage. "Popcorn was simply discussing the idea of going to look for palgraves."

"Palgraves? Aren't those a good distance away?"

"Apple Ridge," Popcorn said. He shrugged. "I think it'd be a good trip to take, and get some work done as well."

The foreman sighed, rubbed his forehead, and shook his head. "I suppose that wouldn't cause any issues. When are you heading out?"

"In about a month. We'll need time to chart our trip, just in case we don't return on time, and will want to get some rations figured out beforehand as well," Popcorn said. "Besides, I'd like to be here for the festivities... no expenses spared, alright? We still have some of that cider from Apple Ridge, yes?"

"Yes. I'll make sure things are prepared and I'll let you know if there's anything more that I need," Park said. He looked between them again. "Is everything alright?"

Jean shifted.

No, it wasn't, as she was suddenly having second thoughts about Popcorn. However, outside of that, they were fine. She sighed and nodded slightly. "Why wouldn't it be?"

"The two of you are acting differently... differently than even after..." Park trailed off as Popcorn lightly wrapped an arm around Jean. She looked away from the foreman at the mention of Ashur, and Park murmured, "I'm sorry, I just want to be sure that the leadership team won't be destroyed by anything."

"It's alright, Park," Jean murmured. She offered him a little smile. "We're doing alright, just figuring out life now."

"The nightmares are bad," Popcorn added. "I've taken to needing some tea and companionship through the night."

"I see... just keep the companionship minimal, alright? The fort was a mess during your fight."

Jean's face grew hot, and she looked away from him. Popcorn muttered something under his breath, far too quiet for her to hear, and she gently pulled away from him to start to the cottage. "Was there anything in particular that i needed to do for the celebration?" she asked after a moment, turning to look at them.

Park sighed and shook his head. "Just keep doing what you're doing, Miss Cassy. If you would be so kind as to determine the best method for removing cockatrices in order to place them elsewhere, especially in avoiding damage to their feathers, we can take that."

Jean gave one short nod before she hurried off. All the while, she could feel Popcorn's gaze following her, and she did her best to ignore it.

She couldn't understand why he was suddenly interested in her. It wasn't as if he'd ever shown any signs of desiring her before, and now, it seemed constant. Jean shook her head to herself and began tidying around the cockatrices. Augur was sleeping beneath the rickety bench she'd put her apron on, and as she approached, he opened one amber eye and then yawned.

"You're feeling rather lazy today, aren't you?" Jean asked, scratching behind his ear tuft.

The griffin gave a yawn and rolled over, exposing his soft underbelly. Jean chuckled and rubbed it. "You know, I'd expect your adult venom to come in any day, now. We're going to want to figure out the best way to counter that before it happens; the last thing we need is to send someone's family a final pay. We should probably figure out a better way to deal with the cockatrice venom and poison, too." She glanced at the pen, studying the litter of petrified frogs and mice that had made their unfortunate way into the run.

Augur chirped at her and began to preen her hand, making Jean laugh. She sat down and continued to rough the chick up, all the while watching his beak to keep from losing a finger.

Eventually, the griffin stood up, preened furiously for a moment, and then hobbled away. Jean couldn't help but smile as he did so, and she returned to her activities shortly afterwards. All the while, she was running through potentials of countering the anticoagulate in great horned griffin venom. It was a high potential, especially in having cockatrice venom at her disposal, that she could use as well.

Jean was so hyper focused on the idea of an antivenom that she didn't realize the day had passed until Popcorn placed a hand on her shoulder. It startled her into knocking her various parchments and quills to the ground, and she narrowly missed the inkpot in her fright.

Popcorn raised his free hand in defense. "I didn't realize you were so lost in thought."

"No... yes." Jean began to gather her documents and waved a couple in the air to dry the ink faster. "I had a realization; we're going to need something to counter Augur's venom when it comes in."

"Do you have an idea on how to do so?" Popcorn sunk into his chair, leaning on his cane with a raised eyebrow. "We don't have many resources to spare, and if we attempt to outsource to Blackrock, they're going to need something solid to work with."

"That's the thing!" Jean rummaged through her documents. "Lots of things in nature have some method of countering it. Charcoal expels most poisons, snake antivenom is made with the venom itself. I don't think there's any way to reverse the venom using itself but—" She lifted a parchment and nearly thrust it into Popcorn's face. "Cockatrice venom has a slowing agent." Popcorn took the page as Jean stood, beginning to pace. "If the cockatrice venom slows and eventually paralyzes, it stands to reason that we could, if we isolate the compounds, use it to counteract the great horned griffin venom. I mean, they're the same family of chimera too; you went on and on about it several weeks ago, and..." She trailed off, realizing that Popcorn was beginning to stare at her. "What?"

"Your mind is amazing," Popcorn said simply. Jean blushed and tucked some hair behind her ear. "I'll see about sending a sample of cockatrice venom to Blackrock. I don't know if they'd be any help, but as they've developed some cures for snake bites... it's a small chance, but one none the less."

"When do you think they'd have an answer?"

"Hopefully before we leave for palgraves." Popcorn handed her the parchment back and crossed his legs. "We'll be going in about a month and a half, due to supply limits Park just informed me of, and the celebration will be this week. Perhaps we could attempt some experiments of our own, too."

Jean paused. That didn't sound ethical, but it certainly couldn't hurt. Popcorn had his blood magic, after all, and she remembered that he was able to counter the large amount of griffin venom she had delt with. A little bit of a bite wouldn't do much harm to a person, which meant the blood magic to be used wouldn't be much, either.

"Let's see if they can isolate whatever it is that helps, and we can start small on mice." Jean finally decided.

Popcorn grinned at her. The smile made Jean's heart flutter, and she turned away before he could see that she was beginning to blush again. There were bigger things to focus on, and how he made her feel certainly wasn't one of them.

Over the build up to the six-year anniversary, Jean found herself spending more time with Popcorn than she had previously expected. They worked closely together, attempting to figure out when Augur's venom would come in and, when that didn't work, braving an adult great horned griffin to collect venom. Popcorn hadn't liked the idea, but Jean was sure that the griffin's saliva, regardless of whether it was attacking prey, would contain the anticoagulate. She herself wasn't entirely positive as to how she managed to approach a great horned griffin and get a small glass bottle of the spit, but when she returned to Popcorn's pale face and shaking hands, she could only give him a grin.

Eventually, the day of the celebration arrived and, with it, a successful experiment; one of the mice injected with a drop of great horned griffin spit experienced normal clotting when a drop of cockatrice venom was placed in the wound.

The two researchers very nearly flung their precious experiment from the table as they jumped up and down in their glee, and Jean stared up at Popcorn with a grin as he held tightly to her. Then, realizing how close they were, Jean pulled away and hurriedly gave an excuse to leave.

The workers from Miss Tamrin's Gilded Cage had arrived early— Ingrid explained that Park and Popcorn had paid an exorbitant amount for their services to last longer— and Jean was more than happy to help them get situated in a spare cottage until they left. Then, amid the bustle, Jean settled under the dead oak tree and watched the workers get makeshift tables, chairs, a stage, and dancing area together. Two boars roasted above the fire, cider was laid out, and Miss Tamrin's group was already entertaining with revelry and song. Jean smiled slightly at the change of pace, punctuated by Park pulling out a fife, and leaned against the tree.

This was a welcome difference from every other day.

As night drew near, and the festivities only grew, Ingrid joined her with a tankard of cider each and a plate. "You certainly look out of place over here, among the nettle mice," she teased as she sat.

"I don't dance, and it seems as though that's the only option now," Jean laughed. She took the cider and drank it, the bitter alcohol stinging her lips and throat. "Why don't you go find a partner?"

"The only one left is Boss Man and, frankly, I think he has eyes on only one partner at this time," the brothel worker replied.

True to her friend's words, Jean found that Popcorn, who was beside the bonfire, was chatting idly as he watched her. He didn't seem to notice that she was staring at him in return, which only brought slight comfort to Jean. She shook her head. "He's been acting strange recently: wanting to spend more time together, resting his hand on my knee, holding me while we sleep... Ingrid, you don't think..."

"I think you need to have a drink and lighten up, Jean," Ingrid replied bluntly. She sipped her cider. "Just keep your head about you and you'll be fine. No harm has ever come from dancing. Aren't you supposed to be the adventurous type, anyway?"

"Ingrid," Jean scolded. "That doesn't apply here."

"Mhm, of course it doesn't. Come on, you need to join the fun."

Jean gave a half-hearted protest as the cote pulled her to her feet and to the fire, where the two began to dance together. Every so often, Jean took a drink of cider to keep her courage up, especially as she realized that Ingrid was moving them closer to Popcorn. Then, without warning, Ingrid disappeared and Jean found herself in front of Popcorn. She flushed as he grinned at her, obviously in a stupor from good drink and food. "Ingrid left."

"I know, she tricked me into dancing and then slipped away," Jean lamented, flopping onto the log beside Popcorn. She took another drink of her cider, swayed slightly, and leaned against the man. "She even pulled me away from the oak tree to do so."

"The nerve," Popcorn replied with a laugh.

The two laughed together for a moment before Jean, unsteadily, took his hand. "Alright, I'm over here and the courage from drinking will only last so long. Dance with me."

"I'm no good—" Popcorn stumbled after her, laughing as he managed to remain upright.

The bonfire was surrounded by a chaotic tangle of bodies, laughter ringing out as they stumbled over each other through the night. Jean knew her mind was slipping, but she didn't care; the warmth of the fire, the drinks, and Popcorn chased away the demons lurking in the shadows. Even their whispers were silenced as Popcorn, as gently as he could, pulled her closer.

It was well after midnight when the festivities died down.

Her mind was far from tethered to reality as she and Popcorn struggled into her cottage and collapsed on the bed. Jean stared up at Popcorn, her gaze unfocused. "I love you."

"Love's a strong word, daito," Popcorn slurred back. He crawled onto the bed beside her. "I wouldn't use it lightly." His thumb absentmindedly traced her lip and Jean giggled as she wrapped her arms around his neck. "But don't tell Park... I love you too."

"It's a secret," Jean breathed.

21

SUCESSES

J ean groaned as she rolled over, pulling away from Popcorn's naked body, and blinked. Her head ached, her memory was fuzzy, and she wasn't entirely sure of what happened that night. Then, as she pulled the covers over herself, the sudden realization of her state, and the state of the staros man behind her, made her fly from the bed in shock. It was then that the blinding headache struck, and Jean staggered towards her wardrobe to get dressed before she found her canteen and drank.

She didn't remember anything after Ingrid got her to the bonfire.

Without another moment to lose, Jean hurried from the cottage and to the courtyard. The fort was eerily quiet aside from snores that trailed from the cottages from time to time. She had no doubt that everyone was nursing rather nasty hangovers, especially as she saw Park stumbling from the lord's quarters, gave her a half-hearted wave, and then turned around to return to the darkness.

As Jean did her best to recall anything that had happened, she could feel her heart was beginning to race. They had to have had slept together, which meant there was a chance of conceiving again. She tapped her fingers nervously against her leg as she scribbled a note down beside the cockatrice pen, her handwriting a barely readable scrawl as she did so. If she got pregnant, it was going to end poorly again... but she couldn't tell Popcorn. He'd already been through enough with her, and there was no say in how he'd react to another pregnancy so soon after losing Ashur. Her stomach knotted and she lowered her gaze.

She could see the shadows were beginning to spin again, bringing an eerie fog around the courtyard. Out of the corner of her eye, she could see the blasted staff was manifesting once more, whispering to her that it could fix her problems.

A chitterling tentatively pushed one paw through the darkness and retreated, quickly, when a dapple of sunlight touched its fur. The staff hissed in annoyance, its sound growing sharper as Jean spotted Osmond, who had been resting near the chimeras' water dish, start to move toward her. Jean tried to ignore it, but the hissing grew louder with each passing second. Finally, without thinking, she stormed toward the shadowy corner where it was hiding. Osmond raced after her, bounding in front of her as though trying to dissuade her, but it was too late; she thrust her face into the face of the shaman holding the staff. "What do you want from me? Why won't you leave me alone?"

It stared at her, a raw laughter rising in its decaying throat. Then, it slowly held the ebony staff towards her.

"Take it...." it hissed, its dark eyes staring into Jean's soul. "One.... of us...."

In her annoyance, and ignorance, Jean reached towards the staff. If she could break it, maybe the damned thing would leave her alone.

Her hand was unable to close around the wood as she suddenly found herself holding one of the lightcasters. It was fully charged and went off without her approval, striking the shaman and staff deftly as though it had a mind of its own.

There wasn't time for the shaman to scream, either, as it went up in a cloud of smoke and the staff, no longer held, disintegrated before Jean's eyes. As quickly as it had happened, the lightcaster was gone and Jean was staring at nothing but shadows. Her eyes were wide and, as she stared, she finally swallowed past the lump in her throat. Osmond bounced in front of her slightly, almost as though he was scolding her, before he circled the shadow and then returned to the water dish. Jean ran a hand through her hair, wincing as she brushed her hand over her horns, and then shook her head.

That was more than she wanted to think about.

The woman turned and returned to her tasks, trying, again, to think things through and remember what happened. As hard as she did, there weren't any thoughts entering her mind and, eventually, she gave up.

It was around noon when Jean finally saw others emerge from their homes. They were quiet, reserved, and many held their heads as the sunlight reached their eyes. Jean chuckled weakly, though that expounded on her headache. Then, she turned to see that Popcorn was coming towards her. The confused look on his face told her everything she needed to know, and she shifted in preparation as he approached.

"Jean... I need to know... I woke up, exposed, this morning—"

"You got so incredibly drunk that you said it was too hot, and you stripped down," Jean said, managing to keep her voice smooth. He didn't know they slept together. She was going to have a stillborn again, or miscarry, and she could manage that alone. It wasn't ideal, but he didn't need to deal with that pain again. Jean brushed her hands off on her pants. "I figured that the best thing was to tuck you in and find somewhere else to sleep."

Popcorn nodded as though he was thinking through her words before he sighed. "Good. I won't lie, I was worried that we might have..." He trailed off. "Not that I'd be opposed, of course, but... you weren't on birth control before, and I don't know if you are now. When I woke up alone, I wasn't sure if you had stayed with me or not."

"No, I didn't." The curseborn shifted as she lied. "I'm finishing up chores, and then I think we need to keep working on the great horned griffin antivenom. Augur is starting to get less friendly when he plays and, while I'm trying to correct the behavior, it's more than I want to test right now."

Her employer nodded again, offered a smile, and started back to the cottage. "I'll meet you inside, then, and we can get to work on that. Oh, and Park is beginning to request supplies for our trip to see palgraves. I hope you don't mind."

"Not at all." Jean watched him go before she released a breath she was holding. That was incredibly close, more than she wished to admit. He trusted her blindly, though, and that was something she hadn't expected. Solaris help her, she was going to be reborn as a curseborn again for lying to him, wasn't she? Jean sighed, stared at the sun, and closed her eyes.

She certainly couldn't win on any front, could she? Between her bad karma already, and losing her son, there was no chance of something better than being a curseborn if she even had a chance for that fate, now. As though answering her thoughts, a chill ran through her spine. She was worthless at this point, and there was no chance of redemption now.

Jean shook her head, pulled her curls out of her face and tied them back, and set to work once more.

When she joined Popcorn in working on the antivenom, she found that he was less pressured to be near her. Yes, he continued to lean into her space, lightly touched her shoulder or hand, but it seemed different now. In a way, Jean missed it. On the other hand, however, she felt like there was far less pressure towards any sort of physicality with him.

The weeks passed before Jean realized it. They spent more time focused on the antivenom once they received a report from Blackrock's Temple of HaMelech, where the doves were able to give some basic information about the cockatrice venom. Jean's theory was correct, both based on the experiments and the report. The true test, however, was when Park rushed to them. "Augur nipped me, and I'm still bleeding— he got carried away while I was roughhousing with him."

Jean glanced out of the cottage door to see Augur, who was now nearly the size of a pony, laying down with his head on his paw. Popcorn wasted no time in grabbing a tourniquet to tie Park's arm off. "Well, daito, it's time to be sure this works!"

"Are you sure it's safe?" Park asked. He was rapidly going pale, his pants soaked with blood from even the small wound as Popcorn tightened the tourniquet.

"As safe as it can be, compared to bleeding out," Jean retorted. She grabbed one of the small glass bottles of antivenom and paused, holding it over Park's bleeding hand. "It might sting, Park."

"Noted," the foreman said.

Jean placed several drops of the antivenom into his wound, watching it anxiously. As it mixed with Park's blood, there was a near instant clotting effect. Then, Jean dropped a little closer to the joint. "It should be entering your blood stream to counter...."

Park grimaced. "It feels horrible."

"I'm sure it does," Jean murmured. "Keep the tourniquet on, Popcorn. I'm not sure what'll happen if the antivenom travels throughout his blood stream, but we should have caught the majority of the venom in order to neutralize it."

"I'm your first test subject, aren't I?"

"No... well, yes, if you don't count mice," Jean admitted. Park frowned and she shook her head. "It's got to be the safest option around, otherwise Popcorn will be using his blood magic, and that, from experience, is a miserable happening." Park shrugged and slowly wiggled his fingers. Jean watched intently as the clot remained, beginning to scab over nicely in the handful of minutes that Park sat there. Eventually, Popcorn released the tourniquet and closed his eyes. The hair on Jean's neck began to prickle as she realized he was performing blood magic, and it subsided as he gave an approving nod.

"Nothing made its way to his heart, from what I can tell; it's still beating as strongly as it was before, and if the wound clotted, I'd dare say that keeping the tourniquet guaranteed that the antivenom did its job in the immediate area of the wound. I think it worked."

"Think?" Jean questioned. "It did! We did it, Baba!"

She ignored Park's eye roll as she embraced the baron, pulled away, and inspected Park's hand again. "We can start placing these around the fort as emergency stations, and keep vials with each worker who leaves for milling. It's not a problem to be too safe, and... I can't believe it!"

"I can... now, can I return to work? I feel like I'm some sort of experiment still," Park interrupted. He pulled his hand away from Jean and rubbed it lightly. "Are there bandages I can use?"

"Yes, yes... I'll start getting things together for those stations..." Jean began to pace, her mind racing as she listed off places she would want the antivenom. All the while, she could feel Popcorn's eyes on her as she talked, and a little smile crossed her face.

It was a rush to get the emergency stations set up, especially as Jean spent as much time as she could ensuring that the antivenom was strong enough to counter Augur's venom as it grew more potent.

Eventually, the supplies for Jean and Popcorn's expedition arrived and they carefully prepared for a month-long trip. A majority of their packs were filled with quills, ink, and parchment, but there was still room for rations, weapons, water, and, of course, Jean's tea. Jean was slightly overwhelmed with the idea of leaving Augur without her; this was the first stint of time that she wasn't in the fort with the griffin, even though she was sure he was more than fine, but it still worried her. The rakow were more self-sufficient as they understood how to hunt for grubs and nettle mice, but Augur hadn't had that chance yet. Still, Popcorn assured her that it would be fine.

When the two left, after giving Park careful instructions for caring for Augur, the rakow— who insisted on climbing into Jean's pack as she attempted to remove one and replace it with supplies— and the cockatrice, Jean could only take a deep breath of the pine scented air. It'd been a while since she'd traveled, and her legs were already beginning to protest. Of course, that was all the more reason for her to push harder. There were a handful of times that Jean and Popcorn stopped to rest, especially as Popcorn's limp grew heavier or his breathing grew worse. Eventually, during one of their stops for Popcorn's heart to rest, Jean ventured a question.

"Baba... are the heart attacks normal?"

"I thought I'd answered you before?" Popcorn asked, one eyebrow raised. "Why do you ask?"

Jean shifted. "It's just something new. People don't have that many heart issues and survive and—"

"And you wanted to know if you need to expect more?" Popcorn finished. She nodded, and he looked at the trees above for a moment. "They're normal for me, a price for the blood magic, I suppose. Either way, they happen often enough that I know how to deal with them."

The answer made Jean frown, and she tapped her foot for a moment. "What happens if you can't deal with it? I mean... you've been conscious for the ones I've witnessed, but what if something out of the ordinary happened?"

Popcorn hummed, stood, and started to walk again. "I haven't thought about that. Honestly, Park doesn't seem to care too terribly much if anyone were to fall dead, and so I never really considered having a plan if something happened. I suppose I would want someone to do something, but outside of that, I don't know."

Jean ran after him, then walked in silence beside him. Finally, she murmured, "I don't know if anyone could do something if they didn't have your permission."

"Hm, that's valid. The doves are pretty firm on consent, though I'm surprised they worked on my leg without my permission. That one was likely a decision I made while delirious." Popcorn shrugged to himself and looked at Jean. "If I were to grant you permission to speak on my behalf, only in those emergencies, would you do so?"

"Would I...? I mean, if I knew what you wanted," Jean said. She frowned to herself. That wasn't what she expected from the conversation, but she certainly wasn't going to argue as Popcorn stopped again, pulled out a parchment and a quill, and began to write. "What exactly would you want me to say?"

"It's permission for you to decide on my behalf if I am unable to do so," Popcorn said. "You've a good enough head on your shoulders, I believe I can trust you to decide if I need to be treated or if I'd rather die. Anything regarding the heart, for example, certainly is something that I'd like to avoid death with. I've done so for a decade, I'd like to continue to do so."

Jean watched him write, nodding quietly. She could remember that— it was easy enough to do after she saw him stop one heart attack. As for other things, she hoped she wouldn't need to bring this permission up. Well, she didn't want to bring them up regardless.

Their trip was rather uneventful as they made their way through the forest, stopping every so often to document little creatures or rest their legs. Jean's particular favorite was the viper weasel, a curiously long creature with fangs that retracted into its mouth. She couldn't help but smile as she watched it poke its head out of a tree's knot, disappear, and reappear several times before it scurried off to find a squirrel.

Eventually, she and Popcorn made it to Londor's Crossing. It was a massive stone bridge crossing an even larger chasm, and, as Jean stared down into the darkness below, she murmured, "Does it go straight through the world?"

"I would say 'yes', but rumors have it that a river leaves the mouth of the ravine many miles away," Popcorn replied. He leaned over the edge of the bridge and dropped a rock, and the two stood in silence as they waited for any sound of the stone hitting the ground.

"How do you think they built this?" Jean asked softly.

Popcorn shrugged. "Who knows. Probably in the First Age, given the weathering of the stone. No one has really put together how anyone did things at that time." He turned to leave, his cane clicking against the ancient stone, and Jean followed him.

"You know a lot about the First Age," she mused. "You commented that you found my lightcasters in an old ruin from that time, and that Fort Haven might be from then."

Her companion paused and nodded. "It was my area of focus when I first started adventuring. I don't do it too much anymore, given my health, but I enjoy looking for relics and ruins as I can. One of the places I'd like to go, if at all possible, is the Empty. Sure, it's hostile, but no one else is willing to go there." A dreamy sort of look covered his face and he sighed. "It would be a trove of wonders..."

Jean smiled at the expression and shook her head. He always got that far off look when he was imagining the future. It was a sweet thing to witness, and she followed him off of the bridge and deeper into the forest beyond.

Eventually, the two made a camp and shared dinner together. It was incredibly difficult to be near the fire as the stew cooked, as Jean's stomach turned with the smell, and she cursed herself silently as she realized what exactly that meant. Popcorn seemed none the wiser as she picked at her dinner, and she eventually said, "Do you know how long it'll be until we find palgraves?"

"Any point, now. We're in the right place; it's only a matter of finding them." Jean nodded to herself, yawned, and settled against Popcorn's side. He looked down at her and wrapped an arm around her to keep her near. "It's been a long day, hasn't it?"

"Mhm," Jean murmured. She sighed and closed her eyes. "A very long day..." She only just registered his hand running through her hair, and as he did, she sighed and allowed herself to relax further. "A rest is needed..."

Popcorn chuckled, the sound shaking Jean slightly, and she smiled a little bit. Then, as they listened to the fire crackling together, she said, "I hope we find a palgrave while here."

"We will, daito. You get some sleep; I'll take first watch."

When he woke her, Jean shifted and rubbed her eyes. The fire was nearly dead, and Popcorn had curled up with his head resting in her lap. She absentmindedly stroked his hair, watching the area around them, as the night animals sung. It got eerily quiet about an hour later, after the fire had completely burnt out, and Jean manifested her lightcaster for its comforting light. Even Osmond was gone, though she thought she had seen him bobbing around.

The feeling of being watched filled her, but there were no sounds or signs of predators, and so Jean maintained her uneasy watch until dawn. Popcorn woke easily, and the two, after briefly eating the stew from the night before, started out once more.

Palgraves

(sciuridae pinnate)

Grasping claws

Palgraves are odd omnivorous creatures that are around the size of a skunk: wood-colored to blend into trees, the males host long, vibrant tails in order to court the smaller, duller female.

Currently, Palgraves have only been seen past Londer's Crossing, near Apple Ridge.

Dark exterior to tail

Feathers are obnoxiously yellow and pink when unfurled. Surprisingly vibrant when compared to its fur.

Courting involves the lifting of the haunches as high as possible before the Palgrave violently shakes its feathers.

TELFARIANS & KINGSMEN

Jean was stopped by Popcorn around noon. He lightly grabbed her wrist, pulled her back, and pointed towards a tree at the edge of the clearing.

It took a moment for Jean to notice what he was seeing, and then she tilted her head.

Plastered to the tree trunk, looking almost like a piece of bark itself, was a creature the size of a squirrel. Its eyes were squeezed firmly shut until it thought it was alone. Then, it opened its eyes, yawned with a beak wider than Jean realized was possible, and slowly climbed down from the tree.

Now that Jean saw one, she was suddenly able to see the other three that hid amongst the leaves and bushes.

The first palgrave slowly moved to the middle of the clearing as Jean and Popcorn slowly sat down in the shrubs. It paused, looked around again, and then began to give a soft whooping call. The other palgraves watched it intently as it thrust its rump into the air and revealed its long tail. Then, with a shake, the bark colored tail opened to reveal brilliant pink, yellow, and blue plumage. Jean's mouth dropped as she watched the palgrave wiggle and move, displaying its feathers. Two of the other palgraves climbed from their tree to inspect it, prompting Jean to whisper, "It must be a courting dance."

"I think so," Popcorn whispered. "It seems late in the season, but it would make sense given the great horned griffins..." he trailed off and pulled out his parchment. "I'm thinking we set up camp closer to them, and watch them for a couple of weeks. Figure out what we can, document it, and go from there."

The palgraves seemed to be used to them by the fourth day, actively coming closer to Jean to inspect her quill and ink before they'd dart off. Jean often perched herself in a tree to watch them move from branch to branch, though she decided that was a bad idea close to dawn as an avalanche of palgraves raced up and down the tree itself. Popcorn remained close to the ground in order to rest his leg, though their notes were always able to give one another insight on the strange chimeras they were watching.

On the fifth day, everything went strangely silent. Jean and Popcorn had been watching a male woo a female when they both stopped, their ears perked, and then raced off. Jean looked around, the feeling of being watched making the hair on the back of her neck stand up yet again. Popcorn, too, was uneasy as he looked around and then stopped.

Without a sound, he pulled Jean into the bushes and covered her mouth. She didn't protest, though she very nearly yelped in her fright. Popcorn was staring through the roots of the bush and she followed his gaze, her stomach beginning to drop.

Slithering into the clearing on hundreds of legs, its segmented body roiling like a horrid wave, was a massive centipede. It lifted its upper half upright to look around, its pincers clicking, before it lowered itself and slowly moved forward again. Jean gripped Popcorn's wrist, beginning to shake, as the creature slowly moved around. As it grew closer to their bush, the sheer size of its pincers were realized and Jean squeezed her eyes closed.

It grew closer, and closer, before it stopped at their bush. Then, suddenly, it turned and raced away.

Popcorn and Jean stayed silent until the birds began to sing again, and then Popcorn struggled to his feet. "We need to go."

"What was that? It was huge!" Jean exclaimed, standing as well.

"Trouble, daito. Come on, grab what we need from camp and let's get going."

He stumbled through the underbrush and Jean followed him, confused but unwilling to be left behind. "Baba, it's just a large centipede—"

"That thing was a demon, Jean, from the blood goddess Telfaria. That means there are Telfarian bandits here, likely a slaving group, and we are their next targets. We need to go, now." Popcorn reached back and grabbed her hand, beginning to pull her behind him. "We have to get back to Fort Haven— they're not going to stop their pursuit until well after we reach Londor's Crossing."

Jean wasn't sure what questions to ask, but whatever questions she was beginning to think of left her mind at a sudden burning in the back of her arm. She dared to look back to see there was a dart with bright yellow feathers hanging limply, having delivered some drug into her. "Baba..."

Already, her legs were beginning to feel weak and heavy.

Popcorn turned to look at her, the grim determination on his face now horror as he saw the dart. "No... Damn it, no..." He pulled the dart from her as one planted itself firmly into his arm. He brushed it off, frantically, and pulled Jean close in an attempt to run further. Jean's body refused to obey now, and Popcorn's slowed as a second and third dart sprung from his chest.

Once the poison took effect, Jean and Popcorn both collapsed.

The wait was the worst part, until Jean heard the bushes rustle behind her. She could only move her eyes, and they darted there and then to Popcorn, who was pale. Then, as the bushes parted, a group of four individuals walking and a fifth riding one of the centipede demons appeared.

They were all in leather clothes, various weapons slung over their shoulders. Jean could just see the twisting centipede tattoos on their forearms, declaring their allegiance to Telfaria, before the man on the centipede swung down just inches from her face. Bile rose in her throat as she realized that his boots were pieced together from stretched and dried human faces, a stark reminder of the rumors of cannibalism that were whispered in settled areas. The centipede curled around her and Popcorn as the man grabbed Jean's jaw and twisted her head to inspect her as though an animal. "We'll get a pretty price for the girl, don't you think?"

A little chuckle ran through the group and a woman stepped up. She leaned in, her wild hair decorated with bones and bits of metal, and studied Jean. "For a curseborn, I suppose. I know there's a buyer towards the north who'll take breeding stock." She gave a cruel grin and then jerked Jean's head to look at her horns. "They're a bit smaller than he'd prefer, but she's got a body he'll take regardless. As for him, he took more than a single dose to slow him down; he's a beautiful specimen."

Jean's stomach dropped and she willed herself to move, to struggle, or even scream if at all possible. The poison, however, forced her to a state of stillness outside of the tears that were beginning to streak down her face.

"Aw, the little one is crying," the man with the boots sneered. "Poor girl, might as well accustom her to the life she'll be experiencing, eh boys? Take our cut while we can!"

There was a general ruckus and chorus of laughter as the other two men approached, their hands wandering, and Jean was only able to squeeze her eyes shut in an attempt to block it out.

When she forced herself to return to reality, her body was numb. She only remembered the pain they caused her, and the shame, that flooded her body as the realization of her rape set in. She wasn't sure when she was moved, only that she was now in a large cage made of bone that housed many others with haunted, distant looks.

Jean struggled to the corner of the cage, doing her best to shield her body to keep from being seen. She was so exposed, so naked, and there was nothing more that she wanted than to hide from the world.

A chitter slowly approached her, flashing between its hulking form and Popcorn. It reached its hand out and Jean shied away. "Please, please, just leave me alone," she whispered, her voice raw. Tears began to streak down her face again. "Please, just leave me..."

"Daito, daito, it's me," Popcorn whispered.

She blinked at him, just able to see through the hallucination enough to see that it really was her friend. He reached out for her again and she shrunk back. "Please, don't touch me!"

"It's okay, daito, it'll be alright. Take my tunic."

Popcorn placed the rough-spun wool shirt over her and she clung to it. It was her only lifeline now, one that didn't touch her with unwanted hands or memories of a better time. Instead, it offered her warmth and a way away from her nakedness.

Jean slowly relaxed before a Telfarian suddenly pressed her face to the cage with a battle cry, scaring Jean, and then laughed. Then, after being entertained, the Telfarian sauntered back to the communal fire and sat down. There were fifteen around the fire that Jean could see, and still more laughs coming from elsewhere. In the dark, just past the fire, Jean could see three shining carapaces of the centipede demons.

The stench of rot and death were overwhelming.

Jean's blurry eyes scanned the camp, lingered on a human leg turning slowly on a spit over the fire, before her eyes snapped to the opening of the cage two spaces down.

A bandit had thrown it open and entered, grabbed a child, and drug it from the cage. The screaming intensified as he tossed the child towards the demons, and then they abruptly stopped as the sounds of bones being broken and flesh being ripped apart filled the night. The only thing that was audible at that time was the sobs of a woman mourning her lost child.

"Jean, can you hear me?" Popcorn whispered.

Slowly, she looked at him. He was staring at her, his gaze earnestly searching her face. "Jean, we're going to get out, alright?"

"How?" Jean whispered.

"You have your lightcasters, right? They can manifest?"

Jean nodded, though she didn't listen to the rest of her words. Instead, she felt the shadows around her begin to solidify. She could see creatures testing the strength of the shadows again, surrounded by the shaman once more. The woman closed her eyes, briefly, and opened them again to see a chitter was blinking up at her. In an instant, she aimed a manifested weapon at the chitter and pulled the trigger.

It refused to go off.

"Please, please shoot," Jean whispered. Popcorn's face turned more panicked as he tried to get her attention, but she pulled the trigger twice more before another chitter appeared, pulling the first one away.

As they moved, the hallucination revealed that Jean had been aiming at a child.

She stared at them, tears beginning to streak down her face, before chaos broke loose. One of the chitters in the shadows began to laugh, and a chorus was taken up by more of the demons in the woods. The Telfarians around the fire froze, looking around as they lifted their weapons. Popcorn cursed beside her and Jean found his hands on her shoulders. "Jean, Jean, I need you to snap out of it!"

Jean looked at Popcorn. "I'm so sorry."

With that, the chitters testing the shadows poured through and surged over the captives. Popcorn shielded Jean and she clung to herself as chitterlings began to bite the hapless prisoners. The bandits' worry crescendo into fear as chitters with daggers flooded their camp and, as this happened, mists rolled in from the trees around them.

Screams and laughter haunted the night and Jean clasped her hands over her ears. "Stop, please!"

"Daito, we have to go!" Popcorn shouted. He looked around widely before spying a man trampled on the ground, riddled with bites. "Sorry, mate, no hard feelings."

The familiar nausea caused by magic flooded Jean as she watched Popcorn rip the man's blood from his wounds, forming a solid, crystalline war hammer. He brought it down on the lock. "Everyone, out!"

Jean was caught in the stampede, which threw her to the ground. She did her best to cover her head and neck as people ran around and over her, her own cries echoed as the others ran into chitters or the centipede demons. Ahead of her, the Telfarians were culling any rabbits they saw, each wielding clubs or swords that were quickly becoming covered with red crystals.

Popcorn returned to her side and pulled her to her feet as the Telfarians looks their direction. "Stop them! Stop the blood user— he's a traitor!"

Jean didn't spend any time trying to understand why they called Popcorn a traitor, especially as he hugged her close to his side and ran with his war hammer through the darkness.

The centipedes were close on their heels, their clicking pincers and creaking joints accentuated by the smell of blood. Other people ran around them, blindly flying for their lives through the darkness and the trees before Popcorn slid to a halt. Jean clung to him as the gravity of the situation set in, and the realization of why those ahead of them disappeared into the darkness.

It was a sheer cliff face that had been hidden in the dark, boasting a drop of more than a hundred feet.

Popcorn cursed and Jean clung to him as the scuttling of demons grew louder. She looked up at him. "Baba, what do we do?"

"We climb. Here, you go first, daito. It's alright, I'll follow," Popcorn whispered. He helped her to the edge, glancing over his shoulder all the while, and gently lowered her down. "You can do it, focus on what you are grabbing onto and where your feet are, alright? It's just like climbing a tree."

Jean slowly picked her way down, stopped, and stared back at him. "Aren't you coming?"

"Get just a bit further, Jean, and then I'll come," Popcorn said softly. He looked behind him again and Jean, as she slowly moved further down the cliff, slowly understood.

"No... Baba, you have to come now. There isn't time to waste—"

Popcorn shook his head again. "Go, Jean." He looked back, hesitated, and then stared at Jean. "Rainome."

With that, before Jean could answer, he turned away from her, manifested a bladed claw of red crystals, and tore off in the direction of ebbing light.

Jean stared up at the cliff edge as the sounds of screaming echoed through the night once more. Her mind spun with a thousand questions, and worries, before a lithe centipede skittered to the edge and very nearly fell. Jean stared at its eye plates, each fractured lens seemingly focused on everything and nothing, before it lunged towards her.

She gave a cry and clung to the rocks as the centipede, misjudging its leap, flew off of the cliff. She could hear a soft thud below her, prompting her to squeeze her eyes closed. Then, as she released a shaking breath, she started to climb down. If Popcorn didn't make it through the night, she had to— if not for her, then for their possible child.

Osmond brushed against her cheek as he appeared, nearly startling her from her hand hold, before the orb floated further down the cliff. He lit various nooks and crannies for her to use, pausing for Jean to make her way, and then stopped just above the bottom of the stonewall. Jean looked down at the light.

There was no movement, and the centipede demon that had fallen was still as well. Jean sucked in a breath.

The bodies that fell laid contorted and broken. Bones were snapped, heads were broken, and rocks had crushed some of them. Jean did her best to keep from vomiting as she picked her way through the fallen. It was eerily silent, and even the screams of Popcorn and the Telfarians above were impossible to hear.

Jean clung to Popcorn's tunic, looked around, and very nearly began to cry. Then, as Osmond lightly bounced ahead, Jean stumbled through the dark after him.

All the while, her mind was filled with fear and questions, many of which around Popcorn and what might have happened to him. She got caught in several brambles, which tore her skin and clothes, before she pulled through again; she had to get out of there and find help.

When dawn slowly approached, Jean was exhausted.

She wasn't sure how far she had ran, but when she looked back at the hazy morning, she could see a large plateau looming back at her.

It was the sound of twigs snapping behind her that made Jean lunge for nearby bushes. They scratched at her, sending the smell of blood in the air, but Jean didn't care. She clung to herself, watching nervously as boots approached.

Were the Telfarians here? Did they find her? Did they kill Popcorn?

Her panic was momentarily halted as a small group of Kingsmen knights stepped out of the undergrowth. Each wore a tabard adorned with a fruiting apple tree, their hands resting lightly on their swords as they patrolled.

She swallowed and stared.

Maybe they could help her? It was worth a chance, though she was terrified that they'd assume she was an intruder on their patrol. Perhaps, if she was truly cursed, they'd take advantage of her, too. Worst yet, they could kill her on sight simply for being a curseborn in this area; not all Kingsmen seemed to like curseborn, and if they all hated people like her, then her body could be easily hidden.

Jean's hands were trembling as she looked toward the plateau again, her stomach dropping. There wasn't time to worry: Popcorn didn't have time, if he was still alive.

With a deep breath, Jean slowly stepped from the bushes. "Please... Please, I need help."

The patrol turned to look at her, many rather surprised to see a near-naked curseborn woman before them while two seemed embarrassed to see her in that state. The final Kingsmen, however, stared at Jean before rushing towards her. She stumbled backwards, her shaking growing worse as he grabbed her by the wrists. "Bind her, she may be working with the Telfarians!"

"Jones, we don't know—"

"I said bind her, Travin! We can figure it out later... her mouth as well, to keep her from cursing us!"

"Please, no!" Jean begged, struggling as they surrounded her. Travin gave her an apologetic look as she began to cry but Jones, who had begun this, growled.

"It's a trick! We'll have Captain Olare speak to her; the camp isn't too far away, and if we need, we can return to Apple Ridge as well," Jones said. He pushed Jean, who stumbled forward and tripped. "Get up!"

"Jones, this is too much," another man said. "She's injured from whatever happened before she found us. Even if this is a trick, we must be gentle; let HaMelech decide her judgement, and not find fault with us!"

Jones glared at them and they looked between one another before the company hurried back the direction they were coming from. Jean struggled to look back at the plateau, which was growing smaller in the distance, before Jones pushed her again. "Focus, curseborn!"

All the while, Jean could only cry through her gag.

She didn't know why they were treating her this way, why they assumed she was a Telfarian before asking questions, and where they were taking her. Popcorn was somewhere, struggling, and she was dealing with this while trying to carry this child. While some Kingsmen had treated her horribly, this was by far the worst and, very nearly, something that made her want to return to the Telfarians.

When they broke into a clearing that was edged in tents, Jones instructed two of his men to find 'the captains' while he would handle the interrogation. Then, he unceremoniously forced Jean into a large tent in the middle of the camp and all but tossed her to the floor.

Jean scrambled backwards, sucking in a breath as her body began to ache, and Jones approached.

"Your fear betrays you, curseborn," he said, his eyebrows furrowed. "The captains won't treat you lightly—"

He was cut off as a flash of movement caught his, and Jean's attention. As she realized that it was a chitter holding a weapon, and several chitterlings that were with it, she tried to scream through the gag. Jones drew his sword, leveled it, and stared at Jean. "You've got the madness!"

He swung the sword twice, dispatching the demonic threat, before grabbing Jean by the hair.

Again, she tried to scream.

Before he could say anything, though, a very stern voice cut through the air.

"Jones, stand down!"

He dropped her and Jean struggled backwards again. The tears hadn't stopped and, this time, it was hard for her to breathe as she saw two more forms enter the tent. Jones saluted them. "Captain Olare! She's summoning chitters, sir. I was just about to—"

"We are not Solari guard or Inquisitors, Jones," Captain Olare said firmly.

As Jean cried, she registered that one of the captains was approaching her. She tried to flinch away, stuck against the tent, before a gentle voice murmured, "Just a moment, friend..." Then, there was a whistle, and a large furry beast pushed its way into the space as a small glowing orb road on its shoulders. As the creature settled with its head in her lap, two hands very carefully untied the gag from her mouth. Jean managed to blink through her tears just enough to see that it was Nettles, the large sheep dog, and his master Rolandus beside her. The old archer gave her a soft but sad smile. "We've got you, Miss Jean, you're alright now."

Telfarian Bandits

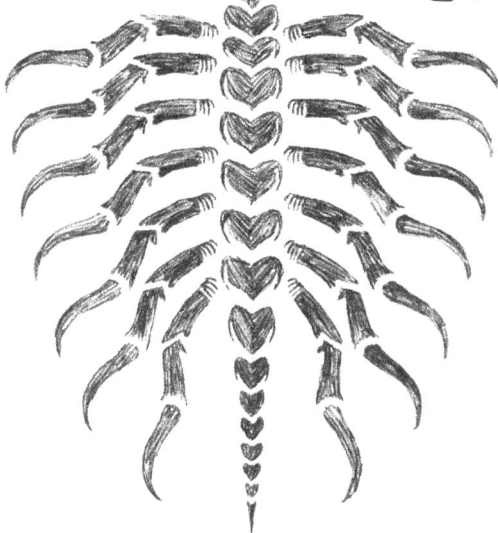

Telfaria is a little spoken about deity, and viewed as highly heretical by those who worship Solaris. She is known as the Blood Queen, and those who follow her are known for raiding and murder.

If individuals pillaged by Telfarians aren't killed outright, they will often be sold into slavery; it is only slightly kinder than becoming food for their dragon centipedes, which are said to resemble Telfaria herself.

Many Telfarians reside past Apple Ridge and the mountains beyond. People don't dare travel to or from those lands, especially as the Telfarians are told to hold to strange customs and afterlife beliefs (my adoptive mother once said that they'll eat the bones of their victims, and, after experiencing the Telfarians myself, I'm not entirely convinced that it is only a rumor).

While Telfarians are allowed to live in Blackrock, they are under strict rules and regulations meant to keep the peace.

23

RESCUE

The relief that crashed over Jean as she recognized a friendly face brought her to hysterical sobbing again. Rolandus's eyes widened, and he pulled her close, allowing her to hide her face in his neck. Behind him, Jean could hear whomever Captain Olare was reaming Jones.

"What on taurus do you think you were doing, Jones?"

"Sir—"

"No, you will not respond just yet. Your patrol mates informed me of the treatment you gave this poor woman prior to any information, any questions, or any actual reasoning outside of your assumptions." Jean began to calm down enough to see that Jones was staring up at a massive redhead.

Captain Olare stood with his arms crossed over his chest, one of them fully clockwork, powered by a kinetic crystal backpack strapped to his back. His tabard, bearing the Apple Ridge motif, was draped over a large suit of clockwork armor, a stark contrast to the standard-issue attire worn by the others.

Jones shifted in front of him, glanced at Jean and Rolandus, and looked at Olare again. "I was trying to keep my patrol safe."

"You frightened a stranger, denied her any semblance of comfort, and allowed her to remain as exposed as she is due to your decisions, Jones. This is unacceptable." Olare's gaze softened ever so slightly. "I recognize you were attempting to do the right thing, but that should never come at the cost of one of HaMelech's creations in this manner. There was no discernment, and no sense of mercy in your actions. Until I have a chance to speak with you privately, with Captain Rolandus, you are to remain in camp. Kindly fetch this young lady something to wear, and see if you can find one of the doves."

"Marin," Rolandus said lightly. He looked back at Olare. "Marin needs to be here."

Olare glanced at him, raised an eyebrow, but then nodded. "Find Marin."

Jean struggled ever so slightly. "Marin is here?"

The two captains, and Jones, paused. "You know Marin?" Olare asked.

Jean nodded. "I do. She was at Fort Haven several months ago, during the Long Night..." she trailed off, her voice catching slightly as those memories, and the surge of new ones, flooded her.

"Rolandus, thoughts?"

"I met Jean during my time in Bleak Hollow last summer," Rolandus said softly. "She wouldn't be lying now. She's the one with the Guardian watching her, the one who I brought to Godric's Rest after leaving Last Hope."

"Very well... May HaMelech send a sign for us to know our next steps, then," Olare said gently. "Rolandus, undo her binding. At the very least, I want her to be able to dress herself when the clothes come."

Rolandus nodded and undid Jean's hands, pausing as he saw the little diamonds on her wrists. Then, he looked at Jean. "What are these from?"

Jean followed his gaze and then met his eyes. Her heart began to pound harder in her chest and she whispered, "I didn't steal them... Popcorn found them while exploring and he gave them to me."

"Can you manifest them?"

She hurriedly nodded and did so, holding a lightcaster in one shaking hand before she quickly dispelled it. "Please, I didn't—"

"Jean, you're fine," Rolandus soothed. He looked at Olare. "She has lightcasters; they've imprinted."

"I'll take that as the sign, then," Olare replied. He approached Jean, who flinched, and then stopped. For a moment, he merely watched her. Then, he crouched in front of her. "You're safe now, little one. Marin, my sister, will be here shortly to tend to your wounds, and we'll figure out how to get you home."

The words made Jean relax, ever so slightly, before she swallowed. She really couldn't go home, not until Popcorn was found. Was there enough time to find him?

"No." Jean mumbled.

Olare and Rolandus shared a glance before Rolandus murmured, "Jean, is the madness...?"

She flinched away from him at the reminder of her condition, doing her best to avoid their prying eyes and potential judgement. Finally, she whispered, "It's Popcorn. He's out there, somewhere, and..." She trailed off, tears beginning to streak down her face again. "The Telfarians have him. He stayed back so I could escape."

"The Telfarians... Do you remember where they are, Jean?" Olare asked softly. "Or how many there were?"

Jean shook her head slightly. "I... I know that they were on a large plateau. There were a lot of them, but with the chitters..."

She trailed off as hurried footsteps raced into the tent and the familiar face of Marin entered. "Olare, Jones said you needed— Jean! Jean, what are you doing here? What happened to you?" The dove healer flew to Jean's side and gathered her in her arms. "Olare, Rolandus, shame on you for not finding her something better to wear before you came in! We can get you something to wear, and bandage you and..." She trailed off, looked between the three and then looked at Jean. "Why are you here?"

Jean sniffled and repeated what she had told the two captains. Marin's face went steadily paler and she looked at the men. "Will there be time enough to find the others?"

"If we leave now, we can try," Olare said softly. "Rolandus, gather all of the camp. We'll return to Apple Ridge as soon as we are done, with whomever we can find. I want us torn down and ready to go in fifteen minutes. That should be enough time for you to help Miss Jean, Marin."

"Of course, Olare. Come on, Jean, we'll get you taken care of."

The healer helped Jean to her feet and the two women slipped out of the tent. As Jean followed Marin, she caught sight of Jones being berated by two female knights before they stormed off. Rolandus whistled and the camp was suddenly full of activity as the well-oiled machine began to tear down. Marin ushered Jean into a separate tent and helped her change, pausing as she saw the various bruises. "Jean, did you tell Olare and Rolandus everything that happened?"

The question made Jean pause. She was already ruined after sleeping with Popcorn the first time, and now there was a prevailing idea that she was broken after sleeping with him again. Mentioning her rape brought nothing but worry and guilt, her mind unable to shake the idea that she should have managed to escape. Finally, Jean whispered, "No."

Marin listened silently as Jean gave her minimal details, her fingers beginning to shake. Marin brushed hair from her face. "Oh, Jean, I'm so sorry this happened to you."

"And now... now Popcorn is out there..." she trailed off and swallowed. There was something there that seemed to whisper that he was alright, a gut feeling that he wasn't dead, but he was tiring. He needed help, soon, but he was still alive. "Marin, we need to go, please."

"Jean—"

"Marin, he's going to die and—" Jean steeled her nerves and swallowed. "I can't go through labor again without him. I just... I just can't. I'm pregnant again, its his, and I... I need to have him there with me. Please, we need to go find him."

She didn't dare look at Marin's shocked face, instead staring at her feet as the healer paused. Then, Marin murmured, "I'll inform Captain Olare that it's time sensitive and we need to go quicker. The camp is nearly done, but those who are not packing need to pull the war rams and get the hounds ready." She hurried off and then returned a few moments later.

Jean had managed to pull on a clean linen dress, though it burned where her scrapes were regardless of how soft it was. The woman jumped as Marin entered and then shook her head as Marin began to apologize. "No, it's alright."

"They're ready. Olare and Rolandus want to speak to you before we leave, they're just outside."

The curseborn took Marin's outstretched hand and followed her, now able to see everyone more clearly as she had a moment to relax. There were three curseborn in the company, one of which a woman, and the others were normal looking. She was surprised to see an even mix of men and women in the group, though it was more noticeable as the female knights had moved away from where Jones was. He, in particular, didn't dare look towards Jean as she approached Olare and Rolandus.

Rolandus turned to face them as he wrapped a bundle of feathers from his bow around his wrist. In an instant, his dark face was covered with brown feathers and two beautiful golden eyes blinked at her. Jean had to pause, briefly, as he took the shape of a falcon cote, but she didn't speak until Olare looked at her.

"Jean, the entire company is going to find the Telfarians. I would never normally ask someone who's dealt with them to join us, but you are the only one who knows where they are and how many there may be. It's going to be impossibly difficult to return, I'm sure, but we need your help. Will you come with us and serve as a guide?" Olare's eyes, which seemed to hold seriousness even when he was speaking softly, made Jean shift.

Could she go back? They were awful, and if they were too late, she'd be forced to witness whatever brutality they had inflicted on Popcorn. She couldn't bare to look at his body lying on the ground, but... if he was still alive, she wouldn't leave him with strangers.

Finally, she gave a little nod.

"Do you feel comfortable enough riding with Rolandus?"

Again, Jean nodded, and the falcon cote in question gave her a gentle smile. "Come along, Jean. Up we get."

He helped her atop a war ram, its wool just visible through the barding that protected it from attacks. It was taller than a horse, and Jean's head swam ever so slightly as she looked towards the ground. Then, Rolandus carefully stepped into the stirrup and pulled himself up in front of Jean. "Hold as tightly as you feel needed; the rams are faster than they look, and if we need to go up an incline, they're faster still."

Jean wrapped her arms around him and stared down at Marin, who gently squeezed her arm. "He'll keep you safe, Jean. If there's anyone I trust watching you today, while I can't, it's Olare and Rolandus."

"Thank you, Marin," Jean whispered. She watched her friend hurry off to join a cart that the doves had claimed before Rolandus' whistle caught her attention.

Nettles joined them, followed by two other large sheep dogs and a pack of 12 smaller hounds. Their tongues lolled, but none lolled as much as Nettles' as he nudged Jean's leg and panted. It made Jean smile despite the situation, and she returned her gaze ahead of them just as the war ram lurched forward and tore through the forest with the company.

"We're going back to where you found Jones!" Rolandus called over the wind. "From there, we're going to have you tell us what you remember!"

"It's on the plateau past that clearing!" Jean said back. "I don't know the actual distance, but it took me a majority of the night to get to where I was!"

Rolandus' chest shook like he was humming, and Jean remained silent as they rode. It wasn't until they reached the clearing she had first seen the Kingsmen in did she speak, pointing past Rolandus' shoulder. "That's the plateau! There's a sharp cliff on all but one side, as they didn't have to climb to reach the peak."

"Then we will circle it when we reach it," Olare said as he pulled his ram beside them. "Did they have centipedes?"

"At least three, but one fell from the top of the cliff as I escaped," Jean said.

Olare nodded, looked at her, and offered a gentle smile. "Thank HaMelech the Guardian led you to us, then. This area is not friendly to even those who live here." As Jean was left wondering what guardian they spoke of, as it had been mentioned again, her attention was brought to the dogs around them.

The pack of hounds seemed excited now, pacing frantically around the rams while the sheepdogs stood attentively and listened.

She was caught off guard again as the war rams took off, followed by the wagons at a distance, and held tighter to Rolandus.

All the while, Jean focused on that glimmer of hope that Popcorn was safe. It was still there, but it was also developing into pain within her chest that expanded and forced the air out of her lungs. She sucked in a breath. "Rolandus, please, we need to go faster."

He glanced at her over his shoulder and called to the rest of the company, and the rams moved faster in response.

They put her original run in the dark to shame as they reached the plateau in less than two hours, stopping once for a quick drink for the animals before they hurried further. Eventually, they group split into two; Rolandus and Jean took a shallower path up the plateau, followed by the many dogs that were led by Nettles. The other rams made their way up the sheer cliff edge while the wagons, still further behind, turned to find a less steep path.

When Jean and Rolandus reached the top of the plateau, it was pure chaos.

Telfarians had noticed intruders coming from the cliffside and had readied attacks. Centipedes scuttled amid them before the hounds following Rolandus split off, biting and tearing at the demons and chasing them through the underbrush. The Knights lowered lances and forced through the ranks while Rolandus, as calm as Jean remembered witnessing in Bleak Hollow, pulled his bow out and manifested a golden bowstring and arrow. He shot it at one running Telfarian and then a second before he looked at Jean. "I don't see any prisoners, Jean, but that doesn't mean there aren't any. Help me lay fire, and we shall move further into the encampment."

Jean manifested her lightcasters at his words and slid from the war ram. It shuffled slightly as she landed beside it but otherwise didn't run, and she pressed near its flank as she began to fire charge after charge into the fray. One of the Telfarians hid before an assortment of boxes and Jean, as she stared at him, realized that it was the man who had begun her assault.

Anger, guilt, pain, and fear coursed through Jean as she watched him lean out from his cover to throw a crystalline red dart towards a knight. He didn't know she was there, and she didn't want him to. She began to fire at him, sending two bolts of energy into his chest. As he stumbled backwards, convulsing, Jean fired four more times. Her eyes were hazy with tears.

She hoped this hurt more than what he did to her. She hoped it burned him, send panic through him at an unknown assailant, before he wondered if death would come. And she prayed to whatever god was listening, Solaris or HaMelech or even the dreaded Black Dragon, that his afterlife was filled with nothing but pain and misery.

"Jean! Jean, he's dead! Kindly focus your fire elsewhere!" Rolandus called amid the din.

Jean blinked twice and looked at Rolandus, and then at the mutilated corpse that she had been firing upon. A brief ounce of remorse flooded her before it vanished.

She sucked in a breath and slowly looked around the area, trying desperately to find Popcorn amid the chaos. Knights were beginning to move people towards the doves' wagon, where a golden dome of light protected them from enemies. They were pulling people from bushes and deeper in the woods, calling to one another as they discovered more Telfarians, and still Jean didn't see Popcorn.

Without a word, Jean slid down the little embankment they had been positioned on and started to run. "Baba? Baba, where are you!"

"Jean, come back!" Rolandus shouted after her.

She barely registered a whistle as she ran, and Nettles bounded to her side. She cast him a brief glance as she hurried into the woods to try finding Popcorn. Something cracked against her side and threw her to the ground. Jean gasped in pain as she breathed, the agony of broken ribs racing through her as she struggled to find her assailant. It was a Telfarian, who's blood-thirsty smile turned to fear as Nettles' hackles raised and he lunged with bared teeth.

With that distraction, Jean stumbled to her feet and began to look for Popcorn again.

When she did find him, it was just before a small group of Kingsmen broke through the tree lines as well. She wasn't sure how startled they were, but she figured that, if she was the baseline, they were even more worried.

Popcorn was standing amid a small pile of bodies, most of which Telfarians. He was covered in blood, his chest heaving, and his hand had been encased in the same red crystals that the Telfarians were wielding. As his head whipped towards the sudden intruders, Jean found that his eyes had been glazed over with the same black void as they were when he was threatening her. A sick grin flooded his face and he dropped the body he had been holding; it landed on the ground in a sickening mass.

"Popcorn, please, stop!" Jean cried out, drawing his attention to her. He stood there for a moment, his head cocked to one side, before the grin widened.

"Look at you, girl... I wondered if I'd be seeing you again."

Popcorn's gait was unsteady and unnatural. Somehow, his arms hung longer than they should have, and his limp was gone despite the work that had been done when Jean had first met him. She stumbled back as he approached, his hand clawed as he grabbed her by the back of the neck. "I've been looking forward to this, girl... you've threatened everything-"

"In the name of HaMelech, I command you to release her!"

Olare's voice split the air and Popcorn froze. Jean took that moment to push Popcorn away from her and then scrambled towards Olare. The knight stood over her, helped her to her feet, and then stared Popcorn down. "Dark one, you have no power here. Under the authority of the King of Kings, you are to leave this man!"

Popcorn began to grin, foaming at the mouth both white and black spittle. His body began to convulse and he took two steps towards them before he collapsed. Jean stared in horror as his eyes flashed from black to green and black again, his hand reaching towards her. "Girl—"

"Begone!" Olare said sternly.

A blood-curdling scream left Popcorn and Jean lunged forward to grab him. Olare caught her shoulder, holding her lightly, as they watched the foam grow heavier and then, after a brief moment, Popcorn went still.

Only then did Olare release Jean, and she raced to Popcorn's side to check him over. "Baba, Baba, please, look at me."

Out of the corner of her eye, a large, eight-legged creature scurried into the trees. In addition, she also saw Knights of the Long Road hurrying their direction, weapons still drawn, as though expecting Popcorn to fight. Jean stared down at the man, the red crystalline claws no longer there but instead a bloody mess all over his arm. Without a sound, she pulled him into her arms and held him tightly. "Please, please open your eyes."

When the knights reached her, she was surprised to see that there was a dove with him. The healer slid to a halt beside Jean and looked for a pulse. Jean, meanwhile, held Popcorn tighter. Then, the man suddenly inhaled and began to cough and choke.

Jean turned him as he began to vomit blood and bile, his body shaking as he clung to Jean's wrists. Eventually, he stopped, and simply looked at her. A little smile flickered over his face. "Diato... you're safe..."

"You are too, Baba," Jean whispered. "You're safe now."

"Remember... what I said about my heart...?"

"Yes?"

"I... I can't fix it."

Jean's blood ran cold and she stared at him, realizing that his body had begun to shake again. "No... no, no! Please, you have to help him! His heart—"

"Move, miss," the dove said firmly. Popcorn's eyes rolled into the back of his head as the dove began to do chest compression, muttering to himself. "We won't be able to do much without his permission—"

"He told me that I have the authority to give permission!" Jean interrupted. "Please, you have to save him!"

"Bring a stretcher!"

"Others are being treated now, can't you heal him?"

"They are stable. He's actively dying," the dove said, not looking at Jean. "I'm doing what I can, but it is HaMelech who is in control now, not me."

Jean's mouth went dry as the bustle of knights and doves hurried. One of the Knights of the Long Road took over the chest compression while

Rolandus gently pulled Jean back. She struggled, briefly, before she began to cry in the falcon cote's chest.

What good were these healers if they couldn't save a man? They claimed their God was greater than any others, and yet they couldn't fix this. Jean sobbed again, finally managing, "Please... please, save him..."

Eventually, the group got Popcorn and the other injured into the wagon. Rolandus helped Jean onto the war ram. "They're doing what they can, Jean. While they may not be able to fix the issue, as the heart is certainly stubborn, they can at least pray to HaMelech for more time."

Jean stared sullenly at the wagon as they rode beside it, a little sheen of gold laying over the injured within. Popcorn was still breathing, though it was faint. Others, as she watched, no longer had breath.

With that, Jean remained silent the remainder of the long ride toward Apple Ridge.

Olare wears a reinforced armored mechanized (RAM) suit. It offers the protection of full plate armor while being 2-3 times thicker than what can be typically carried and offers the user greater strength and endurance.

Rolandus and Olare know my aunt and uncle. Neither told me the whole story, but I know it's from after they left Zanther.

Rolandus and Olare

Two large crystals power Olare's arm and armor.

Mantles for cotes take many forms. Rolandus has a falcon feather bracelet on his bow.

Olare has a RAM fist that can deliver over 1,000 newtons, or 1 ton, of force in a strike. He also carries a standard issue twin-assault dartcaster that is capable of throwing 4 darts a second.

Rather than a traditional bow, Rolandus uses a relic hardlight weapon. When activated, it strings itself and manifests arrows out of thin air.

RAM suits are a common sight in a company of Knights of the Long Road. They are often the backbone of the army and are suited to work as hammers and anvils due to being heavy infantry.

QUESTIONING

The four-hour ride left Jean's body aching, especially with no opportunity to stop and stretch. Rolandus apologized repeatedly for not taking a break, but with the wagon full of injured, there simply hadn't been time. Jean understood that completely, especially as she glanced at the wagon from time to time.

Popcorn was still breathing. It was hard to tell amid the chest compressions, but it seemed that they were doing enough to at least force his body into continuing to function. As for his heart, Jean was uncertain as to if it was still beating or if it had completely failed.

Numbness had set in as they rode, too. The fire that Jean felt while dealing with the Telfarians, the relief that had come when she found Popcorn, and everything between, had faded into apathy. There was no promise that he'd survive, and no guarantee that she, herself, would be safe after the assault. In fact, the more Jean thought about it, the more she was certain that Solaris would punish her for crying out to whatever would listen to her... especially when the other two she attempted to pray to were the Usurper and the Black Dragon.

When they arrived at Apple Ridge, Jean was caught off guard by how quaint it was. Apple orchards surrounded the little town while massive stone buildings dotted the residences. They headed towards the temple of HaMelech, which had a large bell erected above its roof line and a well in front of it. People hurried out of the way as the group came, calling out ahead to make way and to let those at the temple know there were injured. It seemed like a well-oiled machine, especially in that everyone expected something akin to this to happen and reacted in a smooth manner rather than chaos.

The injured were helped out of the wagon first. Then, the knights instructed civilians to enter the temple and see who needed food, funeral rights, or simple comfort. Rolandus helped Jean from the ram and looked to Marin. "Can she go with him?"

"I'll bring her," Marin said. "There's no way I'm allowing her to remain away from him at this time. Come, Jeans we'll check on him first, and then I'll tend to you, alright?"

Jean nodded faintly and hurried after the short red head.

The temple itself was silent aside for footsteps. People prayed over the injured, sending shivers up Jean's spine, while others covered the faces of those who passed. Marin took three turns and then sped up. "Quickly, Jean."

"Where are they taking him?"

"Surgery, I assume. We've got something that could help his heart but... I don't know if they're willing to do it with his inability to speak."

Jean's brows furrowed. When they caught up to the group with Popcorn, one was pacing and the other was praying over him. The third dove looked at Marin and Jean. "Marin, who's this? Why is she here?"

Jean opened her mouth but Marin interrupted. "She's his partner; they're from Fort Haven, I've met them before."

"Partner?" The doves looked between one another and the first spoke again. "Miss, do you know anything about what's going on?"

Jean nodded rapidly. "His heart is bad. He's been keeping it going on and off with some sort of blood magic but before this happened, he said he couldn't fix it. I don't know what's happening, but he had a heart attack a month and a half ago and was fine. When we came this direction, he said he wanted me to be sure that, if he couldn't, his heart was tended to in an emergency." She gripped her arms. "Is there anything you can do for him? Please, please say there's something you can do for him."

She was shaking again, and Marin drew her to her side in an attempt to calm her down. Jean appreciated the gesture, but it did little to soothe her. In fact, it made Jean more frustrated. Everything so far had seemed to be what she needed to recover; kindness, understanding, gentleness, and yet, she was so incredibly angry because it wasn't working. Jean wiped tears from her face and grit her teeth.

"We have an artificial heart we can give him," the first dove said gently, "but we aren't guaranteed that it'll work. Only HaMelech—"

"Then do it, please!" Jean snapped. "He keeps saying that staros take more to be killed, but this is the worst!"

"Jean, you need to calm down," Marin murmured. "They're trying their best."

"It doesn't feel like they are, Marin!" Jean returned. "He's dying! You haven't dealt with someone you care so deeply for dying! Not so soon after losing your baby! Everything keeps happening, and I am so tired of people saying it's going to be okay!" Tears were falling faster down her face now and, for a moment, it felt good to cry. Then, Jean saw the pained look on Marin's face and knew she had overstepped a line.

"I know what it's like to be there in a situation like this, Jean," Marin murmured, "and right now, I know how angry you are. Let them do what they can, and we will rely on HaMelech for the rest. Please; you need a bath and to rest."

Every fiber of Jean's being screamed as Marin gently led her away, her being numb once more. She glanced back to see that the doves were beginning to wash Popcorn's chest and their hands, preparing for a surgery that wasn't guaranteed to work, and then looked at Marin. Finally, she whispered, "Will he be okay?"

"As soon as I know, I'll tell you," Marin said back.

She drew Jean a hot bath and set out another set of clothes. "Do you want to be alone?"

Jean paused and nodded. The last people who saw her naked were not friends, but there was something about even a face she recognized looking at her in that state. It made her feel dirty, used, and even vile. No, she didn't want anyone to see her undressed- Popcorn included. Marin offered a gentle smile and stepped out.

When Jean was alone, she scrubbed until her skin was raw. The water burned, the lavender and chamomile that rested on the surface stung, and Jean's heart ached as she continued to try and clean herself. It was doing nothing for the disgust she felt for herself and what had happened. Eventually, after it hurt too much to even touch her skin with a cloth, Jean left the tub and redressed. She stared at herself in the little steel mirror on the counter, studying the bags under her eyes and the now wet curls that framed her face. At one point, she would have called herself beautiful. Now, all she saw was a tired woman with nothing left to claim as her own.

Marin returned then, knocking lightly on the door. "Jean, are you done?"

"Yes."

She turned to face the dove, who's eyes shone with concern. Jean's eyebrow raised, and then her blood ran cold as the woman murmured, "I need you to return to the surgery room with me; the doves need to speak to you urgently."

"Is everything okay?"

"They'll explain, Jean, I'm not fully sure."

Jean wasted no time in following Marin once more, nearly running into the first dove she had spoken to. "What is it? What's wrong?"

"He doesn't have enough blood to work the heart, even with it installed correctly," the dove said. "He lost enough during the battle, and the blood now—"

"Give him mine," Jean interrupted. "Just give him my blood."

"Will that work?" Marin asked. "I don't know if it could, as we aren't sure of herher blood type, or his."

"Curseborn blood seems to be universal," the first woman said. "We can at least begin the transfusion with her, and call someone else in if needed. We need all we can get to get him going- it's bad."

"Then get going!"

Jean was whisked away and pulled into the surgery room. There, she stared at Popcorn as the doves scrubbed her arm and then placed a needle into the inner portion of her elbow. The blood from her arm swirled through a tube and into a small bag. As soon as that bag was full, the tube to Jean's arm was clamped and the blood bag was attached to a different tube and needle that ran into Popcorn's arm. The dove beside Jean placed a hand on her shoulder. "That's one pint, and about all you can give—"

"It's not going to be enough for him, is it?" Jean questioned softly. The dove hesitated, and Jean shifted. "Take another pint. I will need to rest, anyway, but there isn't enough time for him to be wasted."

"Miss—"

"Please," Jean murmured. "I can't lose him."

The dove looked at her colleagues who, after a moment, nodded. "Alright, but if you begin to feel dizzy, you must stop, alright?"

Jean nodded, watching as she placed another bag beside her and began to take additional blood. Jean was beginning to feel dizzy and cold, but she didn't say anything. It was only when the dove removed the second bag of blood and got it ready for Popcorn to use, and Jean slowly stood, did darkness come crashing over her.

When she awoke, she found herself in a neatly kept bed in a small room. There was a second bed beside her, and two across from her, that hosted only pillows and blankets. Her head was pounding as she slowly looked around, realizing that there was someone in the chair next to her.

Captain Olare was reading a book quietly, tapping his foot slightly. When he realized someone was watching him, he lifted his gaze and offered Jean a warm smile. "Good morning, miss. Rolandus just stepped out to speak to Marin, he's right outside the door." Jean didn't want to admit how much those words meant as she slowly shifted on the bed, and so she avoided his gaze. Then, after a moment, he spoke again. "Marin said you had donated blood to save your friend's life. That was very noble of you."

"I couldn't just let him die," Jean said quietly.

"I know, but it was noble all the same, even if your intentions may have been selfish," Olare said. He shut his book and looked towards the window, his voice contemplative. "Rolandus and I spoke briefly about how the two of you met, and Marin and I spoke about the happenings in Fort Haven. I truly am sorry to hear what you experienced over the Long Night." Jean looked down again. She wasn't surprised that Marin had told him, not after hearing the family relationship. Still, it stung to know that her hurts had been shared with others without her consent. Olare's eyes were on her again. "My sister was not detailed in her recount, only that it was a blessing that HaMelech had halted her travels. Given her expertise, my assumption is that you required her aid."

That made Jean feel slightly better, and she nodded. Then, they sat in silence until Rolandus entered the room again. He had placed his feather mantle on his bow again, which was carefully hooked onto his back. He smiled gently at Jean and sat down. "Sleep well?"

"I think so. I don't remember falling asleep, though."

Rolandus chuckled and Olare gave him a look. Then, Olare said, "You likely don't. Marin said you were carried out after straining yourself too much with the donation."

Ah, that would explain why she only remembered standing. Jean sighed and shut her eyes. "I see."

Again, Rolandus chuckled. "It happens to the best of us, Jean. I cannot donate blood even on a good day; the needles make me so incredibly stressed, they cannot find a vein to use. Either way, Marin's checking on your friend now. Olare and I were hoping to speak to you about what he had witnessed at the Telfarian camp, especially as Olare had watched your encounter with him."

Jean frowned and looked at the two captains. They seemed more concerned now than they were when she first woke up, which made her shift nervously on the bed. as she did so, she realized that her ribs hurt less than they did before; a quick inspection proved that they had been bandaged while she slept. Now that the adrenaline wore off, the pain was noticeably there. She assumed, however, that someone had given her some sort of numbing agent to combat the pain's full extent. "What do you want to know? I'm not sure I can explain too much, but I can try."

Olare nodded faintly. "Perhaps you can start with the blood magic he wields? Have you witnessed this before?"

She looked between them again. Neither of them seemed to be terribly angry looking, simply worried as they glanced at one another. This would prove difficult; even she didn't know where the blood magic had come from, but she'd experienced it first-hand twice now. Did she lie to them, say she hadn't? Would they discipline him or otherwise neutralize whatever threat he was if she was honest? What if she did decide to tell a falsehood? Would that cause additional problems?

Finally, Jean gave a silent nod.

"Was it similar?"

She nodded again, and Rolandus lightly said, "Jean, we aren't going to do anything to him. We just need to know exactly what we're dealing with. Marin said she counted more demons than there were Telfarians, which means that something else was there. What exactly have you seen happen?"

Demon? Is that what the black mist with legs was?

Jean swallowed. "It's his blood magic... he's used it three times before, that I've seen. The first was a claw, from a man he had..." she trailed off, tried to speak past the lump in her throat, and then continued. "The other two times I saw, they were towards me and the Telfarians. It... it would happen when he was angry, but he can do it on a whim, too... and he used it to heal ailments, as well."

Olare sat back and Rolandus hummed. "What did he use the blood magic to 'heal'?" Olare asked.

"Several things. Blood loss, venom removal, his heart..." Jean fell silent again, realizing just how worried she was about him. "Please, you said Marin was checking in to see how he was doing. Is he alright, do you know?"

"Calm yourself, Jean," Rolandus soothed. "She'll be back soon."

Jean nodded slowly and looked between them. Then, she whispered, "Popcorn is a good man. He has a temper, but I know he's a good man. He saved me, he saved the other prisoners."

"You care deeply for him, don't you?" Olare offered her a gentle smile and looked at Rolandus. "I can recognize that compassion and care anywhere.

You are a good friend, at the very least, and I know you want no harm to come to him. Marin and the other Doves will be keeping a close eye on him: between the surgery and what we witnessed, I hesitate to allow anyone near him, for fear that harm may come to them. There is another matter I'd like to discuss with you." Jean bit her lip as he lightly gestured towards her hands and arms, where the black scars were visible. "The chittering madness, how bad is it?"

She knew it would be brought up. Jean shifted, winced at her ribs, and whispered, "Bad enough that the chitters in your camp were there because of me."

"You're manifesting them? That's unusual, even for those rather ill," Olare mused.

Rolandus gave him a look. "It affects people in different ways, Olare. Just because others don't manifest doesn't mean it doesn't happen."

"You're right, my friend, I'm sorry. I'm merely thinking back on what I've seen. Marin will know better than I will, I must admit. Still... this has been happening since your meeting with Rolandus in Bleak Hollow?"

"Yes, sir."

"Yet the lightcasters chose you... which is odd as well."

Jean looked between them before she swallowed. "I have a question for you," she said, desperately wanting to change the topic. "Every Kingsman location I've been to, I hear about how people like you are supposed to uphold grace and compassion as emissaries of HaMelech. Yet I only see cruelty and rejection from the majority. That man treated me like I was a prisoner, and others have treated me just as bad. How can you do and say two different things?"

The question seemingly caught Olare off guard, as he blinked a handful of times at her. Rolandus, however, chuckled. "You have been thinking about what I said all those months ago, hm?" He looked at Olare. "If you'd allow?"

"By all means."

"We're supposed to uphold those qualities you listed, of course, but you must remember; we're still human, Jean. Just as I'm sure Solari tenants call you to behave in certain manners, we are called to do the same. The

Holy Text outlines where our hearts and minds are to align, but there are flaws in our lives simply caused by the nature of the world. We've got the knowledge of knowing that the dove Himself, the son of the Creator, died for us in order to allow our flaws to be made perfect, but that still takes time and management." Rolandus smiled gently. "There's far more to it than I'm sure your interest allows, but I can tell you now that yes, I believe you when you say Kingsmen treated you poorly. And for that, on their behalf, I apologize. Their behavior was wrong, and they certainly didn't demonstrate who HaMelech is. I don't blame you at all for frustration, confusion, or even anger for what was said and done."

Jean blinked at the man. It wasn't what she expected to hear, but she also didn't have anything to counter it with. In her mind, she always assumed that they thought they were perfect and better than others. Now, it seemed just the opposite; they knew they weren't perfect, just like those around them, but they were trying to uphold standards of perfection. It really was confusing, and she'd have to ask Rolandus more about it, but she tucked that away as a soft knock on the door announced Marin's presence.

The redhead had donned an apron for herself and had pulled her hair under a kerchief. Her face, though tired, was gentle and had a soft smile as she stepped in. "I hope I'm not intruding."

"Is Popcorn alright?"

Marin's face grew softer. "He's sleeping in our recovery wing, Jean. The surgery was a success, and his heart was beating stronger than before as I left. The doves said that it was by HaMelech's hand that it worked as well as it did." She looked between Olare and Rolandus, one eyebrow raised. "You're not bothering her, are you?"

"We were speaking to her about Popcorn and his... unique abilities," Olare said. He looked at Jean. "She countered with a rather excellent question regarding Kingsmen behavior."

Rolandus looked at Jean and gave her a little wink, which made her smile ever so slightly. Then, he looked at Marin. "We did want your input on something, as chittering madness was brought up."

"Yes?" Marin came in, looked for a chair, and then folded her hands in front of her. Jean gestured to the side of the bed for her to sit, making the dove smile and sit down. "What exactly is it?"

"Chitter manifesting," Olare said. "When exactly does that happen when someone has chittering madness?"

Marin tilted her head, her eyes flickering as she studied the ceiling. Finally, she looked back at the group. "I've seen it only a couple of times, both of which after a serious interaction with a chitter weapon. Unfortunately, even the remedies I know of only took a fraction of the hallucinations away. Why do you ask?"

Olare and Rolandus looked at Jean and Marin tilted her head. "Are you manifesting them?"

"You're not surprised about the madness?"

"Jean, please know that treating chittering madness is my calling. I knew the moment I first met you that you were struggling with it. Then I saw your hands during the Long Night, and that confirmed my suspicion. Now, are you manifesting them?"

Jean nodded slightly and Marin tapped her leg slightly. "I'll begin by getting you some herbal treatments. Does it happen often?"

"During times I'm stressed."

"Then we'll work on some stress relief techniques as well. Chittering madness is difficult as it's an extension of chittering sickness, and the worse it gets, the worse the symptoms are. Manifestation tends to lean towards the worst cases, while hallucinations are throughout. It's a miserable, miserable curse, and I truly cannot wait for the day that the Black Dragon is cast down. Until then, though, it'll do good to get you treatments and techniques to soothe the issue. The Solari do prevention, I have been fortunate enough to know some treatments... though... Jean, I hope you know that it will never fully go away. Only HaMelech himself can make that happen." Jean frowned as Marin stood, brushed her hands off, and squared her shoulders. "Olare and Rolandus, I'd like for the two of you to let Jean rest now. She's had a very long day and will need sleep more than anything in order to recover. You're welcome to return in the morning. Jean, my dear, I'll be back in about twenty minutes with some herbs and food for you, alright? They're planning on bringing Popcorn back tomorrow morning after a night in the recovery wing, simply due to the nature of the surgery."

She and the two knights left, Olare and Rolandus bidding her a good night, and soon Jean was alone. Well, mostly. A broad-breasted robin had perched on her windowsill and was singing as Osmond rested beside the gas lamp on the bedside table. Jean watched the bird before Marin returned with her medicines. All the while, Jean thought over Marin's words. She'd be like this forever, outside of whatever she could do to make it slightly less awful. The Solari couldn't know, which meant she needed to keep silent when it came to the fort.

"You need to rest," Marin said gently. She held a glass of water as Jean swallowed two pills. "These will help with the pain and the tea that I've brought will help your stress. It's time to begin to heal and to focus on you. I did a quick bit of research, well, spoke to some other doves, and they confirmed that the bout of unconsciousness from blood donation shouldn't affect the pregnancy. Regardless, I want you to remain in bed the next couple of days to recover."

"Yes, Marin."

The dove smiled at Jean who, after a moment, yawned.

"Get some sleep, I'll check on you later tonight."

With that, Marin slipped out and Jean was left with her thoughts once more.

Clockwork
Heart

Artificial atrium

The entire mechanism is wound by a simple key, similar to winding a clock.

Gears are required to engage the hydraulic pump

Kinetic stone holds approximately 36 hours of charge

Screws hold the cover in place

Any part that comes in contact with the body is coated in a nonreactive, glasslike material that lessens the rejection chance.

Key pathway runs through the ribs. A plate on the surface of the chest covers the hole keeping the inner workings clean.

ETHEREALS

J ean awoke to Marin's presence twice. The first was the dove checking her over for fever or any other signs of infection that could have set in while she was sleeping. The second time was when Marin gently woke her up to use the restroom, given Jean had been resting as long as she had. When she finally woke to sunshine streaming into the room, Jean was pleasantly surprised to find Popcorn had been moved into the bed beside hers.

He had bandages crossing the entirety of his torso, his head was wrapped, and there were two machines hooked to him: both had tubes but only one went through his mouth and into his lungs while the other monitored the clockwork heart that had been placed in his chest. Jean could just reach his fingertips with her own and she let them brush together as a silent comfort that they were alright.

As she laid there, she allowed herself to slowly relax. It was quiet in this temple with only the machines beside the bed making a periodic sound. Jean's thoughts began to wander, touching on the pregnancy, Popcorn's recovery, and her chittering madness. All the while, Jean ran through the questions that Olare and Rolandus were keen on asking her as soon as she had awoken.

What exactly was it that had caused Popcorn to go feral, and why did those claws he used look like the ones the Telfarians wielded? The only logical answer was that Popcorn had been a Telfarian, but Jean didn't like that answer. He wasn't as bloodthirsty as they were. Besides, he hated them as much as she did.

Then her thoughts wandered to the creature of darkness she had witnessed, whatever it was that had left Popcorn, that Olare called a dark one. Perhaps that was a dark ethereal? She had heard whispers of creatures like that, but no one was ever able to really see them. Marin could, though, if Olare said she saw demons. Jean didn't know much about the Kingsmen, but she remembered her uncle talking about demons and dark ethereals once, and he used those words interchangeably.

Jean frowned.

Her aunt and uncle hadn't heard from her in several months, and Park was unaware of a Telfarian group this side of Apple Ridge. From what Jean knew, the bandits were supposed to either remain in Blackrock or, if they weren't there, they were to stay to the west of the mountains in the plains. Having them so close to Apple Ridge and Londor's Crossing was worrisome, even for someone who didn't know much about their movements.

The woman shifted, winced, and stared at the ceiling. She needed to write to them; somehow, she needed to get a letter out.

There was also the issue of pregnancy. She wasn't going to tell Popcorn anytime soon, as he wasn't even aware of their laying together. She could always lie once she went into labor, claim it was the Telfarians, but even Ashur looked so akin to his father that the lie was going to be difficult to uphold.

With a sigh, Jean closed her eyes again.

Popcorn awoke several hours later. It was the faint movement of his fingers against Jean that alerted her to his consciousness, and she turned to look at him as he began to cough. A dove was gently removing the tube from his throat. "There you go, good job; keep coughing, I know it's awful but it's helping."

Popcorn choked slightly as the tube was completely removed, then he inhaled deeply and coughed again. The dove patted his shoulder lightly, "Good work, dear. Alright, you rest while I get you some broth... Did you want anything to eat, hon?"

Jean nodded faintly, still staring at her friend. When his coughing fit subsided, he turned his head to see that Jean was there. A little smile flickered over his face. "Hey... you're safe..."

"You are too," Jean whispered. She managed to move slightly and clasp his hand. "You're safe, too. We're in Apple Ridge. How are you feeling?"

"Like I was hit by a wagon," Popcorn answered. He gave a little laugh and coughed again, making Jean wince. "My chest burns."

"They had to do massive surgery. Your heart stopped working, Baba." Jean stroked his hand with her thumb and he sighed. "They replaced it with a clockwork."

Popcorn raised an eyebrow, choked for a moment and then inhaled. "Excellent. More machine than man."

The two laughed quietly together before Jean recounted everything that had happened. Popcorn listened with half-closed eyes, nodded from time to time, and then he sighed. "I'm glad you're safe, daito."

"Me too. There was this awful feeling while I was with Kingsmen, one that felt like my lungs were going to explode, but I knew we had to get to you regardless."

She watched as Popcorn stiffened slightly, his eyebrows furrowed. Then, as soon as it happened, it vanished. "Interesting."

"Yeah... on the topic of interesting... Popcorn, where did you get your blood magic?"

He opened his eyes and looked at her. It was the same look he'd give Augur when the griffin attempted to get away with something, a mix of amusement, exhaustion, and even annoyance clear on his face. "Why do you want to know, Jean?"

"The captains were asking, and I was just thinking about it," Jean answered. She watched his face flash through emotions again, her own worries growing stronger now.

He wasn't answering. Why wasn't he answering? Was there something wrong? Was he really a part of the Telfarians at one point?

As though echoing her thoughts, Popcorn muttered, "You get it as a boon for worship, or acceptance, as a Telfarian." Jean's blood ran cold as he continued. "That was shortly after I left the North, and it lasted several years. Fortunately for me, there was a bit of a betrayal and I decided that I despised that life. I left, found the fort under Telfarian reign, and captured it. I've been doing artifact retrieval since."

He looked at her and Jean avoided his eyes. She would have assumed that he'd tell her after everything that they'd been through, but it all made sense. The knowledge of the centipedes, the fear-based command, the blood magic, his connections in the Telfarian district of Blackrock. It was all there, and Jean just hadn't seen it.

"Daito, please, believe me; you were never in danger while at Fort Haven. That past is far behind me, and I'm glad it is. Look at me, please." Popcorn's voice was so gentle that Jean was unable to help herself. His green eyes met hers and he whispered, "I walked away from that life. I do not wish to go back to it."

Jean slowly nodded, though she didn't believe him. Telfarians were always that way, and if he was one... well... that just told her what he used to do for a living. Popcorn squeezed her hand again before he murmured, "Did the doves check you over? You're sure you're alright?"

"I'm positive. Marin's been keeping a close eye on me."

"She seems nice enough, I'm glad you ran into her again." Popcorn yawned as the dove from before brought two bowls of broth. "Thank you."

"You're very welcome. Do you need help eating?"

"No, I have it."

They ate in silence and then laid down again. Popcorn slept through most of the day while Jean, amid her thoughts, found herself in the company of Rolandus for an hour or so. They discussed the weather,

Kingsmen weapons, and archery, before Rolandus asked, "Do I need to send word to anyone that you will be here for the time being?"

"Please- both my aunt and uncle as well as the foreman of Fort Haven need to know that we are here," Jean said. She watched the falcon cote intently as he scribbled those notes in a small notepad, and then continued as he looked at her again. "The foreman's name is Park- he'll know where Apple Ridge is. As for Uncle Flick and Aunt Anca..."

"Did you say Flick and Anca? The Alastars?" Rolandus asked, his eyebrow raised. Jean nodded and he began to laugh. "You're related to Alastar? I would have never guessed! How's he doing? And Miss Anca? Last I heard from Alastar, Caxton was just a babe. Granted, Marin just got back from visiting them but still!"

"You know my uncle?" Jean asked, blinking in surprise.

"Aye! Alastar and I served together for many years before they moved away. It was the hardest goodbye any of us had to say... but they have a good life in Blackrock! I was grateful to be able to hold Caxton when he was just a wee thing, fresh to the world!" Rolandus wiped his eyes. "If I had known you were going to visit them, I would have sent a letter with you!"

Jean couldn't help but laugh herself at his mirth, and they spent the next hour discussing her family. Then, Rolandus left, and Jean took a nap once more.

She awoke late that evening, well after meals were served, to a soft groaning down the hall. It sounded like someone was having nightmares, and it was echoed through the area as though many were experiencing the same dream. Beside her, Popcorn was sleeping soundly in his own bed.

The woman looked around, trying to decide if any doves were awake to check on them, before movement in the shadows caught her eye. It seemed to be a lithe black cat, not a rabbit, that walked directly on the wall as though as thin as paper. It stopped, looked toward her, and then trotted down the hall without a sound. Another creature, the same black shadow as the cat, made its way through the ceiling and around a corner. Jean's heart began to beat rapidly as she saw a third beast outside of the window.

It was smaller than before, but still had the eight-legs that writhed like tentacles. It climbed up the window, paused on with sill, and then pressed through the glass above Popcorn's bed.

Jean tried to speak but found her throat was too tight to make even a sound. Instead, she watched this demon snake its way down the wall and to Popcorn's face. Two tentacles wrapped around his jaw, a third on his nose, and it forced his mouth open. Popcorn choked as it snaked down his throat, a sinister chuckle slowly covering the sounds of gagging before it was silent.

That was a dark ethereal, the one she had seen before.

Jean looked around desperately for help, but her legs refused to move. In fact, she wasn't even sure if she was actually looking around. Just as she attempted to scream, a soft voice asked, "Are you sure you'll get help if you scream?"

The curseborn froze again, her heart beating louder in her ears as the voice continued.

"Jean, you know they're not going to trust your word. You're Solari, and a curseborn- of course you're trying to cause more problems."

She knew it was Popcorn's voice, but it certainly wasn't Popcorn speaking. The words were wrong.

"Marin and Rolandus trust me," Jean whispered back to the silky purr. "They wouldn't think—"

"How do you know?" The voice snickered softly. "Jean, you're safer to stay here. Why don't you lie back down, and forget all about this? It's just your imagination... just like Osmond."

Jean swallowed. "How do you know about Osmond?"

"I'm a figment of your imagination, Jean, of course I know all about your other friends. Now, be a good girl and close your eyes."

As soon as the voice said that, Jean knew full well that it was the demon within Popcorn. She stiffened, swallowed, and whispered, "You aren't going to hurt him, will you?"

"Oh, Jean, would I be able to hurt him? You made me up; I can't do anything to him. It's time to rest now; the stress is far more than you need in your... delicate state."

The thinly veiled threat made Jean's blood run cold and she closed her eyes, trying to tune out the voice once more. There was a chuckle and then silence from Popcorn.

Around the room, the moans had died away. If not for Jean knowing what she had spoken to, she would have assumed it was entirely a bad dream.

She laid there, silently, for several moment, before there was a door that opened in the distance. She could hear three sets of footsteps, one that seemed similar to Marin's and another like Rolandus'. They walked through the hallway, moving to the far side, and Marin's soft voice lilted toward her. "Something's in here, more than one. I'd like to check each of the patients to be sure they're okay."

Jean couldn't see what they were doing, but as Marin's voice carried again, the feeling of ants marching up her back filled her. "Thank HaMelech that these don't seem too problematic..."

The black cat shadow raced past Jean's bed and through the wall.

Jean swallowed hard. Marin really could see these, too, which mean that they had to be demons. As the small group approached the room Jean was in, she squeezed her eyes closed as though she was sleeping. Marin's hand rested on her forehead and she murmured.

It wasn't any tongue that Jean recognized, but it made her very skin want to crawl off as Marin continued. Then, as Marin pulled away, she stiffened slightly.

"Olare said he had one, and it's back," Marin murmured. "This is a stubborn one."

Jean cracked one eye open to see they were speaking about Popcorn and the thing that had crawled inside of him.

Rolandus stepped to one side of the bed and the second went to the other. Rolandus looked at Marin. "You speak over him; we'll restrain him if anything happens. It's volatile, Olare said it tried to get Jean. Even if Popcorn himself remains asleep, I don't trust that you'll be safe."

Marin gave one short nod and rested her hands over Popcorn's chest. She began to speak quietly again, the words just as foreign as before, and Jean shifted slightly to get a better look.

It was silent for a moment.

Then, in a sudden flurry of moments, Popcorn was upright with a hand grasped around Marin's throat. She began to choke as Rolandus and the other knight struggled to pull Popcorn off of her. Jean could see that Popcorn's eyes were glazed back again, the voids of darkness that held nothing but sinister amusement as Marin struggled.

Jean was about to reveal she was awake when Marin managed to say, "In the name of HaMelech, stand down!" All at once, Popcorn recoiled from Marin and the two knights pinned him down. The dove sucked in a breath. "You have no power here, and you have no right to use this man!" She began to pray again in that strange language, this time with more ferocity, as Rolandus tightened his grip on Popcorn.

The staros gave an unearthly shriek and threw the second knight into the empty bed, prompting Rolandus to snap, "Stand down, dark one!"

Popcorn began to seize, then collapsed, and the darkness in his eyes faded. "What happened?"

Marin didn't move any closer. "Popcorn?"

"What's happening, why did you wake me?"

Rolandus sighed, looked at the other two Kingsmen, and then offered an exhausted smile at Popcorn. "We're going to need you to go to a smaller, more intensive unit, my friend. Your condition is more serious than we thought."

Fear began to creep into Jean's heart as the three slowly helped Popcorn stand, his body unsteady. Were they going to kill him after this? She had done her best to explain that he was a good man but now that Marin had been strangled, she wasn't sure they'd believe anything she said before.

"Will Jean be alright on her own?"

"We'll let her know," Marin soothed gently, "she's also welcome to come and see you while you rest."

Slowly, the group helped Popcorn walk and moved the machine attached to him.

It wasn't until after they left that Jean slowly left her bed and followed them. She hated to think that Marin and Rolandus would execute her friend, but this was more than out of the ordinary. It was the right thing to do, too, wasn't it? Ensure he was safe? That's what she had to do to keep her near. Her heart ached as Popcorn walked, his head hung low and his steps uneven.

They walked through several empty hallways until they entered a room with a single bed. There, Marin gently lowered Popcorn under the covers and pulled them over him. "There you go... I'll talk to Jean in the morning and have someone bring you food once you're woken up, alright?"

"Thank you," Popcorn whispered with a tired smile. "I just... I hope she doesn't get too worried. I hate... hate when she worries."

"She'll be alright, Popcorn, she's a resilient woman," Marin murmured back.

Jean scurried through the darkness just ahead of the three Kingsmen and threw herself into the bed. They finished their rounds and two of the footsteps left. Marin returned to her room and felt her forehead again. Jean tried to appear asleep, but sighed as Marin murmured, "I know you followed us... and you saw everything."

Jean opened her eyes to stare at the healer. There was slight amusement on the redhead's tired face, and she shook her head. "He'll be fine tonight, Jean, I promise."

"What was that?" Jean whispered back.

Marin sighed, looked at Popcorn's empty bed, and then back at Jean. "A dark ethereal. I'm sure Olare mentioned that I saw one before—"

"I saw it, too... and the cat and the spider," Jean whispered. Marin's eyes grew slightly wider and Jean shifted. "And... and it spoke to me. Marin, am I going mad?"

"No, no, you aren't," Marin said softly. "You're not going crazy at all. I'm not sure why you can see them, but you're seeing the same things I am. I haven't had them speak to me, though, and so I need you to be careful; nothing they say can be trusted, as they are here only to steal, lie, and destroy. They are agents of the Black Dragon and nothing makes them happier than someone bending to their will."

"Like Popcorn?" Jean asked.

Marin sighed and nodded faintly. "Like Popcorn."

The confirmation sent chills down Jean's spine and she swallowed again. Then, Marin shook her head. "It isn't for you to worry about, Jean. You have a hedge of protection around you, and you are aware now of the lies it speaks. I need you to rest- Popcorn needs you to rest. I'll speak more to you about this tomorrow, if you wish, but for now, you only need to worry about ignoring the lies that creature speaks over you and resting to maintain a level head. HaMelech has shone favor over you, and I pray that you lean into that tonight."

Jean nodded mutely, allowed Marin to fix her bedsheets, and then stared at the ceiling again.

None of this is what she expected, and all of it terrified her.

26

NEXT STEPS

The first thing Jean did when she woke up was return to Popcorn's room. She sat on the edge of his bed and stroked his hair absentmindedly, thinking through everything that had happened while questioning the future. Marin entered with some porridge, knowing she had been there through someone who likely saw Jean, and she sat down in the chair.

"Do you have any questions for me?"

"Are you able to explain anything about the dark ethereal I see?" Jean asked quietly.

Marin sighed, watched Popcorn, and then shook her head. "I don't know if I can. I haven't met someone who didn't follow HaMelech who had this ability, nor have I had to explain how it works. Frankly, I only received basic instruction that helped me see both sides of the spiritual, but..."

"I can't, can I?"

"Likely not. I don't know if any agents of light, the elohim, would be willing to show themselves to you. They're strange creatures, and HaMelech alone knows why they walk among us. I've only ever seen one, though I know more are around." Marin offered a little smile. "If you see one, though, I'm sure you'll recognize it."

Jean nodded faintly and then paused. "Rolandus keeps mentioning a Guardian- what's that?"

"Elohim, though they seem to have a different purpose than others. Rolandus told me he had seen a guardian in person last fall; was it with you?"

"I guess? I'm not sure what he means whenever he says it."

"Then it likely hasn't revealed itself to you," Marin said. Jean nodded, though she was distracted by Osmond, who was floating behind her.

The two chatted quietly about the next steps in Jean's recovery, which involved nearly a month of rest due to Popcorn's surgery. He woke up halfway through and held Jean's hand as they talked, though he didn't say much. Eventually, Marin excused herself and Popcorn pulled Jean into a lying position beside her. He turned to face her, his nose in her hair, and sighed. "Can't leave for a month, hm?"

"No, but they're going to go find our things. They have a good enough search area that they're hopeful," Jean murmured. "Olare said that would be the best way to make us feel at home while we do stay."

Popcorn nodded slightly. Jean found herself savoring the warmth, though it faded as Popcorn grunted. "My chest hurts."

"I can call a dove."

A dove did come in, just moments after Jean spoke. The man carefully undid Popcorn's bandages. "Alright, it's your new heart. Unfortunately, it does use kinetic stones and has to be wound periodically- you can go 48 hours if you really have to, but we'd suggest no more than 24. You're moving towards 48 hours now." He revealed a port in Popcorn's chest that drove down, ending in darkness, and then pulled out a key. "There's two of these. Keep one on your person and the other as a backup. You insert it into the port and give it several winds..."

Popcorn did as the dove instructed, the pain on his face lessening as he wound his heart again. Jean watched with a tipped head. This wouldn't have had worked any other time, even in Blackrock. Somehow, things had worked out perfectly here.

She returned to lying beside Popcorn, allowing him to play with her hair as he rested. Finally, he murmured, "You're welcome to go explore if you're feeling up for it."

"I think I want to stay with you right now. You're warm, and we're safe. I don't want to lose that until I need to."

Her friend chuckled quietly and pressed his nose into her hair again. "That's fair."

They fell asleep together, and Jean awoke to take Popcorn's advice and explore. Marin found her amid the war rams in the stable, resting against the belly of one while Nettles had his head in her lap. A laugh was shared and Jean, after a while, returned to the temple.

Two days later, a small scouting party returned to Apple Ridge with a handful of Jean and Popcorn's belongings. They'd found his cane, their journals, and one of the satchels; everything else had been lost. Still, Popcorn and Jean were in good enough spirits at receiving what was found.

Once Popcorn was well enough to go outside, he and Jean spent time watching Rolandus instruct younger Knights of the Long Road on their archery. Jean was surprised to find that many of the knights carried small boltcasters with them alongside their glowing swords, which Rolandus patiently explained were hardlight weapons due to their nature.

It was fascinating to see a sword with no edge suddenly grow sharper than steel when it was wielded, and Jean found herself more and more curious about these Kingsmen the longer they remained.

Rolandus also invited Jean to shoot in order to help her hone her shot, and she spent many hours with both him and Marin as they trained the sheepdogs. Olare popped in from time to time, too, to check on healing progress before he returned to commanding the knights.

Eventually, it was time for the two to leave. Jean held Popcorn's hand tightly as they sat in the back of the trade wagon bringing cider to Blackrock. It had been difficult for her to say goodbye to Marin, Rolandus, and Olare, especially as Marin held her tightly and whispered, "I'm so proud of you."

Popcorn smoothed some hair from her face and pulled her close. "We'll see them again, diato."

"I hope so," Jean whispered back. "I really hope so."

She turned into his side as the wagon lurched forward, avoiding the waves that were given from their newfound friends. Instead, she focused on Popcorn's heartbeat and the calming rhythm it provided.

As the wagon set up camp for the night, she and Popcorn stepped away from the firelight to study a small, winged mouse. It perched on Jean's knee, grooming its dainty wings as she sketched it. Popcorn tilted his head, watching her intently, before Jean lifted her head and narrowly caught an acorn that he threw. "What was that for?" She questioned as the mouse scurried away. "You frightened it off."

"I was just ensuring your reflexes haven't suffered is all," Popcorn replied. He stared at her, frowned slightly, and asked, "Do you still feel like everything's alright?"

"I mean... yes? I don't feel like anything bad is happening or will happen," Jean replied. She tilted her head slightly as Popcorn nodded to himself. "Why?"

"I'm just wondering. It's been a hectic month, year, really, and I wanted to know how you're feeling about it." Popcorn stood and stretched, prompting Jean to do the same. "I think, once we settle back in Fort Haven, I'd like to go on another trip with you."

"That soon?" Jean questioned. She frowned again. That was much quicker than she'd think he'd want to leave, especially with his healing heart and bad leg. She touched the key hanging around her neck to ensure it was still there at the thought and then looked at Popcorn. "Where are you wanting to go? Certainly not the Empty?"

"No, not the Empty. Up north, past the Spinebacks."

Jean blinked at him, her mouth hanging open slightly.

That was a dark place. The light from the avatar of Solaris didn't shine there, and she wasn't sure what all lived where sunshine didn't fall. There were rumors of massive beasts and barbaric tribes, but no one really ever tested those theories.

"It's nearing winter, we'll be caught in a blizzard if we aren't careful... besides, what's in the north that you want to see?" She finally asked.

Popcorn took her notebook and flipped through it. "You've never seen an iterin, have you? Or hot springs? Or mushrooms taller than I am?"

"No, but there are dangerous people up there."

Her words got a soft laugh, and Popcorn gently poked her nose. "I'm from up there, diato. My people are up there... and if there's anyone up there I want to see, it's Seldom. He and I have some catching up to do, and I want to show you the place I grew up." His eyes danced slightly with mischief. "I think you'd love it there, diato."

Jean sighed. She was going to have a baby the end of spring next year, leaning to early fall. If they got caught by a blizzard going before winter, that meant they'd be stuck there. Alternatively, she could be incredibly pregnant, wandering through the north with Popcorn, possibly going into labor and recovering far from Fort Haven. None of her options seemed ideal.

"Fine, we can go north... but we'll need to go soon. I don't want to get caught on the other side of the mountains," she agreed.

Popcorn's eyes went wide, and she raised an eyebrow. "What?"

"I was just surprised that I didn't have to argue too hard, is all," Popcorn replied. He grinned at her, paused, and then took her hands. "I didn't thank you for what you did in Apple Ridge, by the way. Once I was really informed..." he trailed off and sighed. "You really shouldn't have."

"Why not? I know you'd do the same for me." Jean smiled slightly at him, squeezed his hands, and then pulled away to return to the camp. All the while, she could feel his eyes on her.

The remainder of the trip didn't take long. Jean found herself in Fort Haven before she knew it, and she and Popcorn spent the majority of the day telling Park about what had happened on their trip. Popcorn was silent about wanting to go north, but he did click his tongue eventually. "I'm going to need you to take on more mercenaries and guards. The Telfarians were further east than they have been, which means they're working their way towards Blackrock," he said. "We'll need to add more shifts, too. I'd rather not lose this fort to them after six years of it being mine... especially when Jean and I will be gone."

Park frowned. "Are you finally going to the Empty, after all this time?"

"No." Popcorn met Park's gaze. "We're going north to the Silverpike tribe."

The ashn foreman spat his drink across the table and Jean grimaced, wiping herself off. "Park!"

His reaction was so sudden and volatile that Jean was beginning to second guess the trip entirely, especially as Park nervously took a drink from his flask and then again from his cup.

"Sorry, Jean... how long are you planning on being gone?"

"No more than a month, before the first snowfall."

Park slowly nodded and shifted. "I assume you'll be back in time to watch Augur attempt a nest this spring, then."

Jean frowned and looked at Popcorn. "He can't, he doesn't have a territory. Nests aren't made without a territory."

Popcorn nodded in agreement and Park chuckled. "You tell that to Augur, then. He picked a fight with another griffin and, as he's been strutting around the property with his tail held high, I assume he won."

The words made Jean laugh, and she excused herself as she wiped her eyes. "I'll be back for dinner; I need to go find a certain griffin."

The men nodded and returned to talking, allowing Jean to slip out to find the griffin. He had gotten plump since they left, the rakows as well, from Park's constant treats. Jean's approach got a lazy tail twitched before she crouched in front of him. The feathers on the back of his neck lifted until he opened one eye, and a thunderous purr filled the air.

"Hi, buddy! I missed-" Jean was cut off as the griffin knocked her over, rubbing against her like a housecat and batting at her. "Easy with the claws, Augur!" She laughed as she struggled to escape his affection. "You're getting big!"

It took a good bit before Jean was able to get out from under him and pet him before she checked in on the creatures of the fort. Neither Popcorn nor Park were at the fire by the time Jean assumed they would be, nor did they show up to eat by the time dinner was done. She supposed it was likely to check the fort's lines in case the Telfarians managed to get this far east.

Dinner was uneventful, but, as Jean settled into bed beside Popcorn, the night was less peaceful than she'd hoped. She woke up twice to see

Popcorn had pulled her into his arms, sleeplessness written all over his face. She figured she'd have nightmares after their earlier conversation about the Telfarians, which he only confirmed with a faint nod before he murmured for her to go back to bed.

Early the next morning, Jean, Popcorn, and Park all set out to Blackrock. They arrived at Flick and Anca's house near sundown and enjoyed dinner with them while Jean's aunt and uncle told stories of those they'd met from Apple Ridge. Park didn't seem to know what to do while there, but as Popcorn passed him a glass of wine, he slowly grew more comfortable.

Anca spent extra time with Jean before she went to bed. After a couple of soft questions, Jean admitted her miscarriage to her aunt and, without warning, witnessed Anca break down into tears. They two cried together and Anca, after a moment, explained that she had spent many years and many miscarriages in pain. It was a moment of closeness that Jean never thought she'd share with her aunt, especially when her mother refused to talk about pregnancy when she was young.

It soothed Jean as she fell asleep, as it was a reminder that her family had some semblance of caring.

The next morning, Jean, Popcorn, and Park split up.

Jean figured that they'd meet in a pub for something to eat close to lunch, allowing her time to find a new journal and medicinal herbs from the Solari district. Popcorn had also offered to escort her through the Telfarian district as he needed to restock on efrage, but she politely refused. Park also declined; he reminded Jean and Popcorn that that was where the ashura were, and he refused to risk his life for some weeds. Instead, he chose to go to one of the banks to check on the Fort Haven investments.

While she wasn't sure why he'd waste a trip to Blackrock for business, Jean didn't argue.

It was a lovely day as she made her way through the city. People were still quiet, as it was too early for crowds, and a handful of vendors treated her as though she was an actual customer. It was a strange change, and she was certain it was only due to the desire to upcharge her, but it was a change nonetheless.

An hour's walk brought her to a vendor outside of a bookstore. His cart had the same whimsical carvings of animals as the store next to him, and it pulled Jean in closer to study the notebooks he had for sale alongside the artwork as well.

"The leather's been taken from various creatures; dear, bear, some cockatrice... basilisk hide..."

"How on earth did you get basilisk and cockatrice hide? Those are illegal to hunt outside of Blackrock." Jean looked at the vendor, frowning.

He shrugged slightly. "We make the journals in store, and so we have a merchant who comes through with leather ever couple of months. Now, were you going to purchase or simply bother me with legalities?"

Jean opened her mouth to reply before the stench of death wafted behind her. She stiffened up slightly, very much aware of someone behind her, and then turned to see a familiar skull mask and dark robes.

Mhoryga's employee, the ascended named Ankou.

The vendor's face had grown pale as Ankou stepped closer, his hand clenched around something. "I'll be purchasing the journal for her, I'm sure it's a rather good price today."

"Of course, sir, what would the lady like?" The vendor scrambled to an upright position as Jean pointed at one of the journals. He nearly flung it at her and, with a shaking hand, took the coins that Ankou offered.

"Thank you... Wait, where are you going?" Jean turned to see that Ankou had started down the street again. Against her better judgement, she hurried after him. "Why did you buy the journal for me?"

Ankou sighed. Never once did he slow down, nor did he look at Jean. "To get the vendor to understand that Mhoryga doesn't take lightly to one of her own getting swindled. She especially doesn't like knowing that vendors in this quarter have decided to take advantage of the situation and your appearance."

That was odd. Jean wasn't entirely sure why Mhoryga would remember her, especially as it had been so long. Still, she held the journal tightly and followed Ankou. "I suppose I should thank her, and you. It was very kind."

"Don't mention it," Ankou said with a shrug. "She wishes for you to join her at your next convenience, should you be able to." He paused, looked at

Jean, and then stepped towards a shadow. "Mind the darkness, won't you? I don't care for demons sharing my territory."

Jean stared at him as he stepped backwards into the shadows and disappeared, her mouth hanging open. So, Mhoryga knew she was in town and wanted to see her? That, and Ankou knew about the chittering madness. That was incredibly ominous, and Jean wasn't sure if she wanted to unpack that. She also didn't have time to think it through, either, before Popcorn and Park raced around the corner.

As soon as Popcorn reached her, he gripped her upper arms. "Are you okay?"

"Of course, I'm okay. Why wouldn't I be?"

"Why do you smell like ascended?" Park questioned, wildly looking around. "Is there an ascended here?"

"He just left."

"Who was it?" Popcorn asked.

Jean looked between the two, her eyes wide at their apparent panic. "I'm fine, really! It was the man who works for Mhoryga, his name is Ankou. He purchased a journal for me after a vendor was causing problems. He didn't hurt me, I was alright."

"Oh, how kind," Park said. He pulled his flask from his hip and took a deep drink. "Let's get out of here; ascended have absolutely nothing good to them."

"He isn't a threat, Park-"

"All ascended are, Jean. If you spent any time in Ashuran, where your blood is from, you'd know this."

Popcorn ushered them off as Jean tried to figure out what Park meant, eventually piecing that Park could tell she was noble, too. It was an incredibly strange idea, especially as she had no clue how they were doing it, but she didn't argue. Instead, she asked, "How did you know where to find me?"

"I figured you were in trouble when you didn't beat us to the pub," Popcorn replied. As they approached the pub, and he checked Jean over again, he sighed. "We're going to leave from here to the north," he said after a brief pause. Both Jean and Park looked at him, Jean's eyes wide as he continued, "There are some things of a rather urgent matter I need to discuss with someone in my tribe, more than ever."

"I thought you were going to think about it and decide later," Park said.

Popcorn fixed his gaze on him, "And I did. I've decided that we need to go now before the weather changes. There's no guarantee when the snow will begin to fall, and I'd rather be in and out before it does. We're still on the other side of snow, we shouldn't be hit by any freak storms until after we return."

"I don't have my things here to go." Jean protested, "I mean, I want to go but Augur, and my things and—"

"He'll be alright," Popcorn said. He kissed the top of Jean's head and then gave her a gentle squeeze against his side. "He will be waiting for you when we get back. It'll only be a month, as long as the last trip ended up being. Besides, I don't want to miss spring when it comes time for him to woo a mate. We can buy a few things for you so we don't need to travel back to Fort Haven. We're closer to the pass than we would be otherwise, meaning it cuts down on travel time by several days already."

Jean blinked at him, offered a weak smile, and then sat.

That took away any additional time to prepare, time that she should she'd have in order to get ready for another trip. Was she going to be alright on this trip?

She was afraid, but as she glanced at the man speaking to the barkeeper, something told her that everything would be okay.

A flicker of light in the corner of her eye made her look towards the door to see Osmond. He hovered there for a moment before moving towards the mountains outside of Blackrock before he faded. For a moment, Jean stared at where he had been.

She wasn't sure what that meant but given the last several times he had wanted her to follow him, it meant that she, Popcorn, and their unborn child, would be going north sooner than she expected.

ILLEROSS &
BEYOND

The Long Night

On the morning of the Spring Solstice, when Solaris reaches the central axis and is perfectly aligned with Illeross, the Long Night officially begins.

Solaris vanishes for the next 24 hours without a trace. During this time, the Black Dragon is freed from its celestial prison to sow death, darkness, and destruction. During the Long Night, all light is diminished by half. A massive bonfire sheds little more light than a lantern would normally.

The Eye of the Black Dragon appears in the sky directly above the viewer regardless of their location and stares with an unblinking hunger.

Anyone caught in its gaze, begins to hear its call and will be tempted to fall to their deepest carnal desires. Those who give into their depravity are empowered by the dark god... at a price.

Illeross

The toroidal world of Illeross is a land of magic and wonder. Its sun is the deity Solaris the Radiant who flies back and forth through the center of the torus to make the days and seasons. Meanwhile his first wife Lunararia orbits the outer ring calling the tides and reflecting Solaris' light to the frozen dark lands of the far north.

Illeross is divided into 5 regions.
1. "The light" this Southern region never sees night.
2. "Dawn lands" this region only sees night as winter approaches.
3. "Central lands" this region always has day and night.
4. "Dusk lands" this region only sees day as summer approaches.
5. "Dark lands" this Northern region never sees Solaris directly.

Instead of flying at a consistent speed Solaris prefers to race from one zenith to the other. If his path was divided into 6 parts from axis to zenith it would look like this.

zenith
2 hrs
18 min
1 hr
48 min
1 hr
6 min
33 min   1 hr each
12 min
3 min
Axis

Solaris at the zenith of the summer solstice

Lunararia has an orbital period of 36 hours.

As the seasons change so does the axis point around which Solaris flies, raising in the summer, and lowering in the winter.

Solaris at the zenith of the winter solstice

Lanther Blackrock
Top
Bottom
(However those on the bottom such as the people of Ashura wrongfully disagree)

GLOSSARY

Ascended- an ashura who has 'ascended' from societal standards. They feast on souls and are seen as highly dangerous

Ashn- an ashura individual who does not conform to societal standards. Often masked by scraps of cloth and relegated to servanthood/slavery

Ashura- an individual from the city-state of Ashuran

Avatar of Solaris- the sun

Black Dragon- the unsanctioned 'deity' of destruction and discord

Boltcaster- a weapon, similar to a crossbow, that is smaller and lighter for use

Chimera- a creature that is not of one 'species'. Example: a griffin

Chitter- a creature of shadow and darkness

Cote- an individual with the ability to change their form from humanoid to a creature/human hybrid

Curseborn- a person with features resembling a demon. Often with horns and reddish skin, they are viewed as 'cursed' by Solaris worshippers

Dove healer- A Kingsman healer

Ethereal, dark- something that follows the Black Dragon as a servant, one of which who can attach to susceptible hosts

Ethereal, light- a spirit or being that is recognized as not following the Black Dragon, often one who serves HaMelech

Fletcher- a tiny creature with the body and head of a hummingbird, and the limbs/paws and tail of a kangaroo rat

Great horned griffin- a huge beast with the body of a tiger and the head and additional features of a great horned owl

Griffin- a creature sharing characteristics of two different animals. Example: tiger and owl, hummingbird and mouse, raven and raccoon

Hardlight- a type of weapon used by Kingsmen; it uses manifested holy light rather than actual steel or metals

Husk- a derogatory term for curseborn

Kingsman- a follower of the god HaMelech

Knight of the Long Road- a warrior/guard who serves HaMelech

Lightcaster- a hardlight boltcaster

Mantle- a skin or hide of an animal that is used in the changing of a cote's form. These are imbued with magic and only work for their owner

Noble- an ashura who is the societal standard in Ashuran. These individuals cover their faces with fine masks

Rakow- a chimera, or griffin, comprised of features from both a raven and a racoon

Solari- a person or multiple people who follow the Solari pantheon

Solaris- the high god in the Solari pantheon

Staros- a people group in the far north

Telfaria- the goddess of blood and death

Ivumi Terms & Phrases

Ae'shaur- Ivumi (Northern) term for curseborn, loosely translates to 'horned one'

Ashkin- Ivumi (Northern) term, loosely translates to 'idiot'

Diato- Ivumi (Northern) term, loosely translates to 'little mouse'

Hishan- Ivumi (Northern) term, loosely translates to 'breath of fresh air'

Irinmo no sunab- Ivumi (Northern) phrase, loosely translates to 'you are not alone'

Lor mi tuni fasta, un mi lash ingtu- Ivumi (Northern) phrase, loosely translates to 'may the hunt be swift, and the bow be light'

Rainome- Ivumi (Northern) phrase, loosely translates to 'my beating heart'. Used as a statement of endearment

Rinki- Ivumi (Northern) loosely translating to 'life'

ABOUT THE AUTHOR

Ellie Lerum is a fantasy author and blogger whose stories blend redemptive hope, emotional depth, and a touch of whimsy. A devout Christian and mother of dragons (well, griffins... and two spirited little girls), she writes tales that wrestle with grief, healing, and courage through richly imagined worlds. Ellie draws inspiration from her faith, real-life loss, and the works of J.R.R. Tolkien to craft narratives that are both adventurous and deeply human. Whether writing or exploring Idaho with her family, she finds the greatest joy in connecting with readers who see themselves in the stories she tells.

Follow her on Facebook and Instagram @AuthorEllieLerum, or at authorellielerum.com

ALSO BY ELLIE LERUM

The Cassy Series

Book 1: Phantom in the Dark
Book 2: Souls in the Ice
Book 3: Specter in the Shadows
Book 4: Wraith in the Light

Tales of Illeross

Turning Point
Gracefully Broken
A Mother's Prayer

Children Books

Animals of Illeross: An A-Z Alphabet

www.ingramcontent.com/pod-product-compliance
Lightning Source LLC
Chambersburg PA
CBHW050923030726
47503CB00007BB/2436